From Cork to the New World

A Journey for Survival

Canada

The Publishers acknowledge the financial assistance of the Government of Canada through the Book Publishing Industry Development Program (BPIDP) for our publishing activities.

Library and Archives Canada Cataloguing in Publication

McCarthy, Michael, 1950-
From Cork to the New World : a journey for survival / Michael McCarthy.

ISBN 978-0-88887-377-4

1. Irish--Ontario--Peterborough Region--History--19th century--Fiction. 2. Peterborough Region (Ont.)--Emigration and immigration--History--19th century--Fiction. 3. Ireland--Emigration and immigration--History--19th century--Fiction. 4. Robinson, Peter, 1785-1838--Fiction. I. Title.

PS3613.C34578B58 2009 813'.6 C2009-902045-9

2nd printing April 2010

Cover design: drt, 2009
Illustrations by Katelyn McCarthy

From Cork to the New World
A Journey for Survival

Michael McCarthy

Borealis Press
Ottawa, Canada
2009

Preface

This story is historical fiction; the subject matter is the lineage of the McCarthy family. The facts regarding the actual journey are not known; however, the dates, locations and certain events have been identified through documented sources. Although the true account of the McCarthy immigration has not been passed down through the generations, some liberties had to be taken to make the story complete. The main characters are real; the story is fictional.

Even though this story does not set out to provide a complete account of the McCarthy and Sullivan exodus, it is a reflection of their character that I tried to identify. I have examined my known points of reference—my grandfather, my father, my uncle, myself, my children, as well as my grandchildren—to determine key, common personality traits. It is their character, built through this examination, that I am presenting, rather than a complete and accurate account of the original immigrants.

Peter Robinson is one of the real characters and heroes of this book. Through his compassion, leadership and determination, he led over two thousand Irish immigrants into Canada and set them up with land, provisions, tools and other resources to achieve one of the most successful immigration projects in history. Appreciation for his accomplishments continues to this day.

Michael Edward McCarthy
2009

Acknowledgements

I would like to thank all the McCarthys through the generations who produced and moulded the current generations and the generations to come. I hope I have done you justice in capturing your essence while taking the liberty to create a fictitious story to illustrate your life.

Special thanks to the Reverend Monsignor Bernard McCarthy, Donna Rockwood and Eugene Seeley, cousins to my father Linus, who assisted with putting the missing pieces in place.

Special thanks to Dee Dee Hogan, who voluntarily laboured through the developing, proofreading and encouragement process, thereby keeping this author motivated and focused through often confusing and difficult periods.

My sincere appreciation to Rodine Dobeck whose editing process made this story come alive.

A special thanks to my wife Ann, whose patience and understanding supported me as I researched, travelled and demanded seclusion to consider all the nuances of this story.

William Sullivan Family

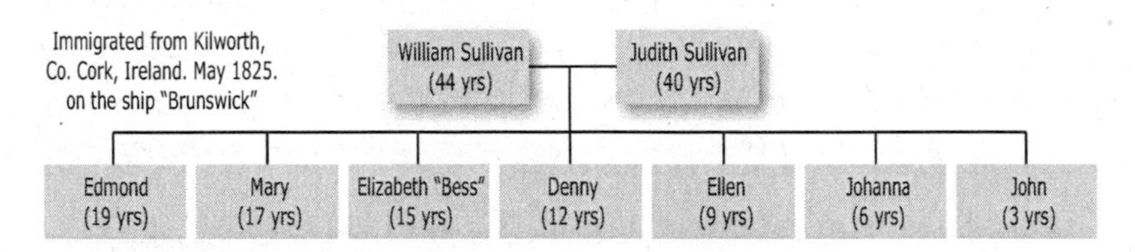

Thomas McCarthy Family

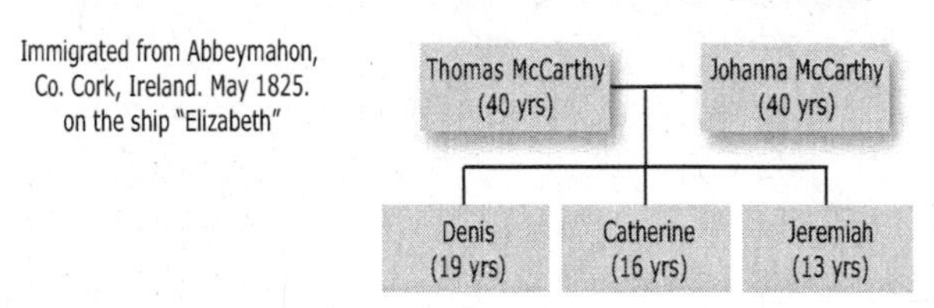

Jerry McCarthy Family

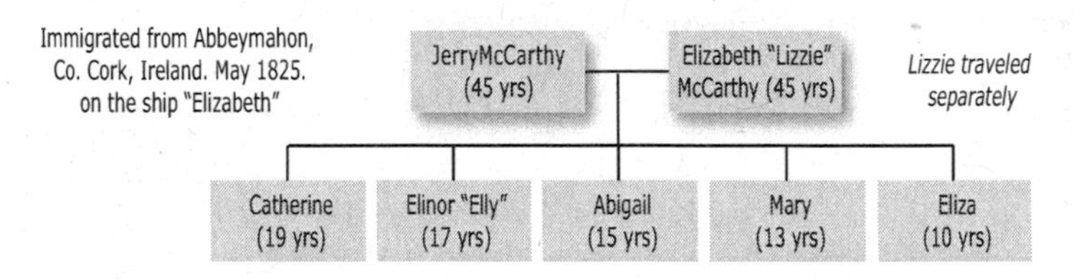

Ages given at time of departure from Ireland

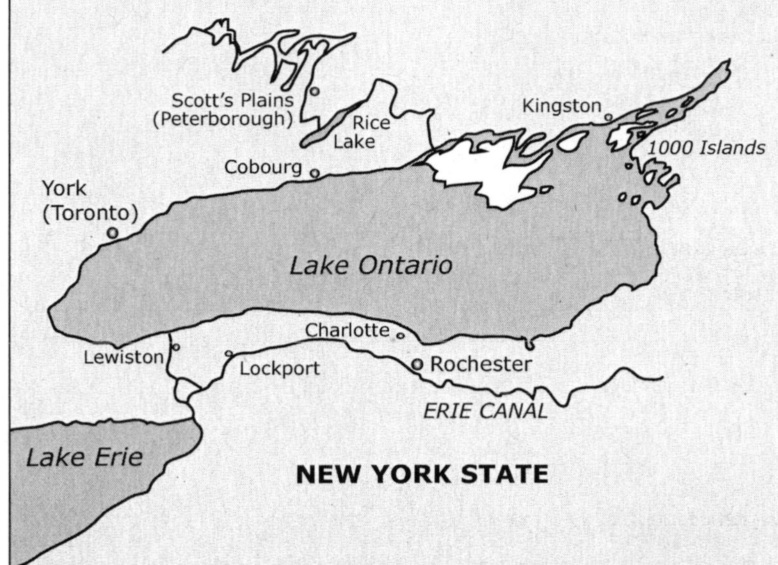

Lake Ontario, 1825.

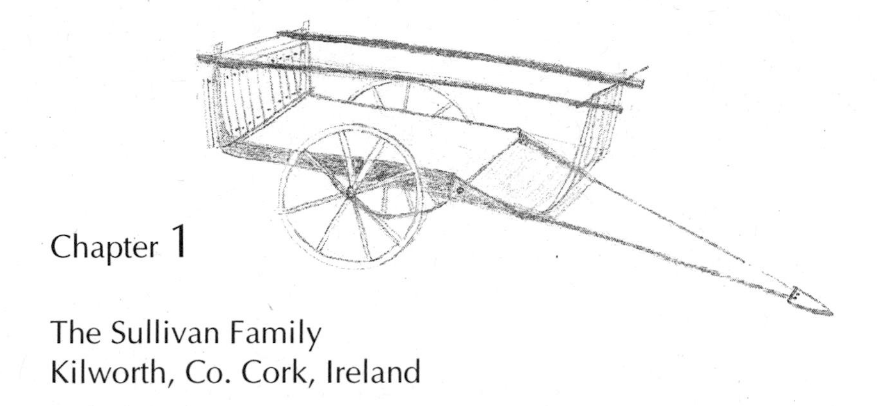

Chapter 1

The Sullivan Family
Kilworth, Co. Cork, Ireland

Four British soldiers smartly exited the front door of the barracks in the village of Kilworth, northern County Cork. Living proof of Irish oppression was about to occur.

This part of Ireland, in the Blackwater River valley in the shadow of the Knockmealdown Mountains, had rich and fertile farmland. The Araglin River flowed south out of the mountains and fed the Blackwater, providing an abundance of fresh water for the inhabitants, cattle and other farm life.

It was just after daybreak and the cool, early morning air made the soldiers quickly button up their bright red tunics, to protect their chests and necks from the dampness.

The sergeant emerged from the doorway and joined his troops, who fell into precise formation of two in front and two behind. The aging sergeant appeared confident as he glanced at his men and ordered, "Let's go." They headed east through the village on the main road.

The inhabitants of Kilworth could only speculate as to the reason for the march. The soldiers served as the local police and the people of the town watched the soldiers' activities. Neither trusted the other.

Their presence on the roadway, along with their formation and stride, drew notice. Routine patrols usually consisted of two soldiers so this march was no daily patrol, and the sergeant's pace was quick and determined. They turned at the edge of the Moore estate, home of the Earl, and followed alongside its ten-foot-high stone boundary wall. For those watching their movement, the mystery of their destination mounted as Sergeant Miller paced his troops towards the northeast edge of Kilworth, a predominantly Catholic area.

Kilworth Parish had its own barracks just outside the small marketplace village. The outlaw William Brennan, a notorious highwayman, had attracted the troops twenty years earlier during his "rob the rich and give to the poor" days when he eluded capture by the English soldiers. Eventually he was caught and hanged but not before a military presence was established in this small farming community. This morning, the soldiers marched in formation past the wall that stretched for seven miles protecting the Earl from the surrounding citizens.

The detachment of soldiers respected their sergeant, who had served in the Kilworth barracks for the past eight years. He was widely known in the British service not only for his leadership ability, but also for his interrogation ability. That reputation of producing results had a direct link to his assignment in Southern Ireland, which was consistently a hotbed of rebel activity.

Sergeant Miller wanted to maintain his reputation and retire within a few years. The practice of rewarding loyal soldiers generally didn't filter down to the sergeant level, but he was hoping that his record of eliciting important information about rebel activity and overthrows would win him a plot of land in Northern Ireland. He had had enough of the insolent southern Irish and he could never rest comfortably where hatred was not easily forgotten.

Meanwhile Judith Sullivan, who lived in a small cottage at the eastern edge of Kilworth with a few acres of farmland, occupied her seven children with their morning chores of drawing water, making tea and preparing porridge for the family. They had been given strict instructions to be quiet.

"Why is Da sleeping so late?" asked little Johanna.

"He is not feeling well this morning," replied her mother. "Now place those dishes on the table without rattling them and making noise."

"Yes, Ma."

The troops continued to make their way through the small town towards the east edge of the village. The village was quiet on this fall morning—until the hard rap from the sergeant's fist hit the Sullivans' front door. The English followed proper etiquette of knocking before entering on a warrant-less entry, but patience was never part of the etiquette. The sergeant did not wait long before ordering one of his soldiers to open the door. The crash of wood splinters flew inward, hitting Judith Sullivan as she approached the door, which now lay in pieces on the floor, half hung on its hinges. The soldiers took satisfaction in causing destruction to their neighbourhood foes.

"Where's Sully?" asked Sergeant Miller as he stepped into the cottage. William Sullivan was known through the region as "Sully." If the sergeant had asked for "William," he would have signalled that he did not truly know who he was looking for.

"He's sleeping—or he *was* sleeping before you rudely knocked down the door," replied an agitated and defiant Judith.

With a wave of the sergeant's hand, two soldiers rushed into the house to hunt for the wanted fugitive. No explanation was given to Judith, or even expected, as to the nature of their inquiry of her husband.

"He won't be much good to you, as he is hung over pretty badly this morning," she warned.

"I'll be the judge of that," replied the crusty officer.

Sully emerged from the back room with his head hanging low and supported on each arm by a soldier. William and Judith's seven children sat in the front room watching the scene. These invasions and forcible removal of their father had happened two times before, as Sully was suspected of being an Irish rebel and an important link in the internal structure of the rebellious movement.

Once out in the front of the house, Sully threw up much of the half-digested beer from the night before. The soldiers backed off until he finished vomiting. Of course, the soldiers thought he vomited on purpose as an affront to their authority and kicked him in the middle of his sickness. The sergeant called off any additional brutality; he had to interrogate Sully and didn't want to smell the rancid odour for the next several hours.

The soldiers retraced their route to their barracks supporting, dragging and pulling their prisoner. The watching residents now realized the intended purpose of the previous march, as they watched Sully stumble along the road back to the British quarters.

Sergeant Miller started the interrogation with, "Where were you last night?" Both men knew Sully was in Doyle's Pub, as that was the purpose of this unpleasant early morning visit. "Who did you talk with?" was the second, anticipated question, and both knew the answer to this too.

Sully decided to give his story without going through the ritual of questions and answers. "I went to Doyle's Pub last night to have a pint. I saw Liam and spoke to him about going to America."

"Who's going to America?"

"Maybe both of us."

"Why?" asked the sergeant, hoping that he was uncovering an international conspiracy.

"To live." Even though Sully wanted to be truthful, part of him wanted to be coy with the sergeant and make him work. It also forced the sergeant to give up what he already knew in directing the questioning.

"You're emigrating to America? And who is paying for this?" Sergeant Miller knew Sully had no money. As a reduced farmer in the service of the Earl, Lord Mount Cashell, Sully had no money or property to sell for transport out of Ireland.

"You are, Sergeant. The British government will pay my way as part of a new settlement in Canada."

The soldiers had heard of the recruitment of poor Irish for the Robinson Settlement in Upper Canada. "So you think the Earl will send you to America?" The sergeant's retort was more sarcastic statement than a question. It also planted uncertainty in the sergeant's mind—whether this rebel prisoner would be granted land before the sergeant was granted his due reward for loyal dedication in His Majesty's Service?

The questioning from England's best interrogator in Ireland continued, with little result. The British had misread William Sullivan for years. He was not an Irish rebel, although all Irish people wished for a free and independent Ireland. His trips to the pub intentionally coincided with visits by those who were active in the resistance movement, to deflect the spies giving information to John Bull's ear. Sully's friends were involved and they tried to recruit him to take a more active role, but he was content to visit and listen to the events at the pub even though the next day was spent in the sergeant's company answering questions. As a sympathizer to the cause, he felt his time with the sergeant was a useful diversion from the real activity.

In all the interrogations throughout County Cork, no one convinced the British that Sully was uninvolved. Sullivan was vocal about Ireland being independent but he was a follower of Daniel O'Connell, a supporter of non-violent political action rather than armed rebellion. At this point in history, the British made little distinction between the two.

The frustrated soldiers often resorted to physical abuse as a tactic. Today, the sergeant did not get overly brutal with his strategy since Sully had the attention of the Earl in negotiating his emigration. For the first time, Sergeant Miller let up his aggressive style in the hope of improving his chances for favourable review with the Earl. He knew he was not going to break Sully. If he were going to arrest him, it would come from somebody else's testimony. However, the process was important as an example to the citizens to avoid rebel goings-on. Sully knew he could not convince the sergeant he was innocent of insurrection activity. The situation was part of living in Ireland in 1824 and, in particular, in County Cork.

A crisis was building in Southern Ireland over living conditions and as a result, rebel activity was mounting. People watched families and neighbours losing land and experiencing deteriorating personal health from lack of proper nourishment. The Sullivan situation was an example of a condition that was repeated throughout Ireland, especially in County Cork, where there was widespread starvation from crop failure. No matter what the fields yielded, the majority of the harvest went to the landlords. The situation was at a critical stage in the early 1820s, when the annual potato harvest no longer sustained a proper diet and disease was widespread.

Human deterioration and death occurred throughout the region—but not from starvation, as that process took too long. First, lack of nutrition caused immune systems to break down, allowing fever and disease to flourish. The poor Irish farmers and labourers were dying at accelerated rates from typhus, relapsing fever, dysentery, cholera and poor politics. The few crops that were produced on the small subdivided pieces of land were taken as part of taxes and tithing.

Secondly, these poor families did not have access to sanitary goods. Within their community, they cared for each other and unwittingly transferred germs and harmful diseases.

A plan was needed to offset the crisis. The visual effect of near-skeleton human forms walking about was too much to ignore.

As Parliament and the Prime Minister finalized the Robinson plan to help the poorest Irish families to emigrate out of Ireland, the politics at the grassroots level was becoming confrontational on both sides. Sully's time spent under the interrogation tactics of Sergeant Miller was a manifestation of the hatred building from years of oppression and neglect.

Now, Sully's walk back through Kilworth was as predicted; he had difficulty maintaining balance and poise. The citizens along the route watched but did not come out to assist, either out of fear or not wanting to be linked to rebel activity. Before long, Liam came running up to Sully as he made the turn at the Market House in the centre of town. The rebels had their own network of information and they had been waiting to hear of Sully's release.

"What happened?" asked Liam.

"Nothing."

"What did you tell them?"

"Nothing."

Liam seemed relieved. "Are you all right?"

"From the ankles down, I'm fine."

"Let me help you," said Liam. He grabbed Sully's arm and helped him walk the next two miles home. As they walked Sully explained the focus of the inquiry.

"Miller wanted to know what was discussed at the pub last night. He thinks there's a rebellion coming and he thinks we are getting help from the Americans."

"What did you tell him?"

"I told him the truth—I don't know anything about such matters."

"Good man."

"It's the truth. Also, he was very interested in our emigrating to Canada. It was like he wanted us to go, but then who would he beat up twice a month?"

Judith opened the door and the two men stepped inside. William's eldest son Edmond had repaired the door by replacing two vertical planks and a cross member. He was in the process of whitewashing the door as his father returned.

"Nice work, son."

"You all right, Da?"

"Yeah, I'm fine." Sully moved towards a chair in the kitchen area and sat down.

"I'll get you some tea," said Judith.

The family gathered around. The two small girls, Ellen and Johanna, sat on the floor next to their father. Ellen placed the youngest, John, who was three years old, on her lap. Ellen, a quiet contemplative child, was nine years old. She had motherly instincts and took care of her younger sister and brother. Johanna, the younger sister, was more spirited and enjoyed laughing. She liked to listen to stories that her father and Edmond told, and fantasized being part of the stories. The baby, John, liked to watch the family dynamics as he sat quietly and smiled at all the chatter and commotion.

Edmond, the oldest at nineteen years, was a mirror image of his father in both looks and personality. They both had perpetual smiles that appeared even when their faces were in a relaxed state. Sully was quick-witted and his son followed suit. Such personalities encourage others to talk and relate. This was part of Sully's problem: the underground rebels, who lived in town and had grown up with Sully, liked him.

So trips to the pub found him in the middle of rebel conversations, but he walked away when the topic of politics came up. They respected his neutrality. He did support the Catholic Association founded by Daniel O'Connell from County Kerry, who was working towards Catholic Emancipation through Parliament so that Irish Catholics could freely express and practise their faith—this was currently outlawed by the Penal Laws. Sully believed O'Connell would achieve their religious freedom. In addition, Sully had demonstrated his loyalty to the cause by accepting the interrogations and not reporting confidential information that he might have overheard or inter-membership connections. Edmond, influenced by his father's troubles, had not been active up to this point in political discussions or actions.

The other children included Mary, seventeen, Elizabeth (called Bess), fifteen, and Denny, the middle child at twelve years. They gathered close to listen to Sully's report.

He always started the story with a warning: "Don't get involved with the rebel resistance unless you are willing to take the punishment that goes with it." The statement was not a justification for his associations or his trips to the pub. Nor was it a command forbidding his children from pursuing freedom from English tyranny. He meant that they should be prepared for the consequences of their actions. The children nodded.

He continued speaking to his family. "You all know that the British government is sponsoring Irish Catholic families emigrating to Canada. We applied to the Earl last week for this program. Sergeant Miller will help us with our application."

"Did he say that he would help?" asked Judith. "I can't believe that he would go out of his way to help any of the Irish, especially us."

"No, he didn't say he would help us. I just didn't give him any information, but I did tell him we applied for the Robinson Settlement. He'll help. He can't wait to get rid of us."

"Won't he thwart the application to keep us here or send us, I mean you, to jail?" asked Ed.

"I don't think so. He has interviewed me three times, all to no avail. He wants to find a spy who will give him the information he wants. He knows it won't be me."

Judith knew the meaning of her husband's words, and this was her greatest fear. Sergeant Miller would be looking to implicate Edmond or any of the children, and either leverage or divide the family. It was time for a change. Their meagre subsistence of farming land owned by the Earl offered no hope for the future. Judith supported the move to Canada for the sake of her family and their freedom.

"What is this Robinson Settlement?" asked Denny.

"Peter Robinson is a member of the Upper Canadian Assembly who took a group of five hundred and sixty-seven Irish last year to Upper Canada," explained Sully.

"Yeah, that's when Billy Fitzgerald left for Canada," said Bess.

"Bess, that's Mr. Fitzgerald," corrected Judith. She turned to Sully. "He lived in town, remember?"

"Oh yes, I remember Billy," said Sully. He continued, "Now, those five hundred emigrants were given land, a home, and a cow in Canada to start farms. The program was successful and they have asked Mr. Robinson again to make a larger settlement in Upper Canada. We have the opportunity to receive one hundred acres, a house, seed for planting, farming tools, a cow and transportation to America, all at the expense of the British government."

"Do we have to go?" asked Denny.

"We don't have to go," answered Judith, "but it's best for us because we cannot stay here. We don't have the food or the land to grow more. Soon we will be sick from the lack of food."

"Will we come back?" asked Ellen.

"No, this move is forever," said Sully. "Like Ma said, it's best for us."

"Now everyone, back to your chores," ordered Judith as she directed the children away from the table. Mary grabbed the empty bucket off the table and headed out the door, along with Bess, to milk their one remaining cow which too, was showing signs of emaciation. Denny's routine obligations for the day were done and he looked around for a chore. Judith pointed to the broom and Denny took the hint by starting to sweep the cooking area.

The two young girls, still sitting on the floor, were hoping for more of their father's story. Ed sensed the girls' desire and said, "Come over here and I will tell you a story about the great cúChulainn's Last Battle." The girls instantly got up and ran over to Ed's chair in the front room. Of course, Johanna was first to move and arrive at Ed's chair. Her love of stories made her giggle with excitement, and little John joined in the merriment.

Edmond started, "cúChulainn, a handsome lad just seven years old . . ."

Johanna cried out, "Oh good."

"Yes, at seven years old," her brother continued, "he had a dream, a dream that called him to battle but warned him of an early death."

He continued the epic tale set in northern Ireland: "Long ago our hero cúChulainn received his training and honed his fighting ability to become the greatest warrior in Ireland. The legend tells us that he had many lovers and battles with jealous husbands, but the biggest challenge of all was the 'Feast of Bricriu.'"

Little John raised his arms and clenched his tiny fists at the mention of a fight while Johanna squirmed with delight over the handsome lover, and Ellen solemnly waited for the details before expressing an emotion.

Edmond continued, "The evil sorcerer Bricriu laid a plan for Ireland's three bravest warriors to fight each other—Conall, Laoire, and cúChulainn—at a feast hosted by Bricriu. The custom was that the greatest warrior received the best meal. When it came time to serve the meal, the three warriors fought for the honour. The warriors were tested for many days; each time cúChulainn outfought and outwitted the other two, but the challenges kept coming. Finally cúChulainn had to fight a giant, a sea serpent and an invasion of raiders, and was then declared the best warrior. After his victory, the king placed him in command of all warriors."

The children were not able to grasp the subtleties of the tale but they enjoyed the story of the handsome hero as he overcame evil aggressors and battled for self-preservation.

On the other side of the room, Judith tended to Sully and his wounds. "Do you really think Miller will help our application?" she asked her husband.

"I don't know. His attitude changed when I mentioned going with the Robinson group."

"I would just as soon he stays out of it, for good or bad. I don't like the man."

"Really? I was thinking of inviting him over for tea," mocked Sully, who disliked Sergeant Miller as much as, if not more than Judith.

Judith looked at him. "Can you stay out of the pub for the next month or so?"

"My absence will be noticed. They'll think I'm mad or something. Besides, you know the saying, 'You can't trust an Irishman who doesn't drink.' I'll have to go once or twice." Sully turned serious. "Worse yet, they'll think I made a bargain with Miller."

"Then keep away from Liam Mahoney." Her caution was received with silence. Judith was not active in political discussions but she was well aware of the Irish plight and the resistance to English domination, as well as the personal cost, especially for her husband. "I can't stand those English pigs," Judith added.

"Now, Judith, you're part English, right?" Sully asked playfully.

"I am not English. I'm as English as St. Patrick was English, God rest his soul. Just because my family lived in England for a couple of generations doesn't make me English. I have lived here all my life, as did my mother and father. English, huh!" Judith was on a fiery roll, her voice was getting louder, and she was talking fast. Sully could not get a word in edgewise to calm her down.

"I suppose if we move to Canada, then you will think that I'm Canadian?"

"Well, yes."

"Well, no. I'm Irish and if I move to Canada, I am still going to be Irish. No matter where I go, I am Irish. And that means I'm not English."

"Well, that settles that," said Sully as he looked around the room towards the kids and raised his eyebrows and drew his chin down as if to say "I shouldn't have said that." The kids in the front room giggled at their father's funny face. Even Ed could not help but laugh. The laughter relieved the tension from their mother's rant.

"Stop making funny faces at the kids," Judith ordered in a less intense voice.

"What face is that, my dear?"

"You know, and don't call me English any more, either."

"You made that clear." All voices were back to normal and the two married partners were done with their jousting for this time. Judith was a large, tall woman, her appearance imposing, and when she talked with determination she was intimidating to most people. Sully knew how to handle his wife with respect yet playfulness. Even though he could get her going on a topic and question her opinion, she knew when he was good-naturedly taunting her. But in any case, her opinion had to be clarified and nothing left to doubt. That was her way.

Ellen and Johanna watched their mother with admiration for her strength and her ability to articulate. Through years of watching, they had taken note of their mother's use of power and authority in the family while always respecting her husband and without undermining his role as head of the family.

It was time for dinner but there was no food for the nine members of this family today. Judith was rationing out their food supply and recently she had been making small, barely sustainable dinners every other day. Most of the inhabitants of Kilworth were poor, reduced farmers who had limited land owned by English lords, and their allotment of food for personal consumption was restricted to scarcely nutritious meals. The English blamed Irish parents for having too many babies and consequently too many mouths to feed.

Such conditions across the country caused mass starvation, sickness and disease, and eventually frequent deaths. Food, especially maize, was plentiful, but most was shipped back to England. Adding to the problem was Irish stubbornness in preferring potatoes as their main diet. Four years earlier, Ireland had suffered a widespread potato blight and they were still adjusting to the effects of damage to that crop and famine.

Ordinarily, a family would complain about such conditions and openly voice their hunger, but Judith did not allow complaining about things that could not be changed. The children were told that this was their sacrifice for being poor, and if they worked hard and long they would reap the benefits. The concept was hard to understand; they saw their father work hard and long with little reward. But Judith's message was one of hope and perseverance.

* * *

Early the next morning Sully and Edmond fed and watered their pig, a sow—the only pig left after the previous litter was sold at the market. Food was scarce even for the farm animals like the pigs, who had to scavenge for insects and new shoots to supplement their diet. The Sullivans' small two-acre farm did not support much planting or grazing. Edmond looked up and saw three English soldiers walk by.

"Why do we have to work so hard while soldiers enjoy the best part of our harvest?" he asked his father.

"That's the way it is," replied Sully without paying any notice to the soldiers.

"Some of the boys down at the market want to firestorm the barracks and burn it to the ground."

Sully looked up, surprised at his son's comment. "And what will that accomplish?"

"They will take notice to treat us better."

"You hope they will take notice, but in reality we will suffer further," Sully said.

"Then we will burn down another barrack."

"You said 'we.' Are you part of this plan?"

"They have asked me to join. I can't stand by while they drag you off and beat you."

"Edmond, think about this. What would happen if you got caught?"

"I will be hanged in the square, but we don't plan on getting caught."

"And if you don't get caught, what will happen?"

"Nothing." Edmond hesitated. "Well, maybe something."

"Right, somebody will be beaten; somebody's house will get burned down—somebody that doesn't deserve it—as an example or a message. Instead of causing trouble for the village, let the politics of Daniel O'Connell work for our rights. It may be slow, but I am confident Mr. O'Connell will achieve change."

"It doesn't seem right," Edmond said. Edmond knew his father was right, but it was hard to be patient at nineteen. He wanted immediate results.

"If you get caught both you and I will be hanged," cautioned his father.

That was the end of the discussion. Edmond was willing to risk his own life for the sake of a rebellion, but to link his father and cause harm to the family was unimaginable.

* * *

Two days passed, and the news came that Lord Mount Cashell wanted to see Sully the next day. Sully was not surprised by the request and he felt prepared to meet the man who controlled whether he and his family would be recommended for the move to Upper Canada. By coincidence, Sully had met Lord Mount Cashell's mother, Lady Margaret, before the current Earl was born. The meeting had a profound effect on the young Sullivan boy—his first exposure to the English-dominated peerage who controlled Ireland.

Twelve-year-old Sully was helping his father sell produce at the market. As Lady Mount Cashell stopped to examine potatoes at the Sullivan display, she took an immediate liking to the young lad who tried to explain the superior taste of the Sullivan potato.

Lady Margaret had had a difficult upbringing and later in her teen years she had learned two important lessons: the value of a good education and the proper treatment of children. This day at the market, she passed on both lessons.

"You represent your crop well, young man," she said with a smile.

Sully was proud of the compliment and could not help beaming his familiar wide smile in return. His father, distracted by another customer, was unaware of the exchange.

"Yes, Madam."

"You seem like a good lad. How old are you?" asked Lady Margaret. As she turned to look at the cabbages, Sully could see that she was pregnant.

"Twelve years old."

"Ah, yes, twelve years, a good age. Do you read?"

"No, Madam. I can't read."

"Oh, too bad. You should learn to read. There's a whole world out there beyond County Cork that you can visit and learn about through reading."

"Yes, Madam, someday I would like to learn to read."

"I see you are helping your father. Is he a farmer?"

"Yes, Madam."

"Do you like farming?"

"Yes, Madam."

"Someday you will be a farmer like your father?" she asked with real interest.

"Yes, Madam."

"Why?"

Sully thought for a moment. "Because I like doing the work and having food to eat."

"And that makes you happy?"

"I guess so."

"Does working with your father make you happy?"

"It does; he shows me things and makes it fun."

"So," a slight hesitation from Lady Mount Cashell, "what is your name?"

"William."

"So, William, it makes you happy to work with your father, and I suppose it makes your father happy to work with you."

"I believe so."

"When you are older, you can teach your children like your father has and make them happy in their daily tasks, too. Life is hard, like working in the field all day, but the happiness you will find is in the work and your family."

"I think you're right."

"William, learn to read so you can read to your children and teach them to read."

"I will, Madam."

Lady Margaret was interrupted by her housemaid. "Madam, I think we should go."

"Yes, and buy a couple of cabbages from this young man."

"Certainly."

When the transaction was complete, Lady Mount Cashell stated, "William, remember to read. It's important for your future."

"I will, Madam."

Ordinarily, such a conversation between an adult and young teen would have little impact, but this was no ordinary encounter. A Countess had shown favour to a peasant boy and conducted a heart-felt conversation about his life and future. Sully remembered the unusual kindness shown by Lady Margaret.

Aristocrats in Ireland commonly belittled and scoffed at poor Catholic farmers with their dirty hands and faces, unkempt hair, worn and torn clothing, and bare feet. But Lady Mount Cashell saw someone underneath the tattered appearance, and she touched a soul that needed hope and purpose in his life, even though circumstances were unlikely to change.

The effect of that experience continued for many years. Although Sully never learned to read, he always had a yearning to learn the printed word. He and Judith often talked of the children's education.

Despite the news of the Earl's demand to see Sully, he was not scared. How cruel could the offspring of the kind Lady Margaret be, he reasoned, since she had reared and nurtured seven children. At the time, it was unusual for nobles to raise their own offspring. Sully felt confident meeting the Earl.

Moore Park, the home of Stephen Moore, the 3rd Earl of Mount Cashell, was a short distance from the Sullivan house in Kilworth. The walk down the long entrance lane brought Sully to the mansion guarded by two British soldiers. One soldier intercepted Sully as he approached the house.

"I'm William Sullivan and I'm here to see Lord Mount Cashell."

"The Earl is in the stable over here." The soldier led William to the barn, where they found the Earl grooming a horse, and Sully's presence was announced. Clearly, the plan was to meet Sully outside of the mansion.

"Sir, I am William Sullivan. You asked to speak to me."

"Ah, yes, Mr. Sullivan. I have received a submission from you for the Robinson Settlement in Canada."

"Yes, sir."

"I have also heard of your activities with rebel insurgents."

Sully interrupted the Earl. "That's a misunderstanding, sir. I grew up with many people in this area, some of whom want to see a free Ireland. I do not advocate their murderous methods to achieve freedom."

The Earl was surprised to hear this condemnation of his compatriots. "So why do you visit and drink with them in the pub?"

"I live here. This area is my home. This is my life." Sully paused to assess the Earl's reaction. A moment of silence hung in the air, with no reply. Sully decided to take the advantage. "If I can be forthright, sir, why do you live here among all this turmoil, hatred and poverty? You have the wealth to move away from all this. I don't have money or the opportunity, at least until now."

The Earl thought for a moment about Sully's bold statements but did not answer his question. "If I recommend your application, are you serious about moving your family to Canada?"

"Yes, sir."

"One of the criteria for recommendation is that you are a good citizen. Mr. Robinson does not want problems at his frontier settlement."

"I understand. I will be a long way away from Doyle's Pub. The only time you hear my name is connected to Doyle's Pub."

"The ships to Canada are leaving in the early spring of next year. If I hear of any problems with you between now and then, you will be heading to Van Diemen's Land rather than Canada."

"I look forward to the journey," said Sully, allowing the Earl to decipher which destination he meant.

The Earl summed up the meeting. "Nothing, Mr. Sullivan, no news what-so-ever of rebel doings."

"My word, sir." Sully stuck his hand out to shake but the Earl just waved him off. Sully left Moore Park confident he would receive the Earl's recommendation.

Lord Mount Cashell recommended William Sullivan and his family for the Robinson Project, along with 82 other families totalling 562 people, which was one of the largest recommendations made by any baron. Rather than writing a letter of recommendation for each family, as Peter Robinson requested, the Earl wrote one letter, dated the 20th of October 1824, in which he recommended the 83 families because they all fit the criteria of "poor and wretched," adding that "they subsisted by tilling the soil."

The Earl further stated, "They are just the sort of person you want in America, and by taking them, you will rid this country of so many paupers." He noted that the oldest of his recommended group was fifty years of age and the youngest was three or four months and that all were Roman Catholic families except one.

The Earl's frank words accurately described the conditions in Ireland, the lack of food and widespread starvation; the country was overrun with paupers. The Robinson Project was designed to alleviate the growing number of indigent people and provide land, shelter and supplies through this relocation effort.

Another unexpected problem surfaced: over fifty thousand poor Irish "paupers" applied for the program. Peter Robinson needed to carefully screen the applicants based on circumstances and trim the number to two thousand emigrants, leaving the remaining forty-eight thousand people to either emigrate on their own with no resources or to endure the current conditions.

The review and decision-making task was daunting for the appointed Canadian official who wanted to make sure that the applicants fit the program standards and that the settlers would become honourable citizens in his home country. As a result, Mr. Robinson relied heavily on the letters of recommendation. In the end, the Sullivan family was chosen for this relief effort, as well as three other families from the small village of Kilworth.

* * *

During the days following the meeting with the Earl, the Sullivans prepared to leave Ireland, and towards the end of the week the door to the cottage swung open and Edmond walked in.

"Hi Ma!"

Judith looked up and replied, "Hi Ed, what are you up to?"

"Nothing. I was wondering if tomorrow night we could invite Father Hannigan to the house? I would like to ask Frank Crogan too, for a night of singing."

"If you like," replied Judith. "What's the occasion?"

"Nothing special; I am just in the mood for fun before we leave Ireland. We don't have much time left to hear Frank's distinctive baritone voice."

"You're right. Go ahead and ask both of them." Frank was used to such requests because of his singing popularity. He did not mind because of the joy and attention it brought him, and having Father Hannigan attend was a sure method to get Frank to accept.

Edmond headed down to St. Martin's Church, with a stop at the Crogan house along the way, where he found Frank. "Frank, would you like to stop by the house tomorrow night for some festive singing?"

Frank replied without asking why, "Sure, I'll be along."

At the church, Edmond asked Father Hannigan, "Father, would you like to come by the house for a night of singing with Frank Crogan?"

"I think I can stop by."

The next night Father Hannigan walked to the Sullivan house, after having a small meal with another poor parish family, as darkness settled over Ireland.

"Hello, Father," greeted Judith.

"Good evening, Judith." Turning to the rest of the family, Father Hannigan said, "Hello Sully, Mary, Bess, and how are the little ones?" he asked collectively of Ellen, Johanna and John.

Frank came by shortly and was greeted by the family. Frank was a celebrity in Kilworth for his singing ability. He sat on the floor and Sully moved the benches away from the kitchen table so the children could sit and participate.

"I think I'll start," said Edmond who broke into song with the words from the old Irish favourite "Ned of the Hill":

"Oh dark is the evening and silent the hour,
Oh who is that minstrel by yon shady tower,
Whose harp is so tenderly touching with skill,
Oh who could it be but young Ned of the Hill."

"Very nice, Edmond," said Judith when he finished, and Sully nodded in approval. The other children clapped and waited for more. Frank followed with another Irish favourite, "The Green Bushes."

"As I was a walking one morning in Spring,
For to hear the birds whistle and the nightingales sing,
I saw a young damsel, so sweetly sang she:
Down by the Green Bushes he thinks to meet me."

But before he could finish the next line, "I stepped up to her and thus I did say," Judith said with a start, "Did you hear that?"

"What?" asked Sully, as Frank continued the song.

"Shhhh," Judith ordered Frank, who stopped immediately.

"Crack," followed by "boom."

They all heard the familiar sound of a gunshot. Crack—boom. "There it is again," said Judith.

"I wonder what it is?" said Mary.

Father Hannigan, like all the adults, knew something drastic was happening in the town, and said, "God bless us."

A series of gunshots followed as Sully rose and went to the door. He stood in the doorway facing the dark of the evening and looked towards the village, where an orange glow danced along the tree line, indicating a fire.

He turned around and glared at Edmond, who stood motionless, looking back at his father. Neither said a word. Sully was pleased that Edmond was home, but now he understood why Edmond had invited the parish priest and the popular Frank Crogan. They were his alibi for the firebombing of the barracks. Underneath, Sully was angry the way everyone had been used, but was also relieved that his son was safe. Ever so slightly, Edmond shrugged his shoulders so only Sully caught the meaning. Judith watched her two men and knew something was going on between them.

Sully stepped out the door and was followed by Edmond and the remaining household. They stood watching the fire and listening to the occasional gunshot.

"Let's sing out here," announced Edmond, seconded by six-year-old Johanna with a "Yeah!"

"Singing is over for tonight," announced Sully, then he added, "Father, you can stay for the night if you like. No need walking into that mess."

Father Hannigan, who was standing in the doorway, looked inside and saw the two small rooms at the rear of the house separated by a hanging blanket. "I think I will walk back to the church, thank you anyway."

"Are you sure?" asked Mary.

"Somebody may need me tonight," Father Hannigan explained.

"I hope it's for a Confession and not the Last Rites," said Sully, looking over to Edmond.

"That would be a change," said Father Hannigan.

"Frank, you can stay if you like," invited Judith.

"No, that's all right, I'll walk with Father Hannigan."

The two guests walked towards town together as the night became eerily quiet. The light of the fire still gave its glow along the southern tree line but nothing was stirring—no animals of the night gave their mating call, no squeals as predator captured prey. The human animal remained quiet too, but surely the hunt was on for the insurgent fire starters.

"Everyone back in the house," ordered Sully. "Ed, stay out here," he added. Ed drifted off to the side as the family filed back into the house. He knew a lashing was coming from his father. "Don't ever do that again," Sully started. "You used two good people in this town to cover your criminal activities."

"Da, I had nothing to do with it," Edmond protested.

"Don't tell me you had nothing to do with it. You knew when, where, and what was going to happen, and to know that, you were there when it was planned. And then you took steps to confirm your whereabouts."

"Da," was the only protest Edmond could find.

"Don't ever do that again," Sully repeated. "What do you think is going on right now? Your friends are being hunted down. Who do you think was at the other end of those gunshots? Edmond, think about what you are doing."

"You can't tell me what to do. I'm a man now and I'll do what I want." Edmond had found his bravado. His young adult hormones were kicking in to turn this dependent teenager into an independent adult.

Sully showed no surprise at Edmond's defiance. "A man does it on his own and does not hide behind good, unsuspecting people."

Edmond's inexperience at defying his father's orders left him speechless. He reverted back to his comfortable role. "Da, I don't know what to think. This abuse by the Crown goes against everything of value I hold within me. Yet you ask me to do nothing."

"Ed, all change comes through a mixture of diplomacy and force, whether real or implied, and that's the reality of human nature. But the force part is ugly, it's horrifying, and people get hurt. The Irish have shown they can be strong, forceful and resilient. Now it's time for the diplomacy."

Edmond shook his head in a half-convinced way; nevertheless, he had no other familiarity with international politics. Sully let his son regain his dignity and dropped the conversation. "Let's go back inside."

* * *

Judith, Sully and their family spent the winter months of 1825 preparing for their departure. Judith reminded them that this was the stroke of luck initiated by the long, hard work of the family. But the winter was not easy on the Sullivans, or any of the families. Sickness exacerbated by the lack of food rampaged across the southern areas of Ireland. Many people died across County Cork, but the Sullivans were spared, in large part by Judith's handling of the household. She was tough in her ideals but dedicated and loyal to her family's needs.

Within a week of the firebombing, two of Edmond's friends were captured, jailed and sentenced to the British penal colony in Van

Diemen's land on an island south of Australia later known as Tasmania. Tensions in the town subsided with the news of the arrests and Edmond quietly breathed a sigh of relief that he was not implicated for having knowledge of the incident.

* * *

In late March 1825, a rider came to the house and informed Sully that a meeting of all Robinson immigrants was planned and they were to report to the St. George's Church in Mitchelstown in a fortnight. At this meeting they would receive instructions on their departure for British North America. Sully and Judith left Mary in charge of the family during their all-day trip, but Judith insisted on bringing Edmond and Bess with them. Mary, the oldest sister, regularly helped Judith with household duties, and she was a strong presence during her mother's absence.

Edmond needed to learn the man's work involved with the move and Elizabeth needed to know the woman's responsibility to help her mother, therefore they would accompany their parents. Two weeks passed and the four Sullivans headed up the road to Mitchelstown for the meeting. Upon arrival, they learned that the location of the meeting had been changed on the insistence of the Bishop, who did not see the necessity of bringing all these Catholics into the Church of Ireland, an Anglican church. The meeting was moved up the hill to the Catholic Church.

Two meetings were held: the night before a meeting for those mainly from Southern Cork, and this meeting of those from north of Cork City. To the emigrants' surprise, Peter Robinson was present and described the program and the expectations for the settlers for boarding the ship, travelling during the voyage, and settling in Canada. Each family was allowed one trunk for all family possessions.

Judith was a practical woman and nodded to Sully. "We can do that."

Sully was thinking about the magnitude of this move and he did not comprehend Judith's question. "Do what?"

"Fit everything into one trunk."

"Yes, I'm sure we can." His mind shifted to what he was leaving behind—the house, the land and their relatives, none of which would fit into a trunk. Those items would soon be just memories. At once, sadness and fear overcame Sully and he looked to Judith. If she felt any fear, no one saw it. Once again, her presence was reassuring, showing hope, courage and resilience. They both shared these characteristics but at different times, such was the balance of their relationship as a couple.

Peter Robinson met with the head of each family individually. He inquired about Sully's family. "Who is your wife?"

"Judith," answered Sully.

"And your children?" he continued.

"Edmond, Mary, Elizabeth, Dennis, Ellen, Johanna and John," listed Sully. Peter listened and made a few notes as Sully described his family.

"Why do you want to move to Canada?" persisted Peter.

Sully thought it was odd that he was asking these questions but he answered anyway. "I cannot grow enough food to feed my family and pay the Earl's tax."

"You are scheduled to sail on the ship *The Brunswick* from Cobh on May 11," Mr. Robinson told him.

"We will be there, ready to go," Sully assured him.

At the end of the conversation, Mr. Robinson gave Sully his boarding certificate for the boat and wished him farewell until May. "I look forward to your immigration to Upper Canada."

"Thank you, Mr. Robinson," answered Sully.

* * *

The meeting in Mitchelstown rendered the move real and imminent. Sully and Judith toured the area to meet with family and friends they were leaving behind. Judith, the eldest of her siblings, gave away family heirlooms that had been handed down to her. Some items had less intrinsic value, while other items were more practical—such as a large cooking pot, which she gave to her youngest sister. But the item that distressed her most of all was a cup and saucer, a wedding gift given to her great-grandmother who had lived in London and handed it down through the generations. She knew the fine porcelain tableware had little chance of surviving unbroken on the journey across the ocean and the wagon ride into the interior. She left it in the care of her next youngest sister, Ida.

* * *

On the Sunday before their departure, the parish priest of St. Martin's Catholic Church in Kilworth Parish prayed for the three families leaving for Canada. Following the service, Judith and Sully said their goodbyes to the new priest who had replaced Father Burke, the longtime parish pastor who had built the church and had married them.

All their children had been baptized by Father John Burke, with the exception of John, who was born after the highly respected priest had died four years earlier. The small stone church, built in the outline of a cross, with an open bell tower at the top of the steeple, was a second home to these families, and emphasized the closeness of this small but important market town in the northeast corner of the county.

"May the peace of the Lord be with you during your journey," Father Hannigan told the gathering of the Sullivan family in the front of the church.

"Thank you, Father," replied Judith.

"I think young John there has the making of a good priest. Make sure he gets a good education."

"We will," said Sully.

"And pray for us at home that the Lord blesses our fields with abundance."

"And ours too," said Sully.

* * *

On Tuesday, May 10, the Sullivans closed the door to their cottage for the last time in Kilworth to head south to Cork. The Earl's men were present to take control of the property, and as soon as the last Sullivan, Edmond, stepped off the property, the men set fire to the house. The family wept at the sight of their home in flames. Judith huddled the children close together and led them away. As they walked down Dublin Road, they watched the smoke billow into the air behind them. Even though Sully could not express his thoughts, he was happy the house was on fire. No turning back at this point, he thought.

* * *

The morning of May 11 the Sullivans assembled on the docks of Cobh after spending the night with Ida in Cork City. A swarm of people clearly recognizable by distraught appearance lined the dock as three Robinson ships were being loaded for departure on this day. Three ships, *The Resolution, The Albion,* and *The Brunswick* lined up along the side of the dock in the deep harbour. Each had a sign identifying its name as well as a hawker who yelled out for those unable to read. Occasionally a family would present their boarding certificate to the hawker for verification, but the hawkers were young boys from Cobh and unable to read.

The lad yelled topside, "Any Kavanaghs?"

"Not on this ship," came the reply, and the boy sent the family to the next boat.

The scene was not one the Sullivan children would soon forget. The people who lined up in great masses were Ireland's poorest and most downtrodden. Their drawn faces and emaciated bodies looked as if they were waiting for medical help rather than a ride to freedom. Even though this group was chosen for being poor, Catholic, good citizens and family-based, they represented the direst poverty.

As they waited, the other shipping business of the port added to the confusion and chaos of passengers hustling back and forth. All ships' masters maintained tight timelines and, when ready, they were leaving regardless of a confused family struggling with trunks and children, trying to decipher which ship to board.

* * *

Out in the centre of the harbour stood a ship anchored with no sails. There were people on board and movement about the ship, with much shouting and cries of pain. The soldiers were happy to inform the curious visitors about the boat. "It's a prison ship," stated a young soldier, apparently proud to have contributed to the population on board.

The *Surprise* had served its time at sea and was removed from commission. Now it sat moored in the centre of the harbour to house prisoners waiting for transport to Australia, the English penal colony. As many as 350 men were locked below deck in overcrowded conditions; here the convicts waited. An observer later remarked, "The hulks were no place for reform of character," as tales of their notorious deeds were told and boasted about—a different form of survival.

Now, Sully looked at the ship and realized his luck that Sergeant Miller had not made a trumped-up charge of treason, which would have sentenced him to the *Surprise* and then separation from his family and transport to Australia. Edmond was sad as he realized his two compatriots from the firebombing were most likely part of the *Surprise*'s population.

"I could've been on that ship," Edmond whispered to his father.

Sully turned and looked at his son with gloom in his voice. "Your mother, nor I for that matter, could not sail out of Ireland with you aboard that prison boat."

"Da, thank you for your guidance with all that rebel action." Edmond lowered his head half in sadness for his two friends and half in relief that he did not end up with the same fate. "But if I had been sentenced to that ship, they would not let you sail out of Ireland."

Sully did not say anything further and placed his arm around his son in comfort.

* * *

Ida and two other sisters accompanied the Sullivan family to their ship. They hugged and wept as each sister realized they would never see their other sister or her husband, nephews or nieces again. Each family member promised to write the other and someday make a trip to visit, although in the quiet of his or her mind, all knew such a visit was unlikely. Two of Sully's brothers arrived from Mallow to wish them farewell.

The *Brunswick* passengers waited on the dock, as Peter Robinson needed to oversee the boarding process on each ship. He worked his way down the dock from the *Resolution* to the *Albion* and finally to the Sullivans' ship. People milled about waiting for permission to board, adding to the commotion of the docks as barrels of food, water and beer were loaded along with crates of tea, spices, medicines and other sundries.

Finally, passengers were called for *The Brunswick* and the nine family members walked up the plank, the thirteenth family to board. Little Johanna was excited by the massive ship with its tall masts and the activity of the crew preparing for sail. Numerous other families were loitering about, either waiting to settle in or set sail. Small children were running about from one side to the other looking over the gunwales and waving to the people on the docks. The ship was alive with activity.

Peter Robinson greeted Sully on the main deck.

"Good morning, Sully." Peter had a knack for remembering names.

"Mr. Robinson, it looks like a good day for sailing."

"Indeed," said Peter, as he turned serious. "Who do you have with you?"

"My family, of course."

"Yes, I see that, but what are their names?" Sully did not realize that he was being tested by Mr. Robinson, as all passengers were asked for detailed information so counterfeit settlers could not sneak aboard. "Who is your wife?" he repeated.

"Judith," answered Sully.

"And your children?" he continued.

"Edmond, Mary, Elizabeth, Dennis, Ellen, Johanna and John," listed Sully as he had done at the meeting in March in Mitchelstown.

Peter checked his notes as Sully described his family.

"Why do you want to move to Canada?" Peter persisted.

"As I told you earlier," Sully said, "I cannot grow enough food to feed my family and pay the Earl's tax."

Peter Robinson finished the questioning. "Do you have your boarding certificate?"

"Of course," said Sully and handed the certificate to Peter.

"Welcome aboard," said Mr. Robinson and stuck out his hand for Sully to shake.

"Thank you," a confused Sully replied.

Mr. Robinson introduced the ship's captain. "This is Master Robert Blake, and this is Mr. John Tarn, from the Royal Navy, who is the ship's surgeon and the government representative in charge of the voyage and passengers on this ship."

"A pleasure," said Sully.

The first mate, Mr. Lewis, who was standing behind Master Blake, stepped up, said "Follow me," and led them below to make berth.

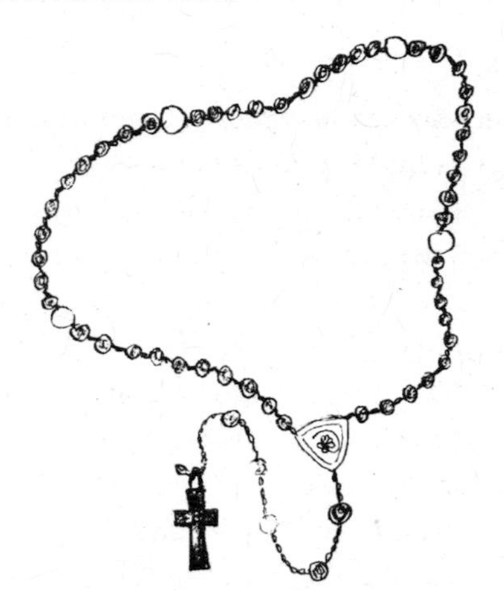

Chapter 2

The Sullivan Family
The Brunswick

Mr. Robinson welcomed aboard fifty-four families on *The Brunswick*, the last group consisting of Mrs. Walsh along with her four children and sister. Mr. Walsh had died during the spring waiting for the voyage to Canada. One more family was scheduled, Darby Guinea along with his wife and four-year-old son; however, their preparations were not complete and Mr. Robinson rescheduled them to take *The Elizabeth* ten days later. Therefore Mrs. Walsh's family was the final one, bringing the passenger list to 343 Irish emigrants relocating to Canada. Of those passengers, 143 were children under the age of fourteen.

Liam Mahoney and his family were also cleared by the Earl to join this project. Peter Robinson questioned Liam for a long time on the dock. Sully could not hear the questions but it appeared Liam was having a hard time. His two young sons watched as his father clarified details in Robinson's lengthy inquiry.

Judith was concerned. "Did you know that Liam was approved for this trip?"

"No, I didn't know."

"Why not—I thought you would know?"

"You told me not to talk to him and stay away. So I did."

"I didn't know you were listening."

"Of course, dear. I always listen—but I don't always follow the instructions."

"Well, as long as Sergeant Miller doesn't get on board."

Sully let out a long breath and lowered his head. "That man could show up anywhere. I say, as long as he doesn't show up in Canada."

"Amen, I pray to Jesus, Mary and Joseph that he is gone forever."

"I'm going over to welcome Liam aboard. They can't possibly think I wouldn't talk to him during the voyage."

Judith leaned into Sully's chest and whispered, "Be careful; there will be a spy on board."

"You're right; someone here will be given an extra acre of land or something of value to spy on us." Both Sully and Judith were right, but the spy remained anonymous throughout the voyage.

* * *

The Resolution was the first to depart the dock. Much cheering and yelling started between the ship and the dock, and goodbyes were waved to families as tears of joy, relief, envy and other emotions were felt on both sides. Then the taunting between the ships began: challenges to race the other two boats to America, as well as boasts of "Our ship is bigger, stronger or prettier" were traded back and forth.

* * *

Finishing his final preparations and notes, Peter Robinson gave his closing instructions to Mr. Tarn, the surgeon and government representative in charge during the voyage. It was now past noon and Master Blake, also referred to as Captain Blake, was getting anxious about taking advantage of the tide and the winds. As soon as Mr. Robinson departed his ship, the Captain yelled, "Make sail."

The canvas from the foresail dropped as sailors quickly set the rigging, which tightened as the ship pulled away from the dock. The ship's crew tied off the lines and hustled to drop the remaining sails as the Captain called out the order: "Drop the mainsail, the mizzen sail, the topsails, the jibs."

Soon the ship was in full sail as it headed to the open waters of the Atlantic Ocean. The sky was clear, which added to their good luck, as the winds were for sailing. Neither the Captain nor the passengers knew at the beginning, but this trip across the ocean would benefit from good winds most of the way and they would conquer the sea in only thirty-two days before landing at Quebec City on June 12, 1825. The time was short for ocean voyages, but it was long for the crammed and overcrowded ship.

The bunks were small and designed for one person, but two and three people were jammed into a single space. One family with two parents and six children had only two bunks because the children were small. No one complained about the close quarters, but the conditions proved fatal for some. The malnutrition prior to boarding, coupled with the susceptibility to illness and the easy transfer of contagious diseases, made this group a breeding ground for medical disaster.

The sickness and death began quickly. The Thomas Rahilly family bunked above the Sullivan family, where one of their young children died from the various diseases of smallpox, typhus and other undiagnosed illnesses. Margaret Lyne, a fourteen-year-old girl occupying the section across the aisle from the Sullivans' housing, passed away en route, as did David Condon, a fifty-year-old labourer from Brigown, County Cork.

James McGuire's family lost one of their children but another was born during this trip. In all, eighteen people died during the thirty-two days between Cobh, Ireland, and Quebec City. In spite of the conditions, seven other children were born. Mr. Tarn was busy during the journey.

Even though there were many deaths, equally prevalent were sick children and sick parents, and many passengers cared for each other's families, thus exposing themselves to even closer contact. The Sullivans were a relatively healthy family compared to the others due to Judith's management of food and family resources, so they became part of the caretaker group. They spent most of the time making the patients comfortable, dabbing their foreheads with cool, damp cloths, and praying.

After the second night on board when the sickness started, James Rochfort prayed aloud. The ship went silent during his prayer for his sick wife, Bridget. Each night thereafter, one family led the ship in prayers as the custom spread. After prayers one night, Judith leaned over to Sully and said, "They should have included a priest on board in addition to a doctor."

"Indeed. Not only to anoint the sick but to care for these grieving families." As could be expected, morale quickly dropped and the hopes of a new life in Canada were re-focused on hopes of just surviving the trip.

The passengers were encouraged to stay below the main deck. The Captain reasoned that the crew needed room to work but he was also protecting the crew from exposure to the diseases. Likewise, with 143 young children, the main deck was a dangerous place where rope lines were constantly being raised and lowered, and there was the enticement for a child to climb on the gunwales and look into the water. The Captain needed to protect his passengers as well.

Healthy men felt the urge to contribute to the voyage since the caretakers were mostly the women and teenagers. The men only got involved with caring for the sick when heavy lifting was needed. Therefore, a couple of the men went on deck and volunteered assistance with the sailing. The Captain realized their need to work and stay active, even though the ocean had been reasonably calm so the ship moved easily, without much need for additional help.

But farmers, like sailors in the nineteenth century, had the ability to adapt to unforeseen difficulties as the situation arose. Their numerous skills for addressing mechanical problems such as lifting and moving made these landlubber farmers and sea-going sailors a similar brand of labourer. The Captain decided to train the men for simple but important tasks in case a storm should strike, so he assigned his sailors to instruct the willing farmers to become assistant sailors. Sully, Edmond and Denny were among the men.

* * *

The two young Sullivan girls watched their mother and older sisters take care of sick passengers. Age seemed to follow age as Judith cared for the adults while Bess and Mary comforted the ill children. The arduous routine as well as the intensity of the care had a profound effect on the two smaller girls. Even though their life had been hard, they always escaped to the various stories and fairy tales that kept reality at bay.

Now they could not escape the misery; they had no place to go. Judith kept watch over the girls as well as young John to monitor their health and any emotional trauma. They were too young to help and too vulnerable to ignore. At least once an hour, she gathered the small children to talk about the things they saw—treatment of the sick. She decided to give them a task.

"I would like you to help these people get better. Can you help?" Each of the children nodded, as now they could be useful. "But not everyone one is going to get better. Some are going to meet the Lord. Do you want to help them too?" The children were ready for their assignment.

"You can pray for each of them: to get better, to ease their pain, or to help them get into heaven." The power of prayer had been instilled in the Sullivan children from infancy. They understood the importance of asking the Lord for help and they equally understood the response was not always as requested.

Judith and William Sullivan taught their children that the Lord always heard their prayers but sometimes He had other plans to teach about pain, difficulty, loss, despair and hopelessness. Judith talked through these life lessons in the simplest possible way for their easy understanding. Faith in a greater power that recognizes good deeds and thoughts and offers eternal rewards after death was the hope these children learned. Now they were ready to assist.

Ellen assumed the leadership role as the three children moved through the aisles and stopped to visit the sick. They approached the Malone family whose father had just come down with a fever.

"We are going to say the rosary," Ellen informed her younger siblings Johanna and John.

"Oh good," said Johanna as John looked on.

Ellen started with the Our Father and the three Hail Mary's. She then went into the first Joyful Mystery.

"I don't think we should say the Joyful Mysteries," said little Johanna. "Mr. Malone is too sick to be joyful. We should say the Sorrowful Mysteries."

"No, we should save the Sorrowful Mysteries for the really sick people." The six-year-old and the nine-year-old had a child-sized discussion and disagreement about which of the rosary's mysteries should be used. John just smiled and sat on the floor with his two hands clasped together pointed towards heaven, ready for prayer.

Mrs. Malone leaned over and said, "Please do the Glorious Mysteries. I believe Mr. Malone will be getting better."

"I don't know the Glorious Mysteries." Ellen was ashamed at her lack of information to help Mr. Malone with the right prayer.

"That's all right," responded Mrs. Malone. She knew the sensitivity of young children and the difficulty they had staying focused through multiple recitals of the rosary. "I'll tell you there're a lot of sick people on this boat. You won't be able to say a rosary at each bunk. I think one Our Father and three Hail Mary's are more than enough for right now."

"All right," said Johanna, anxious to move on.

The three looked around for their next stop. "Over here," said Ellen, leading them to the Mahoney family's bunk. "Can we say a prayer for you?" Ellen inquired. Mrs. Mahoney, who had been crying, just nodded. The children started again.

Judith watched from a distance and called them back after the third prayer session. "That's enough for now," she told them.

"Can we do it again?" asked Johanna.

"Yes, but later," answered her mother, knowing the attention span of youngsters.

"Good," said both girls. John just smiled without voicing any agreement or objection. He was content being part of the group.

* * *

The days dragged for the passengers below deck as *The Brunswick* glided across the sea towards North America. Sudden tragedy struck the Sullivan family, when Sully took sick with a high fever and an intense headache. The symptoms were familiar as many passengers exhibited these warning signs of ship's fever. When the purple rash appeared, Mr. Tarn examined William and determined he had typhus. The news scared Judith, as disease was now closer than ever and the family was vulnerable. She tried to quarantine the family as much as possible because the fever was contagious and deadly.

However, the children wanted to see their father, especially if his passing was a possibility. The hardest to keep at bay was Edmond, whose role as the eldest male was crucial to family survival should Sully die. Edmond needed time with his father for the accelerated learning and bonding inherent in the dying process. Judith was protective but conflicted between these two important elements.

Sully called his son to him and spoke about caring for his mother and family. He then gave Edmond his charge. "Son, you need to help your mother get settled in Canada. You also need to take Denny and guide him into manhood. And then, you can look for a wife and start your own family."

"I will."

Sully talked to each of his children individually and eventually, it came time for Johanna. Usually she and Ellen did everything together but this time their father saw them separately.

"My little Johanna."

"Yes, Daddy."

"I need you to take care of your mother when I'm gone."

"Where are you going?"

"I have to go visit the angels for a while."

"Are you coming back?" Her eyes glistened with unshed tears.

"No matter what, Johanna, I will always be right here." He tapped her in the centre of her chest where her heart lay underneath. "I will always be with you."

Her reply was hesitant but she trusted her father. "I suppose."

"You know when Grandma Ellen passed away, how we thought of her every day."

"Yeah." The first tears started to roll down her cheeks.

"Well, that's how I'll be with you."

"Da, I'm scared. I don't what you to go away."

"God has bigger plans for me. I have to go see him soon."

Johanna reached up and wrapped her arms around him, as far as her little arms would go. She squeezed hard. "Daddy, I love you."

"And I love you too. Now go and see Bess about cleaning your face." The tears had streaked down her cheeks and she sniffled through the conversation with her father.

Judith raised John up to see his father and sat him on the bunk next to Sully. No words were needed. John was just beginning to understand the language but he was not able to grasp meaning from full sentences. John needed to feel affection, a non-verbal connection to his father. Sully reached out and took his hand and smiled at his youngest son. He wanted to hug him closely but Judith would not allow that, for fear of too close contact with his sick father.

Sully reached up and shook his son's full head of hair. It made little John laugh. A tear welled up in Sully's eye. He was going to miss seeing his son's growth, the happy times, the sad but comforting moments, the development of personality, his likes and dislikes. He was going to miss all of it and he knew someday John would regret not having that time with his father too. But life did not conform to wishes and dreams; it dealt on its own terms and to fight destiny was to prolong agony. Sully shook the head of hair again and turned away in grief.

* * *

One major ocean storm blew in during this voyage and it was this day. The intensity started about 11:00 a.m. and continued through the afternoon, as the storm tossed the massive ship across the tips of huge waves and then plunged the boat bow first into the swell, slicing the water into sprays upward and outward, with the streams landing across the ship's deck. Most of the seawater rolled off the deck into the ocean, but some leaked its way below. The passengers were rolling right with the wave trying to regain their equilibrium, when the ship would shift to the left, causing the passengers to grab any fastened object to stabilize their motion, when suddenly it reversed again.

The sick did not have the strength to steady their ebb and flow. Internally, their organs were already fighting the sickness; now the body had to fight the competing force of pitching forward and back, side to side, gravity versus inertia. Seasickness mixed with the fever taxed the body's energy and the seawater leaking below caused bodies to be damp and chilled. The healthy were miserable with the rocking and the moisture.

Judith stayed with Sully, holding him steady to the wooden frame of his bunk. In trying to keep Sully from rocking, she lost her own stability on the wet floor and then did what she had hoped not to; she climbed into bed next to Sully, so the two bodies pressed together would not pitch with the ship. The closeness scared her, although she did not fear her own sickness as much as she feared both of them dying, leaving the children parentless in a strange new world. She had Sully rolled onto his side, facing away from her and she pulled him in tight. They rode out the storm together. Mary gathered the children in the upper bunk for their safety.

A series of wind shears struck the sails as the air currents hit at different speeds along the length of the mast, giving the main sail a twist against Mother Nature's force. It tore the sail's roach, a pocket of excess canvas designed to catch the wind. The reinforced batten could not withstand abrupt wind energy. It started as a small tear and as the second wind hit, the tear ran a diagonal line up through the sail. The Captain called for a jury rig to replace the damaged sail; however, he did not allow his sailors to climb the masts during the storm's height. He called for his volunteer auxiliary force to stand by.

The farmers waited for the order to hoist the rigging. When the force of the storm slackened, the Captain sent his experienced sailors up the ratlines to replace the torn sail. The volunteers proved their worth, as the urgency of the situation called for many tasks to be completed in a short but perilous time frame, which normally caused high stress to the sailors, who had to quickly coordinate and complete their numerous duties. The repair was made quickly and the crew rappelled down to the deck. The ship rode out the storm and stayed on course.

* * *

Only one death occurred as a direct result of the storm, but the stage had been set for three more weakened bodies unable to recover from the multiple assaults of nature in their struggle for survival. Sully was one of the three. He had developed a cough after the storm, a low deep cough sounding as if it came from the bottom of his lungs. Eventually, he moved in and out of consciousness as his condition deteriorated. It took two days before the glazed eyes and laboured breathing indicated the end was approaching. All the children were present while Ellen and Johanna were saying their special sorrowful mysteries for their father. Judith held fast to her husband's hand.

Edmond eased his way to his father's ear and whispered, "Everything will be all right," when the long last breath escaped and no new air was taken in. Sully died on the North Atlantic late in the evening half-way between Ireland and British North America. Mr. Tarn, the ship's surgeon, was present to make the declaration.

Judith's anguish finally hit the surface as she clenched her husband in a tight squeeze, and she released a long, loud "Ohhh no." William's limp and lifeless body failed to react to the intense exclamation and her strong desire for him to return to his mortal self. The embrace continued for several minutes, as Judith let out barely audible wails. The children watched, with their own perception of the interaction.

To the older children, she was saying goodbye; to the younger kids she was pulling him back into life. Somewhere in all their minds, they thought she was addressing the Holy Spirit to negotiate more time or send a final communication. But the end of life is final and no negotiation is allowed. When the emotion subsided and reality took hold, she released and pulled back.

Mary sobbed openly as she reached over and hugged Bess. Ellen went to John and Johanna and said, "Da has died and he is gone."

"But he will be back," objected Johanna. "He told me he was coming back."

Ellen remained firm. "No, he is gone to heaven where he will watch over us."

Johanna would not argue with her sister when she had something more important to say. She leaned around Ellen, who was blocking her view, and said her final words to her father, "I love you, Da."

Denny stood back, alone and unsure how to express his loss. He fought the tears because, since Edmond was not crying, he would not cry either. He watched his older brother closely for the right reaction, but Edmond's stoic stance gave little hint for the proper response.

It did not take long for Edmond's nineteen years of preparation to emerge. He placed his arm around his mother's shoulder. "Everything will be fine. I will get us settled and have the farm working in no time."

"You're a good son, Ed. I'm sure we will be fine, too." Judith had confidence in her son and her children's fortitude. Her weakness, however, was the loss of her husband. She had lost her balancing force: the one who was strong when she was weak; the one who made her happy when she was sad; the one who reassured her of good decisions; and the one who comforted her in the dark of night. Suddenly, she felt very alone.

After a small ceremony and prayers, William Sullivan was buried at sea. The splash of the water as Sully's wrapped body hit the ocean's surface brought sadness and tears for the beloved father and husband. In a fleeting moment, the sea took Sully for its own.

As the ship continued west, Judith was overcome with grief; she could not shake her melancholy mood. While previously she had never showed public vulnerability, now she could not control it.

"Ma, can we play a game?" asked Ellen, trying to engage her mother in other thoughts.

"No, dear, I just want to lie here on the bunk and rest."

"Ma, can you tell us a story?" asked Johanna.

"Why don't you ask Bess to tell you a story?"

The children looked over at Bess, who just shook her head, not in refusing to tell a story but to acknowledge their mother's sadness. Over the next several weeks, the children played calmly around the Sullivan bunk waiting for the voyage to end.

A woman named Geraldine, from a neighbouring bunk, whom Judith had not known during this journey made her way to the Sullivan bunk and offered a gentle condolence: "The Lord truly does work in mysterious ways and, I think, always restores balance." Judith pondered the words, trying to find the balance, but only time would define its meaning.

* * *

Liam Mahoney, along with his wife and two small children, bunked a few rows down from the Sullivans. They, too, had their bout with sickness but an early mild case gave them false reassurance. After Sully passed away, Liam came down with the fever, which did not take long to take hold and overcome him. Within a week of Sully's death, Liam too passed away. The two suspected Irish rebels were now gone. The news reached back to Kilworth Township and Sergeant Miller took credit for eliminating these two co-conspirators on the run from his jurisdiction. The sergeant manipulated the story into the far-reaching power of the British Crown to take victory over two of Ireland's sons. His reputation was intact.

* * *

They saw the coast of New Scotland, known by its Latin name as Nova Scotia, during the first week of June. The sight of land brought happiness for the weary passengers; they wanted fresh air, with room to spread out and start their new lives. Shortly Newfoundland appeared as they passed between the two landmarks indicating the entrance of the Gulf of St. Lawrence. They proceeded slowly, catching the westerly wind off the port side as they headed northwest into the gulf.

An island and other land throughout this area were originally settled by the French and known as Acadia. The British had captured the territory about a hundred years before the passing of *The Brunswick*. Some Acadians had refused allegiance to Great Britain and were dispatched to other areas. The forced separation of family and friends was not easily forgotten and some animosities still existed among the French old-timers. Ships flying the British flag did not always receive a warm welcome.

As this ship sailed through the strait, the volunteer force was called. Edmond and Denny responded to the call. The Captain wanted the top deck cleared, rigging stowed and the deck cleaned, as if King George IV was going to inspect the boat. Of course, the King was nowhere near the New World, as he kept himself in seclusion at Windsor Castle in London. The King had a reputation for preferring lavish parties, women, alcohol and drugs to politics.

His wife, Princess Catherine, was estranged from the King prior to his ascending to the throne and was exiled from England. However, when George III died in 1820 leaving the throne to his son, George IV, Catherine returned to London for the coronation and to assume her rightful title of Queen. At Westminster Abbey, she was barred from attending the affair. That evening she took sick and three weeks later she died of an unexplained intestinal blockage.

The irony of the circumstances was the name of this ship, *The Brunswick,* which shared the name of the German town from which the King's wife Catherine of Brunswick came. Naturally, King George was not about to visit *The Brunswick* off the coast of New Scotland.

Mr. Tarn approached Edmond and said, "This region is all part of the British Empire," as they looked across the water to parts of Nova Scotia and glimpses of Prince Edward Island in the distance. "We are part of the strongest empire in the history of the world." The doctor was proud of his heritage. "Napoleon wanted to rule the world and you see what happened to him. We do not want the world; Britain just wants a few key places to have free trade. You are going to be part of this empire in Canada."

The doctor had no need to lecture an Irishman on the greatness of the British Empire. Edmond took Denny aside. "I don't know much history about this area but I do know that you just heard the English version. Thousands of Acadians were jailed and shipped to various parts of the world because the British wanted to thin out the French. The name of that island over there was Abegweit and the first governor wanted to change it to 'New Ireland'; this is why I know the story. But London wouldn't let them use that name so it was named after Prince Edward, the fourth son of George III."

The boys had learned gratitude while growing up and now the English were trying to give them a better life, so they kept their thoughts to themselves. The two brothers returned below to stay with their family.

The passengers were not aware of the other two ships during the voyage but the Captain had passed *The Albion* soon after leaving Ireland. *The Resolution* stayed mostly in sight of *The Brunswick* during the crossing but *The Brunswick* was a faster ship with larger masts and sails. Even though it was last to leave Cobh, it was now in the lead, with *The Resolution* close behind. Master Blake worked the sails to keep the two ships close. *The Albion* had not been seen since the first day.

Eventually, *The Brunswick* crossed the gulf to the mouth of the St. Lawrence River, where it turned due west. The swift-flowing river led them to the interior of the continent. They stopped at Isle Verte to pick up a river pilot who would assist the Captain in navigating the river upstream to avoid its shoals.

With fresh water nearly depleted, the Captain decided to pick up barrels of fresh water and beer. Even though beer was a dangerous commodity on board, the Captain knew rationing would keep the crew positive and productive. Fresh water, which was used for everything from thirst to personal hygiene and scrubbing the bunks after a death, was another concern.

Potable water had value and because of its careful rationing, the storage area needed protection on board. The situation created many issues, such as adequate storage space, and when empty barrels lightened the load, it disrupted the ballast of the ship. As the journey progressed and the bottom weight became lighter, the ship increased its potential peril during high winds. The ship could easily tip under a strong gust and a rocking wave could upend the boat. The Captain continuously monitored and rationed the supply and redistributed the weight. The ship likely started the voyage with more than sixteen tons of water in storage.

Because of the sickness, the available water was nearly depleted, and the ship's master sent Mr. Tarn to the docks at Isle Verte to barter English tea for water, even though the journey would be over within twenty-four hours. The deal was made for an additional ten casks but they had to wait for the barrels, as this was not a normal re-stocking port. *The Resolution* under full sail sped past the stopped ship lingering at the waterfront.

About two hours later, the ship dropped the foresails and the main sails, navigated into the main channel of the river, and continued the slow move westward towards Quebec City, another 130 miles upstream. Darkness soon approached, which meant the ship had another night on the water.

However, by late Sunday morning, June 12, 1825, *The Brunswick* reached the landing area for Quebec City below the Plains of Abraham. A marvellous view greeted them—of two of the newly erected Martello Towers standing on the cliff's crest. The ship worked its way next to *The Resolution* and they rested together in the channel away from the docks.

"Drop anchor," ordered the first mate.

The heavy chains rattled off the deck and a 500-pound anchor crashed into the river to announce the arrival to the settlers below deck. The current of the river slowly swung the rear of the ship around in line with its flow as the chains tightened and the anchor grasped the riverbed to prevent the boat from drifting downstream.

"We reached here about an hour before dawn," the Captain called from *The Resolution*. "We can't go ashore yet because the transfer steamboat is not here."

"Thanks, I need to check with the harbourmaster," replied Master Blake. A small rowboat was lowered for the ship's master and Mr. Tarn to check in with the harbourmaster.

"Bienvenue à Québec," greeted the harbourmaster with a heavy French accent.

John Tarn was an educated man who spoke three languages in addition to his native English; French was one of those languages. "Bonjour," replied Mr. Tarn. The Royal Navy appreciated his multilingual skills as enhancing his service to the Crown.

"You are scheduled for the steamboat *Lady Sherbrooke* to take you up the river to Montreal," the harbourmaster informed Mr. Tarn, switching from French to English. Most French Canadians were bilingual and were willing to speak in English but they appreciated the effort by others to attempt their language as well.

"Very good, but I understand the boat is not here?" replied Master Blake.

"No, it left yesterday to make a trip. It should be back in a couple of days."

"A couple of days? I have a ship of over three hundred people, most of whom are sick."

"There is no place for you to take them. They must stay on board."

"I need supplies and water."

"There are dock hands running about that can assist you," the harbourmaster said. "How sick are your passengers?"

"We have lost eighteen people during the voyage. Another dozen or so still have the fever."

"Above you can get medical supplies." The harbourmaster pointed up the steep cliff to the fort high above the port.

"Merci," said Mr. Tarn.

The Captain headed back to the rowboat.

"I am going to walk up and see what I can get for the sick," said Mr. Tarn.

"I'll send the boat back for you." The Captain knew this was going to be a long, difficult forty-eight to seventy-two hours waiting for the steamboat.

* * *

Below, a grieving Judith was slowly regaining her composure. Ed and Mary had managed the younger children while their mother restored her spirit as she came to grips with being the sole parent for the family. However strong she appeared, she always carried the loss of William with her. Yet Johanna wondered innocently about her father's arrival in heaven and couldn't help saying, "Da said he went to visit the angels. Is he still with them?"

Judith roused herself. "I believe he is. He will be with them forever."

"Will he ever be an angel?"

"He already is," she said, as tears threatened again. "You know that your father worked hard every day to grow food and keep our home?"

"Yes."

"He was doing other things as well. He prayed every day for his parents, God rest their souls, and he prayed for a successful crop, in addition to a healthy family. He helped his neighbours when misfortune struck and he taught his children to be good people. You see, your Da was training to be an angel while on earth. Now, he is one."

"Oh, good." Johanna was satisfied that her father was happy in his new life. She thought a moment. "Ma, you are not going to the angels, are you?"

"No time soon." She gave a reassuring smile to her daughter. Then added, "God willing."

* * *

The Captain came below and called all the passengers together. "We have arrived in Quebec." A cheer went up through the group. The noise subsided but a few remaining coughing spasms drifted up, left over from the ill trying to cheer.

"Your next boat, a steamboat, is not here. It may be a few days before it arrives, and the harbourmaster has ordered us to stay on ship."

"Oh, no" resounded through the group.

"Make yourselves comfortable. The good news is that we made it and we are in a safe harbour. If you want to walk on the top deck, feel free to go up. Just don't try to leave the ship." The Captain waved his hand and turned towards the ladder to climb above.

Judith turned to Mary and ordered, "Watch the kids." She walked down the aisle and followed the Captain up the ladder. Once above, she called to Master Blake.

"Sir, I don't want to go on a steamboat; they're not safe. I have heard that they blow up and everyone gets burned."

"Mrs. Sullivan, I understand your fear. You have lost your husband and now you're afraid for others in your family. Don't let the fear of new experiences hamper your life, don't become so cloistered within your fear that it saps your energy and holds you down. Don't do that to yourself or your children." He waited and then continued: "Steamboats are safe even though some have caught fire. The *Lady Sherbrooke* is a very safe boat which has travelled this river many times. You'll be fine. I'll have Mr. Tarn contact you so he is aware of your concerns about the boat."

"Thank you, sir. I'd feel much more comfortable if you piloted the boat."

"I don't know the river that well. I'm sure the steamboat captain is a safe navigator."

"Thank you, Captain."

"Godspeed on the rest of your journey."

Judith returned to the lower deck and felt better after being reassured by Master Blake. His warning not to let fear determine life's decisions was something she had always followed in the past. She had not recognized herself slipping into that fear in recent weeks, and now she guarded against it.

"What's wrong?" asked Mary when her mother returned.

"Nothing. I had a matter to discuss with the Captain."

The family sat below with the 330 other passengers in the dark lower deck waiting for the steamboat to return to Quebec. By now the boat had the wear of thirty-two days of cramped family living. A subtle yet pungent odour wafted throughout the living quarters from remnants of human waste, sickness, discarded food scraps and unwashed clothing. There was no wind from the open seas to blow fresh air through the portholes and cleanse the stench. The smell was noticeable from the top rung down into the hold of the ship. Here they all sat and waited for three days.

On Wednesday, news came that the *Lady Sherbrooke* had arrived in the Quebec port and was ready to load and depart. The passengers quickly made their way to the upper deck for transfer to the steamboat. Small dinghy boats rowed the passengers to the dock and directed them onto the *Lady Sherbrooke*. The same process was happening on the neighbour ship *The Resolution*. The passengers hurried as if they were running from some devastating calamity to a ship that might not have enough room for all the settlers. Such was not the case; the massive steamboat took the passengers from both ships as well as seventy-eight other fares going from Quebec to Montreal. In all, 646 passengers boarded and travelled the steamer.

Once loaded, the *Lady Sherbrooke* paddled its way from the dock towards Montreal. The passengers looked back in an easterly direction, where *The Albion* sailed up the St. Lawrence en route to the port of Quebec. The third ship that left County Cork the same day as *The Brunswick* and *The Resolution* had arrived safely. The *Lady Sherbrooke* continued west.

Judith and the seven children squeezed into a small cabin on the steamboat. Edmond announced he would take the children to the top deck to watch the ship churn up the river. After being relegated to the lower deck for the previous thirty-two days, they were anxious to move about and see their new homeland. Johanna stayed behind as she still had questions for her mother. "Ma, I thought steamboats were scary and dangerous," she said.

"No, dear. This boat is a very safe boat that has travelled this river many times. We'll be fine."

"But Ma, I thought you said they were dangerous."

"I checked it out with the Captain. He assured me the boat was safe."

"You sure?"

"Yes."

"Can I go up top now, too?'

"Sure you can, sweetie. I'll take you up."

Judith was surprised that Johanna had heard her concern about the boat, as she never discussed it with the children. Little ears, she thought, amazing how they catch on. Then she finished the thought; I need to be more careful.

The next day at Montreal, the passengers disembarked on the east end docks for another transfer over to the western side of town to bypass the rapids of the river. Three flat-bottom boats took them to Kingston, Ontario. The transfer was slow but the passengers enjoyed the walk through Montreal. People stared at the thin, drawn Irish immigrants, with their tattered clothes, dragging children and trunks behind them. Those observers who had recently made the transatlantic trip immediately knew the distress these people had endured. The Irish, on the other hand, looked at the well-nourished bodies and clean clothes of the settled Canadians and knew better days were coming.

Chapter 3

The Sullivan Family
The Tent Village

The boats chugged out of Montreal against the current of the St. Lawrence River, with black smoke billowing from the stacks. The huge paddlewheel encompassing the entire width of the stern splashed the water back behind the boat until the resistance found its rhythm to push the boat gently forward and head upstream. The trip entailed a rise of sixty feet further above sea level over the 180 miles towards the entrance of Lake Ontario and the bordering town of Kingston on the north rim of the lake.

Today, in late June, an early summer heat wave warmed the area and caused a sudden spring thunderstorm to pass through the river valley with strong winds and lightning. The flat boats with canvas coverings supported by a wood frame protected the passengers from sun and rain, but the wind made the canvas flop up and down, which let the rain sweep through. Many people headed towards the spraying water rather than away from it, as it seemed to cleanse their body and soul. After six weeks confined to the lower deck of *The Brunswick*, the familiar rain comforted their spirits.

There was no fear of the boat capsizing in the middle of the ocean so the small waves generated by the wind along the river basin had little effect on the passengers. Within two hours the rain was over and the wind subsided. The moist calm allowed nature to release the sweet potpourri of spruces, balsam, magnolias and the occasional dogwood that lined the shore. The mood of the weary passengers improved immediately, and the thick vegetation along the shoreline gave a visual boost as the passengers pondered their new homeland. Soon the river was dotted with islands as they passed through the Thousand Island region of the St. Lawrence. The islands also indicated the end of this journey. As the river opened up in Lake Ontario, the pilot kept to the right, proceeding around Wolfe Island, the last and largest of the Thousand Islands, and headed into Kingston.

The English fort and naval port at Kingston were on constant alert against the New Yorkers on the opposite side of the river and lake. Skirmishes were common on this borderline. The English, and subsequently the Canadians, feared invasion from the Americans, who might take the land as part of their expansion of North America. The trouble was internal as well, as some Canadians saw the success of the Americans in gaining freedom from Great Britain and sought the same independence.

The Robinson boats navigated into the opening of the Great Cataraqui River at Kingston, pulling up to the east shore. Looking over a small bay behind them, the disembarking expatriates of Ireland saw the fortified walls of Fort Henry with the British flag flying above. Most passengers looked at the site and kept moving. Judith took no notice until the man in front of her exclaimed, "We will never escape the British Crown."

Judith remained stoic. "Did you not know you were coming to a British colony?"

"I was hoping different."

"As long as our crops belong to us," she said, and the man smiled. Again, as often in the past, Judith's remark fortified the spirit of hope.

The town knew these settlers were coming because the local *Kingston Chronicle* had published an article announcing the arrival of 700 immigrants at Montreal and their imminent arrival in Kingston. The passengers went around the small peninsula to the fort. The flat land behind the fort had numerous tents lined up. A group of officially dressed men and brightly polished uniformed British soldiers waited as the passengers headed towards them. An older man approached and gathered the people together.

"Welcome to Canada," the man announced in a formal tone. "I

am Lieutenant Governor Peregrine Maitland of Upper Canada. You are the first group of immigrants for Peter Robinson's settlement to arrive. You will wait here at Kingston, the capital of Canada, for the arrival of Mr. Robinson. This is Colonel Burke, who is Mr. Robinson's assistant. He will help you as needed."

Lieutenant Governor Maitland looked to the cloudless sky. "The weather is now warm and you will be staying in these tents until Mr. Robinson arrives."

"How long will that be?" came from the middle of the crowd.

"It may be a few weeks, but you will be safe here. We will supply you with fresh water and food." The sweat rolled off the Lieutenant Governor's forehead. His suit was too much clothing for this heat but the official welcome was important. He clearly showed he was happy with their arrival. He ordered a group of men and soldiers to help the passengers settle into their tents.

The Governor saw Judith in the crowd with her family. He approached her. "Good afternoon, Madam, how was your trip?"

"Good afternoon, Governor. I'm the widow Sullivan. I lost my dear Sully on the ship. The sickness took him." Her voice cracked as she spoke and her eyes watered.

"So sorry for the loss of your dear husband. If there is anything I can do for you, please inform me."

"Thank you, but there were numerous deaths on board besides Sully—husbands, wives and the poor children, oh my, the poor children. It was terrible. I feel horrible for those parents who had to bury the little ones at sea." She stopped. The memories and grief overwhelmed her. Mr. Maitland gave her the moment she needed.

She regained her composure and started again. "From what I hear, there were many deaths on the other ship as well. We need . . ." Judith stopped again, unable to form the words.

Mr. Maitland turned to an aide as if Judith had clearly articulated her needs and instructed, "Mr. Baker, please arrange for a priest to come here as soon as possible and perform a memorial service for all the lives lost during this journey."

"Yes sir," said Mr. Baker.

Judith reached out and took his hand. "Thank you, sir, that's what we need."

"Go settle into your family's tent. I'll take care of these matters."

Judith led the children away. Edmond clutched his mother to help her walk; Bess grabbed the other side to help her mother and brother. The three Sullivans led the way as Mary gathered the young children and headed down the row of white tents looking for suitable lodging for this family of eight. At the end of the row, next to the dirt road leading to the fort, they found an available tent.

The next morning Judith awoke just after sunrise to the sound of horses and soldiers marching on the road. It startled her, and it took a moment for her to figure out the noise. Fear had shot through her mind when she recalled the troops banging down her door in Kilworth. She released a gasp of air. One by one the children also woke.

"I think it is just the troops moving about," said Edmond.

Judith was well awake now and realized where she was. "Well, we might as well get up."

"What are we going to do?" asked Ellen.

"The first thing is to clean ourselves. Let's go down to the river and wash our clothes and our bodies."

The family walked up the river a short distance to find a secluded spot where the older girls could have privacy while bathing. The Governor had left numerous supplies with the immigrants, including a load of potash for washing. The family scrubbed the six weeks of ship living off their bodies and clothes. Edmond and Dennis helped John into the murky river water, which raised as much mud as they hoped to expel, and likewise Mary and Bess helped Johanna and Ellen wash. Judith had brought blankets to wrap around them until the clothes dried. The sun rose fast and hot, the beginning of a heat wave that would plague the settlers again. But today, the warm sun was welcome to dry the clothes. As the Sullivans left the river, other families trickled down the banks to start their cleansing as well.

* * *

A temporary cooking and eating area had been set behind the tent area. The section was crowded with passengers having tea and breakfast scones. Mr. Tarn was talking with Mr. Reade, the surgeon from the neighbouring ship, when Judith walked by and said, "Hello."

"Good morning, Mrs. Sullivan," said Mr. Tarn. "This is Mr. Reade from *The Resolution*."

"Top of the morning to both of you," replied Judith.

"Governor Maitland told me that no Catholic priests were in Kingston at this time."

"Oh," said a disappointed Judith.

"He sent a messenger to Montreal to have a priest return with the next boat of immigrants."

"He did, did he?"

"Yes, they should be here the day after tomorrow."

"Oh, my." Judith was surprised the Governor went to the extra effort to have a priest brought in. "Yes, that would be grand."

"The Governor, Mr. Reade and I were discussing the living conditions. With seven more ships arriving soon, this area will become very crowded. We would like to remind you that you may cross the river and walk through the town any time you like."

"You want me to walk over there?"

"No, that is, not unless you want to take your family for a walk."

"Yes, I may do that."

"When the next boats arrive, we will have the remaining area set up with tents and have a memorial service over there," he said, pointing to the far north side of the fort.

"You are most kind."

* * *

The town was well settled as a port and gateway trading area to the interior. Nearly three thousand people called Kingston their home and because of the accessibility, it had become the capital city of Canada. Judith on occasion took the children over to Kingston for a walk through the town.

Within a few days, the passengers from *The Albion* and *The Fortitude* trekked up the hill to the temporary tent city to settle in and wait for the remaining settlers and Peter Robinson's arrival. Father Collins, a young man born in Canada and currently assigned in Montreal, was with them.

The priest went from tent to tent to interview each family about their experiences and losses during their voyage across the ocean. His genuine interest in their stories of suffering in Ireland, sickness and death on the high seas, and fears about starting a new life without one of their family members was appreciated and respected by the families. He informed each group that a memorial service would be offered at sunrise the following morning.

Father Collins knew these Irishmen did not represent those Irish who were drinkers and brawlers but were strong family-oriented souls who believed in hard work and had high moral standards. A sunrise service was not a problem for farmers as the dawning of a new day was an easy metaphor for the priest to deliver and the passengers to recognize. His family was this type of Irish, too. He felt comfort and compassion among his peers.

The next day at 5:30 a.m. the service started. Nearly all the immigrants were spread across the hill, and an altar was set up for Mass; only the sick and those caring for them were absent.

Father Collins spoke of the sacrifices made to achieve freedom and independence. He reminded them that had they stayed in Ireland, the cost might have been greater, with no chance of improvement. He called on the Father in heaven to see their struggles and have pity on their souls. It was the sermon these people needed to hear. Mr. Tarn, an Anglican, stood respectfully towards the back. After the service, the passengers gathered in the central area for tea. A few benches had been brought in for seating but not enough for the entire group.

"This afternoon, I will split a few logs for more benches," said a man from *The Resolution*.

"I will help you," said another.

"As will I, too," said a third. Before long a team of carpenters planned tables and benches to furnish all the expected passengers during their stay.

Father Collins moved through the group. Many thanked him for his spirited message and his deep concern for those who died and those who survived. Even though Father Collins was young, the passion and expertise of his vocation were apparent.

Fifteen-year-old Bess sat down on a bench next to a young woman nearly her age. "A wonderful service," she said.

"Yes, my husband would have appreciated it."

"Your husband?"

"Yes, he died coming up the St Lawrence."

"Oh, I am so sorry for your loss." Bess was amazed that this young girl was married and that she had lost her husband so quickly.

"Thank you." The girl continued, "I don't know what to do. I don't think I can stay here."

"I'm sure Mr. Robinson can help you decide, or find a place for you to work other than a farm."

"How can I work and take care of a baby too?"

"A baby?"

"Yes, I am going to have baby."

"Oh, I see." But Bess did not see any sign of pregnancy.

The girl mumbled, "I'm scared."

Bess turned and looked into the troubled brown eyes of the girl. "Father Collins may help you."

"I don't trust priests. He will just yell at me for getting married so young."

"No, I doubt that." Bess wondered what to do to help. "My name is Bess; what's yours?"

"I'm Rose."

"Rose, such a pretty name." Bess considered inviting the girl to stay with them but thought better of it. Her mother had enough mouths to feed and worry about; another person and eventually a baby might be too much. "Do you have other family here?"

"No, and none to go home to in Ireland either. Daniel and I were going to start a new life. Damn the sickness that spread through that ship."

Bess remained silent. This girl had a hard side and a quick tongue, but she was lost in loneliness and lacked the maturity and support to find her way. Bess gave in. "You can come and stay with us. We will help you as best as we can."

"No, thank you. I'll be all right."

"Come and meet them anyway, even if you don't stay."

"All right, I have nowhere else to go."

Bess took Rose over to her family and introduced her.

"Mother, this is Rose. She was on *The Albion*."

"Hi," said Rose. "I have lost my husband due to the sickness."

"Oh my," said Judith. "I am so sorry. I lost my husband, too."

"Yeah, that's too bad," said Rose curtly. "Bess said that I can stay with you but no thank you." Rose only mentioned losing her husband, but did not mention a baby. After meeting the Sullivans, Rose wandered off. Bess let her go.

Later that afternoon, Bess saw Rose talking with Father Collins. She wondered if Rose told him about the baby or even if she had been married.

* * *

The weeks dragged in the tent village across from Kingston where the passengers had nothing to do. However, plenty of work awaited them up the road and they were anxious to arrive at their new homesteads and take advantage of the summer days to clear, build and prepare for the coming winter.

Mr. Tarn and the British government representatives from the other ships met with Governor Maitland occasionally for updates on the passengers. They were concerned the long delay would make them restless, resulting in a disturbance or placing the project in jeopardy. Word from Peter Robinson was that he had to go to New York and travel to York (Toronto) before arriving in Kingston. The wait was treacherous in the unusual high heat.

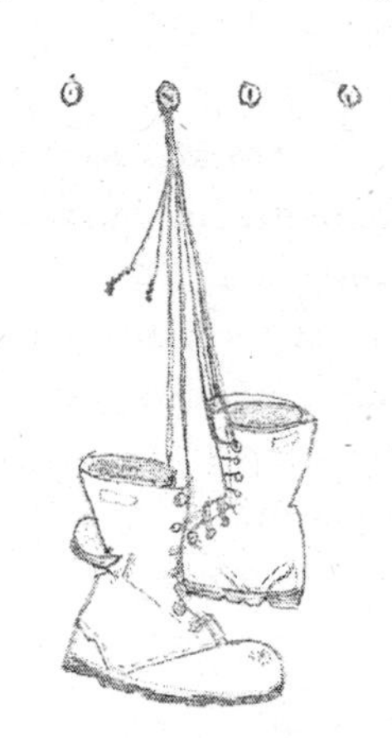

Chapter 4

The McCarthy Family
Abbeymahon, Co. Cork, Ireland

The River Lee runs cold through southern Ireland in late February as the chilled, deep water finds its way to Cork City and into the Atlantic Ocean. Thomas McCarthy felt the cold as the river rolled by while he lay on the ground with his torn and shabby wool coat pulled up over his shoulder. He had spent the night in pain and shivering, sandwiched between the damp ground and the overnight dew, which saturated his body from both sides. His spirit was dampened as well.

Thomas had walked the thirty miles from his home in Abbeymahon two days earlier in hopes of finding work. Out of the two days, he worked one, as a labourer loading freshly woven linen onto wagons bound for the shipyards. The pay was meagre but the opportunity for steady employment was his goal, even though such a goal was unrealistic in the tough times in Ireland in 1825. Just four years earlier the potato crop, the Irish staple, had failed, causing severely reduced food supplies.

Thomas was a farmer whose land was divided and subdivided by the overtaxing Earl of Shannon. Thomas's older brother Jeremiah, whom they called Jerry, had inherited the largest piece of land, six acres, and he had given two of the acres to Thomas to sustain his family. But two acres were barely enough to feed five people and pay taxes to the Earl. Thomas gave priority to feeding his family and the Earl received what was left in profit or food. Since the death of his father and the division of the land, there had been nothing left for the Earl.

When the Earl's constable tax collector came looking for the taxes, he was dispatched with nothing. Of course, threats and intimidation followed but Thomas was not alone; the condition of all southern Ireland was dire, especially County Cork. The Earl did not know or care that many of his tenants were destitute and starving, but the tax collector pushed only so far as he travelled through the county lest he put his life in jeopardy. Jerry was always present at Thomas's house when the collector showed up. He kept a watchful eye out for his younger brother.

Now Thomas was in Cork looking for work because his food supply was depleted. He stood at the river's edge and shook the water droplets off his coat, hoping the dampness—along with his personal troubles—would drop away from his clothes. His wish did not come true in either case.

As he stood looking at the river, he started to cough. It was a dry cough from deep in his lungs. He should have known better than to sleep on the open ground in freezing temperatures, but he had left Sheehan's Porter House on South Main Street at closing time with no place to go. Thomas had been asked to leave the pub because he was out of money even though he tried to buy more beer on his good name with the promise of more work and pay the next day. The money he had already earned was gone.

The pub was a centre for local talk, news reporting and social gathering. He had stopped into Sheehan's for some food and a drink so that he would stay strong enough to work and meet the local businessmen. When prospective employers looked promising, he would buy them a pint. It was an investment in his future. However, when the money ran out and Thomas was clearly intoxicated, Mike Sheehan escorted Thomas out the door.

Now the cough subsided enough for Thomas to descend the short embankment to splash water from the river into his face and smooth back his thinning red hair. He held his trembling hands in front of him to examine the reason for these shakes. His muscles twitched uncontrollably. The trembling was a new condition. It must be the cold water, thought Thomas.

The fear that they would not survive was also tormenting Thomas. He worried about his wife and three children starving and himself not having employment to provide the basics for existence.

"Oh dear Lord, what am I going to do?" he said aloud. In times of trouble, Thomas turned to his spiritual side, looking for divine help to appear from above like magic and take away illness or depression or bestow a lucky pot of gold. The intervention did not come, and Thomas was left angry that he was being cheated for being a merciful and humble man while the heathen English lords had money, stature, comfort and power.

His faith was shaky, but his footing on the edge of the river was firm. He climbed back up to the top of the bank and headed for the city streets in search of a day's labour.

He did not find work, though other men looking for employment were chosen. Thomas smelled like musty, day-old beer. Along with his tattered clothing and now his deep cough, he did not present himself as being sturdy enough for day-long work. The competition was keen and Thomas was not a viable contender as he walked the streets of Cork promoting, promising and pleading. He looked to his spiritual side again as he passed St. Peter's Church. "Dear Lord, please let one boss hire me and I will prove my worth." But business and mercy do not make good bedfellows, and the harsh-dealing world left him alone and jobless.

He approached Mike Sheehan's Porter House and stopped. The pub had not opened yet. Thomas decided to wait; maybe Mike needed help moving barrels or would let him have a glass of brew to brighten his spirits. He slid down the side of the building to sit in the doorway to wait. An hour went by without Mike's arrival. Thomas waited and dozed off because of his lack of sleep the night before on the riverbank. Another hour passed, and Mike woke Thomas so he could unlock his door.

"Tommy, wake up," he said.

"Oh Mike," said Thomas as he started to come to consciousness. "I was waiting to see you."

"What is it?" Mike asked, obviously annoyed that Tommy was back at his bar.

"I was wondering if you had any work for me today?"

"No, I don't."

"Are you sure? Do you need your floor cleaned or anything?"

"No Tommy, you're a drunk. Now get outta here and don't bother me. And don't sleep in front of my pub," was his final exclamation as he unlocked his door.

"Are you sure? I need the work."

"Tommy," Mike started as he put his keys back in his pocket, "you come to my bar every time you come to Cork and drink until you're out of money. No, I won't hire you. You should go home now."

"But I can't. I have no money to take home. I'm here to make money for my family."

"Tommy, if I paid you for a day's work, the money wouldn't make it home. You know that."

Thomas lowered his head. He knew it was the truth. The money didn't stand a chance of making the trip home. "What if I work and you keep the money? I'll send my son for it."

"Tommy, go home," was Mike's only reply.

Thomas headed down the street but in the opposite direction of his home. Mike yelled at him, "Tommy, go home."

Thomas found an open bar and decided to try his luck again, so he wandered in. When he opened the door, three men who were crowded together jumped and turned to look at him. One man looked frightened at Thomas's sudden appearance but it was not fear of physical violence, for the young man could have easily overpowered the exhausted and sickly forty-year-old Thomas. It was a different kind of fear. Thomas had the odd sense that *he* should be afraid, not the men already in the bar. The men spread apart as he walked forward.

The barman, who was one of the three, came around the open end of the mahogany-topped bar. "Can I help you?"

"I was wondering if I could clean your place or do a little work for a drink?"

"No, no work here."

"You sure? Can I stack some barrels or something?"

"I said, no work here."

"Yes, very well." Thomas hesitated. "May I sit for a moment?" and he motioned to a bench on the back wall.

The request was simple enough and hard to deny in a public business. "Yeah, all right."

Relieved to have shelter and warmth, Thomas took off his coat as he sat down. The three men separated even further. One stood at the right end of the bar with a one-page newspaper laid out in front of him. The second man went to a far left table and took two dice out of his pocket, dropping both of them onto the surface before he sat down with his back to Thomas. The bartender turned around, leaned back against the bar, and stared at the whiskey bottles lined up along the back shelf.

Thomas looked to his right again. The man looking at the paper turned his body to the side just far enough to keep Thomas under observation but clearly not to face him. His eyes maintained a steady stare down at the paper without moving. Obviously, he was not reading the paper; it was just a prop.

The man to his left picked up the dice and dropped them again on the table, looked at the numbers, picked them up and dropped them again. He did this repeatedly. The barman kept his back to the bar and to Thomas, a posture that continued throughout the visit.

These men were wasting time in Thomas's presence, sending a message that he was unwelcome, but not because he was some pauper down on his luck. The atmosphere was much larger than that. Thomas realized the men did not want any stranger to have a clear look at their faces, and he concluded the men were Irish rebels in the middle of a clandestine discussion that strangers should not hear or witness.

Finally, he stood up to leave. Immediately the man with the dice on the far left dropped the small ivory blocks into his pocket and headed for the door, cutting in front of Thomas on the way. Cautiously,

Thomas put on his coat and adjusted it. The other two men maintained their positions.

"Thank you," Thomas said to the back of the barman.

"Yeah, you're welcome," came the reply.

Thomas exited the bar past the third man, who stood in front of the building with his head down and turned away from view. As Thomas walked, he scanned the street for any hint that the bar was being watched. Nothing was apparent. About three storefronts down, Thomas stopped abruptly and bent down to fix his shoe. Nothing was wrong with the shoe, but Thomas wanted to glance back and see if he was being followed. The man in front of the bar was gone. Thomas breathed easier and guessed the other three did too.

He continued on, thankful he was not involved in such activity where constant fear was a way of life. He did, however, understand the rebels and their commitment to liberty. He supported the cause quietly, although he could not bring himself to be an active member of the movement. It was too risky to expose his family, and such activity was not his nature.

"I gotta find work," Thomas mumbled to himself. He continued to walk towards St. Patrick's Bridge and the north side of the river. He stopped at the centre of the bridge and gazed into the water. East of the bridge, the river was lined with ships, waiting for loading or unloading. Thomas saw opportunities for many strong men to work along the docks. They refused to hire him, for reasons he did not understand.

He felt strong, but they saw a frail undernourished man. He was proud of his work, but they saw a man in dishevelled clothing. His mind was clear, but they smelled alcohol. He was determined, but they saw a man beaten by the economic conditions of the time. In his mind, Thomas offered the ideal workman, but in his appearance, he was a poor representative, and in his behaviour, he was risky.

Thomas watched the boats move about the river. Employment was so close at hand but he could not reach it. A ship was moving out towards the sea, and he considered hopping aboard a ship to England to find work. But he had heard reports that the Irish had flooded London looking for work and were being turned away in favour of native Brits.

He turned towards the south and looked at the streets of Cork. He saw people move with purpose and self-importance to their duties. He wanted to be like them. His eyes ignored those like him, impoverished, whose idle bodies lined the edges of the street. He paused and thought of his circumstances—Thomas did not want to re-live the rejections. He felt pain but no particular part of his body hurt; and he felt alone amid the busy city. The cough returned with that deep, raspy hacking. Thomas took a couple of steps, raised his head and started his journey home.

The walk from Cork was a day's travel, but with Thomas's late start and his melancholy mood, he barely made ten miles. His feet were hurting so he stopped at the side of the road and took off his shoes. The soles had worn through and the socks did not offer much protection from the dirt and stone roadway. Soon even the socks would wear away. He sat down on the edge of the road to take off his socks and to rest.

A wagon came up the road and Thomas saw that it was the post wagon carrying the mail. William the driver pulled to a stop. "Are you all right?" asked Will.

"Yeah, I'm just resting. Can you give me a ride?"

"No, you know I can't do that in the Post Wagon carrying the Royal Mail. Mrs. Dalys would fire me if she found out." Mrs. Dalys handled the Royal Mail in Kinsale, and she had a reputation for following strict regulations about moving the mail.

"I know," said Thomas, realizing this was just another disappointment and lack of assistance with his troubles.

"I wish I could help you, Tommy. I saw Mike Sheehan and he is worried about you too."

"He's not too worried. He wouldn't help me find work."

"Tommy, it's best you go home."

"Yeah, I know."

Will slapped the reins and his horse pulled the wagon down the road. Thomas got up and continued in his bare feet.

Again he spent the night wrapped in his coat at the edge of a bog. This southern rim of Ireland was dotted with bogs, which supplied plenty of peat for heating. However, Thomas had no protection from the cold night air. The dampness returned to his body and his cough continued, this time more frequently. Thomas knew he was sick but his physical health was secondary to his drive to find work. His mind was distressed and now he had an ailing body. Thomas did not sleep well at the edge of the road.

The next day, he continued towards home. The feeling of hunger was slowing Thomas's progress. He headed off the path to a field of mixed grasses and clover and ate the dry bland vegetation. The meal staved off some of the hunger pains but the grasses were hard for human digestion and he risked binding his intestinal tract. He knew desperation increased perilous decisions even with the known risks, but his survival instincts were strong.

Thomas threw his shoes over his shoulder and headed down the road to Abbeymahon. A wagon came up the road loaded with milk cans. It was Colin Ferguson, whose family ran a dairy farm in a neighbouring town. The farm had remained productive through these hard times and the Fergusons supplied dairy products to merchants in Cork. Colin said "hello" to Thomas as he passed. Thomas knew the family but not well enough to ask for a free handout of cheese or milk. The wagon passed.

Late in the afternoon, Thomas saw a figure walking up the road towards him. As the figure approached, he saw it was a young man of medium height walking with quick, determined steps. Even through starvation and malnutrition, the man with the slender build had confidence, strength and pride, and his thick red-orange hair and wide beaming smile were easy to identify. Thomas watched as his son Denis approached him. As they met, the two men embraced, a rare display of affection. Their concern for each other's well-being was overwhelming.

"I was worried," started Denis.

"What were you worried about?" asked his father, ignoring the reality of his troubles.

"Will, the postman, told me you needed help."

"Damn that Will, he always lies."

"I brought some bread and a jar of tea for you," he said, and reached into his coat pocket.

"You're a good lad."

"What happened?" asked Denis. He and his father had a good relationship and talked frankly about events in their lives. Although Denis was only nineteen years old, he had matured quickly in his teenage years. As the oldest son, he took care of the farm when his father left to find work. Some of those trips were extended when Thomas went on his binge drinking. Denis understood his father and his ways. His "Da" always came home eventually.

Denis cherished the times when he and his father worked the fields together and talked about the crops, the farm, the weather, the proper use of tools, and literature. Thomas could not read but his wife Johanna taught each of the children how to read. The only book in the house was the Bible but Denis found other books in the parish and read extensively. The reading made him a self-taught man of literature, history and arithmetic.

Denis told his father of the stories he read and Thomas listened with delight. He was proud of his son's accomplishments. As Denis grew older he developed a deeper understanding of the Bible and they would discuss passages and their relation to life. He especially liked the New Testament and the precepts of St. Benedict, influential throughout the family parish and abbey begun by the Cistercian monks, whose motto of "pray and work" came easily to the hard-working and well-read Denis. He was the Renaissance man of the family.

At the edge of the road, Denis helped his father to the shade of a nearby bush, as trees were infrequent on this stretch of the road. Thomas quickly ate the bread and sipped from the jar. "This is good."

Thomas continued sipping his tea as he told his son of the lack of work in Cork City. He admitted that he was a poor prospect for a shopkeeper or a businessman to hire. He talked candidly to Denis about his shortcomings and Denis handled his father delicately. Denis knew his father's pride was profoundly wounded because of the lack of food and proper clothing for his family.

"But Da, you stuck with it. You slept on the cold banks of the river."

"I went to the bar; that was my mistake. I shouldn't drink."

"Well, you look none the worse for wear, but let's get you home."

The two started their journey together as dark clouds rapidly blew in and swirled overhead. Thomas looked skyward.

"Rain is on the way."

Denis was used to his father's weather predictions and he was proud of his father's wisdom and talents. Any time low, dark clouds rolled in from the east, west or south Thomas predicted rain. He was usually right. The ocean bordered the land in those three directions and often carried precipitation when the air currents pushed the nimbostratus clouds.

The difficult forecast was weather from the north, with its varying high and low cloud formations. Thomas had difficulty forecasting clouds coming from that direction. Today's wind had blown in low flattened stratus clouds from the southeast. As he looked out to where the Atlantic Ocean meets the Irish Sea, he saw the dark front of rain heading for the coast.

"We're going to get wet."

Denis replied, "Yes Da, low dark clouds mean rain. You had better button up."

Thomas and Denis walked towards Abbeymahon, their home parish, in a typical heavy Irish downpour. The full-length coat worn by Thomas was quickly saturated but the lamb's wool kept his body heat intact. Thomas needed the heat since his body was fighting enough sickness with the cough deep in his chest. He wore his grey tweed flat cap with the visor snapped closed and sitting low on his head. He tried walking in his shoes but with the rain falling and the roadway mud-lined and puddle-filled, Thomas's tattered shoes were gurgling and squishing with each step.

"These shoes aren't worth wearing," he told Denis. He took off his shoes, tied the laces together and again threw them over his shoulder. He would not consider discarding the shoes, as repair could be possible or the leather could be used for some other comfort. Poverty bred respect for every possession.

"Ma will have her fill darning those socks," added Denis as he took out his own flat cap and adjusted it on his head to match his father's. The two walked in silence side by side, matching stride for stride, in the rain, father and son, each proud of the other. The camaraderie of the two overpowered the physical discomfort of the mud and the rain.

Soon the downpour subsided into a light misty rain which was common along the southern coastline. The two travellers approached their hometown of Timoleague. Courtmacsherry Bay appeared on their left as they crossed the bridge where the Argideen River passed under and flowed into the bay. They rounded the turn and headed down the main street lined with shops. Each store had its own distinctive colours, giving the street a rainbow effect in the misty rain.

Thomas felt the familiarity of home, the comfort of knowing each shop, its owner, and the goods available. This small town and every one of its stores had a history with the McCarthy family through social, business and worship connections.

At the end of the row, Timoleague Abbey came into full view down at the bay's edge. The ruins of the 600-year-old friary, run by the Franciscans and built by King Dermod McCarthy, were a prominent feature of the town. In 1642 English raiders had destroyed much of the abbey. That marked the beginning of the end of a long history of McCarthy kings, who had ruled throughout southern Ireland dating back to the third century. Thomas had ancient royal blood, but the family line had been dispossessed and destroyed by the English. Now he was a pauper trying to feed his starving family. He was saddened, again, by being born in the wrong century. He fantasized that if had lived three hundred years earlier he would be a ruler, a landowner, a man of power and strength.

As they passed a pub on the corner, Thomas looked in. Denis tried to distract his father's thoughts. "Uncle Jerry wants to talk to you when you get home, but I don't know why."

"Oh," replied Thomas, still staring into the pub with some inner hope that someone would run out and call to Thomas and Denis for a quick brew. Denis kept up the walking pace as they rounded the corner and headed down towards the abbey.

"So what does Uncle Jerry want?" Thomas asked as his thoughts returned to their journey.

"I don't know but he talked to Ma, maybe she knows."

As they crossed over the edge of Courtmacsherry Bay and headed upwards towards Abbeymahon, Thomas's pace quickened. Denis knew his father was excited to arrive home. They headed up their lane where Catherine, Thomas's only daughter and the middle child, was waiting for them. She, too, seemed unaffected by the rain with the arrival of her father.

"Da, I'm glad to see you," Catherine said as she greeted him.

"And you, too," Thomas replied.

"Ma is mad because you drank the money you earned."

"No secrets in this family," he replied sarcastically.

"I think you are going to get an earful," she added playfully.

Catherine was nearly sixteen years old and blossoming into a fine young woman. She had her mother's habit of speaking plainly what was on her mind, unlike the men of the family, who were more reserved in their words. The red hair and fair complexion were her father's gift, contrasted by dark brown eyes. Catherine was blessed—or cursed in her mind—with the permanent feature of freckles on her face, arms and legs, but her most notable feature was her father's smile which revealed her perfectly aligned white teeth.

Thomas knew Catherine's warning meant his wife was ready to

challenge his actions without waiting or trying to understand his good sense in spending time and money in Tim Sheehan's bar. He was not going to wait or avoid the confrontation by skipping down to Jerry's house before going into his own. He walked up to Catherine and gave her a kiss on the cheek, and proceeded to the front door of his cottage. Catherine giggled as he walked away from her towards his impending firestorm.

"Catherine, knock it off," Denis intervened. "Da had a hard journey. He is tired, cold, sick and soaking wet."

"I'm sorry, Da," Thomas heard Catherine say as he opened the door, took a deep breath and entered his home. Catherine headed up the lane to their Uncle Jerry's to wait out her parents' discussion. Denis waited outside in the drizzle just in case his father needed some support, even though there was never a need to intervene in his parents' relationship. He just felt his presence was more helpful at home than at his uncle's house just now. Besides, Uncle Jerry had five daughters and no sons, and his sister's presence made six girls. He waited in the rain.

"Johanna, I'm home," Thomas announced, touching St. Brigid's cross. "Bless all here." Johanna was standing in the cooking area not six feet from the door.

"I know, I can see you," she replied matter-of-factly.

"Just saying hello," Thomas countered, his tone as demure as when he asked Tim Sheehan for work. His persona was docile and tentative. He was unsure of his words and how he should approach the conversation. It lacked the vitality, strength and sureness of his conversations with Denis.

Johanna asked, "Did you find any work in Cork?"

"Only one day's work."

"Did you bring home the money?" Johanna pressed further.

Both knew the questions and answers before they were asked or replied to. It was the formality of asking, hearing the admission of failure and the transgression of the spent money that had to be expressed and addressed.

"We need to feed this family, not drink to the health of some shopkeeper."

"I know," Thomas said softly.

"Were the men that had jobs buying drinks for the bar too?"

"No, probably not."

"Thomas . . ." Her voice trailed off. No need to beat the downed horse, she thought. Although she was short in stature, Johanna had a direct and firm personality, which made her a determined force despite her size. Her decisions were quick but sound and unwavering. She was also compassionate about her husband's limits, and she understood the devastating lack of available work and opportunities to provide steady income.

Thomas removed his coat, and the change from the damp outdoor air to the dry warmth of the kitchen caused his lungs to heave the bad air out and absorb the refreshing warm air in.

"That's a terrible cough," stated Johanna. "How did you get that?"

"Sleeping next to the River Lee." Thomas hung his coat to dry and moved to a wooden chair. Johanna went behind him and reached up to his five-feet ten-inch frame to massage his back and shoulders. The action was "the touch," a non-verbal connection between them that said "Everything is all right." Johanna had expressed her feelings; she had said her piece. Now, the touch was reaffirming her love, her commitment to Thomas. He raised his left hand to his shoulders and found Johanna's hand. The touch was complete. The communication was reciprocated. He sat down in the chair to encourage the affectionate encounter and relieve the tension.

"You need a cup of tea," she muttered.

"And a good night's sleep," added Thomas.

Just then the door opened and Jeremiah, their youngest son, came skipping in. Jeremiah was thirteen and had spent the day in Clonakilty. He stopped at the door and touched the reed of St. Brigid's Cross.

"God bless all here," he stated, as was the family ritual. Then he smiled as he set a shilling piece on the table. Thomas looked at the money and hung his head low. His thirteen-year-old son had found work, brought money home and placed it on the table in front of him. His self-worth took another blow. He wanted a drink. A shot of whiskey would help; then he forced the idea from his head.

"I worked for Mr. O'Neil digging and stacking peat."

"Can he use more help?" asked Thomas. Johanna looked at her husband. She did not know if he was asking for himself or as future work for Jeremiah.

"No, he said to check back in a fortnight." Jeremiah was excited about contributing to the family income and was obviously proud of his earnings. Jeremiah moved to the back of the small, one-storey house to throw his shoes into one of the sleeping rooms. The house had three rooms: an open front room for the family to gather, cook and eat, and two sleeping rooms in the back. Thomas and Johanna had one bedroom and the three children shared the other room; each of them had a stuffed sack of straw to sleep on.

Johanna took the money and placed it in an empty sugar bowl on the upper shelf. "Why don't you check our peat stack?" Johanna asked her son. He knew the stack was fine and did not need checking but it was Ma's order to leave her and Da alone. Jeremiah left the house. "Your brother wants to see you right away," Johanna told Thomas.

"What about?"

"I don't know but he said it was important. He wouldn't tell me, but Father Brennan went to see him this morning."

Thomas's brother was five years older and had served as the family patriarch since their father had passed on. The meeting seemed mysterious and urgent because Jerry would have told Johanna any family news, and not much escaped Johanna's notice.

Thomas got up from his chair and changed into his only dry set of everyday clothes. His only other clothes were his suit, which was saved for Sundays, funerals and weddings. He placed his shoes to dry out by the fire and left the house in his bare feet. Denis was waiting in front and the two walked to Jerry's house up the hill. As they approached the house, they heard the girls' giggling voices. Denis sighed. They walked in amidst numerous voices, but someone yelled, "Uncle Tommy is here." The girls scrambled to leave the house as if they had rehearsed their exit. Within moments only Jerry, Thomas and Denis remained. Jerry's wife Elizabeth, or Lizzie as she was known, was at her employment in Cork.

Jerry looked at Denis for a moment. "You can stay but keep this conversation under your hat."

"Yes, I will," replied Denis.

Thomas joined his brother at the kitchen table. Denis stood off by the fireplace.

"Father Brennan came to see me this morning," started Jerry. "The English have a program to help poor Irish Catholics."

"Help?" Thomas injected sarcastically. He was not used to the English helping the Irish. The McCarthys were once a powerful and successful family in County Cork. The English had stripped them and most other native Irish people of all control over their own lives and reduced them to a meagre sharecropper's existence.

"The English are building a settlement in Canada for Irish Catholics. The Earl is offering us an opportunity of a hundred acres, a house, cattle and supplies."

"The Earl?" Thomas asked in surprise.

"Yes, the Earl is working with the churches for eligible families. We have been chosen from Abbeymahon."

"I'm sure the Earl wants to get rid of us."

"And we would be getting rid of the Earl."

"So, are you going?" Thomas asked his brother.

"I'm thinking about it. We can't live this way much longer, never knowing when we are going to eat again or if we will be able to keep our land. There is no hope."

"I would hate to leave Ireland."

"You hear the stories from America of fertile land, many jobs, and game meat outside your door. You shoot a turkey in the morning and have a dinner of potatoes, carrots and a stuffed turkey."

Thomas looked over at Denis, who was just listening with a neutral look. "What do you think?'

"I think it has promise, but you need to discuss it with Mother."

"Tommy," interjected Jerry, "you need to think about your family." Jerry was clearly suggesting Thomas needed to take this opportunity. "It won't be long before the Earl forecloses our land and leaves us homeless. This is a chance for us to move on without trouble."

"I'll discuss it with Johanna."

"Let me know, because I have to let Father Brennan know our decision."

"So you have decided to go?"

"Probably so."

Thomas knew he could not survive without Jerry's help. "When would we go?"

"In the spring sometime," replied Jerry.

"I'll talk to Johanna." Thomas rose to leave. "What about Lizzie?"

Lizzie, Jerry's wife, was the only McCarthy to have regular employment. Her job as a housemaid in Cork City was steady income even though it was low pay. Twice a month, Lizzie came home to Abbeymahon to see her family. Jerry did not like the arrangement but the meagre pay was enough to prevent starvation. The prospect of moving to America with land and opportunities would give Jerry and Lizzie a chance to live together again with their girls as a family. Jerry was confident that Lizzie would go.

McCarthy families had lived in this area for over ten centuries and many of them were high chieftains with the kingly title of McCarthy Mor, as the family history was reported to Thomas and Jerry. But that ruling dynasty changed with the invasion of Oliver Cromwell and the conquest of Munster by Cromwell in 1650. Cromwell eventually named himself Lord Protector of the Commonwealth of England, Scotland and Ireland. This Protector took away the property owned by the Irish and awarded the lands to his loyal army commanders.

This booty had two purposes: reward for his soldiers and removal of Irish self-government, replacing it with a ruling English hierarchy of landowners and governors. The McCarthys' land in Abbeymahon was awarded to Robert Gookin, a captain in Cromwell's army, and was divided eventually into twenty-six ploughlands. The McCarthys were no longer landowners but sharecroppers working for English invaders. Even the Cistercian monks lost the abbey and its land to the Crown when the dissolution of the monasteries was ordered.

Jerry said again, "Let me know your decision soon."

Thomas and Denis returned to their cottage below, where they blessed their entry into the house and beckoned Johanna. She was curious about the conversation and its urgency.

"Father Brennan, through the Earl, has offered us a new life in Canada. We will receive transportation, land, cattle and supplies. In return, we give up our land and life in Ireland."

"Just like the English," she replied, "to steal and bargain with the devil in their hearts."

"We must consider the offer, and as Jerry said, it won't be long before they take the land. Our option is to take advantage of free transportation and land now before we are forced to do it on our own."

"How can we leave our home, our families?"

"We must think of the children and their future too."

After careful discussion with each of their families separately and then together as a group, the two McCarthy families decided to emigrate to Canada.

However, the thought of leaving Ireland was troubling Thomas. Even though the prospect of more land and opportunity seemed appealing, his home was Abbeymahon, sitting above Timoleague on one side and Courtmacsherry Bay on the other. Jerry was more comfortable with leaving, but Thomas had uneasiness about moving. Catherine, like her father, had yet to resolve her indecision; Denis was committed to the opportunity.

Young Jeremiah was the most excited about leaving. His vision of the frontier was filled with the youthful dreams of adventure in an exotic and wild land. In contrast, Johanna envisioned isolation and hardship. As time would tell, both mother and son experienced their dreams and fulfilled their own prophecies.

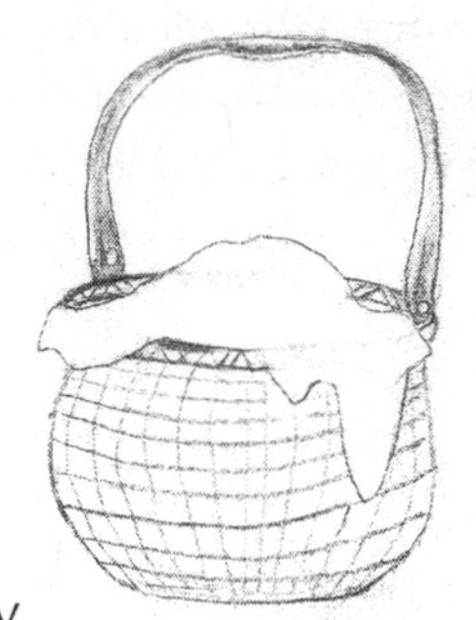

Chapter 5

The McCarthy Family
Timoleague and Courtmacsherry Bay

The news in town of Thomas and Jerry's families leaving Ireland was accompanied by excitement and sadness. The McCarthys had a long history in Timoleague and the surrounding area, which included Abbeymahon. The great McCarthy kings were still revered and their history honoured, and people remembered the McCarthy reign. Now, another unit of descendants was leaving.

But the glory of this once ever-present family's influence throughout the area would never be regained, as the British grip on Ireland remained too strong and their firm power would last for many more decades. Although many McCarthy families would remain across southern Ireland to continue the name and the heritage, the McCarthy brothers of Abbeymahon knew it was time to leave.

Johanna, too, had mixed feelings about leaving, especially on short notice. This move was a major lifetime event and not to be taken lightly, but their future was bleak and the opportunity was now. She headed down from Abbeymahon and across the bridge to climb the hill on the far side to the church to see Father Brennan. St. Mary's Chapel with its stone belfry tower sat on the hill overlooking Timoleague, the river and the bay.

In the eastern distance, Abbeymahon was easily seen over the rooftops of the village and the abbey. Johanna volunteered with a women's group at the church to help clean the altar and pulpit as well as wash vestments, but Father Brennan liked to keep her at the rectory. Her keen common sense and direct manner was helpful when parishioners came to see him. He was not always available and so many explained their troubles to Johanna. They often asked her opinion even though she told them to wait and see Father Brennan.

People also came when they knew Father Brennan was away, so she knew she was the one with whom they really wanted to speak. Johanna was careful not to cross any line of impropriety, often repeating that the person should wait for Father Brennan. But she would sit with the people, having tea, while they explained their troubles. Most were women although a few men confided in her. She reported the visit to the priest when he returned. He asked what the problem was and Johanna explained the issue and any advice she gave. Father Brennan approved of the arrangement.

Now, it was Johanna's turn to appeal for guidance and she requested a meeting in his office. "Father, I am unsettled with this drastic change going into an unknown land," she started. "The interior of Upper Canada has harsh winters; Thomas and I are not used to deep snow and freezing weather. The children can adjust to the climate change much better than we can."

Father Brennan understood her reluctance. "You are afraid of this change?"

"Yes, there are too many unknowns. We have friends, neighbours and family here."

"Jerry and Lizzie are going with you," he reminded her.

"We cannot always depend on them. What if something happens or they live too far away?"

"You are a strong family who has endured many troubles. You will be fine."

"And the children," she continued, ignoring his reassurance, "will need to depend on new neighbours and friends. All those connections are here now."

However, Father Brennan was eager to encourage her to leave Ireland and go to America. "Johanna, your sons and daughter will have land of their own, many times more than they have now. Think of them. The Robinson Project for Upper Canada is a great idea."

"I am thinking of them," she fought back. The priest's reaction troubled Johanna, along with his immediate endorsement of the project without walking her through the dilemma, which was unusual. So she asked, "Father, what are you getting out of this arrangement?"

"Nothing."

"Oh, you must be getting something or you wouldn't be so enthusiastic for us to go. Do you owe the Earl a favour?"

"No, I do not," he insisted. "The Bishop is pushing this project. It is good for the church. We want Catholics—Irish Catholics—to prosper in the New World."

"I knew it was more than just us. What is the Bishop getting from the Earl in return?"

Father Brennan acted shocked. "My dear, nothing." Both of them knew this conversation could head into dangerous territory. The priest did not want to discuss the Bishop's business with a parishioner and Johanna did not want to make unsubstantiated claims against a powerful and holy church leader.

They let the conversation die, even though rumours of collusion between the Bishop and Earl were frequent. And even if some rumours were true, the two men had collaborated for good causes. Catholics were not allowed to openly show their faith in violation of the strict Penal Laws imposed against them. Whereas Catholics were native Irish, British transplants were Anglican, thus politics, heritage, economic stature and religion separated the two groups. This program for relocation of poor Catholics had promise for improved conditions.

"So you want us to go?"

Father Brennan was younger than Johanna but he had the language of a seasoned priest. "I believe it is best."

"And if Catholics prosper in Canada that means the church prospers."

"My dear, don't be so cynical. You will prosper and the Catholic faith spreads. We all have our rewards."

Johanna was angry and disappointed that Father Brennan dismissed her anxiety in order to further the church's expanse. His advice was appropriate for spreading the Catholic faith but lacked a direct connection to their situation. She knew his advice was not personal; it was a prepared message. She left the rectory.

* * *

Jeremiah was excited and told everyone in the Timoleague area that they were bound for the New World. This behaviour was typical for Jeremiah, who openly showed his emotions, but it was his inability to handle the emotion of anger that caused him trouble. He was hotheaded and quick to lead with his mouth, which normally started a confrontation followed by a fight. Even though he was at the young age of thirteen, Jeremiah had learned to react with his fighting skills first, long before rational thinking and a consideration of the outcome could occur. Thomas and Denis attempted to coach him on self-control and both of them knew that he would eventually mature into a disciplined man—but Jeremiah had to develop sooner rather than later.

The difficulty was that Jeremiah could defeat any thirteen-, fourteen- or fifteen-year-old in the Timoleague area. Such success gave him confidence and spurred him to repeat his behaviour over and over again.

Michael O'Leary had little verbal discipline and frequently was the target of a Jeremiah attack when he would poke fun at Jeremiah or his family, especially his father. O'Leary frequently made statements about Thomas and his drinking. Jeremiah's reaction to such statements was fierce, but Michael continued to say things behind Jeremiah's back about his family, and Jeremiah hunted him down to avenge the humiliating words.

The townspeople, however, liked Jeremiah, with his exuberance and outgoing way. They, too, knew he would outgrow his rash and hot-headed ways because they could see the strength of his character and family guidance. He was quick to help anyone who needed a strong back or wanted an errand performed.

At church, he was an altar boy who showed great respect and reverence. Father Brennan was trying to recruit him to become a priest. He also tried to convince Denis to find a calling in the priesthood. Both boys seriously considered the vocation, but neither had a strong desire for the celibate life.

Denis, unlike his rowdy brother, was calm, easy-going and diplomatic. His intelligence and experience gave him a soothing confidence to handle the daily pressure of his father's sickness, lack of food and inability to pay taxes. He felt the burden of duty as the eldest son to take the lead as the surrogate head of household. Denis was helped by Thomas on his good days, by direction from his mother, and by support and encouragement from his Uncle Jerry. This guidance matured Denis into a responsible young man, unlike Jeremiah, who had not yet been exposed to those forces.

Denis worked a couple of seasons on Joseph Donoghue's boat, which taught him fishing in the Argideen River, Courtmacsherry Bay and the ocean. When food was low, Denis went down to the bay and used Joe's rowboat for a few hours of fishing for flounder. The largest catch of the day was offered to Joe and his family in appreciation of the use of his boat. Most of the time Joe declined, but the offer was made anyway. Joe's boat was not always on hand because he loaned it to others so the trips were not a daily routine, nor did Denis want to pester his gracious benefactor.

When possible, Denis stayed fishing as late as he could to catch enough for Uncle Jerry's family also. On trips to the ocean, Denis harvested kelp along the rocky coastline. At other times, especially the evenings, he went to the tidal basin in Timoleague for conger eel; however, the eel was disliked and only fished by area families looking for whatever kind of nourishment they could get. In desperation, large groups of people waded through the shores as soon as the tide receded looking for any clams or even half-eaten fish left over from the birds or seals.

When he returned home, Denis gave his catch, if any, to Catherine for cleaning and preparation for cooking. The seaweed was made into a soup. Fish entrails were given to Jeremiah and he set traps along Ramsey Hill for badgers. The trapping was more a sport than a source of food: the badger was a difficult animal to catch, and more difficult to keep in a trap. They gnawed through rope, cage and most other materials to escape. They were also dangerous animals to approach, especially when trapped, as they were fierce fighters. But Jeremiah's foolhardiness was indifferent to the risks of capturing these mammals.

Badgers did not provide a substantial or tasty meal, so if he could not make the kill, Jeremiah carefully positioned the captured creature and released it from his snares.

* * *

On the road that leads out the north end of Timoleague towards Kilbrittain is a large stand of trees at the base of sheer rock cliffs, just past the outlet of the Argideen River into Courtmacsherry Bay. The area above the cliffs is thickly forested as well, and Jeremiah often spent time in this wooded area. On this day, Jeremiah climbed the rocky hills looking for another nature-related adventure. What he found was more than this thirteen-year-old could bear.

A recent rain impeded his walk over the slick rocky and muddy ground, soaking the path through the hilly terrain. Now the hill's steep grade had a mist blowing over the top edge from the east, cascading delicate droplets of water down and saturating Jeremiah's clothing.

Once at the top, he walked along slowly and quietly so as not to disturb the creatures of the forest, because a slow walk indicates a passive, non-threatening posture to any observing animals. He listened for the birds, as they are the first to indicate the mood of the forest. Birds that hop from branch to branch with an occasional chirp are signalling the woods are tranquil and unruffled. But when birds go to the higher branches or dart away and give squawking noises, it shows they are restless with concern.

Today all was peaceful, and Jeremiah hoped to find the elusive badger. He took a slow soft step and then he heard a noise, a soft crackling sound that made him quickly focus his attention on the dense wooded area to his right. The noise came again; this time it had a familiar tone, like a muffled human cry. He stopped and strained to look. Nothing was there. As he was about to walk again, a second cry was very clear. He sensed the direction of the noise and stepped up into the muddy terrain to investigate. A third whimper, with a movement, caught his attention. He lifted back a branch to see a woman staring at him.

"Leave me alone," she said.

Her arms were folded in front of her and she was holding a baby. The baby cried again and the woman covered its mouth to silence it, identifying it as the source of the noise.

"Oh my, you have a baby there." Jeremiah was shocked. "What are you doing here?"

"Leave us alone, I said." The woman was camouflaged, with mud on her face and over her body and grass mixed into her hair to blend with the lush green bushes and vegetation.

He quickly recognized the perilous threat of exposure to the woman and baby. "You need help," he blurted out.

"No, please do not tell anyone you saw me. They'll take my baby away."

"Why, what have you done?"

"I have done nothing except lose my house. I have no place to live. I have no place for my children."

Children? Jeremiah looked behind the woman where, in absolute disciplined silence, crouched two children, both under five years old. They too had mud strategically placed over their faces and bodies. Jeremiah was shaken and astonished at the sight. The woman's drawn skin and sunken eyes indicated a long time without a proper meal. Now as Jeremiah looked closer, he saw sores on her face and hands, an obvious sign of a lack of proper hygiene, as the soil always has a decomposing effect on organic matter.

"You can't live here."

"I am fine under the protection of bushes," she insisted.

"What do you eat?"

"I am fine." The woman said again, which meant she had nothing to eat except what nature supplied her in her surroundings. Jeremiah guessed that insects and grubs were part of her diet.

"Please come with me. I am going down to Timoleague. We don't have much but at least my parents can offer you a roof over your head."

"Thank you. You are a sweet lad but I cannot." She offered no further explanation except the refusal.

"Oh madam, I cannot leave you here."

"Yes, you can and you must."

Jeremiah had but one choice and that was to leave her there. The other choices seemed not a consideration: notifying the authorities or forcing her somehow to come with him.

Reluctantly, he backed away and down the slope to the roadway. He looked back and again there was no sign of any person at the top of the hill.

He started to run home, desperate to tell someone and provide some sort of aid to this woman and her children. Once at the edge of the river, he felt the urge to cross immediately, taking the shortest route home. But crossing here at low tide, where the riverbed was wet with muck, meant each step would cause his foot to sink into the mud and bog him down. His better judgement prevailed and he took the long route around the river to the bridge. This way was an extra half-mile but the time saved from getting stuck made it much more efficient. He headed up the hill towards Abbeymahon. Luckily, before he reached the house he ran into Denis in the field.

"Denis, come quickly, I need help," he yelled to his brother.

"What is it?"

Jeremiah was filled with the urgency to find help. "Sorry, I don't need help but there's a woman in the woods that does." Denis immediately dropped his rake as Jeremiah gave a quick explanation of his find in the woods. The two brothers ran down the hill and over the bridge. Jeremiah took the lead as they climbed the path to the top. No cautious walking this time, as the birds took flight upon the arrival of the winded and energized pair.

"Over here," cried out Jeremiah, as he retraced his steps and pulled back the bushes. No one was there. "Oh no. She's gone." He moved deeper into the underbrush, but there was no woman and no children.

Denis inspected the underbrush. He found dead straw and grasses gathered into a mat to serve as a bed as well as broken branches used to cover their exposure to sight, wind and rain. There was a small clearing with stones where a fire had been attempted but had not been successful. The evidence around this make-shift home suggested that Jeremiah was right; she had cleared rocks and decaying branches to forage for food. The two brothers searched the area for the family but they were unable to find any trace of them.

"She must've run off," said Jeremiah.

"She had a view of anyone approaching," observed Denis, as he stood at the top of hill with a clear view of the river, the road and the bridge. "She probably watched you run down and the two of us run back."

"Denis, she could be right here within reach of us and we would never see her. She can probably hear us talking now."

"Jeremiah, if we find her, what are we going to do? Drag her down the hill? She's gone because she wants to be gone."

That night, Jeremiah explained his experience on the hill to Thomas and Johanna. Thomas questioned, "What condition has Ireland put itself into that forces a young mother into the hillside? How can we do this to our own people regardless of whether we are English, Anglo, or of true Irish heritage? How could anyone relegate a person, including young children, to live in a mud hole?" Thomas felt that, living in any land, you were part of that community and had a responsibility to promote basic human survival.

Johanna remained silent for a few moments but Thomas knew she had a different outlook. She concentrated on the children who were pawns in the grown-up game of domination and oppression of the lesser people.

"I'm glad you offered them shelter," she told Jeremiah. "Now let's go to bed and sleep on this."

The family retired for the night. Before dawn, Catherine woke up to a noise in the kitchen. The cottage was small so all sounds were easily heard. The noise was familiar, with bowls and pans moving about. She rose to find Johanna baking bread.

"What are you doing so early in the morning?" she questioned her mother.

"Those children need nourishment."

"Can I help?"

"You can go out and get fresh milk from Uncle Jerry's cow."

Catherine was dressed and left the house as the first ray of sunlight hit West Cork. Her cousin Elly was already preparing to milk the cow as part of her morning chores. Catherine explained the discovery on the hill and the need for extra milk.

"You go first," Elly offered.

Catherine returned with a jug of milk as Johanna was covering up bread and jelly sandwiches in linen wrappings. She placed the sandwiches in a basket. The flour and sugar were nearly depleted but that did not matter to Johanna, as the feeding of the woman in the woods and her children had higher priority.

Jeremiah, typical of a thirteen-year-old, was the last one up and rose to the commotion of preparation. "What's going on?"

"Here is a basket to take up the hill."

Before eating his own breakfast, Jeremiah left the cottage with the basket on his arm. The climb to the top of the hill was muddy again with the morning dew. He went to the spot where he had met the woman. No one was there. After pulling back the branches, the living quarters were just as he and Denis had seen the day before. Jeremiah strategically placed the basket in the centre of the matted grass and backed away, leaving the hill.

Throughout the day, Jeremiah's thoughts were focused on the top of the hill. As he worked the field, numerous times he glanced across the river to the top of the ridge, wondering if the woman had found the basket. He decided to stay away to ensure he did not scare the family. The next day, however, he returned to find the basket torn apart and strewn down a small trail under the bush, indicating the small rodents of the forest had discovered the scent and raided the provisions. The jar of milk was intact but rolled through the underbrush, with small teeth marks chipped into the porcelain lid secured by a metal band. Johanna joined in Jeremiah's disappointment that the family had missed the meal after he ran up the lane and delivered the news to his mother.

"What can we do?" he asked.

"We can try one more time, but she may have moved elsewhere."

The second attempt failed as the first had, and the McCarthy household was frustrated at their inability to help. Catherine volunteered to walk the hill in search of the woman, and spent the greater part of two days combing the underbrush and scrub. But this area had a ten-mile radius of thick forest, rolling pastures, and valleys cut by the River Argideen with its feeder streams, making it an ideal hide-out for someone who knew the area.

Johanna told Father Brennan the story of the woman but he had no idea about this desperate woman with three small children. However, Father Brennan's network of information was beyond Johanna's range of the Timoleague parish and she trusted his discretion. He promised he would check for information.

Within the week, he called Johanna into his study.

"The woman you were asking about was found."

"Where?" she asked.

"Further up the river. She and two of the children are being cared for but her small baby died."

"Oh my, sweet Jesus, Mary and Joseph, pray for them," she said as a wash of sadness overcame her.

He comforted her with "You, Jeremiah, and your family did all you could and probably saved all of them from dying. You helped them enormously." Father Brennan waited a moment and then added, "They were taken to a safe place."

Every facet of Irish life had secret societies, from the rebel movement to covert Irish dancing. The Catholic Church was no different in that it could take in a desperate and possibly a widowed mother and her children to feed, house and care for them. It was not illegal to be charitable: the past of the persons, whether they were a debtor or a homeless family, did not matter, and confidentiality was honoured. Johanna knew a gracious family or a nearby convent, possibly as close as Bandon, north of Timoleague, was supporting this needy family.

* * *

Catherine was not happy about leaving her home in Ireland. The hardships were a way of life with her and she saw neither a need to change nor any hope that things might get better. Her family and her cousins who lived up the lane as well as the townspeople, schoolmates, and church were the centre of her universe. The small cottage they called home was familiar, comfortable and a refuge. She was not certain change was good for her father either, as he was already sick. The McCarthys had history and claim to the character and heritage of the area. She fought the move.

"Da, you cannot travel with that cough. You'll catch a death of cold on that ship. We can wait until you feel better and then consider making a move." But her arguments fell short of convincing the family to reassess their commitment.

Catherine decided to walk down to the abbey in town to focus her troubled spirit. The walls of the abbey had been sitting on this site since the thirteenth century. She thought about her forefathers who had shaped this area. Her mind went back to the early kings—Cormac MacCarthy and his son Dermod, who ruled southern Ireland in the 1100s, and Donal Glas McCarthy, who had expanded the abbey in 1312. And even earlier when the McCarthy dynasty started with Oilioll Olum, king of the Munster province in the second century. His rule and descendants continued through his son Eoghan in the third century, and eventually the last name MacCarthy was added, derived from the Irish Mac Cárthaigh, meaning "the loving one," coming from son of Cárthach, lord of the Eoghanacht.

The royal lineage of the McCarthy reign was broken in the 1600s when Oliver Cromwell invaded Ireland and broke apart the Irish rule. Family members and cousins fought and made political manoeuvres to be called "MacCarthy Mor," the ancient title of the family head or chieftain. Eventually, the title was outlawed. Likewise, the family had divided and subdivided through the centuries, leaving Thomas and Uncle Jerry with no known claim to royalty. But Catherine was not looking for royalty; she was hanging onto tradition and a sense of belonging in her corner of the world. She spent her time in the abbey waiting for inspiration, a vision to give her words and plea substance to change minds.

She contemplated the words of Seán Ó Coileáin, who wrote *The Melancholy Man's Meditations on seeing the Abbey of Timoleague in 1813:*

I sat me down in melancholy mind,
And on my hand, my troubled head reclined,
In silent grief my thoughts increased my woe,
And from my eyes the tears began to flow.

I said in the anguish of my troubled breast,
Whilst the round tears each moment had increased,
There was a time when peace and plenty blessed,
This house, when by its Family possessed.

She waited, but no vision emerged.

Frustrated, Catherine left the abbey and walked up to the church. "Maybe God will give me a revelation," she thought. She walked down the row of pews on the left side to the place where her family always sat, and slid into her familiar space. The church was quiet as she gazed above the altar where Jesus hung on the cross. Her answer came: Jesus had died on the cross—his life was over and he ascended into heaven before his work was done. Catherine made a connection from Jesus' death to the McCarthy life in Abbeymahon as being over. Rebirth was necessary in a new country. She accepted the move.

* * *

During their preparation, they learned that Peter Robinson, a member of the Upper Canada parliament, was leading the project to help Irish families emigrate. Each family had to be sponsored by their baron, along with letters of recommendation. The Earl had already made the recommendation and Father Brennan supplied a letter of support for both families. The criteria for eligibility fit both McCarthy households: poor, destitute, Roman Catholic with high moral character, and the head of the family had to be younger than forty-five years of age. Uncle Jerry was turning forty-five soon but he was accepted as a viable candidate. Peter Robinson was coming to Cork to sift through the fifty thousand applications and determine which families represented the best prospects.

As the superintendent of the project, Peter Robinson was resolved to make this assignment successful. The British Parliament wanted to address the devastating conditions in Ireland, and southern Ireland in particular, where death and disease increased at a rapid and uncontrolled rate. They also wanted to expand the population along the Canadian border with the United States. The British feared that the Americans would invade Canada to expand the United States, and these poor Irish homesteaders would protect their homes.

There had been numerous border skirmishes since the War of 1812 and the British government did not trust that the treaty signed at the end of that war would be honoured. In addition, Peter Robinson was a Canadian and he wanted good citizens, not disruptive Irish problems. He wanted settlers who would become productive in the Canadian economy and would be loyal to the area and their new homes, as well as defending their land if necessary. He sifted through the applications and recommendations carefully.

* * *

Uncle Jerry's wife Lizzie had a difficult time adjusting to making this move. She announced her intentions of leaving her housemaid job at the Wakefield home. Mrs. Wakefield was a stubborn and manipulative employer and she did not easily relinquish Lizzie. Servants were thought of as property, not as individuals who could think independently or leave at will. She made the prospect of working another two months a torment. Jerry suggested Lizzie quit immediately, but the money was necessary for the move. Lizzie decided to stick with her duties and her commitment.

Mrs. Wakefield did not like being told the conditions of when and how Lizzie would leave. Her son was planning to travel to America in April and in an effort to exercise power, control and spite, Mrs. Wakefield devised a plan for Lizzie to accompany him. She argued that Lizzie was going to America anyway, so why not accompany her son Jacob to New York? He needed a maid to assist him with his medicine and care for his clothes during the voyage. Lizzie declined the offer. She was going to Canada, not New York.

Mrs. Wakefield contacted the Earl of Shannon, whom she knew and had entertained in her home, and reported the unco-operative and insubordinate Lizzie. The Earl was in a difficult position. Mrs. Wakefield was an influential person who required attention, but he did not want any distraction to disrupt the plan leading to the McCarthys' scheduled departure. He did not want to disrupt the process leading to their scheduled May departure.

One morning a carriage arrived in front of Jerry's house and the Earl's constable stepped out. This was an unusual sight—the collector never travelled in a coach with a driver. Constables were a new force in Ireland, having appeared after the Chief Secretary Robert Peel initiated the Peace Preservation Act of 1814, followed by the Constabulary Act in 1822.

The constable knocked on Jerry's cottage door. Jerry knew he was there; he had seen the carriage pull up. He hesitated in the kitchen; the collector could wait a few minutes. Kate, his oldest daughter, was with him and he signalled for her to be quiet.

Finally Jerry went to the door, after the collector's third pounding. His next step might be breaking down the door; after all, he arrived as a pompous, important person.

Jerry opened the door and said "Yes?" as if he was used to formal guests.

"The Earl wants to see you. Now."

"He wants to see me? And he sends you in a coach?"

"Jerry," the constable was coming back to reality, "the Earl needs to see you right away. We're here to take you."

"What's this about?'

"I don't know, he didn't consult me."

Consult you? thought Jerry. Ha. Jerry turned to Kate. "I'm off to have a consultation with the Earl."

"All right, Da," replied Kate. "Tell him I said hello," she added, loud enough for both of them to hear.

Jerry turned and looked at his daughter. He thought, she will do just fine in this world. Jerry and the constable climbed aboard the coach and it pulled away.

Denis was watching the arrival and departure of his uncle as he was fixing the thatch on the roof. That's strange, he thought. I wonder if Uncle Jerry will be all right. If he had a horse, he would have climbed down and followed them to ensure his uncle's safety, but he had no horse or other means of following. He scrambled to the top of the house to get a better view. He watched the coach move down the hill towards the bay.

Even after he lost sight of the carriage, he could see road dust swirling as it went to the bay's edge. His view was too obstructed by shrubs and other vegetation along the shore to see which way it turned. He mumbled his thoughts aloud this time: "That's strange." He scrambled down the ladder and headed up to Jerry's house. Kate informed him of the constable's visit.

In the coach, Jerry asked, "Where are we going?"

"To the Earl's summer house at Courtmacsherry."

Jerry thought this must be an important meeting, if the Earl came to his summer house on the bay in February to meet with him. Through the years, the taxman and Jerry had had their battles over rent and taxes, so the trip was made in relative silence.

It was not far from Abbeymahon to the coastline along the bay. The carriage turned and headed up the long entranceway lined with cedar trees to the front door. Jerry knew this was special, if it meant using the front door. The carriage came to a stop. Jerry made a move to exit the coach. The constable grabbed his arm and said, "Wait here."

Shortly after, the Earl came out of the house in his flowing velvet cape and feathered hat. The door opened and the Earl entered the coach. The coach started immediately. The driver knew the destination.

The collector made the introduction. "Sir, this is Jeremiah McCarthy from Abbeymahon."

"Ah yes, Jeremiah, 'tis a pleasure."

Jerry reciprocated, "Nice to meet you, sir." He waited to see if a handshake would follow. It did not. The Earl sat back in his seat and looked at his guest.

"I understand your brother has a drinking problem."

"He's a good man," Jerry countered.

"He has been kicked out of every pub in County Cork."

Jerry knew that was an exaggeration but he could not argue that Thomas had his troubles. "What is it that you want, sir?"

"Your brother is behind in his taxes. I could send him to jail at any time but instead I offered to send your family and his family to Canada and give you free land, supplies and seed."

The Earl made it sound as if he was financing the whole plan. Jerry repeated, "What is it that you want?"

"As I was saying, you and your family can go to America or, with the stroke of my signature, your brother can be shipped to a pauper's prison in Van Diemen's Land." Jerry knew he was being put over a barrel. He waited. The Earl continued, "Now there is this matter with your wife. She has been graciously asked to accompany Mrs. Wakefield's son to America. And you are going there anyway."

Jerry interrupted, "We are going to Canada."

"Right, it is next to America. It seems that she can assist the sickly Jacob on his voyage to New York and then she can join you upon your arrival."

Jerry had no knowledge of how close New York was to Canada or where in Canada they were going. The area was known as Scott's Plains, but he had not seen a map.

"So you are offering my brother's freedom in trade for my wife's assistance."

"It seems such a small favour for the benefit you are receiving."

"I see." Jerry looked out the window; the coach had already travelled through Timoleague and was heading north. "Where are we going?"

"To Cork City to talk to your wife, of course."

"Of course," replied Jerry as he sat back in his seat. He contemplated the journey to America. If necessary, he decided, he would go to New York and get his wife. "I guess I will be talking to my wife."

"Good man," replied the Earl.

The journey to Cork was short. The Earl busied himself with papers he was carrying. Jerry looked out the window.

The coach worked its way through the streets. Jerry had never been in an enclosed carriage and he was surprised at people's reaction as the coach passed. Some people waved and some glared as if a magical prince was inside. Then again some showed contempt and disrespect by jeering at the coach or spitting at it. The Earl was oblivious to it all.

Suddenly, they pulled up in front of the Wakefield house. The door opened and Jerry slid out. As soon as he stepped away from the carriage, the constable reached over and jerked the door closed. The coach pulled away.

"Good day," Jerry mocked to the empty space left by the horse and carriage.

Jerry turned and walked to the rear of the mansion, to the servants' entrance, and banged on the door harder than was needed. One of the staff members answered the knock and Jerry asked for Lizzie.

"What's the matter?" asked Lizzie as she hustled to the door, assuming a problem with one of the children.

"I need you to do something without asking why."

"What is it?" she asked, still anxious over the surprise visit.

"Tell Mrs. Wakefield that you'll take Jacob to New York."

"Why?"

"Please do this. I'll come to New York when we arrive in Canada and get you."

"No further explanation?"

"Not now."

"Very well. I'll see you next Sunday," said Lizzie, who needed to hurry because visitors were not allowed.

"I will look forward to seeing you."

Jerry returned to the front of the house and stepped into the street. He looked to see if the Earl was waiting for his return. Neither the Earl nor his carriage was in sight. Jerry was left to walk the thirty miles back to Abbeymahon.

* * *

Lizzie returned to her duties changing sheets on the second floor of the house. She wondered what happened that brought Jerry to the house. She knew Mrs. Wakefield must have caused some ruckus. Even though her anger at Mrs. Wakefield was growing, she tempered her feelings in order not to give the other woman the satisfaction of seeing her emotion. She would wait.

Late in the afternoon, Mrs. Wakefield came upstairs as Lizzie was stacking fresh sheets in the linen closet. Lizzie was ready to confront her but servants were not allowed to address the lady of the house directly; they were supposed to discuss matters through Mrs. Hennessey, the head housekeeper.

Lizzie looked straight ahead into the closet and said, "I'll take Jacob to New York," as if addressing the stack of sheets. She heard Mrs. Wakefield stop. Lizzie turned around and looked directly into Mrs. Wakefield's eyes. Her anger was just below the surface and she knew Mrs. Wakefield sensed the tension.

"That will be fine," Mrs. Wakefield said.

"However, I'll be three weeks ahead of my family. The least you could do is supply me with transportation to Canada. It's only right for the inconvenience, and besides I have to check in with Mr. Robinson."

"Oh dear, who is Mr. Robinson?" Mrs. Wakefield said in condescending tone.

Mrs. Wakefield had taken the bait and Lizzie was ready. "He is our host, appointed by Prime Minister Jenkinson for this Irish settlement."

"Oh dear, every British program is sanctioned by the Prime Minister."

"Peter Robinson is a special envoy, hand chosen by Mr. Jenkinson and serving through Under Secretary of Colonial Affairs Wilmot Horton. We are to meet him here, before our departure from Cork. You know Mr. Robinson's brother is the Attorney General for Upper Canada."

The message was delivered and Lizzie saw that Mrs. Wakefield understood: Lizzie was going to be close to the peerage, the system of nobility in the United Kingdom. Mrs. Wakefield's choice was clear: risk loss of reputation through the words of these Irish peasants who had the ear of the British nobility, or provide accommodations for Lizzie to Canada. The greater good, in Mrs. Wakefield's mind, was to have a positive reputation whenever her name came up in conversation with the nobles.

"I'm glad you will care for my son during his trip to New York, and of course I will make sure you have a safe and comfortable journey to . . . where are you going again?"

"Scott's Plains in Ontario."

"Yes, Scott's Plains. It sounds so desolate, so foreign."

Lizzie disregarded the comment and replied, "Thank you for your assistance."

* * *

The following weeks, through March and April, consisted of making plans for the McCarthys' move to America. The three children were excited, in part because of the exotic thoughts and stories of the wilderness. Another part of them was excited at the hope of a promising future. The Earl's constable and the magistrate's bailiff came around frequently to discuss plans and obtain signatures for land deeds and formal documents. It was a gentlemen's way to foreclose and evict the McCarthys from their land without ugly words and legal proceedings.

* * *

Lizzie was prepared to travel to Dublin with Jacob; she boarded the ship *Brig Wilson* for her voyage to New York. The morning of her departure, they restated the plan. "I will meet you in early July," she said to Jerry. "You are travelling on *The Elizabeth* and your travels will take you up the river to Montreal."

"Yes, the first one to arrive will wait by the docks," confirmed Jerry.

"I'm scared," she whispered into his ear when they hugged.

"So am I, but we will be just fine. If anything happens go on to Scott's Plains and we will catch up there." Jerry's words were spoken in a confident voice although both of them knew the tentative nature of reuniting in a foreign land following a probably treacherous voyage on the ocean for each of them.

Each of the five girls approached their mother for hugs, tears and farewell kisses. Only Abigail found the comforting words that Lizzie needed: "We will take care of Da and make sure he eats regularly."

Lizzie smiled as the tension eased. "Thank you, and take care of your sisters too."

"Yes, Mother," she replied.

Lizzie climbed into the waiting carriage sent by Mrs. Wakefield, and rode down the lane. Jerry and the girls waved at the back of the departing coach. Thomas's family waited in front of their cottage and waved too when the carriage passed by.

"I'm glad you're not going separately," Thomas said to Johanna as the carriage rolled down the hill towards Timoleague.

"I don't think I could do it," she replied. "It would be too scary for me, leaving you and the children to travel across the ocean to New York and then to Canada with only the hope of somehow finding each other."

* * *

Thomas continued to struggle with his health. The cough was now in its third month. It became more intense when he did physical work or when the humidity was high. Bed rest, warm clothes on his chest, and tea helped him feel better, but it did not improve his health. Bloody coughs and sweats were common.

In early April a heavy rainstorm blew over Abbeymahon, with the wind blowing the rain horizontally in continuous sheets of water. The height of the storm was hitting when Jeremiah finished his chores and entered the house. "Holy Moses," he said as his hand glided over St. Brigid's Cross hanging next to the door. With a reprimanding look, Johanna nodded towards the cross. Jeremiah started again with touching the cross. "God bless all who enter here."

"All right, now what were you saying?" asked his mother.

"I said, Holy Moses it's raining hard," replied Jeremiah.

"That's why we are all in here," Catherine said in a mocking tone.

"Ah yes, you are sitting around while I'm doing all the work," Jeremiah countered as he pulled his woollen sweater over his head to shake out the water and hang to dry.

"As I was saying," Johanna turned back towards Thomas, "this cough may prevent you from boarding the ship. Mr. Robinson doesn't want sick passengers who can't make the voyage." They had been discussing Thomas's health and ability to travel under harsh conditions before Jeremiah entered.

"I'm fine with travelling and nothing will stop me from going. This project is important for Denis, Catherine and Jeremiah's future."

"We can go later," responded Catherine, "maybe to New York or Boston."

Denis thought for a moment. "We will do what's best for your health. It's not worth travelling all that way to have you sick, or worse." Denis left the implication of "worse" for his father and mother to define.

"I'll be fine for the journey, don't any of you worry," finished Thomas.

* * *

Nine ships were made ready in Cobh harbour outside of Cork City to carry the emigrating Irish settlers to the New World. Starting on May 10, 1825, the first ship, *The Fortitude*, set sail, transporting 282 settlers. The delays caused by Lizzie's voyage and Thomas's health impeded an early departure for their families on the readied ships. However, by May 21 the eighth ship, *The Elizabeth*, with the two McCarthy families and 198 other emigrants, were ready to sail.

Even though Thomas showed confidence, he was nervous about the possibility of his poor health preventing him from boarding the ship. He made sure he was well rested before presenting himself to the Captain for the trip. He walked along the pier with Jerry leading the way and his own family at his side. Master Donald Morrison, the Captain of the ship, greeted them and guided them to the gangplank leading to the ship. The head sailor in the King's Royal Navy was called a captain but on a merchant ship like *The Elizabeth*, the captain was referred to as a "Master." The crew had great respect for Mr. Morrison and frequently called him "Captain" as a sign of that respect.

Jerry McCarthy boarded his five daughters and turned to watch his brother, escorted by Denis and Johanna on each side of him, walk up the plank, barefoot and unassisted. Catherine and Jeremiah followed behind. Thomas breathed a sigh of relief as he stepped on board, but the difficult task was yet to come.

When all the passengers were gathered on the main deck, Master Morrison came aboard and stood next to an official-looking man dressed in travelling tweed clothes. Mr. Morrison made the introduction: "Everyone, this is the Superintendent of this project for the crown, the Honourable Peter Robinson."

"Thank you, Master Morrison. Greetings. I am here to check your certificates and to meet all of you. So if you would step forward, one family at a time, I will check you in." Robinson was a short man with groomed hair combed forward in the style of the day. He had the air of a prominent aristocrat.

The first family to step forward was John Nagle and his wife Catherine, along with their three older children. Peter Robinson checked each person and asked John a few questions about ages and place of birth. Mr. Robinson was validating the people against the names listed on the certificate. He had found that previous passengers on other ships had sometimes sold their certificates to other families. His questions were based on facts supplied by the families' sponsors, since counterfeit families would not know the information given on the letters of recommendation. Peter's pride and reputation were at stake and he was not going to jeopardize his reputation or the project on a profit scheme by an ungrateful family.

The Nagle family had passed the test and was directed to the deck below. Next, the Buckley family stepped forward and was reviewed by Mr. Robinson. The ninth family to meet Mr. Robinson was Thomas's family. He introduced himself to Mr. Robinson. Thomas waited for the questions but Mr. Robinson appeared troubled.

"It says here your name is Carthy."

"Yes, the Earl thought we should drop the Mc to make it sound less Irish."

"Less Irish? The whole ship is Irish. You are going to an Irish settlement. You needn't try to deceive anyone. And yet, you introduce yourself as Thomas McCarthy."

"That's my name and I would like to keep it."

"Well, your certificate states 'Carthy.'" Peter hesitated.

Thomas braced himself, expecting trouble over his name as well as questions regarding his drinking and inability to maintain employment but, as it turned out, nothing was asked regarding his imprudence. He quietly thanked Father Brennan under his breath for supporting their move without mentioning the drinking. Otherwise, he would be forced to stay in Ireland and Jerry would emigrate to Canada. The ocean would divide the families and Thomas knew he could not survive without Jerry.

Mr. Robinson was a reasonable man and showed he was tolerant of the common man's plight. Even though he was an aristocrat of English heritage, he did not act in a demeaning way or demonstrate animosity towards these poor Irish farmers—unlike so many of the English, who regarded the Irish as sub-human and treated them as such.

"I will make the notation regarding your name." Mr. Robinson turned to the ship's master. "Mr. Morrison, please note on the ship's list that Thomas Carthy will maintain his given name, McCarthy."

"Will do," came the reply.

Thomas was welcomed. "Have a safe voyage, Mr. McCarthy. I will see you in Upper Canada."

The family was directed below to make berth.

Next came a third cousin of Jerry and Thomas's, Timothy McCarthy, and his wife Bridget, from Cork City. They too passed the inspection.

Eventually, Uncle Jerry stepped up and introduced himself as Jerry McCarthy.

Peter looked up and smiled. "Are you related to Thomas who was just here?"

"He's my brother, and I too want to maintain my family name—McCarthy."

"I have an Elizabeth listed on the certificate but she is not here?" Jerry was asked at great length about Lizzie and why she was not present with her family.

The ship had been assigned a surgeon, Mr. Power, from the Royal Navy to accompany the settlers. He was in charge of the passengers during their passage from Ireland to Canada. All nine ships had a Royal Navy surgeon assigned as their doctor and liaison for their delegations.

Upon overhearing Jerry's examination, Mr. Power spoke up. "I have a letter from the Honourable Henry Boyle, 3rd Earl of Shannon, that states Elizabeth McCarthy was to accompany Jacob Wakefield on a previous ship to New York. She will meet her family later in Canada." Mr. Power presented the letter to Peter Robinson.

"I see, Mr. Power. Thank you." He turned back to Jerry. "Mr. McCarthy, we have many McCarthys settling in Canada. Do you have other relatives going over?"

"Just my third cousin Timothy, on this ship."

Mr. Robinson moved towards the ship's master. "Mr. Morrison, please note for Jerry Carthy that he will use his family name, McCarthy."

"Thank you, sir, for your understanding," Jerry said.

"Mr. McCarthy, I see from your recommendation letters that you are a good and holy man. You are looked upon as a leader in your parish. I will be happy to work with you in Canada."

"Thank you again, sir."

"Have a good voyage."

Jerry and the girls were accepted onto *The Elizabeth*.

Mr. Robinson was satisfied that all passengers were genuine. He wished the ship's master and his crew safe passage on their voyage and disembarked the ship.

The Captain yelled, "Set her adrift."

The crew untied the moorings.

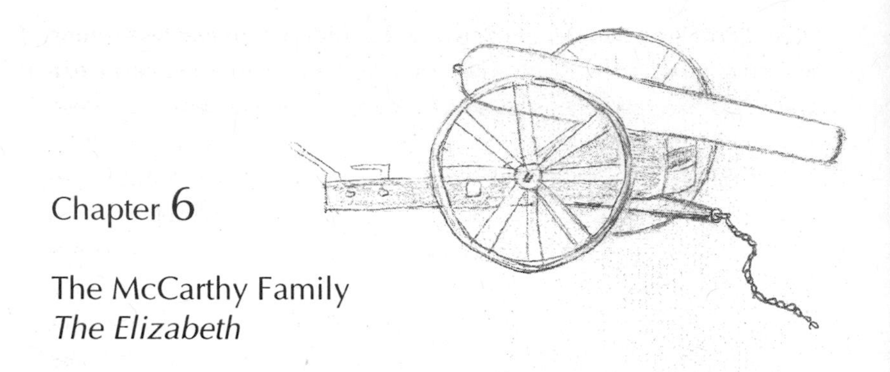

Chapter 6

The McCarthy Family
The Elizabeth

Denis and Jeremiah took the two trunks below as directed by the first mate, Mr. Henderson. Jeremiah climbed down the ladder and Denis handed him the two boxes containing all their worldly possessions. The boxes sat on the floor as Jeremiah examined what would be their living quarters for the next six weeks. The lower deck had bunks stacked three high, open for the full length of the ship, intended for the families to live in a common community.

There was a long table in the central open area with just enough room for two or three families to sit at a time, and benches on either side. A few families had claimed their territory at the front of the ship—the greatest distance from the ladder. Jeremiah was not a sailor but knew the middle rear was more comfortable. He dragged the first trunk to an open set of bunks. Denis joined him, carrying the second box, and loaded them on the port side.

Catherine followed the boys down the ladder. She was wearing her only dress made of white, floor-length, flower-embroidered Irish linen. The dress was a bon voyage gift from her cousins in Timoleague, Patrick and Theresa McCarthy. Catherine felt special in her fine travelling clothes. She walked towards the rear to meet her brothers. "It's dark down here."

"We will be the most comfortable, just past the middle on the port side," her elder brother responded.

"Why?"

"Port side will get the sun and the middle will feel less rolling and shock from the waves." He added, "It will be like the middle of a teeter, less up and down in the middle than the ends. Not much less, but better than the front."

Uncle Jerry's oldest daughter, also named Catherine but called Kate, set up her family's quarters next to Thomas's family. The two Catherines giggled and laughed as they worked on storing the trunks and making the sleeping bunks into a household area.

Other passengers filled the remaining spaces. The open area quickly became packed with thirty-four starving and destitute families making the voyage to fresh opportunities and clean beginnings in the New World. Each bunk adjoined the next bunk with no separation between them. Some families hung sheets, towels or clothes to define their home space. Soon the space was full, with forty-seven children under the age of ten along with an additional seventy-six young people between eleven and nineteen. The sounds of laughing, crying, screaming and arguing were deafening in disjointed harmony.

"This is going to be a long trip," Kate whispered to her cousin. Soon a fistfight broke out at the other end of the ship. Two teenage boys sent their arms flailing, and this was followed by people yelling for them to stop. The boys were separated, one of them bleeding profusely from the nose.

"What was that about?" Kate looked at Denis, who shook his head and shrugged.

Once settled, they returned to the upper deck as the ship prepared to leave. The passengers waved to the small crowd that had gathered on the dock. Families waved to families. Mournful farewells were shouted from the shore to the ship and from the ship to the dock. The two McCarthy families were the lucky ones; they had each other for support.

Captain Morrison ordered the sails. The foremast sail was dropped and pulled the ship away from the dock. As the ship sailed into the river, the mainmast sail fell and caught the breeze. Mr. Morrison yelled and the back mizzenmast sail was released, filling with air as it dropped down. The canvas rotated on the mast to catch the wind, which pulled the ropes taut. Sailors worked the sails and ropes, which tightened as the best exposure to the wind set the ship out to the southern end of the Irish Sea. The topgallant sails were released to give the ship a full set of sails for maximum power.

Mr. Morrison announced that he wanted all passengers on deck in one hour.

The women and children went below; Uncle Jerry, Thomas and Denis stayed on deck. They leaned on the starboard railing of the solid three-mast wooden ship. The ship moved south along the Irish coast as Courtmacsherry Bay came into view.

The three men looked ashore towards the opening of the bay. All three men saw the familiar land of Kilbrittain jutting high and faint on the horizon. At first no one mentioned the view. After a few moments Thomas broke the silence.

"The home of our ancestors."

"Indeed," Jerry replied solemnly.

The morning sunlight shot bright light across the sea, illuminating the coastline and accentuating the rolling pasturelands and the sporadic colourful homes.

"Is it right that we have to leave our homeland?" questioned Thomas. "This land is rightfully ours. We are leaving because we were driven out of our home by foreign invaders. Some day we may get it back after the British are driven from Ireland. And we won't be here to get it."

Jerry countered, "Thomas, we are in exile and have been for three hundred years. The English are just getting around to banishing us from our native country. What is done is done."

"I'd like to be king," announced Thomas.

Jerry and Denis smiled.

"You'd be a prince and I would be king," Jerry reminded him humorously.

"With all the mystery and intrigue of Hamlet," added Denis.

The reference to Shakespeare may have slipped past Thomas.

He showed no reaction as he still had a vision of the crown jewels.

"Not so," Jerry quickly replied. "We are a family that takes care of each other. No murder and back-stabbing here."

Denis was well aware of his Uncle Jerry's protection and support of Thomas. Any disagreement over land or power would be handled by discussion, co-operation and compromise. Shakespeare would have no scandalous story with this generation of the McCarthy family.

Thomas, however, was in a different frame of mind. "I was looking for an easier life. A life where we'd live in the castle, collect the taxes and govern the masses."

"A castle is a building, a sign of the responsibility of the people who live inside," declared Jerry. "Kings," he hesitated, and then added, "and princes, work hard for the people they serve every day. No matter is considered trivial, for their decisions have far-reaching effects on many lives. The true kings and true leaders know their chance of success with their judgement and the consequences of their risks. Great responsibility is expected. You have to be a just man to be a just king."

Thomas looked out to sea as if still daydreaming of lavish parties and huge banquets.

Denis looked at his uncle. "You would have been a great king."

"It was not to be."

"You think we can tell them in America that we are Irish kings?" considered Thomas. They all laughed. Thomas continued, "Jesus came from humble beginnings. We can too."

Jerry directed his remarks to Denis. "You can't declare yourself a king. You have to earn it through who you are. Your words and actions have significance no matter what your position in life."

Thomas came back to the present moment. "'Tis true, Jerry. Even though I have great dislike of the Earl, he knew this move would be best for the McCarthys. He could have chosen the O'Brien or O'Neil families. They are just as poor, and they were just as far in arrears of their taxes. But he chose us."

Jerry grunted. The view of the bay and West Cork was fading away on the horizon. They watched the coastline. Jerry and Thomas said almost simultaneously, "Goodbye," as if rehearsed. Thomas added in a low tone, "the flight of the Earls." His reference was to the banishment of two Irish earls out of northern Ireland two hundred years earlier as the British began their final conquest and authority over Ireland.

* * *

As the one-hour meeting approached, people started returning to the main deck. Jeremiah stayed behind waiting for his mother, sister and five cousins to leave for the Captain's meeting. He finished tying off a lantern line and then slid quietly out of his bunk. He was now the last person at their end of the ship to leave.

A shabbily clothed boy of about seventeen was going through a trunk at the front of the boat. When he saw Jeremiah he slammed the trunk closed and placed something in his pocket. The boy hustled up to the ladder and cut in front of the younger Jeremiah. Jeremiah made no objection until the boy climbed to the second step and an object fell out of his pocket onto the ship's floor. Jeremiah looked down. It was a diamond bracelet. He picked it up and handed it to the older boy.

"Here, you dropped this," he said as he held out his hand. The boy quickly took the bracelet and stuffed it deep into his pocket so it would not fall out again.

"Thanks. I don't want anything to happen to it. It belonged to my grandmother."

"Well, be careful, you don't want to lose it," replied Jeremiah.

"Right," said the boy in a quiet way.

They both went to the upper deck.

Master Morrison started his meeting by making sure everyone knew his first mate, Mr. Henderson. "Mr. Henderson is my right hand. What he says is the same as an order from me." He waited for the thought to sink in. "I expect you to stay below in your bunks during this voyage. My crew needs to work the sails. Once a day I will order time for you to come up and get fresh air and sunshine if God wills it." He hesitated and looked down at a six-year-old boy squirming and talking while he was speaking. He continued, "I don't need you being underfoot as we sail. We will have some strong winds that will push the boat; the winds also create high waves. A rocking boat is dangerous to those who are not familiar with sailing. Therefore, you should not be on deck unless I order it. And, in case you don't know ship etiquette, my word is final. Any questions?"

Master Donald Morrison was a short stout man barely five and a half feet tall, but he had a thick body indicative of a muscular frame. His commanding voice was heard across the length of the ship and no one doubted who was in charge. His thinning grey hair suggested his age was over fifty.

Master Morrison continued, "This voyage may take as little as six weeks or as long as—well, who knows. Let's try and make the best of it." Master Morrison seemed like a sensible and likeable man but he also showed indications that he could be harsh and merciless—which was a good mix for an effective captain.

"We will travel southwest as much as the wind will allow. Reports indicate good weather and a good wind, as it was for the other ships that have gone before us, and with the same good luck, we too will have a fast and safe passage. Now, go below and become acquainted with your fellow travellers."

The sleeping quarters were crowded when all the passengers were on the lower deck. The noise was at a feverish pitch when a man named James stood up and yelled to everyone to quiet down. The attempt was marginally successful. Parents hushed their children and pulled them into their area. But the noise did not go away; it was just muted for a few moments. Soon it was at the same frenzied pitch. James stood up again and starting yelling, using bits of colourful language and showing anger in his voice. "We cannot travel for over six weeks in this hole with this shouting and these uncontrolled children," he said. "Please be respectful of others."

Some mothers grumbled in indignant irritation. Others nodded their heads in agreement that order was necessary. The noise subsided.

Thomas crawled into the bunk and lay down to rest. Denis

pulled his Bible out of the bottom of the trunk to read; Johanna was quietly talking with Catherine and her five nieces as they knitted. Jeremiah and Uncle Jerry were engaged in checkers. After five moves, Uncle Jerry had the younger Jeremiah boxed in. The nephew could not out-fox the uncle. He tried a second and third game; each time he played it differently by moving a checker in a different direction or starting a different strategy on the opposite side, but the outcome was always the same—trapped.

"How did you do that?" Jeremiah demanded.

"Practice."

A teenage girl screamed. Every passenger looked down the length of the ship. A second scream came from the same girl. "My bracelet's gone. Someone took my bracelet," yelled the panic-stricken girl.

"Now, Mary," said her mother, "you must have misplaced it."

Passengers started to disregard the commotion. Jeremiah, however, took notice. He slid out of the bunk and looked down the aisle. The intensity of the young girl's hysteria continued as she frantically looked through her belongings.

"It's been stolen!" she said again.

Jeremiah moved towards her.

His uncle called to him. "Jeremiah, where are you going? Let's play another game." Jeremiah ignored the pleas as he watched the girl and moved towards her.

Uncle Jerry turned to Denis. "Where is he going?"

"I don't know," said his uninterested brother.

Jeremiah was like a dog on point. Nothing was going to distract his focus. There were only two people on the ship who knew where the bracelet was, he and the teenage boy. He moved closer to the girl and when he saw the lack of response from the boy, he grew furious. His face was getting red. He wanted the teenage boy to stand up and return the bracelet.

Jeremiah passed the girl and headed for the boy's bunk. He stopped short of the bunk and locked eyes with the boy. The teenager did not see Jeremiah coming so he could not counter the impending accusation. Jeremiah watched the boy intensely; he did not release his glare to allow him to hide the spoils of his theft.

The girl was oblivious to the exchange between the two boys. The thief was older than Jeremiah and even though he was shorter than Jeremiah, he was stockier, more muscular. But Jeremiah was not measuring the difference in pounds; he was measuring honesty, truthfulness, or the right answer at the time of question. He waited. The girl's voice was in the background fretting over the missing bracelet.

Finally Jeremiah spoke, his voice tight with emotion. "Give the bracelet back."

"What bracelet?"

"The one in your pocket," said Jeremiah, his face flushed and his teeth clenched.

"I don't know what you mean," the teenager sparred coyly.

"I'll come in there and drag you out, if you don't come out here now."

The boy's father came from a side bunk and stepped between the boys, trying to break Jeremiah's eye contact. Jeremiah slid sideways to continue his watch. "You ain't puttin' a hand on anybody," said the father.

"He's got the girl's bracelet in his pocket," countered Jeremiah.

"He ain't got it. You don't know nothin' and you can get out of here."

Jeremiah stepped in closer. "He is giving it back." The father moved his feet into a boxer's stance and raised his arms into a fighting posture.

"I wouldn't do that if I were you," came a voice from behind Jeremiah. He did not have to turn around; he knew his brother's voice. However, if he had turned, he would have seen Uncle Jerry too, followed by Thomas trying to make his way down the aisle as he coughed. But Denis's support was all Jeremiah needed; he bumped the boy's father aside and reached into the bunk.

The teenage boy squirmed, but Jeremiah had thirteen years of daily hard work behind him. His hands were strong, his will even stronger. He heaved the boy out with one tug. The boy landed on the floor and Jeremiah had one arm stretched out and locked in his grasp. He placed a foot on the boy's shoulder to keep him pinned to the floor.

"Take it out or I'll break your arm," promised Jeremiah. With his free hand, the boy reached into his pocket and threw the bracelet on the floor. "Is that your bracelet?" Jeremiah called to the girl.

She looked down and snatched it immediately. "'Tis, that's it. Thank you." The girl disappeared back to her bunk.

Denis turned to a man behind him. "Call Captain Morrison down," he ordered.

The father spoke up. "No, you don't have to do that. He learned his lesson." The father knew his son was in trouble if Captain Morrison found out.

"Call the Captain," commanded Jeremiah.

The man went up the ladder to the main deck. Shortly Mr. Henderson, the first mate, came down the ladder. "What happened?" he asked.

"He stole a bracelet out of that girl's trunk," reported Jeremiah.

Mr. Henderson got the details from Jeremiah and the girl.

"How old are you?" he asked the boy.

"Sixteen," he answered.

"Old enough to know better," said Mr. Henderson as he grabbed the collar of the boy and pulled him towards the stairs.

The girl came back to Jeremiah and threw her arms around his neck and squeezed. "Thank you," she told him again.

"Yeah, you're welcome" was Jeremiah embarrassed response.

A few minutes later, an order came from Mr. Henderson. "All passengers on deck."

They made their way up the ladder. Captain Morrison was standing above the main deck on the bridge and the boy had been tied, face first, to the main mast. The sun was sinking in the western sky and dark shadows were spreading across the deck. Captain

Morrison was in full sunlight, as if he was the main character on a stage. The crew had lined up along the starboard rail.

"Who was the brave man who saw this theft and got the jewellery back?" Master Morrison asked the crowd.

Uncle Jerry and Thomas wanted to snatch Jeremiah out of the crowd and place him out of sight but Jeremiah spoke up: "I did." Uncle Jerry sighed.

Captain Morrison continued, "And you saw him steal the bracelet?"

"No, I saw him in the trunk and then I saw him place it in his pocket."

"Right, that's when he stole it."

"Yes, sir. He did it when you called us to the deck the last time."

"And then you found it in his pocket after the girl discovered it missing?"

"Yes, sir."

"I understand. Does anyone else have anything to say?"

The boy's father spoke up. "He didn't mean no harm."

Captain Morrison cut him off. "No harm, Mr. Brady?" Mr. Morrison had remembered the man from boarding the ship. "He will learn about no harm. Ten lashes, Mr. Henderson," the Captain ordered.

Mr. Henderson ripped the shirt from the boy's back. The crowd braced for the torture as the first blow was delivered. The boy cried. With each crack of the whip, the women sighed and moaned loudly and children covered their eyes. When the first mate was done, Captain Morrison ordered the passengers below. Two crew members untied the boy and released him to his father, who helped him down the ladder in silence. Mr. Power, the ship's surgeon, followed him down with his black bag. Slowly the passengers returned to their quarters.

A hush hung over the passengers. They had seen these events before because the English often made public display of torture to remind the masses of their place and the consequences of committing transgressions. Even though everyone understood harsh punishment was necessary in this case, especially given the close living quarters, watching it being administered offended many passengers. People filed into their bunks in silence.

A man named Patrick walked down the aisle with a violin case in his hand; he stopped at mid-ship and asked to sit on the edge of the closest bunk. His violin case rested on his lap as he opened it and removed the violin with ever so much care. A rag stored in the case glided across the instrument as he polished the wood as if it was his most prized possession. It was a bizarre scene: Patrick in his shabby clothes, dirt embedded on his face and lodged deep under his fingernails. His skinny, drawn appearance made them wonder when he had enjoyed his last meal.

Patrick was obviously a poor farmer, but his violin was flawless and the polished wood shone, reflecting the light from the kerosene lantern. The violin was his salvation, and he treated it with respect and admiration because of the joy it brought him. The bow followed out of the case, along with the rosin. People watched Patrick move with deliberate ease as he set the violin up under his chin and tested four soft and easy notes to make sure the tuning had not changed. Satisfied, he raised the bow and drew it across the strings.

Sad notes of a spiritual hymn filled the lower deck. The timing was right for a mystical moment as the voyagers focused their attention on Patrick. The familiar tune of "Amazing Grace" rang out, reaching the four corners of the deck. Two men stepped out into the aisle and gave voice to the song. Slowly a few women joined in.

Uncle Jerry's second oldest daughter Elinor, whom they called Elly, stepped out. Her singing skills were well honed from her years in the church choral group. Her high soprano voice was an octave above the others, creating the sound of a well-rehearsed, long-standing choir. But such was not the case; these people had just come together for one purpose—a ride across the ocean to a new world. Tonight, they united. The music brought the emotions of fear, sadness, heartache and oppression, yet hope, faith and unity, to the surface. They were one. All voices joined in, from the oldest man of sixty to the youngest child able to hum along.

The noise floated up to the main deck and across the darkened ocean. The ancient kings of Ireland must have heard the chorus and the resolve of their people. The brightness of the stars shone across the water as *The Elizabeth* headed through the vastness of the North Atlantic. The scene was magical, divine and calming.

Captain Morrison was at the helm talking with Mr. Henderson when they heard the music and singing from below. Mr. Henderson said, "I'll check on them."

"Let them have their pleasure," the Captain replied.

"I'll check anyway." Mr. Henderson moved towards the ladder. From high above in the crow's nest, a crew member named Jake was singing at the top of his lungs. "Pay attention to what you're doing," the first mate yelled up.

Jake waved an acknowledgement but continued:

> "Through many dangers, toils and snares. . .
> we have already come.
> T'was Grace that brought us safe thus far . . .
> and Grace will lead us home.
>
> "Amazing Grace, how sweet the sound,
> That saved a wretch like me . . .
> I once was lost but now am found,
> Was blind, but now I see."

Mr. Henderson climbed half-way down the ladder and stopped to have a full view of the lower deck. The scene was orderly, almost reverent, as if the Bishop were on board holding a High Mass. He smiled at the crowd. He felt the urge to join in but thought better of it. He was a man of authority and he was not about to get suckered into participating in their pleasure.

People clapped and howled when Patrick ended the hymn. Before the applause stopped, Patrick started again. The traditional folksong of "O'Reilly's Daughter" was next. The violin sound started slowly but the tempo increased and the singing began. When the chorus hit, starting with the "Giddy aye-eh, For the one-eyed Reilly" followed by the rapid clapping associated with the song, the mood of the passengers changed.

As the song started, Patrick's five children knew what to do and headed down the aisle. They had special tap shoes that clicked when they walked. Those people at mid-ship heard and saw the children coming and pushed the heavy wooden eating table out of the way. The children, who ranged in age from four years to eighteen years, lined up and waited.

Daniel, a young man seated across from the McCarthys' bunks, retrieved a boudhran, an ancient Irish drum with a goatskin covering, from his trunk. He carried the haunting-sounding instrument to mid-ship, picking up the beat of the song as he moved next to Patrick. The crowd was singing as loud as they could; some folks were off-key, some were clapping, but all were tapping their feet. As soon as the first verse ended and Patrick went into his instrumental bridge, the children started their traditional Irish step dancing. The clicking, tapping, and shuffling of the shoes created their own rhythm as they moved in unison around the open table area.

Others joined in at the sides, so as to not interrupt the movements of Patrick's children. In the aisles other dancers bumped and twirled to the beat. The music softened to indicate the bridge was over, and the singing resumed. The hardships of poverty, the fear of travelling into an unknown world, the sadness of separation from family and country were temporarily forgotten.

The first night was full of action. Denis saw at least three whiskey bottles being passed around. He declined a drink as one bottle passed by and he quickly kept it moving so his father would not see it. The singing continued. A young man named Bill stood up and sang a traditional Irish song. And so the night represented the Irish plight—sadness and joy closely intertwined.

The ship was rocking, not from the waves but from the celebration on the lower deck. Feet were pounding on the floor in a cadence that matched the beat of the music, and hands clapped in a stationary dance from the seated passengers. Soon a slower, softer pace overcame the assembly as a group of men stood and crooned Irish heritage songs. Children started to fall asleep. The party was losing momentum as people started to settle into their bunks for the night. Eventually, Patrick played a soft O'Carolan planxty, which signalled the night's end. The passengers settled in for their first sleep on *The Elizabeth.*

* * *

The following morning families rotated in groups for breakfast tea. Later on, one main meal of the day was served near noon. These passengers were used to starving and one regular meal was a treat. Occasionally, fresh water was available from a barrel later in the afternoon. The English had promised them a passage, not a luxury voyage, but for those who had to wait to eat every other day, this seemed like a luxury.

The group had much in common—they were all Catholic, they were poor and destitute, and they were a thorn to the English nobility. Their journey was not born out of some vision for a new adventure and new opportunities or a drive to excel. This trip was an alternative to total destruction. Many folks latched onto hope but most were weary, struggling for survival.

This trip was not like that of other explorers and immigrants who needed a plan once they arrived in America. The future of these families was already decided; their destination was known, and they had land and materials waiting their arrival. All they needed to do was wait.

The days were long, with little activity, and the closeness of strangers living within a few feet of each other was strenuous. Tolerance for noise, opinions, social engagement and habits was strained. A few arguments broke out but most were kept within civil control, especially under the watchful eye of Mr. Henderson.

The passengers' immune systems were already low due to their lack of proper nourishment, which made sickness a very real threat to the cluster of families. Sickness spread, infecting many, and Thomas had already been sick when he boarded the boat. Now with the dampness of the sea and the occasional soaking from a wave that leaked into the lower decks, Thomas's cough was in full force.

Mr. Power examined him and determined he had chronic bronchitis. He suggested staying in the bunk and using a spittoon for his phlegm production. Jeremiah was dispatched to find a spittoon and he returned with an empty tobacco can. "A fine substitute," the doctor told Jeremiah as he started to walk back to the ladder. Then he added to Thomas, "Now you get your rest."

Johanna was sceptical of the doctor's diagnosis because of his nonchalant manner. "British doctors," she said aloud sarcastically.

"What'd you want him to do," asked Thomas, "perform surgery and take my lungs out?"

"He would have liked that."

In the early afternoon, Denis went to the top deck with Jeremiah during their fresh-air time. The two brothers watched the swells of the sea raise and lower the boat as good wind came at the boat from the south. They were on the port side facing the wind.

"Wind from the south has rain in its mouth," quoted Denis from the weather folklore. Denis had been waiting for an opportunity to talk to his young brother, and started, "You know you could have gotten hurt last night over that bracelet."

"Naw, I had him all the way."

"You need to learn how to approach people without threatening them."

"He had it coming."

"Jeremiah, he was three years older than you. You are not stronger than all sixteen-year-olds. You were lucky not to get hurt."

"You were there and it all turned out all right."

"Jeremiah, I'm not going to be there all the time. And if you had lost control, you could've hurt him. Then where would you be? *You* would have gotten the ten lashes. You need to learn tact."

"I don't know. I guess you're right. It was just easier to grab him and force him to give it back."

"Easier is not always right."

Captain Morrison walked over. "Is everything all right?" He looked suspiciously at Denis as he slapped the back of Jeremiah.

"Yes, sir," replied Jeremiah as he tried to catch his breath. "This is my brother, Denis."

Denis stuck out his hand to shake. His hand was quickly lost in the grip of the Captain, whose hands were enormous and strong. He hung onto Denis as if he were pulling a yarn of rope attached to a sail. "Good to meet you, boy. You have quite the brother here."

"'Tis, we were just talking about that," Denis said.

"He's a courageous kid," Captain Morrison said, with a sailor's drawl. "He can work on my ship any time."

"As you know, we are heading to Canada for a new life," Denis said, "on solid ground, not on the sea."

Captain Morrison laughed. "Ah yes, landlubbers. Good luck." He walked away as deliberately as he had approached.

* * *

Johanna, Catherine and her cousins spent most of the time on board chatting, knitting or sewing. In the early morning, Johanna spent some time reading, especially from the Bible. Throughout the day, she kept a watchful eye on Thomas, who was mostly quiet except when coughing. Uncle Jerry and the boys were most active and restless. The other passengers found the McCarthy clan enjoyable, level-headed and mainly good people. They maintained a positive attitude except for an occasional grumble against the English, and most Irishmen made those slurs.

Uncle Jerry's youngest daughter Eliza, who was ten years old, missed her mother. Uncle Jerry tried to console his daughter and Johanna reminded her they would meet Lizzie in Montreal soon. But Eliza was fixed on her missing mother. She missed her house and all its familiar surroundings, and the vastness of the journey was too much for her to comprehend.

Denis called the girls together for a story. They appreciated their cousin's stories, as he was well read and his simple accounts were always interesting, with great detail and a thread of life lessons. The five daughters of Uncle Jerry, along with Catherine and Jeremiah, sat along the bunks on either side to hear the story.

"Today I'm going to speak of the Patroness of Ireland."

"Oh, the story of St. Brigid," said Eliza, distracted already from thoughts of her mother.

"Yes, St. Brigid, born of a pagan king and a slave mother, but as a young girl she was converted to Christianity and baptized by St. Patrick." He continued the story of this fifth-century real and legendary hero: "She also started a convent of nuns dedicated to helping the poor and converting pagans in Kildare. Even though St. Brigid had wealth and luxuries through her father, she disregarded those possessions for a simple and pious life."

"She had an easy life and gave it up," said Catherine, who had heard the story before from her brother. "I wouldn't have done that."

The younger girls giggled at the contrasting opinion.

Denis started again. "Even more significant, St. Brigid was a beautiful girl. She had suitors coming from far and wide, charmed by her graces, but she wanted nothing to do with them." He stopped for a moment and then asked his sister, "Don't you think that is odd?"

"Yes, I would have waited for a prince or a chieftain, maybe even an earl," said Catherine coyly.

"Oooh, no," said little Eliza as she lifted her nose at the thought, "not an earl." The girls giggled again.

"Well anyway, I would have enjoyed the attention and the romance," replied Catherine.

"St. Brigid had so much attention," continued Denis, "she wished herself ugly." Again the girls moaned and groaned at the thought of having such easily acquired qualities as beauty and wealth and rejecting them. Denis proceeded, "Her focus was to help the poor, and she gave food and drink to paupers who came to her door. Her father disliked the free charity and eventually made her leave the house."

"That was nice of St. Brigid to give food to the hungry," said Mary, the thirteen-year-old.

"Yes, it was," acknowledged Denis. "Once she gave away her chariot to a leper, but she asked if she could keep it for an hour to take a sick man to the convent. The man refused to give back the chariot and left Brigid and the sick man alone. However, Brigid's faith and healing powers caused the man to become well again."

"I wish I could heal people like that," said Elly.

Denis was pleased to hear Elly personalize the story. "I suppose there's a lot we can do for sick people to help them feel better."

"Yes, I think there is," she agreed.

Jeremiah, who had been sitting and listening, broke in, "Yeah, and why would she wish herself ugly?" returning the story to her beauty.

"It was a distraction to her work," answered Catherine.

"Actually, she did become ugly after a bout with smallpox; her face became severely scared," added Denis.

"I don't think she became ugly at all given the work she did," Catherine said.

"Yes, the beauty was in her work," finished Denis.

Jeremiah scoffed, "Oh, that's a daft connection."

"Not silly at all," pressed Catherine, "she became a saint for her charitable work."

Jeremiah changed the subject. "So tell us about St. Brigid's Cross."

"Oh, yes," said Denis. "This strong and outgoing saint was wild enough to handle a chariot but calm and reverent enough to sit with a dying pagan, converting him on his deathbed using the simple symbol of a cross made from a rush plant tied together by strains of reeds.

"She was trying to comfort him in his final hours, and at the same time she pulled a reed from the matting on his bed. She wove the reeds into a cross. The man, who was a pagan, asked what she was making so she explained the cross that Christ died on and its meaning for Christians. The man was converted to Christianity on his deathbed and St. Brigid's Cross remains a reminder of her selfless work.

"So," Denis continued, "St. Brigid showed us that it's easy to be charitable when you're rich and beautiful because people want to be in your company. But after all that worldly substance is removed, she still did good things to help people in their day-to-day struggles. And like Elly said, we can too."

The children acknowledged the lesson in the story by nodding their heads.

* * *

The days and weeks went quickly and the trip was smooth. Only one storm, lasting nearly eighteen hours, rocked the boat. Many people were seasick and most belongings were soaked. After the storm, clotheslines were strung throughout the bunks. Some belongings were ruined. On June 29, after thirty-seven days at sea, Captain Morrison called all passengers to the main deck.

"We should be seeing land within the next day or two," he announced. "We have made good progress and according to our calculations, America and Canada are just ahead. We should see glimpses of Newfoundland soon," he added, as he pointed up to the lookout in the crow's nest. "We will be releasing a bird here soon to see where it flies."

Catherine turned to her older brother. "Releasing a bird?"

"Ah, they have a cage with a crow in it at the top of the mast," Denis explained. "As we approach land they release the crow and see which direction it flies. The flight tells them the shortest distance as the crow flies."

"Oh, I have heard that. Da used to say, 'the walk to Cork was short as the crow flies.' I always thought that was funny."

"I'm surprised they will release it for Newfoundland and not wait for mainland Canada."

Captain Morrison yelled up to the watchman, "See anything yet?"

"No, sir."

"Go ahead and release the crow."

"Aye, aye, sir."

The bird flew out and circled the ship. It soared to about 100 feet above the ship, where it turned on a northwest flight.

"I believe it sees land, Captain," yelled the sailor from the nest. "North by northwest."

"Good sign," replied Captain Morrison. He turned aft towards the helmsman: "To the starboard, fifty degrees north."

The ship swung right and the crew adjusted the sails. Everyone watched over the bow on the starboard side with great anticipation.

After an hour Captain Morrison yelled from the bridge, "You can go below if you like—we will let you know if land is sighted—or stay on deck to watch, but it may be a while."

Many passengers stayed on the deck. It was a warm day in the sun and most were happy to spend time out of the "the hole," as the passengers called it. But the clouds rolled in rapidly from the south and it rained hard for ten minutes, then abruptly stopped. The wind shifted from the southwest and the sky cleared. Passengers went below for the rain but quickly returned to look for terrain signalling safe harbour and arrival.

However, what they saw was an enormous island of ice floating closer and closer to the ship. The iceberg was several hundred yards long and towered over the ship. The vertical pillars of crystalline ice reflected hues of soft blue and magenta, which gave a spectacular view to the passengers. The ship passed within a half-mile of the iceberg, allowing a close enough view but without placing the ship in jeopardy of ramming the massive frozen structure. The temperature, however, dropped ten degrees.

Catherine leaned in to her brother again. "Do you think the crow landed on the iceberg?"

Denis smiled. "No, his feet would get too cold."

Catherine was not certain whether Denis was being flippant or not in answer to her serious question. She shrugged her shoulders and grumbled.

* * *

Several hours later, the lookout yelled, "Land ho. To the port."

Those still on board all turned to their left. All they could see on the horizon was the light blue sky meeting the dark blue ocean. The lookout had the advantage of height. A passenger from up near the bow yelled, "I see trees." As Denis strained his eyes, he could see land. Cheers rose among the crowd. Soon passengers from below filled the deck. Excitement swept through the crowd as people yelled, danced, hugged, kissed and cried.

Captain Morrison came down from the bridge. "What you are looking at is the coast of Nova Scotia. We will use that as our landmark to guide us into the St. Lawrence River."

People watched the land as they moved northward to swing around Cape Breton. The exuberance of seeing the New World lasted into the evening, with singing and dancing, which started on the top deck and continued when the Captain ordered the festivities below because the party was disrupting the crew's work. The wind died down and the boat slowed. Some remained on deck just to watch, maybe in disbelief or maybe in belief of something bigger, more powerful. Either way, their lives were about to change.

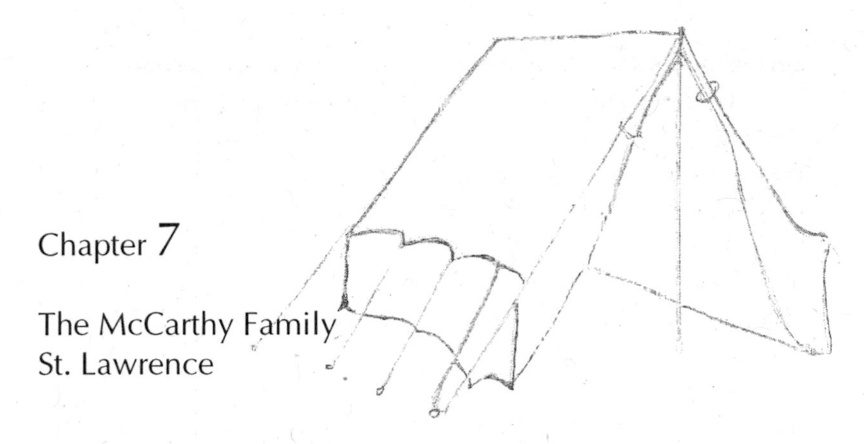

Chapter 7

The McCarthy Family St. Lawrence

The ship ran north along the coast of Nova Scotia to the tip of the Cape. As they rounded the eastern edge of the continental landmass of North America and turned west into Cabot Strait between Newfoundland and Nova Scotia and then headed towards the Gulf of the St. Lawrence, the wind calmed. Even though Mr. Morrison had the ship under full sail, they began to luff as the wind died down. The sun was setting in the western sky, showing the passengers their first sunset in the New World, illuminating the land with hues of crimson and gold.

"What a welcome," pondered Thomas, who had worked his way to the deck to see the treasure they had endured so much to see.

The ship sat at the tip of the Cape—an unusual place to lose wind because the prevailing westerly winds usually blew continuously unabated across the expanse of the St. Lawrence Gulf. Likewise, the open waters of the Atlantic and the constant influence of the Gulf Stream all merged at the tip of the Cape. Wind was always present from one of those directions, but not this day.

It was eerie, and it worried Mr. Morrison. With little wind and no power, the waves kept rolling against the starboard side of the ship. For every foot of slow forward progress, the ship was pushed two feet closer to the rocky shoreline of Cape Breton. The sails hung like limp sheets on a clothesline. An occasional breeze filled the sail but before it could give any push, it died down again. *The Elizabeth* sat rocking against the waves.

"Mr. Henderson, I don't like sitting in irons like this." The reference was to losing the wind and being unable to move.

"Aye, Captain, a wind better blow soon or we are going to be sitting sideways on a sand dune."

The first mate's assessment was troublesome. At high tide the ship could hit the rocky shore; at low tide the ship could run aground and be battered by the receding waves, most likely tipping on its side. The longer they sat powerless in the water, the more likely the ship would get caught in a tidal change. Either way, they would be shipwrecked.

Captain Morrison came up with a plan. "Order all the passengers to go as far forward as they can. I want as much weight in the bow as we can get."

"Aye, Captain."

"I want the stern light in the water, so the waves can push the stern around towards the shore and the bow to face the open sea."

"This is a dangerous move, sir."

"I know, but it will give us a little more time as the waves flow alongside of the ship rather than pushing us from the side. We will be least resistant to the waves."

"Aye Captain," said Henderson as he left the bridge to make the ship ready.

All passengers were ordered out of their bunks and were told to press as far forward as they could go. Captain Morrison calculated an additional three thousand pounds was shifted forward. The bow fell deeper into the water as the stern lightened. He was gambling against time that the wind would pick up before the stern hit rock or sand.

Mr. Morrison waited. His tactic was giving him what he wanted, more time in deeper water as the darkness of night fell, and all passengers were kept in the bow pressed against each other. Babies and children were squished in. Mothers argued for more room. Fathers argued back for the safety of the ship. Thomas coughed. He felt the tightness in his chest but he could not move. They all prayed for wind.

A fog was settling and visibility grew poor. The Captain's tactic lasted for hours, with everyone holding their positions. As it approached 11:00 p.m., something thudded against the back of the boat. Everyone gasped and a silence fell throughout the ship. The Captain's voice came above: "Check the stern."

"Nothing, Captain," was the reply.

"It was a rock, we hit the shore," a woman yelled.

"No, we are still floating," replied a man as the ship bobbed up and down.

"Could have been a whale, Captain," a crew member reported.

"Naw, I doubt it. I believe we are too close to shore."

"There are plenty of whales in these waters; one of them could have hit the boat," the man argued.

Another voice said, "It was a mermaid pushing us back out to sea."

Some laughed, some scowled at the absurdity, and some wished it were true. The thud remained unexplained as the passengers and crew waited. An hour later, Master Morrison announced midnight. The crew shifted duties. A fresh sailor climbed aloft to the crow's nest even though visibility was poor. Mr. Morrison wanted all hands ready if conditions changed. Another boatswain took the helm.

"Nothing to be seen up there," reported the relieved watchman, pointing towards the coast.

The remainder of the crew lingered on deck awaiting orders. The passengers were restless and enduring the pounding of the waves against the bow, one after another. They were exhausted, but the importance of their task to the ship kept their spirits strong. Another half-hour went by.

A young man named Mickey was at the back edge of the group near the middle of the ship and he kept pushing forward. He felt as if he was not contributing because of his distance from the front of the ship. So he pushed his weight forward. The people in front were already squished as far as they could go and yelled back to stop pushing.

Mickey became discouraged because his slight build and his position at the back of the crowd made it almost impossible for him to affect the ship's weight distribution. He decided to go topside and climb out on the bowsprit, a spear-like pole that jutted from the bow of the boat and anchored the foresail. No one saw Mickey leave the jammed group; they just knew the pushing had stopped.

Mickey knew he should not be on the main deck, so he snuck across as the sailors tended the sails, waiting for a breeze. The fog created cover for his movements; he climbed out onto the narrow bowsprit and positioned himself among the ropes to support and balance his weight.

He found peace in his decision to give more weight to the front bow in this manner. He enjoyed the quiet of the night away from crowded passengers while on his little perch. The bow dipped into the ocean, as Mr. Morrison had hoped. Mickey lay prone a few feet above the rolling waves that slapped against the bow and he, like the rest of the crew and passengers, waited.

"I can see the shoreline," came the news from above. The shore was a dark line against the reflecting waters of the ocean. The ship bobbed up and down as it sat atop the water.

Mr. Morrison called to Mr. Henderson, "If we get much closer to shore we must weigh anchor."

"Aye, Captain." Mr. Henderson did not want to challenge the Captain's order, but both of them knew the risks under these conditions of fierce bobbing in the rough waters. They waited, and the atmosphere was tense. The passengers were not accustomed to navigating through turbulent waters. Being crunched together added to their despair. The sailors' fear, on the other hand, came from their belief in the superstitious sailing lore as ancient as the Greek Poseidon, the god of the sea, or other mythical beings living under the ferocious waves seeking revenge for sins of past deeds.

Likewise, the sequence of the waves was important to some sailors, as every third wave had extraordinary powers and produced a roar emitted from the ocean. Others believed the roar of the waves came from the spirits of those who had died at sea, crying out for a connection to loved ones and a proper burial on land.

The Captain was a practical man; he did not believe in sea serpents seeking revenge or long-lost watery civilizations like Atlantis at the bottom of the sea. The known dangers of rough seas were his worry, with the responsibility of the ship, passengers and crew. Each person waited with their own thoughts and perceived interpretations of the dangers they faced.

The waves never stopped rolling against the ship, and Mickey had a death grip on the rigging as each wave tossed him up, off the bowsprit. Then the ship dropped down after the crest of the wave and Mickey crashed onto the wooden pole. He could not move from his prone position for fear of slipping into the water, but he was losing strength as he tried to hang onto the ropes and minimize the impact of hitting the bowsprit. His chest and thighs ached from each slam. It was not wind that he needed; he needed calm water so he could back off the bowsprit without falling. The waves kept coming.

Shortly after 1:00 a.m. the main sail flapped. A breeze shook the canvas like a rug being beaten on a line. A moment later, the foresail flopped, followed by the upper jumbo. Silence. "Come on," whispered Captain Morrison, "come on."

"Here it comes," came the news from above. The watchman felt it first. With a slap of the linen, first the rear sail and then the main sail filled with air.

"Come on, Mother Nature, come on," repeated Mr. Morrison.

A snap, a tug, a jerk came all at once: the sails were full. Beams swung, ropes tightened and sails adjusted as the ship moved forward.

Cheers came from below. Captain Morrison ordered everyone back to their bunks to even out the weight of the ship. The crew worked steadily to right the ship. This wind came from the west, the least helpful for the voyage but a lifesaver for the ship. They sailed back out towards the ocean. Once there was no longer danger of going aground, Mr. Morrison ordered the ship to head back into the gulf, giving wider berth to the land. The crisis was over; Mr. Morrison's gamble had proved risky but successful. The passengers returned to their bunks.

Mickey's mother, Margaret, was the first to recognize her eldest son's absence. She was taking inventory of her seven children: five girls and two boys. All were accounted for except for Mickey.

"Where is Mickey?" she asked her husband.

"I don't know; the last I saw him, he was pushing the group forward. He must be with another family."

Margaret Connell looked up and down the rows of bunks but she could not find her nineteen-year-old son. She called out, "Mickey," but there was no response. "Michael?" still no response. Her worry increased after her third trip along the full length of the lower deck. "I will go up above and check," she told her husband, William.

"No, you stay here; I'll check."

William climbed the ladder and he was not off the top rung when Mr. Henderson saw him. "Keep below," was the sharp order.

"I am looking for my son," replied William.

"He is not up here. Now, go below."

"But he is not below either."

Mr. Henderson was unsympathetic to William's pleas. There had been numerous cries of missing children who were then found shortly after, mixed in with another family or sleeping under a blanket. Mr. Henderson ordered again, "Go below. I'll be down in a few minutes."

The waves increased with the wind but Captain Morrison hit them head on as *The Elizabeth* sliced through the water under full power. Mr. Morrison took a deep breath and slowly let the air escape, and with it the stress for the safety of the ship, its passengers and crew—but the relief was momentary. A flash of light reflected on the horizon: he had more than wind; he had a storm coming.

Mr. Henderson along with Mr. Power went below to meet William and Margaret. By this time all the passengers were aware of Mickey's absence. They checked all the storage areas and the privy areas. Mr. Henderson checked the hatch that led to the bottom of the ship where all the provisions and supplies were stored. The lock was intact.

"The only place for him to be is above," assumed Margaret.

"No one is on deck; we would have seen him," reported Mr. Henderson. "But I'll check." Mr. Henderson went above and ordered two sailors to search the boat from top to bottom. He then went to Captain Morrison and reported that a nineteen-year-old was missing, not a small child.

"Where do you think he is?" asked the Captain.

"I don't know," replied Mr. Henderson. He looked up to the crow's nest. "Did you see anyone go overboard?" he yelled.

"No, sir."

The sailors returned. No Michael was found. "Did you check the bottom deck?" The Captain wanted assurance that all areas had been scrutinized for a hiding person and nothing overlooked.

"We checked the lock on the lower deck, all secure, but we did not go down below."

"Check it."

"Aye, aye, Captain." The sailors left to re-examine the bottom deck.

The Captain enjoyed a moment of satisfaction as the wind pushed the ship through the strait off Cape Breton into the St. Lawrence Gulf. Meanwhile, the sailors opened the hatch to the lower deck and climbed down with lanterns to inspect the area. The deck had barrels of fresh water, crates of food, stacks of extra ropes and sails, and any extra critters they picked up along the way. Mice were common but there was the occasional rat or two that had stowed away in a crate. They used caution because they did not want to surprise a cornered rat during their search.

The bottom of the boat from the keel half-way up the gunwales and along the full length of the ship was lined with bricks. The bricks were stacked three deep, which gave the ship significant weight as ballast to counteract the forces of the wind on the sails, thus preventing the ship from blowing over sideways.

Bricks were a common cargo on ships coming from Europe because passengers did not add the stable weight needed at the bottom of the boat. Many times the return trips to Europe with goods made in America did not need the bricks for the added weight, so they were unloaded on the docks and carted into the cities.

Eventually the colonists found a way to make use of these stacks of bricks to pave the streets of the city, where excessive horse and buggy travel made frequent mud ruts. It also allowed the ships to cleanse the crevices of the ship of unwanted stowaways. The sailors returned with no news of the missing passenger.

Amid the urgent situation of Mickey's disappearance, new dangers confronted Captain Morrison. The swirling wind at the convergence of the gulf and ocean created high waves and the same unpredictability as a storm—should he go close to shore and look for safe harbour, or face the storm on the high seas? Prince Edward Island lay southwest of them; it offered protection, but he did not have time to reach the safety of its eastern shore. He decided to remain on the open sea and face the storm.

As the thunder and lightning approached the ship, the Captain ordered the sails down except for two headsails to allow steerage. The gales of these North Atlantic waters blew hard against the ship. Five sailors on each side of the main mast climbed the standing rigging to the upper sail.

Once above, they lined up along the crosstree, supported in a three-point stance—each foot was balanced on a rope that traversed the horizontal pole, and their third support was their upper body draped across the mast. At twenty feet above the main deck and thirty feet above the water, the sailors steadied their weight against the swaying of the ship and forty-mile-per-hour winds. It was a perilous duty. They rolled up the sails and secured them to protect against wind damage in the impending storm.

The storm tossed the ship about. The passengers became sick. Seawater mixed with vomit frequently flowed past the bunks. The lower deck's rancid smell made even more people sick. Going above was not a choice, as Mr. Morrison would not allow it because of the dangers of going overboard in an intense storm like this. It continued for over an hour before one final wind blew the storm out to sea and the gulf water settled. Michael was still missing.

The crew inspected the rigging and sails, while Mr. Power checked the passenger quarters. Buckets of seawater and potash mixed together were brought below to swab the deck of the vomit and neutralize the odour.

All the hazards of a long voyage were converging in one night. "Anything else?" Captain Morrison cynically questioned Mr. Henderson.

"We have had a full night," agreed the first mate. "Time for you to get some rest."

"Wake me if any other disasters come our way," said Mr. Morrison as he left for his quarters. He did not retire to sleep yet, but opened his journal to enter the day and night's events. It was another hour before he rested.

The sun rose in the eastern sky behind *The Elizabeth* as she made her way across the Gulf of St. Lawrence towards the river's mouth. Even though the night had been long, people rose with the light of day. The excitement of arriving in Canada overpowered the need for sleep and the missing teenager added to the restlessness. A renewed search for Mickey began. His mother Margaret was beside herself with anxiety and fear. The worst of thoughts came to her mind and she pleaded with the Captain, "Can't we turn around and search the waters?"

"I'm sorry, but we must proceed. These waters are vast, covering many square miles. I cannot retrace the exact route. Last night we were under darkness and tossed about with the waves; we cannot determine the same route."

Mr. Power explained the need to proceed and said if her son went into the water, the likelihood of his survival was remote. She did not accept the explanation; her son's life was in jeopardy. It was unbearable to think that he was struggling in the ocean, waiting for rescue.

* * *

Denis and Thomas went topside as Captain Morrison, who also rose at sunrise, allowed them additional time on deck because of the calmer waters. As they approached the river the Gaspé Peninsula was on the south, and then Quebec came into view on the northern shore as they passed the Isle d'Anticosti. This area formed the St. Lawrence estuary where the fresh water of the Great Lakes met and mixed with the salt water of the ocean and created a biologically enriched environment.

Further west, the shorelines became obvious and birds were common sights now. Denis spotted a large bird with a wide wingspan soaring on the edge of the southern shore. He watched the bird as he talked with his father. The bird swooped towards the water but at the last minute turned and rose again. Mr. Morrison walked up next to Denis.

"He almost made the plunge to grab a fish," commented Captain Morrison.

"Yeah, that's a huge bird, beautiful and graceful. I never saw a bird like it in Ireland."

"It's an eagle, a bald eagle."

"Funny name, it doesn't look bald."

"It has a white head and dark feathered body."

The eagle swooped a second time, skimming just above the water, then reached down with its sharp claws and snatched a fish. The bird rose and disappeared along the tree line.

Thomas hacked as he stood along the rail. "How are you doing, Tommy?" asked Mr. Morrison.

"I can't shake this cough."

"The doctor thought it was bronchitis but it should have cleared by now."

"I get coughing so heavy it makes my lungs bleed."

"You cough up blood?"

"Only when I cough hard."

"Which is all the time," added Denis.

"I hope getting your feet on solid ground cures your ailment," commented Mr. Morrison. He looked forward and continued, "It is going to be a difficult trip up the river."

"Why so?" asked Denis.

"We will be travelling against the wind and the downstream current. And the French possess the land on both sides of the river: sometimes they are friendly and sometimes not."

"How far do we have to go upstream?"

"About two hundred miles to Quebec City, but they will be hard miles. All the water from the five Great Lakes empties into this river and flows out to the ocean. Have you ever heard of The Falls at Niagara?"

"Of course."

"All the water that flows over those falls is travelling underneath this ship. The drag is significant and the currents are deadly. I'd rather fall overboard in the middle of the ocean than hit the water here. The chances for survival are better in the ocean."

Denis looked over the side of the ship. It looked passive and tranquil.

"Captain," came the voice from above. All three men looked up. "Man-of-war. British," came the additional news as the watchman pointed north.

Captain Morrison went to the starboard side. Henderson brought him a telescope so Mr. Morrison could see the two-mast brig with cannons lined along the side and a British flag flying overhead. "One of ours," stated Captain Morrison.

Denis raised his eyebrows; he did not see a British warship as one of his. He turned and said, "Father, let's go below."

"Good idea," said Mr. Morrison as he turned and headed down the ship towards the bridge. As the two parties separated, there was a cannon blast. Denis and Thomas stopped on deck. The cannon ball had hit the water before the arrival of its sound. Mr. Morrison turned just in time to see the splash settling from the eight-pounder hitting the water. A puff of white smoke rose from the far shore identifying the source of the cannon fire. It came from the French fort at Sept-Iles. *The Elizabeth* was far out of range of the fort's cannon, but it sent a message of unfriendliness and need for caution. The British man-of-war, which was further east, turned to escort *The Elizabeth* into the river.

Captain Morrison returned to Denis and Thomas. "Don't worry, it was just a warning shot. Not unusual for these waters."

"Welcome to the New World, where the French and the British are sniping each other," observed Denis. "How unusual."

"New place but old hatred," replied Mr. Morrison. "Once we enter the river proper we will be in solid French-Canadian territory that's controlled by the British. The danger will be minimal. The ideals of settlers are the same—survival, hope and opportunity. We will pass through in tranquility."

Captain Morrison ordered the flag turned upside down to signal the warship of trouble. Shortly the warship *HMS Boyne* caught up and pulled alongside *The Elizabeth*. Mr. Morrison yelled, "We believe we lost a passenger overboard during a storm last night. We can't find him anywhere. We were about fifty miles due east and eighty miles north of Prince Edward Island."

The naval commander yelled back, "We will check the area."

"Godspeed," Master Morrison replied. The *HMS Boyne* sailed east to look for Mickey. A British ship named after a significant Irish battle, the Battle of the Boyne, went in search of one of Ireland's lost sons. "Life has its ironies," thought Denis.

* * *

The ship left the open waters of the gulf and headed up the St. Lawrence River towards Quebec City. The watershed that fed the river started over nineteen hundred miles inland, in the far western reaches of Ontario and Minnesota, and drained into Lake Superior. The flow began in the interior of northeastern Minnesota with the North River, and flowed down each of the Great Lakes into the St. Lawrence. Each lake that was passed had its own watershed, draining over 200,000 square miles of land from 10,000 miles of shoreline. Eventually 20 per cent of all freshwater in the world became part of this flow.

Even though this was a major river in North America, sailing upstream to Quebec City was only possible twenty-four weeks a year. The other twenty-eight weeks the shipping lane was closed because of ice jams and damaging ice flow during the spring months. Ships had to vacate the waterway in early fall before being trapped, lest the ice rip apart a moored vessel.

Now, the course of the water was passing the ship to its eventual destination in the ocean. But yet another natural force was occurring just above the surface—the wind. Prevailing westerly winds came head on towards the ship. Sail manipulation and tacking allowed Master Morrison to overcome these two strong natural forces.

The river had frequent ships passing inland and out to sea. Two ships were in front *of The Elizabeth*, making their way upstream tacking back and forth the same way *The Elizabeth* was. However, three other ships passed going downstream with wind and current at their back; they moved straight ahead, making great progress. A French naval ship passed with gun ports exposed, a reminder of the homeland disputes that carried over to the rest of the world.

The passengers were abuzz with anticipation of their arrival in Quebec. Yet Mr. Morrison still limited time on deck because of the constant tacking and working the sails. They were travelling two or three miles in the water to make one mile of progress up the river.

Catherine and her cousin Elly went on deck to take advantage of a little fresh air. There they watched the birds along the southern shore. Numerous species of birds flew along the water's edge, the most notable being the seagulls that circled overhead. Catherine and Elly were used to seagulls from the coast of Ireland. They were annoying scavengers that swooped down close to people like beggars looking for a handout. They were accustomed to ships throwing garbage overboard or passengers who tossed scraps into the air for them to catch.

But this was a different type of ship and a different kind of passenger, who rarely had scraps of food, and if there were pieces of food left over, they were used for other productive purposes such as soups or fishing bait. Feeding pesky seagulls did not happen on this ship. But the seagulls still vied for the attention of the two girls rather than bother with the experienced, harsh reactions from seasoned sailors.

"Get away," ordered Elly as she swatted the empty airspace of a long passed gull. The bird's cry squeaked, then sounded like laughter, which riled Elly further.

Another gull quickly dove by as if waiting his turn for a handout. A young sailor stepped up and swung a broom at the birds. "Damn gulls, get out of here."

The girls were taken back at the vulgar language of the sailor. "Oh my," said Elly, "you shouldn't talk like that even to those annoying seagulls."

"My apologies, madam," said the sailor. "I was just trying to help."

"Well, thank you for your help, but we don't talk like that."

"There are plenty of birds to enjoy in this area; you don't need these filthy scroungers laughing at you."

"I don't think he was laughing at me even though it sounded that way."

Catherine looked at her cousin and the sailor. "More than bird talk going on here," she said to herself.

"Those gulls, the white ones with the orange legs, black cap and black beak, are actually terns, common terns, and that laugh is their identifying feature."

Catherine turned to look towards the shore again. She did not need or want a lesson in seagulls from a smelly sailor in tattered clothes pretending to be a bird expert. Elly, on the other hand, was absorbed in the explanation of the migratory habits of the common terns of the North Atlantic. He explained the breeding habits of the birds in the northern regions and summer feeding along the coast of both North and South America.

The sailor was launching a verbal barrage and getting comfortable with the attention of his own prey when, unexpectedly, a whack on the back of his head sent him sideways. Neither the sailor nor Elly had seen Mr. Henderson approach, but the smack on his head realigned his focus.

"Get back to work," Mr. Henderson ordered. He glared at the wayward sailor but said nothing further. Additional chastising would occur later, out of the earshot of the passengers. It was a fundamental rule not to fraternize with the passengers. This infraction was not a whipping offence because the passengers would not be allowed to defend the friendliness of a sailor, but it had its punishments. The sailor knew something drastic was coming.

Elly turned to the ship's railing and Catherine looked at her. "What were you thinking?"

"He was interesting and I never knew about the terns or whatever, birds."

"Elly, save your romantic encounters for Ontario."

"Oh, I wasn't being romantic. With him? Oh no, not him," she said as she defended her conversation.

"Yeah, if you say so," was Catherine's short reply.

Denis and Jeremiah came from below.

Catherine coughed while standing along the gunwale and Jeremiah responded, "Da has that sickly cough again."

"Is he all right?" asked Catherine.

"He is still coughing up blood," said Denis.

"Ma is going to have the doctor look at him again," said Jeremiah.

The doctor had been busy on the ship during the voyage. Numerous ailments and sickness—mostly fevers and agues—had taken their toll. Three deaths occurred from illness: the father of one family, a child in another, and a newborn that did not survive his first day. All three were buried at sea. Captain Morrison could not allow preservation of the bodies for later burial on land because of diseases, odours, security of the bodies, and superstitions.

He performed reverent and respectful services for those who passed before overseeing their interment in the enormous cemetery of the North Atlantic, which held the souls of many sons and daughters who found death on the high seas. Mickey was now presumed dead from falling overboard and drowning. On a happier note, two healthy births were added to *The Elizabeth*'s family.

"Mother is worried about the length this sickness has held on," stated Jeremiah.

Catherine tried to keep an optimistic perspective. "Actually, Da has shown a lot of strength in fending off all the fevers spreading through the lower deck."

"I hope the doctor can help, although there is not much he can do once the infection hits." Denis added the pragmatic viewpoint.

The three McCarthy children stood at the rail and pondered the hopes for their father's recovery and his realization of his dream of independence and self-sufficiency for his family. Each child considered any sacrifice they could make for the sake of their father. They would have swum the entire distance behind the ship if it would make a difference to Thomas's recuperation. But they were helpless, full of energy to fulfill any task with no direction to go. They experienced the pain and frustration of powerlessness. Waves lapped against the ship as they stood and watched, each in their own thoughts.

"It is God's will," said Jeremiah.

"No, it's not God's will or even God's manipulation," answered Denis. "It's life, it's hardships, and the role that God plays is in guiding us through these hardships," Denis continued as he looked at the passing water and spoke to anyone who cared to listen. "Our faith is earthly as well as heavenly. We have to believe in our own ability to remain good people through challenges and disappointments. Do you think God allowed his Son, Jesus Christ, to be tortured and hung on a cross for some sadistic lesson? No, He does not interfere with the process of an imperfect world and the lives of imperfect people. The reason we are not kings any more is because we lost some battle along the way; it is not because God wanted us to be poor. We have to accept the hardship of poverty; likewise we have to work hard to gain prosperity.

"There are always forces working with us and against us—good against evil, health versus disease. Like this ship: the water and wind are forcing us backwards but the decision of man is to use the wind to drive us forward. We work to overcome the disruptive force. Our father is fighting for each breath he takes, taking air in with each breath. Some of the air is clean and good, but it has sickness mixed in. He fights the good air against the bad air."

Denis continued, "Likewise, Mother tries to make him comfortable against a hard bunk and the rolling of the ship. It is always a fight against competing forces. It's what's inside you that determines the outcome. God is there to show the good side, He is there to comfort us when the destructive force gains temporary control. He is not there for us to throw our hands in the air and say, 'It's God's will, and therefore I am not going to try any more.'"

"But there is nothing we can do," said Jeremiah.

"You're right, we cannot make the sickness go away."

"So prayer has no meaning?" asked Catherine.

"The way I see it, prayer is a reflection, a quiet moment to push all the distractions away and seek all the possibilities of what I can do and what I cannot control. I don't believe that my prayer can cause a flash of light and a bolt of thunder that will make Father well again. I believe that through prayer, the moment of silence with positive thoughts, I can think about Father, the good man that he is, the good man he made me, and the love and respect I have for him. I believe those thoughts have an inherent transcendent power between Da and me. As I sit next to him, he can feel my support without any words being exchanged. You can call it spiritual inspiration if you like. It doesn't exclude God but it also doesn't relinquish all my power either."

"Denis, how do you know all this stuff?" asked Jeremiah.

"I paid attention, I guess, when Mother and Father were telling me stories, reading the Bible, or correcting me when I needed a talking-to."

"I wish I had more time with Da."

"You can. You can right now."

"But he is not going to teach me anything today."

"Oh yes, if you listen, if you watch, if you pay attention, you will learn many things."

Catherine chimed in, "Oh Denis, don't be such a philosopher."

"The difference between you and me," was Denis's reply.

Jeremiah said, "I'm going down below to be with Da." Denis looked at Catherine as if to say, "See the difference that makes." Jeremiah headed over to the ladder, leaving Denis and Catherine alone along the gunwale.

"Denis," started Catherine. But he was not going to have her distract them from the moment.

Denis interrupted, "Catherine, Jeremiah is thirteen years old. He needs guidance. If there is one thing we should have learned on this voyage it's that Father is not going to be here forever. And whatever we can do to ease Father's responsibility and help Jeremiah become a good, honest, moral man, we need to do it."

Denis knew that his plea was for Jeremiah but that his words were meant for Catherine's growth as well. She was getting to an age where marriage and starting a family were a possibility. Her character development as a mother needed perspective as well.

"You know, you and Jeremiah are a lot like Uncle Jerry and Da," Catherine said.

Denis was happy with her link of a family member helping a family member. "And you, too."

She nodded, acknowledging her inclusion in the family. Denis and Catherine went below at the order of a sailor to clear the deck. Mr. Power had already examined Thomas again.

"What did the doctor say?" asked Catherine.

"He said your father will be fine once we get to shore."

"That's all he said?"

"Yes, clean country air will clear his lungs."

Catherine shook her head, crawled into the bunk, and leaned against the post that supported the Rooney family above them. "I'm tired and I'm going to rest for a while," she said. Catherine rolled over, grabbed the family Bible sitting on their platform, and started leafing through it.

The ship was weaving back and forth through the river catching the angles of the wind. The excitement of arriving in Canada had lessened and a number of families were tending to their sick relatives. Coughing, moaning and Hail Marys were heard everywhere. Anyone who was not sick but had a momentary cough was looked at immediately. Such was the case for Jeremiah; he had a brief cough and all was well.

When Johanna heard him, she reacted, "Are you all right?"

"Ah Mother, just a small cough."

A little while later Catherine coughed and placed her hand on her chest, indicating the cough hurt or was causing difficulty. Thomas looked worried and Johanna asked Catherine, "Are you well?"

"Ah, I think so, just a small cough." Catherine quickly dismissed her second cough as nothing.

Denis asked, "Are you feeling all right? The last couple of days you seem to have caught an illness, with some coughing and heaving."

"No, nothing." Catherine was not a complainer and she endured pain quietly because she saw pain as part of life.

The day wore on and the heightened concerns of sickness were on everyone's mind. Jeremiah continued with his challenge to Uncle Jerry over a game of checkers. He announced that he had figured out his uncle's strategy and laughed that he was going to beat him this game, when out of nowhere, two triple jumps and he was out of game pieces. He leaned back in the bunk while Uncle Jerry had the laugh once again.

Catherine lay down next to her father. Thomas was not better but he was able to fight the cough with enough strength to keep the deathly plague away. Catherine felt herself on the verge of sickness and willed her good health to her father so he could be strong again.

Time seemed to drag as eagerness built for the arrival in Quebec City. The evening hours of July 1 came and Mr. Morrison announced that they were still many hours from Quebec. The passengers started to bed down for one more night on *The Elizabeth*. Most, however, were still awake with enthusiasm at 10:00 p.m. when Captain Morrison ordered the sails down and anchor weighed. The ship was still rocking gently in the river's current so the change in motion had little effect on the sleeping passengers, and those still awake were unaware of the ship's landing. The boat had arrived at Quebec with little fanfare. They moored about 200 yards from the dock for the night. Mr. Morrison ordered extra patrols on the ship to prevent anyone from leaving or coming aboard.

On the morning of July 2, with long days and short nights, the sun rose early. Within a half-hour of sunrise, an early rising farmer yelled, "We're here." The word spread quickly and within moments the passengers were on deck cheering the beginning of their new life.

* * *

The anticipation soared again at their arrival, with the added excitement of standing on solid ground after a fearful ocean voyage. It would be good to get off the constantly swaying ship and move around without congestion.

The noise had awakened Thomas and Johanna. Catherine lay still next to her father. Johanna decided to wake her for the news and preparations to disembark. She reached over and shook her.

Her body was cold and her face was blue. Catherine had passed her will to live during the night and her only hope in her final moment was that her father capture her positive spirit. Johanna gasped for air. Thomas turned and looked at his lifeless daughter. He knew immediately that the angels had come and taken his Catherine.

Mother and father sat there speechless. Thomas reached over and grabbed Johanna's hand. Tears watered each of their eyes. "Why her?" they asked. "She had so much life to live; why her?"

Denis and Jeremiah rolled over and saw their parents with tears in their eyes next to their sister. "What's the matter?" asked Jeremiah.

"Your sister passed away during the night," Thomas explained. "Some sickness comes quickly without warning."

"No!" yelled Jeremiah, who refused to believe the news.

Denis hung his head in sorrow. "I don't think she was feeling well the last couple of days. She wouldn't say anything because Father is so sick. May she rest in eternal peace."

"Amen," they said together, making the sign of the cross. Johanna was the first to react: all her energy gave way, causing her to fall from her sitting position to the floor. Thomas sat motionless, unable to move to help his wife, but Denis quickly went to his mother.

"Ma, are you all right?" he asked, and reached under her arm to support her and lift her up. She did not reply. Her body twitched and then her stomach heaved. She had nothing to vomit but the contractions continued anyway. Denis propped her up on her knees as she tried to expel the pain and shock from her body. The contractions continued even though dry air and the gagging sounds were the only things being emitted.

Soon it stopped, but Johanna remained limp on the floor with her son holding her. Thomas looked lost; he had his own coughing spell, but the movement of oxygen in and out of his lungs kept his mind clear and his immediate emotional reaction in check.

After monitoring his mother's strength, Denis lifted Johanna back to the edge of the bunk and said, "I'll get Mr. Power." He continued with an order to his brother, "Jeremiah, keep watch on Mother." Jeremiah nodded.

Denis left the bunk and returned shortly with the doctor. Mr. Power immediately quarantined the area. He had Catherine's body wrapped and removed from the ship.

Meanwhile, Mr. Morrison called all the passengers to order, to prepare to disembark: "Congratulations. It was a tough journey, with many challenges, but we made it. I would like to wish you well on your continued journey and your future days. First, we have to wait for the dock master for an orderly transition to your next boat. Please go below and get your belongings together and wait for my order to disembark." He called to the cook, "Make some tea; this is going to take a while."

Within ten minutes the bunks were cleared and people stood with their bags and trunks ready to step on the solid land, which held promise for their future and success for generations to come. They were excited—even the sick managed to smile. Thomas's excitement made him cough. After a while with no movement the families started sitting in their bunks again.

The cook served tea and made scones with leftover flour, sugar and other supplies. The breakfast was a treat not normally served. After two hours, when they still sat waiting, Patrick broke out his violin and started playing music. Finally, word came down that the sails were up and they were moving towards the docks.

Once more time dragged as the crew tied up the ship and prepared the gangplank for departure. At last they were given the "all clear" to go above and leave the ship. The passengers jammed the ladder to go up.

Denis turned to his family and said, "We can wait. They're not going anywhere without us." So they sat down again and waited in melancholy silence. It took nearly another hour for families to hoist up their trunks and assist the sick to the main deck. A few scattered families remained, each insisting the others go first, but at last the McCarthys made their way topside. The day was warm and the sun permeated their skin. Thomas took a deep breath, which caused a short cough, but the dry air of land felt good. They stopped at the top of the gangplank and addressed the Captain.

"Master Morrison, you are a fine sailor and I appreciate your dedication to getting us here safely," said Thomas.

Mr. Morrison added his own compliment, with sincerity and compassion. "You're welcome. Mr. and Mrs. McCarthy, I'm sorry for the loss of your daughter."

"Thank you," said Thomas and Johanna.

"I wish you improved health," the Captain said to Thomas.

"Thank you."

Thomas and Johanna led the family down the plank but the Captain called to Denis. "Denis, I understand that you like to read and tell stories."

"Yes, sir."

"You may take this book, written by two German brothers, which has tales of old folklore. You may find it interesting for your story-telling."

"Thank you, Captain," said Denis as he looked at the book: *Tales of Children and the Home* by Jacob and Wilhelm Grimm. He waved the book in the air as an additional thank you to the Captain and slid it into the waistline of his trousers to carry it down the gangplank and join his family.

Uncle Jerry and the girls stopped to bid Captain Morrison good-bye, as well.

The only passengers left on the ship were William and Margaret Connell with their six other children. Mr. Morrison had promised a full sweep of the ship after it was completely unloaded. Once again, the parents' hope of finding their son went unfulfilled.

William told Mr. Morrison, "We will wait here for the warship to return."

Captain Morrison took William's arm and escorted him aside. "I pray too that Mickey is found, but the chances are very unlikely."

"I know."

Captain Morrison performed a service for Catherine on the dock and offered a prayer: "May the Good Lord take this soul to eternal rest."

Denis added, "May we always remember Catherine's humour and spirit for life, in God we pray."

"Amen," recited the three McCarthy families, and a number of other passengers who stood by during the transfer to the steamboat.

Her body had been taken for a quick burial, the usual procedure for cases of communicable diseases, and now the family was feeling an emptiness with the sudden absence and shocking turn of events. Like the Connell family, they would long remember the sadness attached to their arrival in North America. There was nothing more the McCarthys could do. If they stayed in Quebec City to mourn, they would not be able to continue the journey with their own resources. Catherine's spirit needed to be a source of guidance, not a burden to hold them back.

Quebec City stood on top of a high cliff with a commanding view of all shipping traffic from the east and the west. The city served as the gateway to the interior of Canada and the United States, so it was a strategic point off the North Atlantic, which was well guarded. The passengers were going from one boat to another, so they did not see much of the city. However, the harbour was down at sea level and was busy with shipping traffic.

Both the British and French navies had ships docked along the piers, an unusual compromise arrangement. Canada was a British colony but Quebec was nearly solid French descendants with strong allegiance to their mother country. The arrangement was tenuous. A smaller French ship moored next to the larger British ship symbolized the circumstances of the French Canadians as well as the dominion of the British Empire.

Thomas and Johanna stopped to wait for Uncle Jerry, which allowed Thomas a moment to catch his breath as well. The two families were assembled together and moving their possessions along the dock, when they heard a scream coming from *The Elizabeth*. It was a short, muffled scream, but identifiable as pain-ridden.

"What was that?" asked Abigail, Jerry's twelve-year-old daughter.

Shortly Mr. Henderson escorted the young sailor who had engaged Elly in the seagull conversation to the gangplank. The sailor walked down the gangplank alone, holding his left hand. Elly ran up to him and asked what happened.

"I was branded and kicked off the ship." He showed her his hand burned with the "E" symbol of *The Elizabeth.*

"Why did they do that?" she asked, pointing to his hand.

"So other captains would shun me as a sailor."

"What for?" asked Elly.

"For talking to you on the ship."

"They can't do that." She turned to Mr. Henderson, who was watching from above. "You shouldn't do this. He didn't mean anything," she yelled.

"Don't bother," said the sailor. "It won't make any difference."

Uncle Jerry walked over. "Daddy, can he come with us?" Elly asked.

"No, we can't take him."

"But we have to take him."

"He'll be all right."

"But he got kicked off because of me. We have to do something for him."

"He got kicked off because he decided to do what he did. We are not responsible for him and he is not part of our group."

"I'll stay here with him."

"Don't be ridiculous."

Elly's sister Kate spoke up. "You don't even know his name."

Elly glared at her older sister for her lack of support. She turned to the sailor. "What's your name?"

"Willie."

"Willie, that's his name, now are you happy?" Elly was angry, disappointed and confused at the day's events, not in control of her emotions. No logical explanation was going to settle her feeling of responsibility for Willie's punishment; of course she was also enamoured of Willie.

Uncle Jerry put his arm around Elly's shoulder. She shrugged it off. She did not want pity. Tears welled up in her eyes and she covered her face with her hands. Her father again placed his hand on her shoulder and directed her away from the gangplank. Jerry looked back at Willie. "I'm sorry for you losing your job."

Willie nodded, not knowing what to say. Finally, he said, "I'll be all right," as the father and daughter walked away.

The passengers of *The Elizabeth* were ushered down the dock to a waiting steamboat. Most had heard of steamboats but none of them had ridden on these new mechanically powered boats. Smoke billowed from the stack as the Captain heated the water to power the paddleboat up the river against the strong current.

Passengers were directed to a plank that connected directly to the lower deck. This plank made the entrance to the storage hold much easier. As they entered, the other passengers were milling about.

"We have to stay down here," one passenger reported.

"What do you mean?" asked Uncle Jerry.

"We have to stay down here in this sooty mess and this awful heat."

The Peter Robinson group was confined to the bottom deck and was not allowed above. People were using their trunks as seats and for blocking off private areas. A shoemaker from Cork spoke up: "We're paying customers. Just because King George is paying the fare doesn't mean we can't have a proper berth."

"We're Irish, what'd you expect?" asked another man listlessly.

The passengers moaned about their lack of comfort for the 150-mile trip. The next day and a half was spent below in the open cargo area and engine boiler room. The temperature had already risen above the hundred-degree mark in the confined space.

Thomas moved over towards the firebox to soak up the dry heat, which comforted his lungs. He sat on the floor leaning up against a steel support pole, closed his eyes, and drew in a full expansion of air. He had not been able to do that for months. A short cough spewed from his lungs expelling the new air. "Don't worry, I'm fine," he announced to all, but really meant the words for Johanna, who was rearranging the trunk. The heat and the noisy bottom deck were secondary to her sadness.

But Thomas's cough seized her attention. She left the trunk blocking the makeshift aisle and hurried over to Thomas. "Tommy, are you all right?"

"Ah dear, I'm fine," he repeated.

Mr. Power went above to speak to the ship's pilot about the conditions of the passengers. "We don't have room for all the passengers," explained the pilot.

"We had reservations through Superintendent Peter Robinson for these settlers. I think it is best you find them rooms."

The doctor's message was clear to the pilot that the superintendent would hear of his scheme to give poor accommodations to his passengers. But the pilot also knew from past trips with settlers that they could be dirty and leave a mess in the rooms after their arrival. Often they tried to fit a family of nine or ten people into a room designed for three or four people. Likewise, the engine room was easier for the crew to sweep out and wash down. The pilot was in a quandary over letting the Irish settlers into vacant rooms; he tried to ease out of his predicament.

"I understand you have some sick families. I may have a room or two for them."

Mr. Power knew that more than two rooms were available. "You need to find rooms."

"I'll see."

The pilot called for a cabin boy and ordered him to find rooms for families as directed by Mr. Power. The cabin boy was perplexed at the new orders but went about making the adjustment. Twenty-three of the thirty-four families were moved into rooms. Thomas declined moving out of the engine room. Jerry's family was healthy and they stayed with Thomas, Johanna and the two boys.

After the cargo and passengers were loaded aboard *The Quebec,* the ship sailed out of Quebec City port to head west towards Montreal. Excess steam was channelled into a small pipe and a high-pitched whistle announced its departure. Elly went to a starboard window and looked back at the dock. There stood Willie waving goodbye. Elly started crying again. Kate stood next to her and consoled her. She apologized for her insensitivity on the dock.

Uncle Jerry started to show signs of anxiety. He was short with the girls. His words were quick and sharp. Everyone thought the stress of Catherine's death, Thomas's sickness and Elly's attraction to an unknown sailor were the sources of his irritation. However, Thomas knew what was on Jerry's mind. He was worried about Lizzie. As the time neared for Jerry to meet his wife in Montreal, he was nervous.

The two-day trip meant one night's sleep on the steamboat. The churning of the paddlewheel and the engineers working the boilers kept most remaining passengers awake—they were scattered over the floor of the boat. Thomas kept close to the engine for the dry heat but Johanna and the boys could not stand the high temperature during the long night and moved further away.

The night on the boat was long and sad for the McCarthy family. Catherine's death overwhelmed all the family members, but especially Jeremiah, who was devastated by her passing. His emotions were raw and he reacted with anger to the food served to the *Elizabeth* passengers. It was poor in quality and most of it was gone by the time it reached the passengers in the engine room. "We are being treated unfairly," he shouted.

Thomas looked up at his son and said loudly, "Jeremiah," hoping the mention of his name would stop the rant.

"I don't care; this food is cold and there is little meat left and they put us in this heat box. We are being treated unfairly by being put in this fire trap." He then shouted, "We were served last even though the kitchen is just down the hall." Jeremiah's parents did not see the next move coming because Jeremiah had never displayed physical rage, but he grabbed the edge of the table and flipped it over, sending the few remaining bowls of cold chicken broth into the air.

Johanna yelled, "Jeremiah, stop it."

Thomas placed his hand on the floor to gain leverage as he tried to get to his feet; however, Denis moved quickly and grabbed his brother in a bear hug before more damage occurred to the boat or people. Without releasing him, Denis manoeuvred Jeremiah out of the engine room to the bottom of the stairs leading up to the main deck. Jeremiah had regained his composure and Denis released him but blocked his brother's ability to return to the engine room. "Go up the stairs," Denis ordered.

Once on the main deck and at the railing, Denis was livid. He searched for the right words to reprimand and counsel his brother but in his anger, nothing came to mind. "What are you doing?" he finally asked.

"I don't know," replied Jeremiah, who was equally surprised at his own behaviour. After a moment, he found the only phrase that described his feeling. "It's not fair," he repeated.

"What's not fair? Throwing the only food we have onto the floor?" asked Denis.

"I don't know what's fair." Jeremiah clenched the rail tightly, waiting to sort out his thoughts, but the thought of Catherine's death and his uncharacteristic explosion in the engine room did not connect. Denis missed the connection as well, thinking Jeremiah's anger was solely due to their mistreatment by the steamboat operators.

"Are you all right?" asked Denis.

"Yes, I'm fine," reported Jeremiah in a calmer voice.

"Let's go back downstairs," said Denis.

Jeremiah returned to the engine room and apologized to the group. "I'm sorry for disrupting your meal." He grabbed a broom to sweep the eating area but everything had been cleaned. After a couple of strokes, he sat down.

Now the family was sitting around the engine room with a huge emptiness that Catherine's exuberant presence customarily filled. Little conversation took place. Denis started saying the rosary in a soft, barely audible voice: "In the name of the Father, Son and Holy Ghost. Our Father, who art in heaven, hallowed be thy name; thy kingdom come; thy will be done, in earth as it is in heaven."

Jeremiah heard the beginning prayer and joined in: "Give us this day our daily bread. And forgive us our trespasses, as we forgive them that trespass against us. And lead us not into temptation; but deliver us from evil. Amen." Denis continued to lead the family in the five sorrowful decades of the rosary.

Afterwards, the scene became an impromptu memorial service and Thomas spoke about Catherine and her life. "She was too young to die, and all the while she was worried about me and whether I could survive the journey. Before we left Abbeymahon, Catherine begged us to wait for another time. Maybe if we had waited . . ."

Johanna interjected, "What's done is done. She's gone and we can't bring her back."

Thomas slid over to his wife and placed his arm around her shoulder and pulled her in. She buried her head in his shirt. She did not want anyone to see her crying. They spent the remainder of the evening in solitude.

* * *

The next day, July 2, 1825, they arrived at the port of Montreal. Ships could not go further upriver because the Lachine Rapids impeded the passage. A portage of people and goods was necessary. Even though the city was opening a narrow canal to allow small vessels through, this steamboat was too large for the channel. The passengers disembarked and loaded their belongings onto a waiting wagon.

Thomas stood and stretched. The air filled his lungs without producing any coughing. From a practical point of view, the heat had healed his lungs. However, Thomas thought of the spiritual point of view: perhaps Catherine's youthful strength had transferred to him, making him well again. But regardless of the source, Thomas was feeling better. He walked off the boat feeling sound and vigorous.

The short trip through the city was a welcome change for the sedentary passengers who were accustomed to walking as a way of life. The temperature was a comfortable 78 degrees Fahrenheit as they left the ship, but this was early morning and today would be hot, with temperatures reaching 90 degrees Fahrenheit.

Uncle Jerry was anxious to leave the boat so he could look for Lizzie. People were everywhere about the port—some were workers, some were waiting for loved ones, and still others milled about because they had nothing else to do. Jerry examined the crowd but did not see Lizzie. He was scanning each person along the docks, hoping she would jump out from behind a crate of flour or some other obstruction. A man in tattered clothes approached him and asked for a shilling. Jerry dismissed him with an abrupt gesture to step aside.

Across the wharf stood a woman with a rose-flowered kerchief covering her dark Irish brunette hair. She wore an ivory dress that flowed to her ankles, with black shoes supported by a two-inch heel. She was well dressed, with a classic, refined appearance. Jerry's gaze passed her by, thinking that could not be Lizzie. The woman was also looking for someone in the crowd but was watching a boat that was unloading passengers from Three Rivers, Quebec—half the distance between Quebec City and Montreal.

Jerry returned to the family group and said, "Lizzie must be down at the next dock waiting for us there. She is not here." The woman also turned and walked off the wharf back towards the city, unseen by Jerry.

Jeremiah was watching for Lizzie too when he noticed Jimmy Brady, his wife and four children headed in a rush up the Rue St-Pierre, which was away from the portage route above the rapids. The eldest son John was the same boy who had stolen the bracelet on the ship.

"That's strange," he said.

"Where are they going in such a hurry?" asked Denis.

Jeremiah did not like the family but he had kept his distance during the voyage and there had been no additional problems.

"Something's going on with that family," he said.

They continued to pack the cart, when Mr. Power ordered the group together. "Where are the Bradys?" he asked.

"They headed up that street over there," said Jeremiah, pointing in the direction the family was last seen.

"Where were they going?"

"I don't know, but they were going in that direction. What's wrong?" Jeremiah asked.

"It looks like they absconded and stole the ship's blankets as well." Mr. Power raised his voice and made a plea: "Could I have two volunteers to track the Brady family down?"

"I'll go," said Jeremiah immediately.

"Oh no," broke in Denis. "You're not going."

"Why not?" Jeremiah demanded.

"You will hurt somebody."

Mr. Power spoke. "I think Jeremiah will be helpful, if he goes. He will present a strength the Brady family does not to want face." He turned to Jeremiah. "As long as I have assurance that you will control yourself."

"I'll control myself."

"Then I'll go too," said Denis.

"Wait!" interrupted Johanna. "I cannot have both of you going to catch a thief and absconders. I cannot lose all my children."

"That's all right, I'll go with them," spoke up his cousin Timothy.

Denis said, "I'll wait here," and leaned over to Timothy: "please keep an eye on Jeremiah."

"Good, settled," said Mr. Power. "Let's go." The three men started towards the main district of Montreal.

Uncle Jerry told Thomas that he was going to walk around looking for Lizzie. "I can't leave Montreal without Lizzie. She will be looking for me here."

"You should have some time before the doctor returns."

"I'll be back soon," said Jerry, and he walked east away from the group.

The three-man posse walked the streets of upper Montreal looking in shops and alleyways for the Brady family. Jeremiah was the first to spot them a block away.

"Good, let's go," announced Powers.

"No, wait," said Jeremiah. "If they see us coming, they will run and then split up. Let's circle around the alley and come at them head on."

"Good idea," said Mr. Power. The three hustled down a side alley and met up with the Brady family at the next corner. "Where are you going?" demanded Mr. Power.

"Nowhere," said Jimmy Brady.

"You're coming with us," said the surgeon.

Jimmy Brady looked at Jeremiah and Timothy. They both nodded to Jimmy but neither said anything. Soon the posturing and positioning began that would lead to a fight. But what Jeremiah had failed to learn in strategy on the checkerboard, he had learned by reading people in conflict.

Jimmy's eldest son John was sizing up Jeremiah. He had been surprised and embarrassed in their last encounter. He had not forgotten the ten lashes that cost him weeks of pain and discomfort on a rolling ship. Every time a splash of salty seawater leaked down into the hold and hit his skin, he was reminded of the punishment from Mr. Henderson. Two of the ten cuts had been infected and took more time to heal. John was looking for an opportunity to avenge his pain.

Jeremiah moved his right foot back, strengthening his position. John noticed the subtle move and understood its meaning. The younger McCarthy stood erect, confident and strong. He was ready for battle. The Brady family had shown their deceitful nature and that bothered Jeremiah. The sting of Catherine's death lingered just below his Irish skin. He could feel the emotion rising again. He asked himself, "How could a good person like Catherine die so young and crooks like the Bradys stay healthy?" Jeremiah's fair skin was flushed with anger. His facial and arm muscles tightened. Adrenaline was kicking in.

Timothy McCarthy saw the intensity building between John Brady and Jeremiah. A fight was almost certain here on the streets of Montreal, and he regretted volunteering to join this search party. Mr. Power also saw the danger of a fight brewing.

"Jimmy, we don't need a fight here in the street," he suggested to the elder Brady.

Jimmy looked at the two boys and then down to his two youngest children, who were six and four years old. "All right," he said. "I'll go with you."

Jeremiah knew there would have been a fight, a chase or both if the two small children were not there. Mr. Power led the group down the hill towards the wharf. Timothy and Jeremiah followed behind. The woman with the kerchief from the wharf came walking around a corner. She did not pay attention to the small group walking past her.

"Aunt Lizzie!" yelled Jeremiah.

"Jeremiah, what are you doing up here?"

"I am with Mr. Power taking these people back to the boat."

"Is Uncle Jerry with you?"

"'Tis, down at the boat. He was looking for you but, I'm sure, he wasn't looking for you dressed like this."

"Yes, they bought me these clothes. Nice, huh?"

"Yeah. Let's go. I have to keep up with these people." The encounter with Lizzie dissipated Jeremiah's negative emotion. Even though Lizzie did not know the history between Jeremiah and the Bradys, she could control Jeremiah with one verbal command. Timothy was happy to see her.

"I thought I missed your boat. How was your trip?" asked Aunt Lizzie.

Jeremiah stopped. "Not so good. Catherine died yesterday."

"Yesterday?"

"'Twas, just before getting off at Quebec. It was sudden. There was a lot of sickness on the ship."

Once at the wharf, Jimmy Brady was handed over to the authorities and taken to jail for stealing the blankets. His wife and children were left behind in Montreal. The promise of free land, tools and provisions was over for the Brady family.

* * *

"We're going to head up the street to the next quay," announced the surgeon. He called for the wagon train to begin. Four wagons were stacked with the trunks and belongings of the now thirty-three families. They reached the departure dock on the upper side of the rapids and reloaded onto a new steamboat. Mr. Power took an accounting of the travellers. All were present except Uncle Jerry.

"He is out looking for his wife Lizzie and she is right here with us," Denis informed him.

"He had better hurry. The boat isn't going to wait," replied Mr. Power.

The boat's boiler was building steam and the engines were ready. The Captain ordered the paddleboat to leave. The crew jumped to the dock to untie the moorings. Denis and Thomas stood at the railing watching for Uncle Jerry. They looked down the dock area and saw Uncle Jerry coming down the avenue.

"There he is!" yelled Denis.

Uncle Jerry was waving his arms, telling the pilot to go ahead. He ran up to the edge of the dock and said, "Go ahead, I'm going to wait here."

Denis was yelling back, "Jump on board, Aunt Lizzie is here."

"What?"

"Aunt Lizzie is on the boat."

"Really?"

"Yeah, jump on the boat."

Uncle Jerry ran and jumped on deck just as the gap started to widen between the ferry and the dock. He was reunited with Lizzie. They hugged and kissed. The passengers applauded the couple and their thrilling reunion.

The steamboat headed up the St. Lawrence River towards Kingston, Ontario, their next stop on the journey. A few rapids inhibited the progress, as they navigated around rocky white water and proceeded west.

Eventually they came to Cornwall on the Canadian side and New York State on the south side of the boat, their first glimpse of the United States. Many passengers were in awe of this sight. The McCarthys were surprised to learn that many people had plans to leave Canada and emigrate south to the States.

As the boat approached Lake Ontario, the river widened out. The boat passed numerous islands dotting the river. The area, known as the Thousand Islands, actually had eighteen hundred islands in the river, and knowledge of the main shipping lane was critical for the pilot, to take account of the hazards of shallow and hidden dangers. The islands provided a scenic panorama of blue water with dots of green islands scattered along the river. The passengers lined the railing and watched the variety of islands passing by. The end of the Thousand Island passage signified the opening of Lake Ontario and their approach to Kingston. Beginning with this first week in July, the Kingston area was their holding place for the next two months, to wait for Mr. Robinson to arrive.

The end of the journey was close and the thrill of starting their new life was near.

Chapter 8

The McCarthy Family
Kingston

As the flat-bottom steamboats called bateaux navigated the many picturesque islands where the upper St. Lawrence River meets Lake Ontario, the first boat kept right of the largest island, Wolfe Island, and headed along the coast towards Kingston. This town was the guardian of the Canadian entrance to the Great Lakes and the interior of British North America. The remaining boats followed, loaded with the people and their few possessions.

The largest possession on board the steamboat was the sense of wonderment and excitement the travellers felt travelling through the Thousand Islands, as the clear blue skies and warm weather welcomed them with the beauty of paradise. At the end it laid before their eyes the tidy village of Kingston, with its formal English gardens of green vegetation and colourful flowers contrasting with the blue water of the lake and wide opening to the Great Cataraqui River—a grand welcome for weary travellers.

The boatman headed to the western shore, the landing site for the village, because along the eastern shore the guns of Fort Henry watched their approach and guarded the naval yards of the British fleet along the shoreline. The first boatman landed and threw a rope ashore.

"Are these the new immigrants from Ireland?" asked the harbourmaster on the dock.

"Yes, on transport from Montreal," replied the boatman.

"They are to be quartered at the fort," the harbourmaster said, and pointed across the river.

"Fort Henry? Can I land there as a civilian craft?"

"Yes, that's where the other immigrants are staying."

"Thanks," said the boatman as he pushed off, wheeling the boat in the direction of the western shore.

"And keep them on that side of the river," yelled the harbourmaster as they left.

"Oh, it sounds like they had trouble," Denis said to Thomas.

"Yes, it does," agreed his father.

The boats headed across the river and around the naval docks into the bay that separated the Navy docks from the Army fort. They heard a voice yelling from the ramparts of the fort wall; a soldier was calling for them to continue on around Point Henry into the next bay. Again the boat steered away from landing to head back east for the opposite side of the point. Once on that side, another soldier at the water's edge directed them to a landing.

Thomas looked up the hill and behind the fort to a sea of weathered tents with imbedded beige streaks from a mixture of airborne dirt and rain. The tents had probably been white when pitched but after weeks of baking in the unusually hot sun of June, the canvas had faded into a light brown mosaic of weathered huts spread over many acres of land.

"Oh my," said Thomas.

"My gracious," exclaimed Johanna.

"Look at all the people," noted Jeremiah as the slow movement of bodies intermingled among the tents.

"Head up the hill and grab an empty tent," ordered the soldier.

"Hold on," Mr. Power yelled to the first off. "We want to stay together, so I will find an area for all of us. Stay here and wait for me to return."

Mr. Power disappeared over the crest of the hill, as it was clear that more tents were further up out of view. Shortly, he returned.

The available area for *The Elizabeth* passengers was over the crest of the hill in a tall grassy area facing west. The smoothly contoured ground consisted of broken rock with sparse grass growing through the small chunks of limestone, as the hill was a human-made summit with the fort situated on top. The vegetation-free land was designed to give a clear view to the north of potential invaders.

In addition to being an important military and naval base, Kingston was a small trading and shipping centre on the edge of Lake Ontario. Goods were shipped and received from the interiors of the north along the Cataraqui River and from the western Great Lakes. Fort Henry, positioned noticeably on the east side of the river, protected the town.

As the residents learned of the new settlers living close to their town, many showed disapproval for these newly arrived Canadians. But the dislike was not necessarily because the new people were Irish or poor farmers; it was because of their numbers. A tent village had sprung up abruptly for the latest immigrants to wait for Peter Robinson's arrival, which they learned was going to be delayed. Peter had business in New York so his ship travelled a different route, which eventually led him through New York State to The Falls at Niagara and then to the Village of York, later known as Toronto.

The residents of Kingston originally thought these people would be stranded in their town and they did not have the resources to house or feed them. This latest was the eighth ship to arrive, full of large families with small and teenage children, pulling into the village docks in full view of the town. Over two thousand new people had descended on the outskirts of Kingston. They had no money, food or lodging if they stayed. Many of the immigrants were sick with fevers that could spread through the masses. The order for the encampment had come from Lieutenant Governor Peregrine Maitland of Upper Canada: they were to await Peter Robinson's arrival here. The townspeople were concerned.

The settlers frequently ferried over to Kingston to visit and walk through the village to pass the time, and they sensed the concern of the townsfolk. Added to this unenthusiastic tone was a clear view from the town of the canvas-lined hill. The sight of the hundreds of white tents lining the hillside was a constant reminder of their presence.

Even the welcome into the tent village by some of the new arrivals' fellow Irishmen was cordial only on the surface; people gave pleasant greetings and asked about their trip across the sea but underneath, people were protecting their turf. Some did not want a sick family or noisy children moving into the tent next to them, and still others had had their fill of living in congested quarters for long periods. However, these were few, and the great majority extended the Irish hospitality of social acceptance and the philosophy that life was a pursuit of happiness and laughter, even when the basic necessities were lacking.

The *Elizabeth* passengers, eager to spend a night on solid ground, were directed by Mr. Powers to a series of empty tents fashioned from old or excess canvas sails. The dry July heat was overbearing and sweat soaked their clothes, attracting mosquitoes, black flies and no-see-um gnats that buzzed annoyingly around the face and head. Their instinct picked up the scent of exposed skin, which led to a blood-sucking attack along the back of the neck, behind the ears, and on the wrists or ankles. There was no escape from the barrage of swarming insects. The open-ended tents offered protection from the direct sun but not the bugs, which nested in the grass.

By midday the tents' temperature reached between 90 and 100 degrees, adding to the discomfort. The healthy immigrants spent a mix of their time outside in common gathering areas, wishing for a breeze to cool the skin and blow the flying insects off course, and in the tents out of direct sunlight. Frequently, families walked down to the edge of the lake to bathe, swim and cool off.

Intense sun on a treeless hill became the prevailing problem as the dry heat took the moisture from the air and made breathing difficult, as if there was not enough oxygen, and even deeper, laboured breathing did not help. These fair-skinned Irish were used to humidity, and a day without some sort of rain in Ireland was unusual, but now the sun continued to deprive them of the needed moisture.

Adding to their discomfort, many experienced various degrees of sunburn, because two hours in the sun turned their fair white skin into a blaze of red. The settlers who had been there the longest were in the skin-peeling stage. Babies and young children cried openly. Two thousand people crowded at the edge of the lake and river looking for relief. Peter Robinson needed to rescue his people soon for the sake of their own comfort and health as well as whatever goodwill he still possessed from resident Canadians.

The first arrivals from the ships *The Resolution* and *The Brunswick* had been there the longest. They had ventured out and made contact with the Mississauga Natives. The two peoples shared much of the same emotions, history and discomfort of living under British rule. One of the first evenings of their encampment, people sat and conversed after a meal of fresh lean venison from a moose, a gift from the friendly Mississauga hunters.

Denis was with a group that had gathered in an open area away from the tents. These long hot days of summer solstice kept the settlers outside late into the evening.

A young girl, Máire Fergus, about the same age as Denis, caught his eye. They talked about their trip on the ship. Denis started, "On the first night my brother Jeremiah caught a boy stealing jewellery while everyone was on the upper deck. The Captain ordered ten lashes and we all had to watch."

"Oh, that's terrible," said Máire.

"Yes and everyone on board the ship felt gloomy afterwards, but Patrick Leahy, who lives down there"—Denis pointed down the row of tents, where Patrick's tent could have been any one of a hundred tents—"played 'Amazing Grace.' Have you ever heard of it?"

"Yes, but I don't know all the words," replied Máire.

"Well, it is a beautiful, reverent song about redemption. And he played it with all the passion we were feeling about the boy being whipped. Even if someone didn't know the song, the haunting yet compassionate verses gave us relief."

"I wish I had been there," Máire said with empathy.

"After that Patrick played upbeat songs that got us singing and dancing." The conversation erupted with laughter when Denis described the various attempts at dancing. "Yes, some of these farmers hadn't danced in years and their rusty moves made all of us comfortable with getting up and dancing."

"Let me see," asked Máire.

Denis stood and made a couple of hops mimicking a jig. Máire laughed out loud at Denis's uncoordinated steps. He quickly sat down as they both laughed at his attempt to dance.

"We had some music," informed Máire, "but no parties like that."

"It wasn't all partying. Certainly there were significant events; once we almost ran aground and later that same night, we think a boy went overboard during a storm."

"Oh my!" Máire said. "I travelled on *The Albion*, which carried one hundred and eighty-seven new settlers, and we also had a lot of sickness. So we were a pretty serious group, because we tried to keep the sickness from spreading. And, speaking of not having any fun, I've been bored just sitting around this tent village for the past three weeks with nothing to do. I'm glad you came along."

Eventually, Denis mentioned his sister's death. He was not normally quick to announce that kind of information. The sting of her death was still fresh and Denis was not eager to share the still-raw emotion of grief. But he found Máire easy to talk with, and he softly spoke of his sister. "My sister died just as we arrived in Quebec. She was a lovely girl and a lot of fun."

Máire, like Denis, was mature for her age, so their conversation had a refined and compassionate tone unusual for teenagers. "I am sorry to hear about your loss; I wish I had known her."

Both Máire and Denis had seen sickness and death move rapidly through the immigrants. The overwhelming grief and commiseration were sentiments engulfing the entire group daily. Denis continued, "She tried to keep her sickness private because she felt my father needed the attention. I only wish I had known what was going to happen—maybe I could have done something."

"I'm sure there was nothing you could have done or that anyone could have done to save her."

Denis needed to speak of the happy moments to keep his own melancholy at bay. "Catherine often walked over to a friend's house, Ellen Collins who lived down the lane, to feed and play with Ellen's baby lamb. The two had a special liking for this lamb and named it Fuzzy. Ellen told Catherine she could bring Fuzzy with her to British North America but Catherine knew the lamb would not be allowed on the ship, so she asked to have a raft built for the lamb to float behind the ship. My father asked her, 'How are you going to feed her?' Catherine would answer, 'I don't know' and think about the lack of grazing and potable water. Finally she would say, 'it could be big raft.'"

Máire smiled gently as Denis reminisced about his sister.

* * *

The summer heat wave of 1825 in Kingston reached 100 degrees in the shade of the tents and the suffering continued to reduce immunity in the intense heat. Thomas, on the other hand, had shaken his cough since encountering the warmth and dryness on their arrival. His lungs were able to take in air and exhale even through the uncomfortable heat. The absence of alcohol may have helped too. His muscles, though, were still weak. He became winded quickly when he exerted himself. He ordered Jeremiah to do the hard labour of carrying their trunk and fetching water, and said, "That's what he's here for."

Another group sitting in the open area included Lizzie, who sat next to her sister-in-law. The sun was setting on the eastern end of the lake and spreading pink and red hues across the sky. She told Johanna, "I was so sorry to hear of Catherine's death."

Johanna thanked Lizzie. "I appreciate your thoughtfulness. Catherine was close to your girls. How are they doing with their cousin's death?"

"They are very sad and pray for Catherine's soul every day. How did it happen so fast?"

"We don't know. She wasn't feeling well for a couple of days.

Denis noticed, but she didn't say anything. And then she started coughing, like Tommy, but she still denied anything was wrong." Johanna struggled describing Catherine's last few days. She looked down as she spoke softly, fighting the tears.

"How awful. I hope she didn't suffer."

"I don't think so. She didn't complain of pain or show that she was in any discomfort."

"She was such a good girl, full of life."

"She was. You know that dress that Theresa made for her?"

"Ah yes. The one with flowers."

"We made sure she was buried in the dress. She looked so elegant when she was on the boat. It made her happy." Johanna filled with emotion, her eyes watered.

Lizzie reached over, took her hand and spoke delicately, matching Johanna's tone, "She is with the Lord now."

"I'm sure of that, bless her soul," Johanna agreed emphatically.

The two women sat there with no further conversation for many minutes. The pain was predictable but the public acknowledgement of grief was not customary nor expected.

"How did Thomas take it?" Lizzie finally asked.

"He was so sad for his little girl. He blamed himself for giving her his cough, although the doctor said it was not his fault."

"Poor man."

Johanna felt pain but she did not know how to channel the grief except to bury it and not talk about the loss of her child, her only daughter. She wanted to deflect both their thoughts. "How was your voyage?"

"It was very good. Mr. Wakefield was much kinder than his mother. When we arrived in New York, he wanted me to stay with him and work at his new home. I told him that I couldn't because I was meeting Jerry here. He said that he would send for Jerry and the girls and provide housing for all of us. I knew Jerry would never go for that. Jerry wants his farm, his independence. He would never consider living in the service of someone else."

"Thomas is the same, his life is the land," Johanna agreed. "It bothered him to look for work in the city."

* * *

So the family members grieved each in his or her own way. Denis remained guarded in his sorrow, Johanna buried the pain deep inside so no one could see her vulnerability, and Jeremiah acted out his sadness with destructive behaviour. Thomas remained sad both in visage and in his speech. As a man of religion, he separated himself from the group and prayed quietly that his daughter's soul reach heaven, which she so richly deserved.

* * *

The days were long and moved slowly for most people as the inactive group awaited Mr. Robinson's arrival. Denis, however, found himself travelling over to Máire's tent frequently to visit. They became a constant pair. A bond of similar likes and habits formed between the two and soon, if either one hesitated in speech, the other would finish his or her sentence with accuracy and comfort. Time did not matter to Denis. Máire had his attention and time spent with her was all that mattered.

A week after the McCarthys' arrival in Kingston, a man from *The Resolution* called for a meeting of all the Robinson settlers. The man wanted to set up an association for the settlers with a compact similar to that of the pilgrims on *The Mayflower*. The long wait in the heat had made the earlier settlers impatient, and now the impatience was turning to contempt and distrust. Many settlers felt they needed a unified statement demanding their immediate move onto their lands.

The group of assembled passengers listened and argued over the need for a compact and coalition representatives. The Irish were not keen on just making rules for the sake of having a law. The issues of politics and elected officials produced scepticism and a fear of unwanted control.

Colonel Burke was Peter Robinson's deputy superintendent in charge of the camp at Kingston and he, like Peter Robinson, was respected for his fair treatment. Many settlers argued that a separate pact was not needed and might hamper relations with Peter Robinson and his project.

Thomas, Denis and Uncle Jerry attended the meeting and remained silent until a man, William from one of the earlier ships, spoke up. "They are going to leave us here. They just dumped us in a field in British North America and we are going to be left here," he repeated.

Denis spoke up. "I don't think so. Mr. Robinson has been very particular to make sure everything has proceeded smoothly and we have received news that he is coming soon."

"They have said that before," countered William, "but he is not here."

Denis decided to take a stand. "We were taxed so highly that we had to forfeit our land. Had we stayed in Ireland, we would be walking the lanes without homes or food to feed our families. Mr. Robinson came to help us, as he did two years ago for the first wave of Irish settlers. Now you want to create a pact which demands certain rights. That goes against the fairness and generosity Mr. Robinson and Colonel Burke have shown us.

"This pact is an ultimatum, my friends." Denis was trying to reach the rational members of the group. "You are applying old British standards from Ireland against Mr. Robinson, who represents the Upper Canadian government. I think Mr. Robinson will be here shortly to take us to our new homes. We must be patient. Our ships made quick passages across the Atlantic. Most voyages take much longer, and we need to wait for Mr. Robinson."

The bickering subsided and the pact lacked consensus. The group realized an accord was not going to happen and most felt one was not needed. Even though the level of disagreement was intense, the matter was dropped because only a few remained convinced of the need of a statement of grievance and demands. However, certain members of the group talked after the meeting about an idea to occupy the children during this waiting period.

"What might help," started Patrick Leahy, "is setting up a school for the children. Keeping the children occupied will help the impatience and provide an education. Do we have anyone who can teach, someone who can read and write?"

Most parents liked the idea of a school; however, some voiced an opinion about transmitting fever among the children, and consequently many parents were reluctant. Thomas nudged his son. "You can help with this."

Denis volunteered, "I know how to read and write; I would be happy to teach the children."

Thomas was pleased his son committed himself to the general welfare of the group. "Good for you, son. I'm proud you stepped up to help."

* * *

At the other end of the tent village, Judith Sullivan saw the new passengers arrive from the remaining ships. The tent village swelled into a sea of white. It was now July and the heat had not broken. Tempers were sharp and people stayed close to their own area. Word spread that a man wanted to form some sort of union or pact among the passengers. Judith thought this was an odd idea but she went to the meeting to discuss the thought.

The meeting was held but nothing came of it except the idea of a school for the children. Judith supported the idea of classes for Ellen and Johanna. At the end of the meeting, Judith approached the young man who had volunteered to teach the children:

"My husband died of the fever and I can't care for my seven children alone and teach them to read at the same time. My two youngest daughters would enjoy your class. Would you teach them?"

"Sure, we can get started tomorrow morning."

The next day a schoolroom was fashioned in the centre of the meeting area for the young children. Bess walked the girls over for their first day of class. Denis McCarthy met them at the bench.

"Good morning, who do we have here?" he asked the children.

"I'm Johanna."

"And I am Ellen. I am the older sister."

"Yes, I see. Welcome. Are you ready to learn new things?"

"Oh yes," said Johanna, then added, "I love to hear stories."

"Ah, and I love to tell stories."

Johanna giggled with excitement.

Soon the centre area, covered with a tarp, was filled with many more children. Even though the overcrowded tent village had several hundred children, only about twenty attended. The first day of class was started with a story:

"Once upon a time there was an old goat. She had seven little kids, and loved them all, just as a mother loves her children. One day she wanted to go into the woods to get some food. So she called all seven to her and said, 'Children dear, I am going into the woods. Be on your guard for the wolf. If he gets in, he will eat up all of you, even your skin and hair. The villain often disguises himself, but you will recognize him at once by his rough voice and his black feet.'

> "The kids said, 'Mother dear, we will take care of ourselves. You can go away without any worries.'
>
> "Then the old one bleated, and went on her way with her mind at ease.
>
> "It was not long before someone knocked at the door and called out, 'Open the door, children dear, your mother is here, and has brought something for each one of you.'
>
> "But the little kids knew from the rough voice that it was the wolf."

Denis continued the story from the book that Captain Morrison had given him, known as the Brothers Grimm fairy tales, and he described how the children outsmarted the wolf by feeding him food that contained stones, which gave him a stomachache. "The kids led the wolf to the well for water and the heavy stones made him fall in and drown."

The children were captivated by this German mythical story,

which was not widely known throughout Ireland, and they cheered the ending. The children needed the reinforcement that good overcomes evil, even though real life experiences are often contrary. The fantasy, the use of their imagination, the belief in good things, and having hope instilled in them was necessary for their development and maturity. Denis knew to do otherwise was a disservice to children.

Johanna and Ellen went back to their tent excited about their first day at school. "He told us stories about talking goats and wolves," yelled Johanna. "And there were seven kids, I mean baby goats."

"It was rather about paying attention to your mother and being careful with strangers," corrected the more serious Ellen.

"I know that," said Johanna. "But he made the goats and kids talk."

"I am glad you enjoyed your first day," commented Judith.

"We can go back tomorrow?" asked Johanna.

"Of course."

"Yay!"

The next day, instead of more children there were less. Denis wondered what happened. He questioned his teaching methods; maybe the wolf story was too much for these children. His two favourite pupils were waiting for him but the others were slow in coming.

He asked a nearby woman, "Where are the rest of the children?"

"Mr. McCarthy," she said, "people are afraid of the sickness spreading among the children. They liked your class but not with the other children so close."

"I see." He turned to the children. "We are going to do some counting today." Adult problems were not meant for the children and he knew how to keep those two issues separate.

"Goody," squealed Johanna.

* * *

Eventually Denis tutored just Ellen and Johanna while the other children stayed away. The arrangement worked well and Máire joined them in the classes and various excursions through the area around Kingston. It was a joyous time for Johanna and Ellen, the fun and adventures occurring on a daily basis as they studied arithmetic by counting steps or clouds in the sky, and the natural world by looking at insects and flowers.

During the first week, Judith introduced Denis to her eldest son. "This is my son Edmond."

Denis stuck out his hand and said, "Nice to meet you." Edmond responded by gripping Denis's hand for the shake. Each grip was firm, confident and strong. Their eyes locked in the moment, confirming sincerity, friendliness and unity. Their physical appearance reflected their common background of tough Irish farming, but Edmond's easy smile and Denis's congenial response set the connection within the first moments of the introduction.

"You are teaching my sisters?" asked Edmond.

"Yes, they are good girls, I enjoy being with them. Ellen is so serious and Johanna is so exuberant. I appreciate both of their qualities," Denis said, as they turned and walked among the tents and Judith turned to her other children.

Edmond added, "They are different in many ways yet they have some similar traits, such as both liking stories of heroes and heroines, liking fun games—and both of them like their new teacher."

"Good to hear," replied Denis, and then added, "My regrets on the passing of your father. It must have been difficult on the ship and all."

"Indeed, but the hardest was the burial in the sea. It was so quick and the sea . . ." Edmond hesitated; he had not expressed much grief since his father's death. He had remained strong for his mother and the other children and not allowed his own sorrow to show. On his father's deathbed, he had promised that he would become the patriarch and he showed little grief, believing strength suppresses emotion. Now he was speaking away from the family to a peer who showed an easy empathy and, from the stories he heard, a talent for wisdom. "The sea," he continued, "seemed like an unnatural place to bury my father. It has no place of memorial, no headstone, no 'here lies a great man.'"

Denis was equally restrained. "I know, they took my sister at Quebec. I am not sure where they buried her." Silence fell on the conversation; each man hung his head lost in his own thoughts. After several steps of walking Denis started again, "The Lord has both of them now."

Edmond looked up at Denis and said, "Teach my sisters well."

"I will," replied Denis.

Edmond reached up and placed his hand on Denis's shoulder as a gesture to show camaraderie. Even though this movement was foreign to Denis's style, he understood its meaning.

* * *

On hot, lazy days with low human energy, Denis and Máire went with the two girls through the tent village to the edge of Lake Ontario or the river when the heat became overbearing. The children waded in the water away from the busy boat traffic at the town piers. They would count the little minnows swimming around the shallow water. Occasionally Ellen or Johanna would try to catch a minnow, but the baby fish were too quick and scurried off, only to return a few minutes later to tease the girls again.

About a hundred feet down the shore, they watched a Great Blue Heron stand motionless at the edge of the water. With one quick bob of his head, the large bird grabbed a fish and raised his head, stretching his neck to swallow his catch.

"How come he can do that and we can't?" asked Johanna.

"He practises all the time. If he doesn't catch the fish, he doesn't eat," explained Denis.

"Oh, he's lucky," said Johanna.

"Lucky to eat raw fish straight out of the water?" asked Máire.

"Oh, that's terrible," said Ellen.

"We are the lucky ones. We can cook our fish," said Denis.

The lessons continued through the hot summer.

In the evening when the heat of the sun diminished and people gathered for talk, a larger group formed for music, singing and dancing. Michael Leahy and his children from the first ship, *The Fortitude*, and Patrick from the McCarthys' ship, *The Elizabeth*, brought traditional Irish music to the group. The music lifted the settlers' spirits as the melodies, songs and voices drifted across the tent village. These daily enrichments brought entertainment, distraction and renewed hope to the settlers.

* * *

Bess had been troubled about Rose for a long time. Her story of being alone and pregnant was almost impossible for innocent Bess to understand, so she consulted her mother for advice.

"What can we do for her?"

"For one thing, it is her trial and tribulation. We face our own ordeals all the time and we must learn to grow through them. Secondly, she is in trouble and we can help, if she is willing to let us," Judith counselled.

"So are you saying to leave her alone?"

"No, I am saying that we can offer to help but if she declines our offer, then we leave her alone," Judith said firmly.

"She can't clear a new farm and raise a baby," Bess insisted.

"I'm sure Mr. Robinson will make other arrangements. However, this problem sounds bigger than starting a farm. This girl needs help in making decisions, like where she is going to settle, and how she is going to provide a home, food and other necessities for herself as well as the baby."

"She has no one to talk to."

"You can slowly work your way into her confidence, so she will talk and listen to you."

"It sounds like a lot of work."

"How bad do you want to help her?"

"I'll try." Bess pondered her approach to Rose, because the girl kept to herself at the bottom of the hill. Bess decided to seek her out, and headed down towards her tent. Rose's tent had the front flap pulled back and Bess looked in. Just inside, Rose was seated out of the direct sun.

"Hi," Bess said, trying not to be shy.

"Oh hi," came the reply from Rose.

"How are you doing?"

"I'm fine." Rose did not offer much in the way of conversation.

"I saw that you met Father Collins."

"Yeah, he was all right."

"Did he help you at all with your . . ." Bess stumbled on phrasing her words.

"No, I didn't tell him anything."

"I am glad you're still here."

"There's no place else to go. Although I did see a new brewery has opened in town. I wonder if they would hire a girl?" Rose considered out loud.

"I don't know," said the inexperienced Bess.

"Of course, I could work in a bar. Where there is a brewery, there are bars."

"I suppose, but a bar is no place for a girl like you."

"What kind of girl am I?" Rose challenged gruffly.

Bess thought maybe Rose was the right kind of girl for a bar. "I meant, having the baby and all."

"Don't mind my problems." Rose lay back on the bare ground inside the tent as if the conversation was over.

Obviously Rose did not have good communication skills. In fact, her life's training was anything but good. Had she explained her past Bess would have been even more bewildered at how to help this girl. Rose came from a household where anger was the common trigger point from which words were formed. Shouting was a way to make yourself heard and threats were tossed around as a way to win an argument or remind the family you still existed. Beer or whiskey, and commonly both, were the staples at every meal for her parents, and some form of alcohol was a midday refreshment to maintain equilibrium.

She was the youngest child, with an older brother and sister who offered her no assistance in learning or managing her life, because survival for all of them was strictly an individual accomplishment. Either you made it on your own or you went without.

Rose did not announce her marriage to Daniel or the fact that she was leaving for Canada until the night before departure. Even then, her parents only stopped arguing long enough to say, "Oh really." Perhaps Rose's parents didn't believe her and therefore didn't give the statement much thought. But Rose took the lack of response as ambivalence.

Now Bess was trying to inquire about her plans and Rose simply closed up, as if Bess's concern was an intrusion or an attempt at manipulation. To Rose the gesture of genuine concern and friendship represented unnecessary exposure to some future ridicule.

Bess watched Rose lying on her back. She could see the formation of her pregnant abdomen but was still uncertain how she could help. Bess thought for a few moments and then walked on past the tent because she felt unable to react or guide with confidence. Rose took the departure as a sign of what had always been given to her from others— indifference.

* * *

One morning in mid-July, the McCarthy family was sitting inside their tent and did not see the young sailor coming their way. Will, the sailor who was dismissed from *The Elizabeth* for flirting with Elly, was going tent to tent looking for the girl who had shown an interest in him. However, Will did not know the girl's last name so when he asked for her, especially by the nickname "Elly," no one knew who he sought.

With close to four hundred families encamped, his search was tedious and frustrating, but he was determined to find her: he had walked nearly two hundred miles from Montreal and another one hundred fifty miles boat ride from Quebec in his quest to find the pretty young Irish girl who had flirted with him. Eventually he found his way to the McCarthy tent, and Elly was shocked at his unexpected arrival.

"What are you doing here?" she demanded, conscious of her family staring and listening.

"I came to get you," he said.

"Get me, for what?" Elly said with a mixture of surprise and annoyance.

"So we can start a life together."

"A life together? I don't think we are ready for a life together."

"But you said on the dock that we should be together."

"I felt that we needed to take care of you. I'm not ready to leave my family."

"You don't have to leave; we'll live close by," he assured her.

"You have this all wrong. I am not going anywhere with you," she insisted.

Will was stunned at the rejection. He thought her father had influenced Elly at the dock and that she was secretly waiting for him to find her and run away together. Now she rejected him entirely. "Are you sure?"

"Yes."

Perhaps she was just shy because her family was so close. He thought that must be it, so Will leaned in and spoke softly, "I will be waiting later tonight at the ferry dock for you."

Elly was astounded at his misunderstanding of the incident at the dock in Quebec. The shock distracted her from her father's raised eyebrow at Will's appearance and Jeremiah's scowl of concern for his cousin's welfare. Will, likewise, was not paying attention to the family's reaction.

Will left the tent fully confident that Elly would reconsider and meet him at their rendezvous on the dock. However, Elly had no plan to leave the tent or her family to meet and run off with Will. Meanwhile Jeremiah contrived his own plan to thwart Will's strategy. As dusk approached, he slipped away to head down the hill and over the path leading to the ferry dock. When he arrived, Will was standing on the dock waiting. "Elly is not coming," he announced to Will.

"Oh, and she sent you?" he challenged.

"No, I'm here to make sure you get the message."

"What message?"

Jeremiah thought this dumb sailor was an egit. He moved in closer to make sure the message had intensity and firmness so there was no confusion. "She does not want to see you again."

"Really," Will said with a smirk.

"Really. Stay away from her and our family," said Jeremiah, standing squarely with his face inches from Will's nose.

Will may have been confused about the original message but he was not confused by Jeremiah's intimidating posture. Will however was not intimidated. "And you are going to do what?"

With a push on Will's shoulder, Jeremiah said, "I'll . . ."

He never finished his sentence because Will punched him with a jab to his right cheek. Jeremiah was a tough thirteen-year-old who was used to fighting. But Will was older, fit and strong; he had spent many of his teen years on a ship lifting fifty and sixty pounds of rigging routinely and pulling and hoisting sails many times each day. The labour made him quick, agile and tough. And fights were common events when in port and a night of drinking turned violent. Jeremiah did not stand a chance against Will's powerful blows to Jeremiah's ribcage.

Jeremiah swung and hit Will, but Will seemed unaffected. Instead he delivered a punch to Jeremiah's left eye that impaired his ability to react. Will followed with a left hook, which moved Jeremiah's nose an inch to the right with a snap. Jeremiah lost his footing and his ability to focus, and he landed on the dock. Jeremiah had lost his first fight, which was mercifully short.

By the time Jeremiah regained his senses, Will had turned and climbed aboard a small fishing schooner, which he had bought earlier in the day with his severance wages. Will left and never returned to Kingston or his lost love, Elly.

Jeremiah hurt. He hurt from the pain and he hurt from defeat. He rose slowly from the dock and each breath ached from the blows to his ribs. He headed back along the roadway towards the fort with just enough daylight to navigate his route. Passers-by saw the bloody boy from the settlement on the hill staggering, crying and holding his chest. They left him alone, until he came upon a townswoman coming from the opposite direction. She offered a towel to wipe his eyes—the left one was swollen shut. She sat Jeremiah down on a tree stump left over from clearing the area.

"What happened?" the woman asked.

Jeremiah had years of training from his father and older brother about using good judgement rather than fighting. The question from this woman brought this painful lesson to mind. "I learned that fighting is not the way to deliver a message."

The woman was confused by the facts, but understood Jeremiah's words. She wiped the oozing blood again. "I'll help you home," she said, as she lifted Jeremiah to his feet and they started up the hill. They worked their way across the open field as the Robinson settlers watched, astounded at the sight of the tough kid from southwest Cork in his defeated march past the crowds. Denis was sitting with Máire in the open area and he was the first to see Jeremiah coming.

"Jeremiah, are you all right?"

"I think so."

The woman spoke. "He came up from the docks but I don't know what happened."

At the mention of the docks, Denis knew his brother had gone to meet Will. "What did you do?"

"Not much, as you can see."

Denis thanked the woman for her kindness and held his brother around the waist to help him walk. Máire helped from the other side. At the tent, Johanna was angered at her son's aggressive behaviour and at the same time heartbroken for his suffering. She started to lecture him, and thought better of it. She did not have the energy. Seeing his pounded body and recently having been reminded how fragile life was, she comforted him and cared for his wounds.

Thomas too was at odds with himself, seeing his son. On one hand, he felt Jeremiah deserved and needed the thrashing; on the other hand, he too was drained at the sight of his son in pain. He pinched his son's nose with both hands and gave a jerk to the left, which made Jeremiah yelp in pain. The nose was reset to the centre of his face.

The woman who had helped Jeremiah back to his camp returned. She had a bucket with a towel stuffed down into the bottom. "I brought you some ice," she said as she unwrapped the towel that was insulating a chunk of ice. "I went to the ice house and talked Mr. Barrett into giving me a chip."

"An ice house?" wondered Thomas.

"Yes, they cut blocks of ice in the river during the winter and store the blocks in a warehouse for summer use," she told them.

"That's amazing," responded Thomas.

"Yes, the winters are cold and the river freezes solid. You will be able to walk across the frozen water in January and February. It's fun to slid around on the ice but you have to be alert for areas where the ice is thin. People break through and drown in the water or freeze to death trying to get out."

"Life is going to be different," said Thomas.

* * *

It was a few days before Denis talked to his brother about the brawl. "Why did you feel you needed to fight Will?"

"I don't know, I guess that's what I was used to."

"And?" his brother pressed.

"I learned my lesson. I won't fight any more, I promise."

Jeremiah truly believed what he said, that his fighting days were over. And he was right; he never did fight after that day on the dock. The memory of the pain stayed with him even though his body healed. There were times when Jeremiah was tested and he remained strong in the face of a challenge; indeed, his wits and verbal savvy always won the day. His passage from boyhood into manhood could be traced to the dock at Kingston and the frivolous sailor who misread Elly's affection.

* * *

Denis continued to see Máire. Their private time was spent in the evenings after the day's lessons with the Sullivan girls. After a walk down to the ferry dock one warm night, the two returned up the hill. Denis reached out and offered his hand to help Máire over a rock. He did not let go of her hand after she safely stepped onto the firm sod, but squeezed her hand and held firm. She squeezed back.

Denis knew the relationship had just entered a new dimension and their close friendship had evolved into romance. He smiled at Máire; their eyes locked in an unspoken communication as excitement filled their souls. Denis was unsure what to do with the moment. He wanted to take her in his arms and just hold her tight, but he was a man of restraint and this unfamiliar warmth of connectedness left him in a state of confusion.

His mind raced for words, perfect words that would not confuse or mislead, words full of poetry and tenderness. Nothing came to mind. He felt awkward, and stared at Máire to see if she was feeling the same affection. A wave of fear came over him—of making a false assumption.

If Máire felt the same way as Denis, she was not showing it. She smiled and squeezed back but she was not going to take the lead. These two Irish Catholics stood frozen in a foreign moment of courtship and moral indecision. Denis found words of less intensity. "Are you all right?"

"Yes, I'm fine."

"Good, let's go," said Denis as he pulled her forward. He released her hand and as she moved in front of him, he reached behind her to place his hand in the small of her back. He gently guided her forward. In an uncharacteristic movement, Máire turned back and looked at Denis with a wide glowing smile. He knew then that she felt the sensation, the phenomenon, the wonder of the moment. His spirit soared as they walked in silence. Routine conversation seemed out of place now.

Denis knew he was entitled to acreage in Scott's Plains and he could imagine Máire as part of his settlement. Though it was too early in their relationship to speak of marriage, his thoughts of the future now revolved around Máire.

* * *

Jeremiah's ribs were still sore the day after the fight; Mr. Power examined his upper torso and felt that only one rib was actually broken. The two ribs on either side were merely bruised, but the surgeon warned Jeremiah that his left side would need a long time to heal. At the same time, Jeremiah's eye swelled with black and blue colouration under the skin, and now the cut above his eye was oozing infection.

After the doctor left, Thomas went out and returned shortly with a half pint of whiskey.

"This will help," he announced to Jeremiah.

"Tommy, where did you get whiskey?" asked Johanna.

"Never mind that," he said to his wife.

He found two glasses and a clean cloth. Tommy poured whiskey into the glasses and handed one to his son. They both drank to his health. Tommy took the cloth and poured whiskey on the cloth and cleansed the wound. Jeremiah yelled. Thomas poured two more shots. He dabbed the wound again but Jeremiah made no sound. The whiskey was gone but the wound was clean.

Johanna was mad. "Thomas, don't give the boy whiskey!"

"It was only used as a medicine," he said defensively.

"I'm telling you, don't give a thirteen-year-old boy whiskey!"

Thomas thought for a moment. He was not going to win this argument. "Very well," he said.

* * *

The heat wave during the peak of July was overbearing. Having to endure the ships, the closeness, the waves and storms had been tough enough on the immigrants, but now the heat became the latest health hazard. Luckily for the group they were close to an abundance of water and they all made multiple trips down to the river, carting buckets back to the tents to keep them cool in the intense heat. Still, many people had low resistance, and sickness took a new toll as they sat and waited.

If they knew where they were going, many might have walked, as they were only a hundred miles from Scott's Plains. A hundred miles was an easy walk for people who travelled this way all the time, but maps and the destination were unknown, so people waited.

Some waited with patience and some did not: inactivity became the devil's playground, as the saying went. A few went into town to hawk and beg for beer money, while others had exhaustive discussions on planning the farm and future household strategies, and still others lay in the sun. At first laughter was common among the group but as time went on grumbling was more often heard.

* * *

The settlers waited for Peter Robinson in Kingston as Mr. Robinson completed his travels to New York and then proceeded to York. Before leaving York, he decided to inspect the route he would use for his settlers. He travelled 62 miles east from York and arrived at Cobourg, a port town along the north rim of Lake Ontario, by the third of August. Cobourg was his staging area for the trip into the interior. He went north into the interior to inspect the roads and waterways for the 31 miles passage from Cobourg to Rice Lake and up the Otonabee River to the Scott's Plains area.

At the same time, he mobilized previous settlers from his 1823 settlement project, as most of their summer work was complete; the only thing left to do on their farms was the harvest. So Peter appealed to their appreciation of their gift from the government, and many of the earlier settlers turned out to assist. He improved the roads to transport the heavy-laden wagons carting the boats over land, along with the personal goods of the settlers, from Cobourg to Rice Lake. He planned on using the boats to continue the transport north towards Scott's Landing, where he had a depot constructed to manage the process of the settlement. Peter now felt prepared to lead the settlers into the interior, so he headed for Kingston.

Peter's arrival at Kingston on August 9 sent excitement through the tent village. As he stepped off the steamer that brought him from Cobourg, he was flooded with warm welcome. "Mr. Robinson, we are glad to see you" was a common greeting. They were indeed happy to see him, since his arrival signalled a movement out of their tents.

People complained to him about the heat. "The sun and heat have been unbearable," said a widow from *The Albion*.

Peter informed them, "You were much safer and more comfortable here even though the temperature was hot. Because you were near the shore of the lake, which caught the breezes, you had some cooling effect. The interior was just as hot but the trees absorbed any breeze that came along. Besides, the intense summer heat caused the bugs and flies to infest the interior. I've never seen it so bad. You had much more comfort at the lake's edge."

"Well, regardless," said one man, "we are anxious to start settling in our new homes. When can we start the trip to the interior?"

"In a day or two," replied Peter. "Tomorrow we start loading the first boats."

Peter had arranged for flat-bottom bateaux to carry passengers from Kingston to Cobourg, where the journey north would start. Only five hundred passengers were allowed on the boat at a time, so the first arrivals were taken on the initial trip. *The Resolution* and *The Brunswick* were the first two ships but, combined, they had 570 passengers. Some settlers needed to be left behind for the second trip. Mrs. Sullivan who was on *The Brunswick* had lost her husband early in the voyage across the ocean so she approached Mr. Robinson and introduced herself. "Due to the unexpected loss of my husband and my extreme grief at his passing, please call me Widow Sullivan."

"I am sorry to hear of William's death," replied Mr. Robinson.

"You remembered his name?" she asked with surprise.

"Of course, we chatted briefly when you boarded your ship."

"But there were so many."

"Yes," he replied. Peter was a genuine person so when he added, "Your husband impressed me," he was serious about the compliment and at the same time gracious to the grieving widow.

"I will volunteer to wait for the next boat," she told the superintendent.

"All right; why?"

"Two of my daughters are being tutored by Mr. McCarthy, who will not be leaving yet. Their schooling can continue if we wait here together."

"That's fine with me." He turned to Colonel Burke to make note of the request.

* * *

The tent village shrank as families gathered their belongings to carry them down the hill to the waiting boats. A few families discarded unwanted items that they did not want to carry any more, while others who saw some potential use quickly snatched them up. Clothes passed from child to child, so these were seldom cast aside. Rose had little to carry and she gave away her departed husband's clothes.

Bess walked down to assist. "You headin' to the interior?"

"Yes, I thought I'd get my land, ride out the winter and then sell it in the spring."

Bess was surprised that Rose had such a detailed plan. "Can you do that?"

"Sure, why not? It's my land, isn't it?"

"I suppose," answered Bess. "When is your baby due to be born?"

"I figure in November or December sometime."

Bess saw her mother standing up the hill. "Hang on a minute; I'll walk down with you, but first I have to tell my mother where I'm going." Bess ran up to her mother. "Ma, would it be all right if I rode ahead with Rose to Scott's Plains and met you there?"

"Now?" Judith asked in surprise.

"Yes, she is leaving now."

"But it may be one or two weeks before we get there."

"I know, but it will be good for her."

"Bess," Judith said in her firmest voice, "I can't let you go. We are heading into a wilderness area. I don't know what to expect. I can't let you go under such uncertainty."

"But please, for Rose's sake," Bess pleaded.

Judith thought for a moment; she would be with hundreds of other settlers. How great could the danger be? If Bess didn't go, perhaps they would be putting Rose in danger. But Judith's final thought had to be for Bess, a fifteen-year-old on her first trip to the backwoods of Canada.

"No," said Judith. "And that's final."

Bess knew the words "that's final" meant the request was refused and no further discussion would be tolerated. "Very well," she said dejectedly, "I'll walk her down to the boat."

"That'll be all right."

Bess headed back down the hill but Rose had picked up an escort, a young man whom Bess did not know. He was carrying Rose's bag and she was hanging onto his arm, her long brown hair flowing in the quick breeze coming in from the lake. Bess quickened her step to catch up.

"Hey, wait for me," she yelled.

Rose turned. "I have a young man to help me with my bags."

"I see. And who is this man?" Bess asked.

"I don't know his name yet." She turned to the older teenager, who looked about eighteen. "What's your name?"

"George."

The three walked in uncomfortable silence down to the docks. Once they reached the boat, Bess said to Rose, "I'll meet you in Scott's Plains."

"I'll see you there," she grinned and grabbed George's arm again, and the two boarded the boat.

Bess stared after them. "Maybe it's best I didn't go with her," she thought.

* * *

The steamboat returned a week later to pick up the next five hundred settlers. Mostly the passengers from *The Fortitude* and *The Albion* were loaded on board to head down Lake Ontario to Cobourg, where they started the inland journey to Scott's Plains. Máire and her family were scheduled for this trip.

Denis walked her down to the dock and said his goodbyes. Little Ellen and Johanna Sullivan insisted on going to the dock with them. He promised to find her as soon as he arrived in Scott's Plains. As he was finishing his goodbye, he wanted to kiss her and leaned forward, but she didn't offer her lips. Finally he quickly kissed her on the cheek. Máire bent down and hugged each of the girls. She turned and boarded the boat. Denis, along with the two girls, watched her walk up the ramp. He liked her style, the way she walked and carried herself. He stood holding the hand of one Sullivan child on each side, and watched his hoped-for future board the ship.

After the boat left, Denis took the girls back towards the hill that led to the tents. Johanna was dilly-dallying as they walked, watching a bird in a tree. Her older sister tried to hustle her along.

"Johanna, keep walking."

"I'm coming," she said, but didn't move. "Denis, would you tell us a story?"

"What story were you thinking about?" he asked.

"My favourite is Cinderella."

"Oh yes, one of my favourites too," Denis agreed. "Why do you like Cinderella?"

"I like Prince Charming." Her face shone at the thought of her hero. In her young mind, Prince Charming looked a lot like Denis.

"Johanna, you are such a dreamer," Ellen rebuked her.

Denis found a shade tree and sat the girls down for yet another telling of Cinderella. "Once there was this beautiful girl," he started, "but her mother died." The girls listened intently, especially now that they had lost a parent too. "This girl was as old as Máire," he pointed out to where the departing boats had been, "and just as beautiful, with soft yellow hair and engaging blue eyes."

Ellen immediately understood who he was describing but Johanna was a little slower. "I thought Cinderella had brown hair?"

"Johanna, he was talking about Máire," explained Ellen with a huff.

"Oh," said Johanna, taking a moment to figure out why Denis would describe Máire. "Oh," she said again, and laughed.

Denis turned serious and narrowed his eyes to change the tone of the story. "But her father married another woman, who was mean and treated Cinderella badly. The woman had two daughters, who learned to be just as mean towards Cinderella as their mother."

"Who could be mean to Cinderella?" asked Johanna rhetorically.

"Shhh," said Ellen with a stern look, "listen to the story."

"I am," countered Johanna, glaring back at her sister.

Before any further bickering could occur, Denis started again. "Cinderella had to do all the work in the house—scrubbing the floors, washing the clothes and cleaning the dishes—while the other two sisters did nothing to help." Johanna let out a sigh and Ellen looked at her sister ready to correct any interruption.

"When news came of a ball at the palace of the king, Cinderella's mother and two stepsisters were happy to be invited."

"Cinderella couldn't go," said Johanna.

"Shhh, don't spoil the story," repeated Ellen.

"That's right, Cinderella couldn't go," said Denis, "even though she had to help make the dresses for the other girls." Denis looked at his audience; he had their full attention. "Cinderella was sad and missed the comfort of her mother. She watched the others leave for the ball in their bright gowns and polished shoes. After they had gone, Cinderella sat by the hearth and cried—until a Fairy Godmother appeared."

"Yeah!" exclaimed Johanna. Ellen looked towards the sky and let out a long sigh, as she realized Johanna was going to keep interrupting the story.

"The Fairy Godmother asked Cinderella if she wanted to go the ball but she said, 'I can't, I don't have a gown.' With a wave of the Fairy Godmother's wand, Cinderella had a beautiful gown and shiny glass slippers. 'If you want to go, you have to promise to be home by midnight,' instructed the Fairy Godmother. 'I will,' said Cinderella."

Johanna opened her mouth to say something, but looked at her sister and stopped any words from coming out. Johanna raised her nose and shook her head with a defiant shake, as if saying, "I am not going to say anything." She looked back to Denis. Ellen just smiled at the minor victory.

"The Fairy Godmother made a coach out of a pumpkin," explained Denis. Johanna giggled. He continued, "And the attendants were mice transformed into handsome coachmen." Johanna giggled again and Ellen tried not to smile at the thought of handsomely dressed mice, but the corners of her mouth involuntarily turned up. "Once at the ball, she met Prince Charming, who asked her to dance."

"Ahh," said Johanna.

Denis rose from sitting on the grass and started shadow dancing as if he had Cinderella in his arms; he twirled around the girls who sat there watching him go around and around. All the while he was humming a waltz to supply the music.

Johanna giggled out loud and even Ellen laughed openly. Denis reached down and lifted Johanna up into his arms. He twirled again with Johanna's little feet dangling from his waistline; she was laughing uncontrollably with each exaggerated dance step as he moved graciously around the tree and into the open field. Finally he set her down in the same spot where he had lifted her.

"Do it again," she begged. He moved towards Ellen.

"Oh, no," she said sliding back away, "not me."

He didn't push it and moved away, continuing with a couple of twirls just for added effect. The girls laughed again. He stopped and took a deep breath as a number of people, who had been watching along the top of the hill, started clapping. Denis turned in surprise to see the people acknowledging his silliness. He took a bow in thanks to his audience.

"We will finish the story later," he said. "Let's get back."

Johanna remembered these happy times in Kingston with Denis, her teacher, for the rest of her life.

* * *

Each week the steamboat returned to Kingston after the previous passengers made their way to Cobourg and on to Rice Lake. The flat boats returned to the steamboat and the process repeated. The remaining families started to get restless. The summer was ending and they must prepare for fall and winter. They had no idea whether their houses were ready or even built. The inactivity was playing hard on their imagination. These farmers used the calendar to track their livelihood. Their intuition was telling them to prepare for a change in season but they had no way to do so.

Finally, some of the families decided to settle in Kingston. A few more absconded from Kingston and headed across the tip of Lake Ontario to Cape Vincent, New York. They thought the United States offered more hope or perhaps a meeting with previously immigrated family members.

* * *

A few weeks passed. The passengers of the long and deadly voyage moved into the interior of Upper Canada to become the settlers of Peter Robinson's project. Only the hearty would survive this transition from Irish to Canadian farmer. The cleared and established farmland of Ireland, with its temperate winters warmed by the Gulf Stream, was incredibly different from the cold Arctic streams that produced harsh bitter winters in Upper Canada. The coniferous forestlands had yet to be cleared into rich humus loam for farming, and the long-lasting deep freezes affected the planting, tilling and storage of crops in Canada.

These experienced farmers were about to face vastly new experiences; they would have to change their old practices. The environment had many other differences besides weather and undeveloped soil. The notorious deer ate the tops of plants, while moles chewed the crop from below. Other animals, insects and parasites waited for the latest food source to appear.

Mosquitoes were not prevalent in Ireland, yet in Canada they mass-produced under the ideal wet conditions and abundant animal blood. Now, two thousand new animals in the form of settlers gathered in close proximity, causing these vector organisms that carried the deadly malaria to flourish.

But these obstacles were an inconvenience only in their new test of endurance. The Irish were accustomed to a difficult life. These challenges were mere impediments to deal with or overcome. Disease, starvation and death were familiar. They looked to the hope and promise of rising out of those conditions and daily trials to a life of nourishment, abundance and freedom as well as a good life for future generations. The settlers moved inland undaunted by the prospect of hardship.

Four cycles on the steamboat took the remaining nineteen hundred settlers and they made their way to Scott's Plains.

The two McCarthy families, along with the Sullivan family, boarded the boat. Judith had her hands full controlling the small children and making sure all the siblings remained together. Edmond and Mary helped find an unused area for them to assemble and ride out the day-long trip.

The first thirty miles went smoothly, as rough water was kept in check by a jutting and outcropped shoreline. However, as they passed a series of protected islands and peninsulas, the wind came from one hundred fifty miles of unchecked open water. Four-foot waves hit the boats head on, rocking the flat-bottom bateaux forward and back, up and down, as trunks slid into other trunks and people.

People screamed, trying to maintain their footing and hang onto their luggage at the same time. Mothers clung to their children. No one was lost during the trip. One trunk belonging to the James

Mahoney family hit the water and sank within moments, taking with it their meagre possessions and any mementos of their past life.

Johanna McCarthy made her way towards the back of the boat to see if Judith could use an extra hand. "How are you doing?" she asked.

"We are managing," answered Judith.

"Anything I can do?" pushed Johanna.

"No," was Judith's quick reply. She didn't mean to be curt, especially to Denis's mother, but she felt the children were under control at the moment and the answer was merely a straightforward "no."

Johanna said, "All right," and returned to her family, wondering if Judith was always that unfriendly or just under these circumstances.

After the rocky trip on Lake Ontario, the boat pulled into the safety of Cobourg harbour. The boats were loaded on wagons, which were the reason for the flat bottoms, and prepared for the next day's journey into the interior. Overnight, they again stayed in tents.

The next morning at daybreak, the passengers were wakened for a quick cup of tea and a small breakfast. Johanna McCarthy again walked over to the Sullivan group. "Good morning."

"Good morning," each of the Sullivans replied, but Judith made no attempt at furthering the conversation, as she kept busy preparing the children for the day's journey. Again Johanna returned, unsure of the cool reception from Mrs. Sullivan. Johanna made no further attempt at establishing a friendship with Denis's acquaintances.

The huge wagons pulled out of Cobourg, dragged by a team of horses and loaded with the boats and all the luggage. The settlers walked behind. As they approached the interior, Thomas and Johanna saw the shoreline of Rice Lake. There the boat hauled their meagre possessions and future neighbours across the lake towards the Otonabee River. Peter Robinson's plan to mix boats and wagons as a method of traversing this rough topography was working exceptionally well. The heat had broken in a thunderstorm the day before, cooling the area. Now, the moderate temperature at the end of August offered a comfortable ride and a pleasant view of the lake.

"This is paradise," remarked Johanna.

"The lake is beautiful; I hope we settle near water," Thomas said.

The families continued to Scott's Plains and checked into the depot in town. The room had tables of maps and charts of the various townships. The McCarthys had been originally assigned to the Douro area east of town, but Thomas asked for land near water. Peter Robinson looked at him.

"I don't know. Most of that land has been assigned and you are with the last group. I'll see what we can do."

Judith spoke up. "Yes, and I would like to be close to the McCarthy family."

Peter reworked some of the remaining assignments. "I'll have to separate you from your brother Jerry."

Thomas was not enthusiastic about creating distance between him and his brother. He had depended on Jerry his whole life. "I think I'll stay with the original assignment."

"Wait," Peter stated as he continued to transfer the land consignments. He pointed to a map. "I have three adjoining lots in Smith Township. Two are side by side for you and Denis on the 11th line. On the back side along the 12th line is a lot for Jerry. These properties sit on a hill above Chemong Lake," he added.

"Just like Abbeymahon," said Johanna.

"It will feel like home," noted Thomas.

Johanna asked Mr. Robinson, "Why do you have three properties left together in this area?"

"This plot along the 11th line has about five acres of swamp. No one wanted swampland and the access is limited on this side of the road." He pointed to the map and then continued, "It was assigned but the family backed out. There is good news, though; the houses are being built now and are near completion."

Jeremiah knew most of the settlers were farmers and swampy areas cannot be farmed, but he also knew from spending his time in the woods and hunting badgers that animals like to hide out in swampy areas. He spoke up. "The swamp will be good for game."

"You're right," stated Peter's deputy, Colonel Burke. "You'll find moose in that area."

Uncle Jerry looked at the map. "Perfect," he said.

Denis walked over to the table and asked Peter, "Where is the Fergus family?"

"They settled in Asphodel, further east," Peter told him.

Denis looked at the map. Asphodel was twenty miles east of Scott's Landing and Smith Township was another twelve miles north. He noticed that Asphodel was the next town after Douro. He looked up at Judith, whose land was situated on the other side to the northwest. "That's fine," he said, "we're in the middle."

"Denis, your house on your land is not started yet. Is that all right for now?" asked Colonel Burke.

"That's fine, I'll stay with my parents for a while," replied Denis, who had some very specific and definite thoughts about his house and his future.

* * *

Peter addressed Judith. "You are in the next town of Emily on a neighbouring lake, Pigeon Lake. Here, let me show you."

Peter showed the widow her plot. If one traced a line from the Sullivans' land to the McCarthy plots and then to Máire's family in Asphodel, the line would form a northern border east to west above Scott's Plains.

"Very good," she said, appreciatively but not enthusiastically. The widow with seven children was scared of isolation away from Scott's Plains and not immediately close to Denis. "What about Edmond, my son? Is he entitled to a land grant?"

"Yes, his land is just below yours." Peter showed Judith on the map. She was more comfortable learning that Edmond's land was adjacent to hers and if he married soon, he would remain close. "I think this will work," said Judith with more confidence.

Johanna McCarthy looked at Judith and said, "If you need anything, let us know. We can help."

"I will," said Judith. "Thank you." And she smiled at Johanna for the first time.

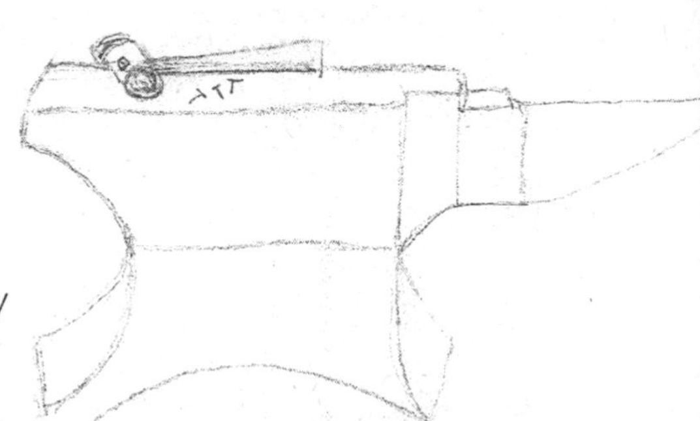

Chapter 9

The McCarthy Family Smith Township

Once the land assignment was made, each settler signed for his land grant as well as the provisions given to him by the British government to start his household. Thomas and Denis sat down in the depot with Colonel Burke to sign the land deeds, one deed for Thomas and one for Denis.

"Mr. McCarthy, you can sign right here," said Colonel Burke to Thomas, pointing to the page.

Denis leaned over the paper, showing his father the specific place on the paper. "Da, just make your mark. Colonel Burke and I will witness it," said Denis.

"I've never taken possession of land like this except from my brother, who gave me a piece of land that was handed down to him from my father and his father before him. This is truly a remarkable day."

"It's been a long time since we acquired land instead of losing it," agreed Denis.

"About two hundred years," Jerry said in a direct and loud voice. "We haven't had our own land since Cromwell overran southern Ireland two hundred years ago." Jerry was showing signs of disgust that Denis had not seen before. Maybe now that they were away from Ireland he was loosening up old sentiments.

"You sound angry, Uncle Jerry," said Denis.

"Of course I'm angry. If it wasn't for that murderous butcher Cromwell, we would still have our home in Ireland. All of us who were on these ships came because we were losing our land because of increasing taxes and every day got closer to foreclosure." Denis had never seen his uncle speak so forcefully about Irish politics or give such a public display.

"Now, Jerry," said Lizzie from the back of the room.

Peter Robinson spoke up. "I can't change history but I can tell you that the British government is trying to help."

"I know, and I appreciate the help, but there is some terrible history here," explained Jerry.

While Judith was still signing her papers, Mr. Robinson stepped away from the table in his calm yet controlling manner and addressed his fatigued and frustrated traveller from across the room. "Jerry, I have travelled to Ireland twice and both times I saw the horrible conditions of people dying of starvation, children without parents, crop failures, the class differences and religious persecutions. You will not find that here. Upper Canada is a place where you make it through your own hard work and the gracious assistance of your neighbours."

"It's been a long and difficult trip," said Jerry as a way to explain his uncharacteristic outburst.

"I understand, and I realize you have much work ahead of you, but life will be better here," Peter reassured him.

"There," interrupted Judith, "all the papers are signed."

Peter looked at Jerry for any lingering comments. When Jerry said nothing, he turned back to Judith to finish her processing.

Because he was over eighteen years old, Denis was entitled to a land grant as well; his settlement was next to his father's property also on the 11th line in Smith Township.

"Denis, now I need your signature for your deed," said the Colonel.

Peter Robinson sat down with Jerry for his deed assignments on the 12th line. "Jerry, if I remember correctly, your land slopes to the east so there is no sitting water."

"That's good," said Jerry and then changed the subject. "Is there a Catholic Church in town?" Jerry still had sharpness in his tone, as if he had not calmed down from his fiery rebuke of Oliver Cromwell.

Peter Robinson addressed the question. "Right now we are bringing in a priest when we can but I am promised a full-time priest for Scott's Plains by the New Year."

Thomas wanted to bring the mood of this meeting back to an optimistic tone. "I still think this is a historic day, not only for our family but all our fellow countrymen who have received a new opportunity for land and survival."

"I agree, Tommy," said his older brother, returning to his normal congenial temperament. "We should rejoice in our good fortune and be thankful to our benefactor, Mr. Robinson."

Peter just nodded the acknowledgement as he worked on Denis's final papers, and then said, "Now, each of you will get your allotted provisions of a cow, feed, corn, wheat and potatoes. Your shanties are being built on the land now. In addition, you will receive the necessary farm implements to get you started. These supplies will be available outside when you leave."

Peter then turned to Judith. "Mrs. Sullivan, we will hold your provisions until you settle on your land."

"This is truly remarkable," said Thomas again. "I am amazed that the British government has supported this effort so thoroughly."

"We are appreciative," Jerry said to Peter. "Thank you for your help."

"You are welcome," replied Peter. "Now let's go outside and load your wagons."

* * *

The McCarthy men loaded their wagons outside the depot.

"Gentlemen, your supplies," said the driver as the last sack was positioned and a cow was tied to the rear of the wagon. The driver checked off the promised goods on a piece of paper and said, "Please sign the receipt." In addition, he reaffirmed, "A group of volunteers from the earlier settlement are building your homes now, so let's get started."

Uncle Jerry showed the drivers the maps of their assignments.

"I know where that is. I was out there yesterday on a delivery," one driver said.

"Good," said the other. "Let's go."

The two families headed north out of Scott's Plains. Meanwhile, Judith and her family stood by. "We will see you soon," yelled Denis.

"Bye, bye," called out Johanna, waving her arms.

Peter Robinson had built a number of buildings in Scott's Plains; one such building was a government house to be used as temporary housing for settlers waiting for their plots to be cleared and homes erected. Judith's house was one of those that had not been started. Peter made arrangements for the Sullivan family to stay in town.

Scott's Plains was buzzing with activity. With the construction of the government buildings and the influx of settlers along with merchants, traders, millers and lumberjacks, the town was being transformed from a small milling operation into a village of regular commerce.

* * *

Meanwhile the McCarthys headed north along the Otonabee River to Lakeville Township and then they turned left towards Chemong Lake to the eastern border of Smith Township, where the roads marking the 11th and 12th lines took them to their homes. Uncle Jerry's girls rode in the back of the wagon mixed in with the sacks of feed and grains until the jostling of the rutty road was too much.

"Ma, this hurts every time we hit a bump," said Elly, and pointed to boxes and sacks that shifted with each rock they struck. "Can I walk?"

"I want to walk too," said Abigail, the fifteen-year-old, followed by each of the other three girls who preferred to deal with the uneven terrain on foot. The five girls got out and walked the remaining distance with the men. Lizzie and Johanna each rode on the front buckboard of their own wagon, which was bumpy enough, but the pounding was not as jolting as the girls experienced in the back.

The driver of Jerry's coach introduced himself.

"I'm Jake," said the thinly built middle-aged man. "I live over in the Bathurst section of Upper Canada. A number of you Irish came here two years ago with Mr. Robinson. Did you know that?"

"Yes, we were aware that a smaller test group came two years ago."

"And that's why you're here," said Jake, "because that settlement worked so well. Most of those folks are my neighbours and they're good honest farmers."

"Are you Irish, Jake?"

"No, I guess you can call me a Canadian. My grandparents came to the New World over a hundred years ago. They were trappers from Sweden. I don't know why they came, they just did."

"How come you're helping Mr. Robinson?"

"He's my neighbour and now you're my neighbour. Anyway, Mr. Robinson hired me because of my knowledge of the backwoods. My next trapping season will start when the snow flies."

"Snow," said Abigail, "that'll be fun."

Jake looked down at her and smiled that knowing smile of "you'll see how much fun the snow will be."

"So Mr. Robinson takes care of his people out here?" asked Jerry.

"You betcha," said Jake. "He will be around frequently to check on you. He's a man of his word: if he says he'll get you a barrel of seed, he'll get you a barrel of seed."

"Yes, he seems like a good man," added Lizzie.

"He is highly respected in the backwoods. I wish all the government people were as high-quality as he is."

Jerry looked over to Lizzie and said, "I should keep my comments about the British Crown to myself."

"Yes, you should," was Lizzie's direct reply.

* * *

Meanwhile, Thomas took off his old worn shoes, as he was comfortable walking in his bare feet on the dirt road. The warm ground, with small rounded rocks embedded in the packed clay, held the heat of the sun and felt soothing to Thomas's feet.

The thick forest of conifers intrigued the families. These Southern Irish farmers were from a land of sparse woodlands. They were not used to seeing trees huddled so densely together up to the edge of the road like a long evergreen curtain extending for miles on end. The visibility into the thicket was only a few feet before branches interlaced, cutting off not only the view, but access as well. The older men saw the forest as an endless supply of wood for heat and building. Jeremiah saw the forest hiding game that he would put on his family's dinner table. The women saw an abyss of darkness, a mysterious unknown that held some good but mostly evil surprises.

Abigail was the first to hear the rustle. The sound came from the left in the wood and moved parallel with their movement along the road. The noise was slight, but there was definitely something moving in the branches. Abbey alerted Jeremiah, who was directly behind her. "Jeremiah, did you hear that?" she said nervously just above a whisper.

"Yes, I heard it too," Jeremiah said, concerned but not frightened.

"What is it?" she asked him.

"I don't know."

Denis heard the conversation, stopped, and watched. "There it is," he said.

Two small black-capped chickadees hopped from branch to ground and up to the branch again as they searched for seeds among the pine cones and other vegetation. One bird stopped long enough to give its famed chickadee call that sounded like its name: "chick-a-dee-dee-dee."

A grey squirrel, the actual source of the rustling, followed the two birds a short distance behind. The scavenger squirrel was an opportunist on a scouting mission. The birds hid their seeds for later meals, and the squirrel was letting the birds do the gathering, so he could feast later at his leisure. The birds ended with only a percentage of their labour.

"What pretty little birds," Abbey said, to hide her embarrassment that these tiny birds had caused her alarm.

"They're friendly too—look how close they are," said Denis.

The squirrel was cautious and not as friendly as the birds. Maybe he feared competition for the food or maybe he thought they were scavengers who saw him as food. The group started again, and Jake laughed at the novices to the area.

The tall, long-needled pines were interspersed among the smaller and thicker short-needled spruces and the air was filled with the sweet smell of the balsam fir. They continued on the trek north for another two miles, and arrived at the intersection of the 11th line.

"We turn here," said Jake.

"How far to our road?" asked Uncle Jerry.

"It's the next road up," answered Jake. "I'll tell you what. Both of us will turn here and we'll take the Selwyn Road to your place, Jerry."

"That's fine," answered Uncle Jerry. They wanted to stay as close together in their new environment as possible.

Another half-mile down the muddy road they came to another intersection. The wagons stopped. "Tommy, here you are," announced his driver, Matthew.

The families stopped and looked over the land. There was thick forest on two southern corners of the intersection. The far northern corner had a tree cluster, but a clearing appeared through the trees. The fourth corner was the swamp with a few trees growing up through the water. A stand of dead and decaying trees was interspersed with the living ones, and thorny bushes clustered around the edges of standing, stagnant water, with green algae over the top of the quagmire. Although the families didn't know it, the still pools of the swamp were a breeding ground for mosquitoes that transmitted malaria to humans. Many of the residents in Upper Canada had been infected and died of "the fever": much of that fever was malaria. Beyond the intersection, they could hear voices followed by the pounding of a hammer.

"Your house is being built over there," said the driver, who pointed and started the wagon towards the noise. They walked over to see a small cottage, or a shanty as Mr. Robinson called it, being built on the clearing. Two workmen were on the roof nailing down boards.

The roadway had been packed down from frequent travel but the lane leading into the house was rutted mud. Yesterday's rain had left puddles in the ruts, and Johanna and Thomas hopped from dry spot to dry spot heading towards their new house.

"What have we gotten ourselves into?" asked Johanna, as the realization of what she had given up by leaving the old, comfortable surroundings of Abbeymahon became stunning reality.

Thomas and the family walked around the property inspecting the house and the lay of the land. Thomas looked up to the roof. "Hello, I'm Tommy and this is my wife Johanna."

"We will be down in a minute," said the larger of the two men, as they laid down their hammers and climbed to the edge. Once on the ground further introductions were made.

"I'm Marty Ryan," said the large man, "and this is Danny Regan."

"Welcome," said Danny.

"The land seems good for crops," said Marty. "We cleared many trees, as you can see, and the soil is rich. So farming it for wheat, oats, corn or potatoes will be fine."

"I see I have a few stumps to burn," said Thomas, looking at the scattered stumps where large maple, oak and beech formerly grew.

Danny added, "You have a lot of firewood throughout your property, too."

"Well, thank you for your work," said Thomas. "We appreciate you being here."

"That's all right," said both men.

All the settlement homes had the same basic structure; they were a twelve-foot by twenty-foot, one-floor shanty with a slanting roof to the rear. The house was small for four people, but many families had seven or more children in the same-sized house.

The men had built an outhouse, or backhouse. "Your backhouse is done; you just need to dig a hole," Danny reminded them.

"I can take care of that," said Thomas. He reached into the wagon and pulled out the shovel, one of each settler's implements.

The work started immediately. Denis cleared an area and fashioned a storage box to stockpile the grains away from the weather and foraging animals. Jeremiah, who had not been tested by physical labour since his fight with Will, went to the wagon to unload the forty- and fifty-pound sacks of corn.

His chest muscles tightened with the lifting movement and the pain shot through his chest and along his ribcage. He moaned as he realized his sore ribs had not healed and would not allow him to lift heavy weights. So Jeremiah decided to dig the pit for the outhouse. He picked up the shovel and tried to spear the blade into the ground but again the pain made him stop. Jeremiah felt helpless.

Jerry called his family together and they headed up the dirt road to his settlement. The mile distance between Thomas and Jerry's settlement would soon be a well-worn corridor for the two families on the north-south route between Smith Township and Young's Point. With nothing for him to do at his own house, Jeremiah decided to go with Jerry to see if he could be helpful at his uncle's home. His mission was to scout out the trail and see Jerry's land and house.

* * *

The next two weeks at the Thomas McCarthy settlement were spent finishing the house and building a fireplace. Thomas had developed his cough again; he was sometimes short of breath or had bouts of wheezing. The cool damp weather of Upper Canada brought back his bronchitis in full force.

Denis wanted to go to Asphodel to find Máire but there was too much work to do, with Jeremiah injured and his father sick. The work went slowly but he had to keep going. The cooler weather of September was setting in, and making the house weather-tight was essential.

Denis walked up the road to the north where his plot of land was located. Even though the land remained wild forest and waited to be cleared, Denis scouted out a good position for the house. He wanted to bring Máire over and show her the terrain and decide on a layout of the homestead. These thoughts made him anxious to arrange the adult pieces of his life—marriage, home and even children. He spent an hour walking to the various corners of the property for perspective.

One corner had good protection from wind, while another had a greater exposure to the sun. Another corner was low and wet so he decided to stay away from that area. He checked the soil for crops. The Canadian loam was a different soil than he had known in Ireland. He did know the staples of corn, wheat and hay would grow in this soil. He hoped for potatoes and other root crops as well. He returned to his parents' house with his head full of plans and visions of the future. Those plans included Máire.

As Denis returned home, he spotted his father in the back of the house stacking small leftover sticks from limbs used in the construction. "We will use these sticks as firewood," Thomas explained.

"Yes, there are plenty around the house and in the back woods," agreed Denis.

"I'd rather have the peat for our heat and not all this chopping."

"Yeah," Denis answered. "I was wondering what you thought about Máire?"

"Nice girl. Why?"

"Yeah, she's a nice girl, but I meant what would you think if we got married?"

"Oh." Thomas thought. "I guess you have to ask yourself," he said out loud, "'Is this the woman I want to live with for the rest of my life?'"

"Oh, I'm sure I can live with her for the rest of my life and then some. But I was wondering what *you* thought of her?"

"Denis, it really doesn't matter what I think or what your mother thinks, or the town matchmaker for that matter, it's how you feel about her."

"I love her and I can't stop thinking about her."

"The old Irish way is that if you don't pick a wife, the matchmaker will do it for you. If you know she's the right one, then ask her."

"Thanks Da, I will as soon as I see her."

* * *

The McCarthy families received word that a priest, Father Crowley, would visit Scott's Plains on the third Sunday in September and they all decided to attend the Mass. The two families rose early and headed into the town. The morning air aggravated Thomas's lungs and he coughed frequently along the way. Johanna wanted to turn around and return home, but he insisted on continuing.

They had no carriage or horse to ride, so walking was the only option for this journey. They made the Mass, which was held in a newly constructed building along the river, but Thomas was exhausted and coughed and wheezed continuously. He spent most of the time outside the building, sitting on a rock, trying to regain his breath.

Denis successfully maintained his reverence during the Mass but whenever possible he looked around for Máire. There was no sign of her. After Mass, he approached his mother. "I'd like to walk to Asphodel to see Máire if you don't mind."

Johanna knew Denis was trying to make time for Máire and his plans for marriage. "I suppose; when would you be back?"

"Late tomorrow. I'm sure I can sleep in the barn."

"All right, but be careful. Uncle Jerry and I will get your father home safely," said Johanna.

Before Denis left, Judith approached and asked about his settlement. "Are you settling in to your new homestead?"

"Yes, we are working on my parents' lot. I won't do anything with my acres for a while."

"Oh yes, it would be too much trying to settle both places at once. We will probably do the same with Edmond's lot, too."

"We are finishing the fireplace before it gets too cold and Jeremiah is clearing the land and burning stumps for spring planting." As Denis explained the work he had to accomplish before winter, Judith's apprehension about moving onto a plot of land seemed to be growing.

"It seems like a lot of work, and you have three men and your uncle close by," said Judith. "I just have Edmond and young Denny."

"I can help whenever you need me, just let me know," Denis reassured her.

The two girls, Ellen and Johanna, saw their mother talking to Denis so they raced over to see their former tutor. He was quite happy to spend a few moments with the girls talking about their new adventure in Canada.

"What have you girls been up to?" he asked.

"We live in this building with a bunch of other families," said Johanna. "It's noisy in there."

"Are you making the noise?" Denis pushed.

"No, not us," said Ellen firmly.

"Oh, I see, you go outside to make noise."

"Right, all the noise we make is outside with all the saws, horses and hammering going on," asserted Ellen again. Denis laughed.

Denis finally started the twenty-mile walk from Scott's Plains to Asphodel. He did not mind the walk and kept a brisk pace to make good time. The directions he received from Peter Robinson to Máire's house were handy, even though the route was fairly direct, and he completed the journey in about four hours. He was excited to see Máire and found her homestead easily. The house sat on a flat lot and he noticed that most of the terrain in this area was flat.

He approached the front door of their house and knocked. Máire's mother answered the door and recognized Denis immediately. "Denis, how are you? It's nice to see you."

"I'm fine. I came to see Máire. Is she home?"

"Yes, she is." She turned and called to Máire in the back of the house. "Máire, Denis is here to see you."

"Denis, how nice of you to stop by. Come in."

Denis stepped inside the home. The house was similar in design to the other Robinson homes—a small, one-room house quartered off to a kitchen area, a daily living area, a sleeping area for the parents, and a sleeping area for the children. Máire's parents and her five siblings were in the house. There was also another young man present, who was about Denis's age. Denis had seen him before but could not place him.

Máire made the introduction. "Denis, this is Paddy. He was with us on *The Albion* and now he lives next to us."

"Nice to meet you," said Denis, as he stuck out his hand. He remembered seeing Paddy in the Kingston tent city.

"Come into the kitchen. I am making bread." She led Denis towards the back of the house. The two made small talk about their trips up the Otonabee River and to their settlements as Máire kneaded her dough.

"We, I mean I, have a nice plot of land in Smith Township right next to my parents," said Denis nervously, stumbling on his words. "I have a lovely lot and I found a sunny location to build our cabin, I mean my cabin." He was still nervous.

"Máire, I want you to see my land. Actually I want you to come and make it our home." He could not wait any longer as he fidgeted for the words. He blurted, "Máire, I want you to marry me and settle down on our assigned lot." It was not a question, although it should have been. Either way, the answer was going to be the same.

"Oh Denis," she hesitated. "I can't marry you. I'm going to marry Paddy." She and Denis looked in the living area. The house was only twelve feet deep and all of Máire's family, including Paddy, had just heard the conversation. The two youngest children started laughing and soon Máire's parents and the older siblings joined in. Paddy was the only one not laughing.

Denis looked at the scene. He felt embarrassed and foolish. He had assumed Máire was waiting for him to come and propose marriage. He had been sure that Máire would say "yes" and they would have a life together, happy and united. He was shocked. When he opened his mouth, nothing came out. "I don't know what to say," he finally cried.

Máire replied, "Denis, there is nothing to say, I'm sorry."

Any words after that Denis did not hear. He half smiled at Máire and headed for the door. Even with all his embarrassment and disappointment, Denis did not forget his proper etiquette. "Goodbye," he said as he walked out the door.

He headed west towards Scott's Plains. This time he did not have a spring in his walk or joyful anticipation for his future in his heart. He was devastated by the encounter in Asphodel. His pride was shattered. His beloved had rejected him.

The walk was long but straight. If the route had had turns and twists, Denis would have lost his way. His pace was slow and there were many moments of stopping to review that last conversation and the previous weeks in Kingston. He was confused and wondered what he had done wrong. Was it him? Or did he misunderstand her companionship? Denis had not been in enough romantic relationships to know what to do. His feelings were unfamiliar and unbearable. Máire's rejection cut deep.

The sun dropped in the western sky and dusk approached. Denis did not know where he was, how far he had come, or how much further he had to go. Compounding the situation, he did not realize his dilemma with the prevailing conditions. He faced nightfall in the wilds of Upper Canada in late September and clouds were rolling in.

When darkness and a misty rain hit at the same time, instinct prevailed. Denis found a tall, full-branched spruce tree and crawled under the low-hanging branches. He cleared dead limbs off the lower trunk and made a bed of fallen pine needles. He curled up under the tree, alone with his distraught thoughts. Alone, hungry and now wet, he lay on the ground. The pain of this night would never leave him.

At dawn, Denis set out for home in a drizzle of rain. His anguish was still deep within his soul. He tried running to relieve his pent-up energy and expel his feelings as if they were raindrops to drip away, but all he developed were blisters on his feet from his worn shoes and the uneven ground. He avoided Scott's Plains by taking the east side of the river and then proceeded north. Crossing the swift-moving river was difficult, especially after a night of rain, but he found a boatman near the source of the river at Lake Clear to take him across. Denis returned home late Monday morning. As he walked down the 11th line to turn in to his parent's home, he stopped and gazed up the road towards his plot of land. His plans and dreams were now pain and agony. He turned and headed in.

His parents were surprised at his quick return. "Why are you home so soon?" asked his mother.

Denis did not feel like talking, but that would only postpone the task of revealing the heart-wrenching truth of rejection. "She is going to marry someone else," he announced without mentioning Máire's name, and then he explained his visit.

"Better to happen now than live with trouble later," advised Thomas.

"Her loss," said Johanna. "She could not find a better man than you. Someday she will realize that."

Denis appreciated his parents' support and advice but the sting of his humiliation and disappointment remained. His ability to build a trusting relationship was now hampered. Eleven years would pass before he had the confidence for another intimate relationship. Consequently, Denis never built a house on his property.

* * *

Peter Robinson made a surprise visit to the Thomas McCarthy homestead in late September. He was checking on his settlers to make sure that they had the provisions needed and that the promised work had been performed.

Peter asked, "Denis, are we going to build your house in the spring?"

Denis replied, "I will be staying here with my family. We will use my land for farming only."

"Why is that?" asked Peter.

"I don't know, I just want to be with my parents with Da sick and all," he explained.

"If we don't build your house in the spring then you will be on your own later to build it," informed Peter.

"That's all right," said Denis in a melancholy voice.

Peter turned to Thomas, who only shrugged his shoulders. Thomas left the decision to Denis whether to explain his change in plans. Nothing was said.

Peter was satisfied their needs were met and left to visit Jerry's homestead. Thomas expressed his appreciation for Peter's interest and visit: "I'm glad you came out and checked on us."

"Oh, I'll be back occasionally," said Peter, who did visit on a regular basis.

* * *

September rolled into October as the days shortened and the weather cooled. Thomas still had his lingering cough even with the added rest and warmth of the cabin. Jeremiah's ribs were healing, and he was able to do some work if he pushed his efforts through the pain. Such was the case when he was chopping wood behind the house. One day, he thought he heard his father coughing and stopped. But the coughing noise turned into multiple sounds that were more honking than coughing. It grew louder and he looked to the sky.

A great number of large birds were flying in a "V" formation overhead. He had never seen a sight like this or heard such noises. He ran inside to fetch his mother and father. They all stood in front of the house watching the passing of Canada geese heading south for the winter. As soon as the first group passed, the second group followed. They were captivated by the experience.

Thomas hobbled back into the house. His condition had deteriorated over the past several days. He laboured for his breaths and his chest hurt. Actually, pneumonia had set into his lungs, and Johanna did what she could to keep him warm in the house. In the evening, the family gathered around and said a rosary for his quick recovery. It was obvious his days were numbered, as everyone knew this episode was serious. Jerry and Lizzie made frequent visits to see him and the nieces stayed at the house and helped Johanna with cleaning, washing and making meals.

In October, amid the golden hues of the fall season, Johanna sensed the worst and gathered her two sons. Denis spent time with his father reading the Bible, while Jeremiah sat close by holding his father's hand. "Father, I have a passage to read for you," said Denis.

"What's that, son?" said Thomas in weak frail voice.

Denis recited the passage without looking at the Book. "Mark, chapter 12: 'The stone that the builders rejected has become the cornerstone'; Da, you are my cornerstone."

"Now son, don't get carried away," whispered Thomas.

"You need to know," said Denis, "you have always been my rock."

"Well, then," Thomas leaned in to make the point, "do the same for your children."

"I will," said Denis.

Thomas's breathing became shallower throughout the next hour as both sons sat with their father. Thomas, now in his weakened state, looked at his wife as she whispered "I love you," and let out that long exhale of air signifying his last breath. Thomas died with dignity in his new home with his family around him.

Johanna decided to bury Thomas on the family plot rather than carry his body into Scott's Plains for burial there. Denis and Jeremiah dug the grave as Johanna found white linen to wrap her beloved husband.

The following day Jerry performed a brief ceremony as Denis and Jeremiah lowered their father into the grave. Thomas's brother read from Psalm 106:

> "O give thanks unto the LORD, for he is good: for his mercy endureth for ever. Let the redeemed of the LORD say so, whom he hath redeemed from the hand of the enemy; And gathered them out of the lands, from the east,

> and from the west, from the north, and from the south. They wandered in the wilderness in a solitary way; they found no city to dwell in. Hungry and thirsty, their soul fainted in them. Then they cried unto the LORD in their trouble, and he delivered them out of their distresses."

"Thomas," he said, "was like the man on the journey wandering the wilderness, hungry and thirsty, looking to find a new home, meanwhile the Good Lord watched over this man and protected him. This parable is like Thomas's journey and voyage to Canada, and his distress is over." He ended the service with Psalm 22.

Elly stepped forward and sang the ancient Irish hymn *Be Thou My Vision*:

"Be Thou my vision, O Lord of my heart;
Naught be all else to me, save that Thou art.
Thou my best thought, by day or by night,
Waking or sleeping, Thy presence my light.

Be Thou my Wisdom, Thou my true Word;
I ever with Thee, Thou with me, Lord;
Thou my great Father, I thy true son;
Thou in me dwelling, and I with Thee one.

Be Thou my battle-shield, sword for my fight,
Be Thou my dignity, Thou my delight.
Thou my soul's shelter, Thou my high tower.
Raise Thou me heavenward, O Power of my power.

Riches I heed not, nor man's empty praise,
Thou mine inheritance, now and always:
Thou and Thou only, first in my heart,
High King of heaven, my Treasure Thou art.

High King of heaven, my victory won,
May I reach heaven's joys, O bright heav'ns Son!
Heart of my own heart, whatever befall,
Still be my vision, O ruler of all."

If observed properly, nature can be intuitive. Jerry looked up and about a hundred yards behind the house at the edge of the wood stood a ten-point deer. With his head held high, he watched the funeral service. Jerry nudged his wife, who alerted Johanna. The scene had a poignant effect on the family. The McCarthy family crest, handed down from the kings of Ireland, was the head of a stag. The kings had sent their farewell.

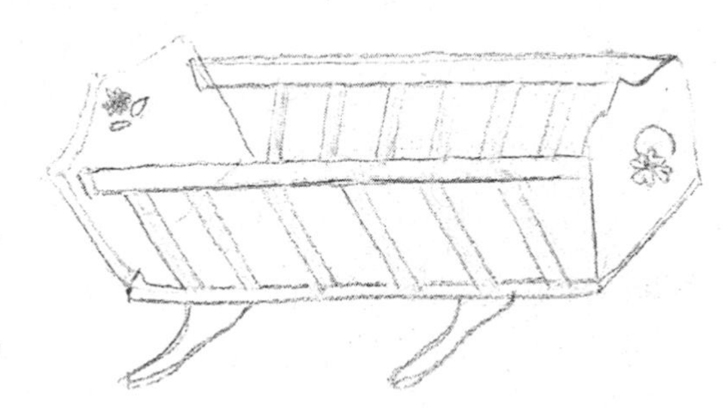

Chapter 10

The Sullivan Family
Scott's Plains

The Robinson Project depot in Scott's Plains in August had been busy with settlers going in and out as arrangements were made for each settler. Eighteen hundred seventy-eight people had made it to the interior of Canada—one hundred forty-six people lost their lives in the three-month journey from County Cork. Judith had entered the building to receive her assignment with Denis McCarthy and his parents and his Uncle Jerry.

Judith listened carefully as the McCarthys inspected available plots and made changes to their original assignment. Denis's father, Thomas, wanted land close to water because their homestead in Ireland was close to Courtmacsherry Bay. Close proximity to water was important to Thomas.

The final assignment that Judith agreed upon for herself and her family was on a hill overlooking Pigeon Lake, a neighbouring lake to the McCarthy homestead. She accepted the land from Mr. Robinson, but the maps and the land descriptions all sounded the same to her and she knew Edmond had much work ahead of him regardless of where they were assigned. Denis paid attention to the Sullivan plot because he knew Judith's interest in being close. He nodded approval when Mr. Robinson showed her the position on the map. As she left the cabin, Judith joined her family outside.

"We are going to live in a town called Emily."

"That sounds nice," said the six-year-old Johanna. "Where is Mr. McCarthy going to live?"

"Our home is on a hill overlooking a lake. Mr. McCarthy is going to live on the next lake over."

"Oh, that should be fun." Little Johanna did not consider the thickly forested land that needed to be cleared nor did she have the maturity to understand the work involved. She understood the fun of spending time with Mr. McCarthy and remembered the happy times by Lake Ontario during their waiting period; this arrangement sounded ideal.

Then she remembered her father. I wish my Da was here, she said to herself, and everything would be perfect. She wished Mr. McCarthy had met her father and the three of them could laugh together and go on adventures into the woods or go down by the lake to chase minnows at the water's edge.

She missed her father, his laughter, the gentle stroke of his hand running through her hair, his support of her crazy fantasies—but most of all, his loving way. Life was never the same for Johanna after her father's death, and Denis McCarthy eased that pain of missing her Da. Denis did not know how much she loved and needed him. If he did, he might have withdrawn his affection so as not to replace her father or interrupt her grieving. Johanna was very happy that Denis was settling close.

Here in the muddy street while waiting for directions to their next stop, Johanna experienced a sudden wave of melancholy over her departed father. She felt alone because no one else mentioned missing her father except her mother, Judith. She let go with a sudden rush of feelings. "I miss my Da."

Bess was the first to respond. "I do too. I was just thinking about him coming up the street here and wondered how he would like Upper Canada."

"So was I," interjected her older brother Denny, "this morning."

Judith just listened to her children voice their thoughts and recall their father. It made her miss him also, but this was their time to speak and she listened.

"Do you think Da would like the land, Ma?" asked Mary.

"I think so," said her mother, "but we have to think if it fits our ability to handle it."

"When are we going out to our new house?" asked Ellen.

"The house has not been built yet. We have to wait for them to clear the land and build our shanty, which may take a while because other settlers need their shanties built too."

The tiny quarters the shanties represented were designed only to get the family away from exposure to the weather.

'Where are we going to stay?" asked Bess.

"They have buildings here in town for those of us waiting."

"How many?" Bess wondered if Rose had made it to Scott's Plains or whether she continued with George wherever he was headed.

"I don't know how many are staying in the Government House, as they called it. Let's go see."

The Sullivans walked down Water Street to the corner of Simcoe Street, to the Government House that had been erected in the small town to serve as temporary housing. Two other buildings were still under construction: the roofs were intact, making the building weather-tight, but the interior walls for privacy had not been completed.

A market area had been established in the centre of town for the new businesses of this growing and expanding district, and it was full of partially built shops. Once again, tents were erected as temporary housing or businesses, as daily deliveries were increasing with the demand for more goods and materials. Near the river, a blacksmith shop and livery barn operated by Andrew Dennehy had served the area for the past two years. His shop was next to Adam Scott's sawmill and gristmill on Water Street; Adam Scott was the first to settle in the area and the town had been named for him. Mr. Scott was a big man with a strong back and a booming personality. He was the rugged frontiersman who knew the area and provided a resource for new arrivals.

Many families visited his shop to ask questions about the area and its land, as well as to hear the truth about rumours of the Indians and, of course, about the British. He enjoyed a good relationship with the Indians and the British and encouraged the settlers to do the same. The Irish came to appreciate their British benefactors who had removed them from their impoverished homeland and given them opportunities to improve their standard of living. Many settlers were vocal about their appreciation and let Mr. Robinson know the depth of their feelings.

The families of the Robinson Settlement worked hard once they arrived at Scott's Plains. Time moved quickly as they were now fighting the calendar; winter was approaching, and all the townspeople helped in the relocation project.

Judith settled her family in the Government House. Their assigned area was small, but they looked forward to the shelter, warmth and nourishment provided for them. All settlers supported the development of the area, including those living in the government houses. The women and older girls looked after the children, cooked and sewed clothes and blankets for the upcoming winter, while the men travelled throughout the district constructing shanties, delivering materials and clearing land. A small group of men had been assigned to design and build a bridge over the Otonabee River.

Once they settled in the Government House, Bess soon learned that Rose had settled in a room above the Sullivan family. Bess went up the stairs to visit her.

"Hi Rose, how was your trip up the river into town?"

"We made it," came the reply in typical laconic language that lacked further explanation.

"Where is George, who was with you?"

"Who?" remarked Rose sharply with an annoyed tone.

"George, the boy you left Kingston with on the boat."

"Oh, him. I don't know. He just carried my bags. He went to live with his parents somewhere."

"I thought he would stay around."

"I am pregnant with my husband's baby. Have you forgotten?" Rose was clearly annoyed at the thought of George.

"No, I haven't forgotten. Sorry," Bess sheepishly answered and then changed the subject. "We are living downstairs."

"How nice."

"If you need anything, stop down."

"Do I look like I need anything?" Even Rose realized the harshness of her tone, but an apology was out of the question.

"See ya." Bess said as she left and went back downstairs.

"How's Rose?" asked Judith.

"Miserable," was the lone report.

"Ah yes, a pregnant woman. It's her nature, being with child and all," her mother explained.

"She can be miserable all by herself."

Judith chuckled as the next generation learned the moods of maturity.

* * *

At the end of September, the Sullivan family attended Mass, as they did whenever the visiting priest was in town. After the service, Judith approached Denis, whom she spotted across the aisle.

"I was hoping the children could continue their lessons. You are such a good teacher and the children look forward to your classes."

"I'd be happy to help out but I will not be coming into town regularly—maybe once a week or once every two weeks."

"Yes, I see. You know I cannot pay you but I might be able to come up with some sort of compensation."

"Oh, what do you mean?"

"I was talking with Edmond—you know my son."

"Yes."

"And now that Sully has passed on, Lord bless his soul, we may not need all of those one hundred acres. The original grant of seventy acres is all we need and with the thirty additional acres, we can make a trade."

"I don't need more land."

"No, not a trade with you. Edmond thinks we can take ten acres of the additional thirty and make a barter with Joe Seaver for three mules. He said one of them was good for riding."

"I see, sounds like a good idea," said Denis.

Judith continued, "I will keep two of the mules for the farm and I will give you one in exchange for teaching the children."

"A mule? For teaching the children?" Denis thought the mule was an extravagant payment because his time spent teaching was enjoyable and hardly felt like work. A mule seemed like an overly valuable recompense for such a pleasurable job.

"Yes, if you could dedicate one day a week for the three little ones."

"Let me think a moment." Denis pondered the offer. At this time he was thinking about Máire and the two of them settling on the land. His parents had their one hundred acres. A mule would be helpful for ploughing and working the fields. Likewise, Johanna had encouraged Denis to use his talents for things other than farming, and a mule would give him transportation into town for the lessons. Mules had a long life expectancy, far beyond that of horses, so for Denis this arrangement was worth considering.

"I like your offer, but are the mules good and healthy?"

"Yes, Joe says the mules are good yearlings and Mr. Dennehy has agreed to examine them for me."

"Oh, you have checked this quite thoroughly."

"Yes, I wanted to make sure of these things before I talked with you."

"Well, if Mr. Dennehy decides the mule is healthy, we have a deal."

"Thank you, Denis. And one more thing: could you teach them in English and not Gaelic? Before you taught both ways but we have to leave the past and our old-world thinking. As we look forward, we must think about the new life we are giving the children and that means being educated in the English language and the Canadian ways."

"'Tis sad to give up the old and familiar," remarked Denis.

"Yes, but we need to look ahead. Everything here in Upper Canada is English. And there is too much sorrow to hang onto the old. The British people here are much kinder and treat us with respect and dignity. We have to find our way in a different world."

"Indeed, and English it is."

Ellen and Johanna ran up to Denis and gave him a hug. He explained with much enthusiasm that he was travelling to see Máire at her new settlement. The girls and Judith said to say hello to Máire for them.

"I will," said Denis.

"I will see you when I return," Denis informed them as he headed down the road towards Asphodel.

Word quickly spread to other families that Denis was tutoring and that he allowed other children to attend his classes. His success in teaching the children sparked the community to start a formal school the following year. Nevertheless, Denis continued to tutor the Sullivan children.

* * *

Denis was not seen in Scott's Plains for several days after the agreement was reached at the church. Judith thought Denis's absence was unusual. She had made arrangements for the barter of land for the mules and Denis's mule was waiting for him at Dennehy's livery. The second week Denis arrived.

"How was your trip to see Máire?" Judith asked.

"It didn't go well," Denis replied, an unusually short answer. This was the fateful trip where Máire refused Denis's proposal. The events of this day would have a profound effect on Denis and change his life as well as the lives of the Sullivan family—in particular Johanna.

"Oh," Judith said, and decided not to inquire further. It was after all, she felt, none of her business. "I have made the arrangement for your mule."

Denis's thoughts were elsewhere. "What mule? Oh yes, the mule. Of course."

"Denis, what's the matter?" He was forcing her to ask.

"Máire decided to marry someone else."

Judith understood an unexpected love loss. "I'm so sorry to hear about Máire." She touched his arm and added, "There will be others but it will take time." Denis just grunted to show he heard the words but did not necessarily believe another Máire would come along.

Of course Judith's thoughts considered her own daughters as likely future love interests—such as her oldest, Mary, or even possibly Bess. Denis was a fine gentleman and a good candidate for a Sullivan girl, but those thoughts were for the future, and nature would have to take its course.

"Come, I'll walk you over to Dennehy's livery."

Denis took a deep breath. Obviously his thoughts were still lingering on Máire. "All right, let's go," he finally said.

Andrew Dennehy's livery and blacksmith business was thriving with the influx of the settlers. The stable was filled with horses and mules and Denis looked around as Judith made the introduction to Andy, as he was known by the townspeople.

"You are getting a fine mule, Denis," started Andy as he led the year-old brown gelding out of his stall. "I've looked him over very carefully and he looks to be in good health and strong of body. His dam was a quarter horse so he should be good for riding."

Denis knew that mules were bred from a horse mare and a male donkey, and that many people felt the mixture was ideal and superior to a horse, especially for a working farm. A working mule is highly intelligent, requires less food, and is less prone to ailments than horses, besides living longer.

"I was hoping for a good riding mule," said Denis as he gently stroked the mule's nose. "He's a beautiful creature."

"He was a little rambunctious when he arrived, but you seem to have a gentle way with him," Andy said.

Denis walked the mule out of the livery stable and rubbed him with long strokes down the muscular legs, finally lifting the leg to examine his hooves. The mule allowed the examination without any fuss.

"You're a good horse man, Denis," remarked Andy.

"I have some experience with horses but not much."

Judith said, "He needs a name."

"Yes, he does." Denis looked him over and stroked the animal again. "I think he should be named after your husband. How about Sully?"

Judith winced at the statement. She was honoured in one sense but the name "Sully" had a reverence she wasn't willing to give up. "I don't know."

Denis sensed the reluctance. "How about Willy?"

"Sounds fine to me," she said with a smile.

Denis mounted the mule and walked him down the street, then returned to thank both Judith and Andy for the gift. Andy knew Denis's reputation for tutoring the children from Judith, and now that Andy had met the man who was not only gentle with children but gentle with mules as well a thought came to mind. "Denis, do you need work?"

"Why yes, of course."

"Do you want to work for me? I can use the extra help."

"Sure, I tutor the children once a week and I have to help my mother and brother with the settlement, but there are other days I can work."

"Good; how about two days a week?"

"Yes, that's fine."

"Your first pay will go towards a bridle and saddle."

"Deal."

* * *

Rose's pregnancy continued through the fall. As November approached she was quite large, and this limited her ability to move about. Bess made frequent trips up to Rose's room to help her bathe and make the small single room into living quarters ready for a baby. Edmond, who had good carpentry skills, fashioned a small cradle in his spare time and presented it to Rose.

"Thank you" is all Rose said, but her voice was soft with gratitude for his thoughtfulness. She rocked the tiny cradle as if the baby was already born.

In late November, the contractions began. Rose let out a yell that was heard throughout the Government House. Bess and Judith ran upstairs and pounded on Rose's door. During a brief reprieve from a contraction, Rose worked her way over to the door and let the two Sullivan women into her room. The three women worked into the night to make the birthing process as comfortable and safe as possible.

Then one major yell and "Ahhh" was heard throughout the building. Everyone knew a new Canadian was born as the sound of a baby's cry was heard. Shortly Bess stepped out into the hall and presented a new baby boy: "Meet Martin, Rose's son." The residents of the building expressed their joy and happiness with the newborn baby by laughing and sneaking looks at the tiny infant wrapped in a blanket Judith had made.

The next few weeks, Bess was a constant companion to Rose because Bess had had a great deal of experience with her younger brother and sisters. The aid she willingly gave Rose and Martin was a great benefit to Rose while she recuperated from her pregnancy and delivery. Winter had settled into Upper Canada and the immigrants were adjusting to the constant frigid temperature. The cold and the consequent limited activity allowed Bess to stay close to Rose and the baby. Rose joined the Sullivan family for their first Christmas in Canada and Martin's first Christmas ever. Because this was the first Christmas in the New World, all of Scott's Plains was joyfully celebrating this festive time of year.

On Christmas Day, Denis McCarthy rode Willy into town to deliver a special present to the children. The children eyed the brightly wrapped linen gift. "My mother made the wrap," he said. Ellen opened the gift to see a book of stories. They yelled with glee at the thought of new and fresh stories to last them the year. Even though the book was used, Denis was happy he was able to get it. "I had to order it from Kingston," he told the family.

He shared a glass of milk with a touch of nutmeg; spices were hard to get and eggnog was an unthinkable luxury. After the drink, he wished everyone a happy and holy Christmas and left to return home, a twelve-mile journey.

The trip home was lonely because few travellers were on the road for the holiday. As Denis rode north towards Smith Township, he sensed something behind him. He turned around expecting to see another rider coming up behind him, but instead he saw a wolf about fifty yards behind, with its distinctive bushy tail and yellowish-brown body with black fur along the top of the back. Denis scanned the area to the left and right but he saw no other animals.

Wolves move in packs, and it was unusual in this case for the other wolves not to show themselves, as they like to intimidate with their numbers and rarely hunt alone. Denis reached down and, with a reassuring hand, stroked Willy, who showed no sign yet of recognizing the danger. Denis maintained the same even pace because running would indicate fear and the wolf or wolves would run with them, waiting for the prey to exhaust itself. The wolf neither gained nor lost distance between them.

Denis approached the intersection of Smith Township, where he turned right to head east and watched to see if the wolf followed. As he approached the turn, a second wolf came into view from the west, as if he were stalking from the left flank. So there are at least two, he thought to himself. Denis made the turn as Willy looked back and recognized the additional company. The mule stopped. Unlike horses, mules are not prone to panic so it was not unusual for Willy to stop and assess the situation. Denis pulled the reins to the right, forcing Willy to turn and face the foe straight ahead. Willy did not object to this change. Two wolves against a man and mule did not frighten Denis; he knew Willy was strong, brave and protective. Even though he had no weapon, Denis was confident of the odds.

Then Denis heard a noise behind him and he became frightened, because a third wolf could change the dynamics of the situation. He slowly turned his head and looked over his shoulder. An older man on a horse was coming down the hill from the east. Denis was relieved and raised his hand in warning to the rider. The wolves stopped their advance and waited.

The man on the horse moved wide to Denis's right, creating a unified but spacious front. Out of his peripheral vision, Denis could tell the man was making movements on his horse but he didn't know what he was doing. He glanced quickly. The man had removed a black powder musket from a saddle holster and was loading. The long moments were tense as he waited. Again he reached down and stroked Willy, reassuring his partner that all was well. And then a blast from the gun pierced the silence.

The closest wolf went down and yelped, but immediately the animal jumped back up. Denis knew there was no time to lose while the man reloaded. He kicked Willy in the side and yelled, "Go." Willy responded and the two charged forward. The stunned and disoriented wolves turned and ran. One hobbled as he ran into the wooded thicket west of the roadway. Willy ran after the animals up to the edge of the shrub and stopped. Denis reached down and stroked him again: "Good boy."

He returned to the other rider. "Thank you; you came at the right moment."

"I hope they're gone because that's the direction I am going," the man said.

"I'll wait a few moments, if you like."

"No, I'm fine. I'll keep my musket loaded and ready. I don't like to shoot animals but they were on the prowl."

"I'm Denis McCarthy from up the Selwyn Road."

"Nice to meet you. I'm Michael Leahy from Douro, originally from County Cork."

"As I am—a Corker too. Merry Christmas." The two men bid farewell and each continued their Christmas journey.

* * *

The depths of winter set in as January brought continuous snow and deep frozen days, and eventually it rolled into February. During this time, Rose was troubled and distraught with indecision. Since the birth of Martin, she realized she was not ready for motherhood and lacked the knowledge to raise a child. Bess was a heaven-sent angel to help her through the first months.

Now, two formidable forces were pulling Rose in opposite directions. The decisions facing her had lifelong implications, not only for her but also for her son. Her first choice was to keep Martin and raise him by herself. But she realized she had limited capacity to take care of herself, let alone handle the responsibility of raising a baby: the thought was overwhelming.

Besides, growing up in a house with fighting, yelling and alcohol gave her few skills for developing a well-rounded child. The time she spent watching Bess and the Sullivan family showed her that parental guidance was a skill that she had not learned, but this was more than missing knowledge of child development. She lacked patience and was quick to anger, and her anger showed when she didn't even realize it. She blamed her parents and home life for forcing her to believe that life was better across the ocean.

She was angry with her husband for dying and leaving her alone. After going through the pregnancy and the pains of a delivery, life was not easier. She found life much more complicated, with far-reaching and more significant consequences. The sudden cry of young Martin who was looking for nourishment pierced her soul. To Rose, his voice was screaming to be freed of the doom she saw coming.

And that was the other dilemma she felt: how could she give Martin to another family to raise him? To let go of the life she created was counter to nature and she felt a tremendous sense of responsibility and connection to the child—far beyond all the other things she had let go, including her family in Ireland.

All logical sense told her to find Martin a home to be raised properly but her inner voice said "this boy is yours and yours alone." These thoughts tormented her and she had no one to confide in. Bess was too close and she always knew the right answer for herself, but these were significant dilemmas far beyond Bess's experience. Rose did not trust anyone else.

In early February, the muddy streets of Scott's Plains were frozen into solid dirt trenches left by wagon wheels and icy lumps of horse manure. Rose walked the streets with Martin in her arms. The rough, uneven roadway was a symbol to her of her quandary in facing her future. She looked for a sign.

Maybe some mother would run up to her and offer all the right answers and relieve her of her burden—but her anger seethed with each step. She found herself at the top of the hill where the new Catholic Church would soon be built. For a moment, her mind blamed the church for her troubles, but then she thought if she had been closer to the church, this situation might not have occurred. Then a third thought struck—I can give the Catholic Church my baby. She dismissed the thought quickly as too uncertain for Martin's future. They could send him back to Ireland—unthinkable.

She went to the Coleman household and knocked on the front door. Mr. Coleman was a businessman involved in banking and land deals who had settled in the area as part of the growing community.

"Oh Rose, come in," offered Mrs. Coleman, opening the large wooden door. Rose stepped in with Martin wrapped tightly in her arms. Mrs. Coleman continued, "The wind will chill your bones in a moment today. Now, how can I help you?"

"Is Mr. Coleman in?"

"Yes, I will call him. How is your baby doing?"

An innocent question, but the answer took some formulating. "He is fine, thank you."

Mrs. Coleman left the hallway and in a moment Mr. Coleman appeared. "Rose, a terrible day for you to be walking about."

"No trouble, sir. We must get used to these conditions."

"Ah yes. What can I do for you?"

"A while back you offered to buy my land. Are you still interested?"

"Yes, I would consider buying the land but you can't sell it yet. You have not taken possession of it."

"I will sign the deed giving you rightful ownership."

Mr. Coleman pondered the offer. "What do you want for the land?"

"What's fair?" Rose knew that Mr. Coleman was a shrewd businessman with a keen sense of a bargain, but he was also a trustworthy resident of Scott's Plains.

"I can give you fifty cents an acre. Fifty dollars for your land."

"Can you draw up the papers?"

Mr. Coleman was concerned. "Rose, what do you plan on doing?"

"I can't stand the cold. I am going to move south into America."

"You can't travel in the winter with the baby."

"We will be fine." The statement was troubling to Mr. Coleman—that a woman who did not like the cold would set out in the deepest part of the frozen Canadian winter and think it was no trouble for her or her baby.

"Your young baby can't travel at this time of the year," he repeated.

"He will be fine, we will be fine." Rose had an air of hardness, the one strength given to her by her family.

"Come and see me at the office tomorrow."

"Is it a deal then?" She wanted to know the answer now.

"Yes, I will talk with Mr. Robinson and draw up the papers."

Mr. Coleman knew the character of this project was against Rose's success and he believed Peter Robinson would allow her to sell her commitment of settling the land. Rose left the Coleman house resolved that a partial decision had been made. The decision was to leave Scott's Plains.

* * *

The next morning Rose went to Mr. Coleman's office to finish the deal. All the arrangements had been made to sign the papers, and Mr. Robinson was there.

"Good morning, Rose," Peter greeted her.

"Oh, Mr. Robinson, I didn't know you would be here," said a surprised Rose.

"Rose, I understand your situation in dealing with a young child settling on undeveloped land in the cold north. I am willing to release you from your obligation."

"Thank you," said Rose. "You're right, it will be too difficult."

"You can stay in Scott's Plains until spring thaw," he added.

"I will consider the thought, especially after this morning's temperature dipped below zero degrees. It's pretty cold out there," Rose said with a smile, her first open positive expression in recent weeks.

"You are getting a pretty good deal, Mr. Coleman—one hundred acres for fifty dollars," said Mr. Robinson.

"Yes, and I get the cow and feed, right?" asked Mr. Coleman, testing Peter.

"No, you are not a settler, so you will not be getting anything additional," said a firm Peter Robinson.

"I just thought I would ask," finished Mr. Coleman.

Rose left the meeting energized by having the burden of developing farmland lifted from her shoulders. She tucked the blanket tight around Martin and walked home with fifty dollars in her pocket. She felt rich.

Rose had to work fast. The town would soon hear of the land sale and know she was holding a large sum of money. Even though these were good people, Rose's experience told her that people had evil in their hearts, especially when it came to money. Rose had a plan. She knew the stage's schedule, and today it was leaving town for York and going on to Buffalo. She returned to her room and bundled her belongings. One more item needed to be taken care of before leaving, so she took Martin downstairs to Bess.

"Bess, can you take care of Martin? I need to do something right away."

"Sure," an enthusiastic Bess replied as she took the baby, still bundled from the trip outside. Rose returned upstairs and grabbed her belongings.

"Thanks, Bess," yelled Rose as she ran out the door and headed down Water Street, with her belongings wrapped tight in a blanket held in her arms the way she always carried Martin.

"I need a ticket to Buffalo," she told the agent at the freight office.

"Here you are, madam," the agent said as he handed her the ticket.

Once outside, Rose saw Ellen, Johanna, John and Mr. McCarthy pass after leaving their day's schooling. "We are leaving," she informed the group as she pulled the wrapping close to her breast. She leaned down to Ellen. "Tell Bess thank you for everything and for being a good friend."

Rose boarded the stage and the driver slapped the reins as the coach jumped forward. She looked out the window at Martin's future aunts and uncles. A tear rolled down her face as she made one final wave to the group and the coach rolled west towards York.

Denis and the children walked home as they normally did—in a playful manner. Today they rolled the snow into small balls and threw them at each other. They yelled with glee as the cold snow struck and dribbled across an exposed cheek. They picked up more snow and rolled it in their hands, hoping to return the chilly favour.

They arrived home and Denis walked them into the house. All four were surprised to see Martin sleeping in a makeshift crib.

Denis explained, "We saw Rose and Martin getting on the stage coach at the freight station."

"No, Martin is right here," said Bess.

"But she had the baby wrapped up in a blanket," said Denis. "I guess baby Martin was not in the blanket. Rose left without her son."

Ellen turned to her older sister Bess. "Rose said thank you for being a good friend."

Denis interjected, "Rose wanted you to have, and raise, the baby."

* * *

Once again, Judith did not miss a beat, even though her daughter had just been burdened with the greatest responsibility in life. "You will raise him as your own."

From that day forward, Martin was a Sullivan. He was accepted as if born to Bess and he was loved and raised in the Sullivan fashion. Every fibre in his personality was developed to the Sullivan standard, just as Rose had hoped. Bess did not hide from Martin the fact that he was adopted into the family but it did not matter to either of them. She was his mother and he was her son. Bess loved him unconditionally until her death.

Martin would become a man proud of his Sullivan heritage. All the important elements of adulthood were passed down to him through the years of his Sullivan upbringing, in the same way as to any other family member. Rose, with all her dilemmas, troubles and sadness, had performed the greatest act of love for her son.

Chapter 11

The Sullivan Family
Emily Township

The townspeople of Scott's Plains could not wait until spring of 1826, which they greeted with great anticipation. For some of the Robinson settlers, this was the first time they would plant fresh crops in the New World; for others, like the Sullivan family, preparations were still being made for settling into their new homestead. Even now others were still fighting the fever that maintained its grip on the settlers, especially those in close quarters at Scott's Plains.

The government houses were a breeding ground for the diseases and, in spite of all the precautions taken and improved nutrition, people continued to get sick and die. Cold and influenza were common and often confused with the fever. Judith kept the children clean, fed and isolated in their room as much as she could, and thus far it had kept the fever away even though they experienced a couple of scary episodes of the flu.

Through this time, the Sullivan children were as tolerant of each other as possible in the tight quarters in Scott's Plains Government House, but impatience and minor aggravations were plunging the close-knit family into daily skirmishes. The seven children, along with newborn Martin, needed room to let their energies loose.

As the snow and ice melted, the children ran through the streets mingling with the other youngsters, and after six months of good and steady nourishment their energy level was high. People were anxious to be outdoors after hibernating and adjusting to their first frigid

Canadian winter. Now spring warmed the temperature and invigorated the spirit of children and adults alike.

* * *

Edmond and his younger brother, Denny Sullivan, were gone most of the spring and into the summer as they helped build their shanty and prepare their land. As the project was ending with the roof construction, Edmond split cedar strips into shingles and passed them up onto the roof to Denny, who nailed them down. The settlement schedule proceeded quickly as the men of the district became experienced in the systematic process of cutting, clearing, milling and constructing farms.

The whole village bustled with activity. The noise from most blacksmith shops consisted of the tink, tink, tink of hammers striking iron. However, from Andrew Dennehy's shop came different noises, of loud voices and laughter, just as often as hammer strikes.

The two men Andy Dennehy and Denis McCarthy possessed the typical Irish wit and saw life with all its oddities in a droll and humorous way. They were likeable and friendly, and the townspeople gravitated to the shop to chat and catch up on news each day with these two intelligent, hard-working, funny men who could turn to the serious in a moment. Pat Collins, the barman at Collins' Pub, wanted to move the bar into the livery to keep his customers.

The talk of the town during these days was the completion of the Erie Canal through New York State, which was just across Lake Ontario. People marvelled at the engineering of an inland waterway that could carry freight and people to the western frontier, or back the other way to Albany and on to New York City. Upper Canada was also designing a canal system that would carry goods through the Scott's Plains area, connecting the many lakes and rivers of Upper Canada. The Canadian interest was high, as they watched closely to see if the American adventure was feasible or not.

* * *

Each day Judith walked down to the settlement office building and checked the progress of the construction of the farm. She did not harass anyone, but Mr. Robinson was well aware of her anxiety about moving onto her land.

On Wednesdays, the only day available that Denis did not work at the blacksmith shop, he made visits to the Government House and tutored the three young Sullivan children. Ellen, who was now ten years old, was learning rapidly and reading books independently of Denis's instruction, and stopped only to describe the story or tell a funny anecdote. Occasionally she became stuck on a word and Denis helped her with the pronunciation and meaning.

Seven-year-old Johanna was still learning simple words and a basic sentence structure using good grammar. Little John was developing a command of words and their meaning, along with the social concepts of sharing a toy, sharing attention, and the basics of good behaviour. Johanna showed her motherly instincts by practising her reading and showing John letters of the alphabet in the story.

Time was set aside during each visit for Denis to tell a story or read a passage from a book. Many times he picked a favourite story from the New Testament and they discussed the account. It was important to Denis that they know the story but not necessarily the significance of the lesson behind it. As their parent, Judith could teach the moral meaning, which she often took time to explain.

The balanced system between Judith and Denis worked effectively, as the joy of the story could be learned first and then retold and shared by the children with their mother, who followed up with real-life examples. Their education was lively, and many of the examples came from lessons learned during the voyage across the ocean, with many people, young and old, crammed together and under high stress. The examples it provided were plentiful, regarding life, death and human behaviour.

In early July, Judith received word that the house was ready and she made preparations for the move with her family. The Sullivan household bid its farewell to the remaining families in the Government

House as they prepared the wagon with their belongings. Martin's small crib was loaded and Bess climbed on the front bench seat with Martin in her arms. She had responded well to being thrust into motherhood. Even though Martin had been left with Bess, Judith and the oldest sister, Mary, shared the feeding times with her for the now eight-month-old child.

Peter Robinson came out of his office to say his goodbye to the departing Mrs. Sullivan and her family. He promised he would soon visit them in the new homestead in Emily Township and make sure they had the necessary provisions to start their new life.

"Mr. Robinson, thank you for all the work that you have done for me and all of us," Judith said.

"You are welcome," was his humble reply. "You are the future of this country; it's important that you succeed."

"You are a good man." Judith was not only expressing her personal sentiments but the appreciation of all the settlers as well. Peter Robinson had taken extraordinary measures to make the project successful for the British government and also the Irish settlers. He did have a problem, though, with the British government: he overspent his allotted budget. But the settlers were the beneficiaries of the miscalculations of cost. He meticulously recorded his spending and accounted for every dollar, but the conditions, medicines and necessary expenses went over the limit.

To the people, he was a hero and rescuer from a famine disaster—so much so that the name of Scott's Plains was changed to Peterborough in his honour later in 1826.

Denis McCarthy left the blacksmith shop and livery barn and walked up Water Street to the Government House to wish the Sullivan family well as they settled into their new home. He told Judith, "I will be out to see you and the children soon. Will you be all right on the homestead?"

"Of course," said Judith. "I am not a helpless individual, you know," she said with a grin.

"Indeed you're not," acknowledged Denis.

Edmond came around the edge of the wagon to say goodbye.

"Goodbye," said Denis. "If you need help with anything, let me know."

"I will."

Ellen and Johanna were standing there behind their brother waiting for their turn to see Denis.

"You take care of your mother," Denis said to the girls.

"I will," said Johanna quickly.

"Oh Denis," said Ellen next, "you know mother has to take of us."

"Oh yes, but you can help."

"We will," acknowledged Ellen.

The wagon left town heading north towards Smith Township, the same road Denis McCarthy used daily to come and go from town. About two miles out of town, the wagon reached the Lindsey Road and turned left off of Denis's route, and headed to Emily Township. Edmond led the family as he and his brother had made the trip several times during the construction.

They headed around the southern edge of Pigeon Lake and up the grade to their new homestead. Once there, Judith, the older girls and the young children realized the magnitude of their endeavour. The land was cleared but a feeling of isolation was everywhere.

Edmond took the lead. "Ma, while we were working on the house, we also planted a few crops. Here we have some corn and over here we have potatoes." Weeds had already begun to encroach on the crop, and immediately Judith sized up the work needed.

"I'll have Mary and Ellen start the weeding tomorrow."

"Good," said Edmond. "Over there is the pasture for the cow, which should be coming this week or next."

"I see." Judith was starting to get the feel of the farm and envision its layout, which made her more comfortable with the land. Suddenly there was an eerie, rapid cry in the distance. Judith looked up in concern and wonder. John and the other children bristled and shook in surprise.

Edmond smiled. "That's a loon. We have heard them during the day and through the night."

The loon let out a second cry. This time it was a long haunting wail as if part of a sad song. "Oh my," said Judith.

"Actually it's quite comforting to listen to at night. Denny and I have been down to the lake and the loons are beautiful black and white birds. They disappear under the water for a minute or two and then pop up several hundred feet from where they started. They are fun to watch."

"Can we go watch?" asked Johanna.

"Not right now," said Judith. "Maybe later Edmond can take you to the lake." The loons let out another wail as if calling the newcomers to come and visit—but in reality they wanted people to stay away. They were recluse waterfowl.

The house sat on a hill above the lake; however, they could not see the lake because the thick evergreen trees made the view impossible. The various lots and farms between them and the water's edge added to the isolated feeling, but families were filling in and settling the area and neighbours were closer than they realized.

* * *

The next day, Denis McCarthy came by the new house with Willy, his faithful mule. Even though he knew they were still settling into the house, Judith appreciated the break for the children. "I didn't realize you were on such a sharp hill," Denis told Judith as he looked over the land.

"Yes, but not so sharp that we cannot farm. Our farm back in Kilworth was on a hill, which gave us good drainage for the crops."

"True, our home in Abbeymahon was on a hill too."

The three small children ran out and wanted to take Denis down the hill to the lake. He looked at Judith for an answer.

"Sure," she said.

"All right, let's go," he announced to his eager pupils. The trip to the lake was the start of a new era for the teacher and students. The children had matured in their learning and ability, and Denis relaxed into a routine involving the natural world, the literary world and social fun.

The new village of Peterborough was starting a school after the fall harvest and Denis encouraged Judith to enroll Ellen and Johanna. Judith was reluctant because of the relationship Denis had established with her children but he convinced her that his talent, resources and time were limited. He promised to continue tutoring with the youngest son, John, until he was ready for regular school. Judith wanted her young boy to be well educated and, if possible, she secretly wanted him to become a priest. Denis and his style of teaching were perfect for her plan.

* * *

During the next several years working the land became a routine for all the settlers as they established themselves within the region. This end result of their journey was the success they were looking for, but came at great cost to health and life. The families improved the conditions from which they had come even though for many that meant hardship and loss. Now, the farms were productive, and more tillable land was cleared as part of the one-hundred-acre parcels. Morale, hope, health and prosperity all flourished as each season progressed.

Denis still made frequent trips to the Sullivan farm even after little John had started school. During a trip he made in 1828, he found Ellen tutoring Johanna with her reading.

"What types of books are you reading?" he asked.

"Whatever we can get from town," said Ellen. "Mostly stories about the lives of the saints."

"I like fairy tales," interjected Johanna, who was now nine years old.

"I see, and I am not surprised you like the fairy tales, Johanna," said Denis. "So I have a gift for you." He reached into his pocket and pulled out a book. It was the Grimm Brothers' book,

Tales of Children and the Home, given to Denis by Captain Morrison. "Here; I want you to have this."

"Oh no, we couldn't take that book," said Ellen. "That's your book you used to read to us from."

"Yes," said Denis. "And now I don't need it. I have read it many times over and I know nearly every story in my mind. I want you to have it here for your reading."

Johanna took the book, opened it, randomly picked a story, and started reading aloud, struggling with a few words, with which Ellen helped her:

> "There were once two brothers who both served as soldiers; one of them was rich, and the other poor. Then the poor one, to escape from his poverty, put off his soldier's coat, and turned farmer. He dug and hoed his bit of land, and sowed it with turnip-seed. The seed came up, and one turnip grew there which became large and vigorous, and visibly grew bigger and bigger, and seemed as if it would never stop growing, so that it might have been called the princess of turnips, for never was such an one seen before, and never will such an one be seen again."

Johanna stopped reading and looked up. "I'll finish reading it later. Thank you for the book."

"I can see you will put it to good use," said Denis.

Six-year-old John said to his sister, "Can you finish the story?"

"I will in a few minutes," said Johanna, looking at Denis as an acknowledgement of the value of his gift.

"I will leave you with your stories," said Denis.

He rose to leave the Sullivan house and Judith came over to thank him again.

"Denis, I appreciate all that you have done for the children. They will get many happy hours from the book. Thank you."

"It is my pleasure to share the book," he said, then left. Such was his style—to make short visits to check on his pupils and the Sullivan family.

* * *

In mid-1830 after Johanna had turned eleven years old, she noticed a change in her older sister Ellen, who was now fourteen. The change was first noticeable when secretive and mysterious conversations were taking place between Ellen and her mother during walks and other private conferences. Johanna waited for her sister to confide in her but after several weeks of waiting, her seemingly best friend did not divulge the topic of discussion. Johanna's next approach was to ask, "Ellen, what's going on? You and Ma are discussing something; what is it?"

"Oh nothing," was Ellen's curt reply.

"Nothing? It has to be something because it happens all the time."

"No, really it's nothing, just Ma and me talking," said Ellen.

Johanna let the subject go, knowing that if it was anything important she would find out soon enough, but then her sister's behaviour changed, too. She withdrew within herself and spent time alone either at the top of the hill with a view of the lake, but with hardly a glance in the direction of its picturesque view, or walking down to the roadway where a small bridge carried the feeder stream to Pigeon Lake. The stream carried tiny twigs and small bugs floating on top for minnows to snatch as eight-inch-deep water meandered under the simple two-plank bridge.

The location had no particular appeal except the serenity of an empty roadway with an occasional farmer or family travelling by. On this one occasion, Johanna followed Ellen to the bridge, where her sister sat on the bridge, removed her well-worn shoes that had been in the family for over ten years, dipped her feet in the water, and sat for over an hour just swaying her feet in the cool water.

Johanna could see that she was mumbling to herself but could not make out the words until she saw the rosary beads in her hand;

then she knew her sister was praying. Johanna watched from a distance down the road. Finally Ellen said aloud, "I know you are there, Johanna."

"I was wondering what you were doing," Johanna said.

"I'm spending time alone."

"I see that," said Johanna, as she walked closer and tried to find a spot to sit next to her sister, but the small bridge was not wide enough for the two sisters to sit side by side. She brushed away a clump of weeds at the edge and sat down. "You are acting so mysteriously."

"I'm thinking," said Ellen.

"About what?" asked Johanna.

"My future and what I should do."

"About what?" repeated Johanna, pressing further.

"Oh, I don't know."

"There you go again being mysterious and evasive," observed Johanna.

"Well, if I had an answer," Ellen's voice was sharp, "I'd give it to you but I don't, so are you happy now?"

"Sorry." Johanna let the conversation rest. After a few minutes Johanna restarted the talk. "Is Ma helping you?" Johanna thought she would add a little more to the question: "Is Ma helping you decide your future?"

"Why are you so nosy about what I'm doing?" chided Ellen.

The question clearly told Johanna to leave her sister alone. "No reason, I guess."

Johanna waited a minute in silence and then rose from the weeds. She looked at Ellen, who sat stoically watching the flow of the minute tributary of Pigeon Lake. Johanna turned and walked up the roadway towards her home.

The encounter with Ellen at the stream signalled a change in the development of the girls. The three-year difference in age was now apparent. Ellen was facing a decision of significant burden and Johanna realized their youthful frolicking had transformed into consequential decisions. Johanna was still too young to understand the growth and maturing process but aware enough to see the effects.

A week later, Judith announced that she and Ellen were going into Peterborough the next day. Normally, such a journey was undertaken with great planning to determine supplies and other incidentals to make the time and effort of the trip most efficient. However, the statement was a surprise and no offer was made for the others to join the excursion. Johanna asked her mother, "Why are you going to Peterborough?"

"Ellen and I need to make this trip together, that's all."

The secrecy was continuing, and it bothered Johanna, because usually this family openly discussed topics within the house, but Judith's deflection and Ellen's refusal to discuss her apparent problem was discomforting to the entire household. However, Ellen gave a hint when she asked her mother, "Are you sure Father Crowley will be there?"

Judith was more cautious but answered the question, "Yes, I'm sure he will be there."

The next morning, Judith gave final instructions to the effect that Bess was in charge, even though all knew that Bess, now twenty years old and with strong motherly habits from raising her five-year-old son Martin, had always been in charge. Denny brought the wagon hitched with their two mules from the small barn in back of the house as Ellen flipped a travel bag into the back of the wagon. The bag contained sandwiches and two sweaters for the trip.

"No shenanigans while I'm gone," Judith said, but her eyes fixed on the young ones, starting with Johanna.

"Yes, Mother," answered Johanna for the group.

Judith slapped the reins, giving the unconventional order to the mules: "All right, let's go." The wagon jerked ahead and headed south along the road for their three-hour journey into Peterborough.

As soon as the wagon was out of sight, Johanna turned to Bess. "Why are they going to Peterborough?"

"I don't know, she didn't say," replied Bess. "It must be important though, to leave so suddenly."

"Why is everything such a mystery?" asked Johanna.

"We will find out in due time," said Bess, taking Martin's hand and leading him back into the house to finish his oatmeal and maple syrup breakfast. Johanna joined them at the table and sliced a piece of bread. She took the knife and dipped it into a bowl of butter just churned that morning by Bess, and watched her sister work in the kitchen. Johanna leaned back in the chair and looked at Martin, who was eating the oatmeal as fast as he could before it could disappear from some food snatcher.

"Now Martin, slow down," said Bess. "You'll get a tummy-ache if you eat too fast."

Martin did not reply; he just looked up at his mother and then glanced over at his Aunt Johanna to see who was watching. He set the spoon down for a moment and then picked it up again for another large scoop. Bess shook her head at the short attention span of a five-year-old. Johanna broke off a piece of bread and tossed it into her mouth. Martin giggled because he apparently had a comrade in bad eating habits. Bess, whose back was to the table, said, "Johanna, be a good example to the young ones."

"You sound like Mother," said Johanna. "And you can see with the eyes in the back of your head like Mother, too."

"It's not hard," said Bess, leaving the secret parent trickery out of the explanation.

Johanna was impressed with Bess and her loving way with Martin. She watched her take a towel and gently wipe Martin's face and then, still holding his cheeks, examine his face, move his head down, checking his hair for lice, and finally, peer into his ears for cleanliness. "Today we will have a bath," she said.

"Oh, do we have to?" protested Martin.

"Yes, we have to," she said firmly.

After a moment of watching the gentleness mixed with the firmness of Bess's style, Johanna said aloud, "You're a good mother, Bess."

"Thanks. Your time will come too, and I'm sure you'll do fine as well."

"When that happens, will you come over and show me?" asked Johanna.

Bess laughed. "There will be no need, you'll know what to do."

"Well, I want to do it as good as you."

"We will talk when you're ready, but that's a long time away," said Bess.

"And you'll have to show me that 'eyes in the back of your head' trick too," added Johanna.

"Sure," laughed Bess.

* * *

The wagon carrying Ellen and Judith arrived mid-morning at the Government House in Peterborough. Father Crowley was waiting for them, as he knew they were coming from a parishioner who had been the liaison between them.

"Good morning, Judith," greeted the elderly priest.

"Good morning, Father," she replied.

The priest turned to Ellen. "And how are you, my child?"

"Very good, Father," said Ellen, nervous at meeting the priest and becoming the focus of an adult conversation.

"Come in and sit down," directed the priest, who had made arrangements to use the office in the Government House for such meetings. "So, tell me what's on your mind."

Judith started, "Father, Ellen has . . ."

The priest waved her off. "Let her tell me. I am interested in her telling the story."

"Yes, of course, Father," said Judith.

Ellen sat up in the chair and cleared her throat before beginning. "Father, I have been thinking and praying," emphasizing the praying piece.

"Yes, go ahead, dear," said the priest.

"I have been thinking about becoming a nun. I think I can do good service as a sister."

"I see," acknowledged Father Crowley. "Keep going."

"I don't know what to say other than I can read and write and maybe someday teach."

"Many young girls know how to read and write and they also raise and teach children. Those are mothers, like your mother here. Why is it that you what to enter a convent and serve the Lord as a sister?"

"I guess it's because I have always admired St. Brigid."

"Oh yes, St. Brigid, a truly great saint."

"Yes, Father, and she helped the poor and cared for the sick. I think I can do that too."

"Judith, what are your thoughts?" the priest said, indicating it was time for her to speak.

"Father, I am very proud of my daughter but I cannot afford to, and do not even want to, send her back to Ireland to enter a convent."

"There are convents on this side of the ocean. I am aware of a fine women's academy and Ursuline Convent in Boston run by Father Thayer. There is another Ursuline Convent in Quebec but they are mostly French speaking. Do you know French?"

"No, Father," said Ellen.

"Well, that wouldn't work," he agreed.

"Do they care for the sick?" asked Ellen.

"No, they mostly teach young girls," said Father Crowley.

"I see," said Ellen. "I am not sure whether I want to teach or help the sick."

"Those are very different vocations; therefore, your training would be very different. Likewise, your choice will affect which of the order of nuns to enter."

"I understand. Do I have to choose now?" asked Ellen.

"No, I don't think you're ready for that. You go home with your mother and think about how you want to serve the Lord and his people. Pray daily for inspiration."

"Yes, Father," said Ellen.

"Thank you for your help, Father," said Judith.

"I will check for other orders in Upper Canada that may serve your calling," he said to Ellen. He ended the conversation with, "We will talk soon. Goodbye."

Judith and Ellen left the Government House. Once out in the street, Judith un-tethered the mules and asked, "What do you think about your vocation choices?"

"It's hard to figure out whether to help the sick or teach."

"Remember, you have three choices: help the sick, teach, or live your faith through marriage and children. Ellen, I think you would be happy with any of the three."

They walked a few steps leading the mule-team down the street, and Judith added, "Let's go see if Mr. McCarthy is at the livery."

"Should we talk to him about my dilemma?" asked Ellen.

"The decision whether to enter the convent or not is your decision. I think Father Crowley gave us some thoughts about determining your vocation and I think we should keep this decision in the family."

"All right," said Ellen, as the two Sullivans walked the team to the livery.

"Hello," said Judith as they entered and saw Denis.

"Hello," replied Denis, as he set his hammer down.

"Hi," yelled Andy from the back as he continued to pound an iron piece on the anvil.

"We were in town and stopped to say hi," said Judith.

"Good, glad you did," said Denis as he lifted each of the mule's feet and examined them. "The team could use a little cleaning and scraping," said Denis. Without waiting for an answer, he grabbed his blacksmith tongs and pulled the nails from the first hoof. "What brings you into Peterborough?"

Ellen remained silent but Judith took the lead. "We had to conduct a little business today."

"Oh," said Denis. He looked up because of the short uninformative answer and gave a lack-of-understanding look.

Judith knew she was being evasive. "And we saw Father Crowley."

"Ahh," said Denis, knowing that matters of religion were personal. He took a file and started scraping the hoof. "How's the rest of the family?"

"All are doing well, and getting older, you know. They are trying to decide how to live their lives," added Judith.

"Oh, yes, indeed," said Denis. "You never know where you might end up. Look at me. I thought I was going to be farmer and here I am working as a farrier."

"And a good one at that," yelled Andy from the back.

"Mind your hammering," yelled Denis back at his boss, and then he looked at Ellen and as if prompted to the thought asked, "What special things are you thinking of doing?"

"Oh, I don't know," said Ellen, looking up at her mother, trying to figure out how far to pursue the conversation with her tutor, who knew her quite well.

"She's young," interjected Judith. "Like you said, those decisions can change down the road."

"Yes, they can," said Denis, "but Ellen is very smart and disciplined. I always thought she would make a good teacher. And we need good Catholic teachers here in town."

Ellen smiled at the man who had a great impact on her development; now the statement would weigh heavily in her decision. Judith also knew the gravity of Denis's statement and tried to temper the unsolicited comment. "She's not sure how she will serve the Lord."

"Oh," said Denis. In his mind, Denis made the immediate connection of serving the Lord and the visit to Father Crowley. "I see. I wish you luck in deciding."

Even though Denis was outside the family circle, Judith always appreciated his connection to the family and his contribution to the good of her children. The dilemma with Ellen was a secret guarded from the rest of the family because of the sizeable impact the decision would have if she were to leave the household.

Judith wanted Ellen to have a clearer direction before informing her siblings and having them add their opinions. To announce the dilemma to Denis before others in the family was contrary to Judith's view of family structure and dynamics. She knew he would find out in due time, as all the family would.

Denis finished shoeing the mules and said, "There you go; have a good journey home."

"Thank you, Denis. You are always a great help to us," said Judith.

"No thanks needed," replied Denis.

Judith and Ellen headed north towards their home in the Township of Emily and rounded the west side of Pigeon Lake as the sun set on the western horizon. They headed up the hill as dusk was setting in.

John, the eight-year-old, was the first to welcome them home. "Guess what Johanna did?" were his first words.

"I don't want to hear any tattling," said Judith.

"She broke the handle off the barn," John reported anyway.

"Oh that old thing, it was going to break anyway," said Judith.

"Yeah, but then she threw it at me and told me not to tell," he continued.

"And you told anyhow," Judith persisted.

"Well, it could've hit me and that would've hurt me."

"Go play, John, while I unhitch the wagon." Judith said, dismissing the report of the irresponsible and near-fatal behaviour.

Denny came out of the barn. "I've got the wagon, Ma, and don't worry about the handle. I fixed it."

"Thanks, Denny," said Judith, realizing that order had been maintained in her absence.

Judith entered the house and Johanna immediately said, "I broke the handle on the barn."

"Yes, I know, and it's fixed. And I also know John almost got hit with it."

"No, he didn't. I threw the handle into the fire pit. He just thought I threw it at *him*. It was nowhere near hitting him."

"All right, leave it alone," said the exhausted Judith.

"How was your trip?" asked Johanna, looking at both Judith and Ellen for a reply.

"It was all right," said Ellen. Judith sat down in the chair and let out a long breath, with no intention of adding to Ellen's report on the trip. After waiting for a reply and not receiving one, Johanna shrugged her shoulders and went out the door to help Denny in the barn.

Now just Bess, Martin, Ellen and Judith remained in the house. "Are you going to tell us what this trip was all about?" asked Bess.

"I'm too tired tonight," said Judith. "Tomorrow we will have a family meeting."

The following morning, the children rose to their chores and kept busy through the first half of the day. Around noon, when the children gathered for their noon meal, Judith approached the mysterious subject they had waited to hear. "Ellen and I went to see Father Crowley yesterday."

They all listened with anticipation for the news.

"Ellen has been contemplating entering a convent."

"Oh!" said Johanna, surprised at the topic of concern.

"We went to discuss whether this is the right decision and if so, what order of nuns is available to her."

"Wow," said Bess. "That would be something—to have a nun in the family."

"Yes, it would, but only for the right person. Ellen has to decide if this is right for her."

"You're going to let her decide for herself?" Denny asked his mother. "Mary Cannon's parents *told* her she was going to be a nun."

"Yes, well, Ellen has to decide this question, but it does not have to be decided right now. She has time to think about it. And I don't want any of you putting unnecessary pressure on her, either."

"Yeah, like Mary Cannon's parents did," added Denny.

"Mary went to the convent because you liked her, that's why. I'd go into the convent too," smirked Johanna.

"All right," said Judith, "enough of that." And then she added, "That's why I want you to keep your opinions to yourself."

Later in the afternoon, Johanna found Ellen in the field harvesting beans off the vine and filling two baskets. "Have you made any decisions about going into a convent?" she asked her sister.

"No, I have not decided. I was thinking of bringing God's grace to the sick or teaching young girls in a school. I don't know which, or if either of them is right for me."

Johanna noted the difficulty of Ellen's thoughts. "I know this must be hard for you because you normally make quick, sound decisions."

"This is not easy," agreed Ellen.

"I know Ma told us to keep our opinions to ourselves, but do you want to hear what I think?" asked Johanna.

"Yes, of course."

"First of all, if this is causing too much confusion then it must not be right. Usually a vocation is a clear calling from God. You just do it."

"I suppose," said Ellen thoughtfully.

"Secondly, I don't want you to go. I will miss you too much," said a sombre Johanna.

"Oh, Johanna, you always have a flair for the dramatic," said Ellen, letting her hands float through the air. "You'll be fine. You are outgoing, energetic, make friends easily and are fun for everyone. I am not worried about you." Ellen hesitated for a moment, "I am worried about Mother."

"Mother?" said Johanna. "She can handle herself. Do you remember when Da died? She was devastated and carried on."

"Mother is going to miss us when we're gone and if I go into a convent, I can't come home whenever she needs me." Then Ellen added, "Or if she needs any of us and we're grown and gone."

"*Now you* have the flair for the dramatic. The rest of us are here to take care of her and we're not going anywhere," said Johanna.

"Well, I am going to think this through and I think you're right, a vocation should be a clear calling. And where did you come up with that thought?"

"That's what Father Crowley always said: 'You'll get a clear calling from God.' He hasn't called me, I know that," Johanna said flippantly.

"Don't be sacrilegious," warned Ellen.

"I won't," replied Johanna.

The two girls continued to pick beans from the row in the garden. Johanna thought of her sister's ability to become a nun. She had patience and ordered thinking, which made her an excellent candidate to be a nun. But she also felt closest to Ellen, and her absence in the household would have a dire effect on Johanna. Ellen was her trusted friend and companion, even though they had opposite personalities. Johanna would be lonely without her big sister.

* * *

During the formative adolescent years, Johanna lived a normal teenage life for that period. However, her activities were severely limited in the summer of 1832.

It started on a warm day in May. After chores were completed in late afternoon to prepare the vegetable garden, the four children, Ellen, Johanna, John and Martin, were hot and sweaty. They decided to head down to the lake and go swimming to cool off. As they approached their favourite swimming spot, the ever-exuberant Johanna took the lead in a dash to grab the rope swing hanging on the black cherry branch overhanging the lake.

Denny had fashioned the swing about five years earlier, when he climbed the tree and attached a manila strand rope to the branch. Over the course of five years, the rope had rubbed and worn with each swing. In addition, the rain and freezing winters had deteriorated the rope at the top, so when Johanna grabbed the rope at full stride, the last strands holding it gave way. Johanna lost her balance, sending her sideways and out of control into the shallowest part of the water. Coming down, she placed her right hand out to brace her fall. Upon impact, all the children heard the snap of the bone.

"Ouch," shrieked John at the thought of Johanna's pain.

"Help me," were the first words from Johanna as she rolled to a sitting position in the water holding her arm.

Ellen rushed down the bank and into the water to comfort her sister. When she saw Johanna's forearm taking an odd angle to the left, she knew her sister had a broken arm. "John, give me your shirt," she yelled. Ellen took control, as she had seen her brother Edmond reset Denny's leg in a winter fall a few years earlier. Ellen grabbed the wrist and gently pulled to reset the arm. Johanna screamed, "Don't do that."

"Be quiet," said Ellen as she found the proper fit. After resetting the break, she folded Johanna's arm into the sling made from John's shirt. Ellen tied off the sling around Johanna's neck. "Help her up," said Ellen to John, who grabbed her left arm and lifted.

"Ooh, that hurts," screamed Johanna as her body movements disturbed the arm.

"Let's get her home," said Ellen, as they headed back up the path to their farm at the top of the hill. Every few steps Johanna moaned about the pain, but each of her siblings was doing everything they could to make the steep climb less painful.

John kept a grasp on her left arm to steady her pace. Six-year-old Martin kept running in front to help and then fell behind to catch her if she started to fall. His excessive energy and willingness to help kept him in constant motion. Ellen maintained her position on the right side, making sure the arm stayed as motionless as possible.

Once at home, Martin ran ahead to announce the injury and the escort party coming up the lane.

Judith met them at the doorway. "What happened?"

"Johanna swung on the rope and the rope snapped," said Ellen. "Her arm is broken."

"Get her inside and I'll take a look," said her mother. She cleared a space at the kitchen table while Ellen guided her into a chair.

"It hurts, Ma," said Johanna, half tearful.

"I will go slow," said Judith as she unwrapped the sling. "Oh my," she said as she looked at the break point. In the trip home, the arm had started to swell and the blood under the skin was prominent, coloured black and blue. "You did a good job, Ellen," said an impressed Judith. She rewrapped the sling tightly in fresh white cloth to immobilize the break.

Judith then told Johanna, "Lie still. You don't want to disrupt the break or we will have to contact the doctor to take the arm." Johanna did not want to lose her arm, so she obeyed the order to remain as still as possible. For six weeks, she lay almost motionless. After six weeks, she exercised it lightly without putting strain on the arm.

The accident at the swimming place laid Johanna up for most of the summer as she waited for the arm to heal. She used the down time to read extensively, as Ellen made frequent trips to the rectory, where the priest had a vast library of various classics of literature.

Denis made routine trips with books for Johanna to read and then he would spend time discussing concepts. One such discussion occurred after reading St. Thomas Aquinas. Denis asked, "Do you recall the cardinal virtues?".

"Yes, I found them quite interesting," said Johanna. "They are prudence, temperance, justice and fortitude."

"Do any of these mean anything to you?" he quizzed the thirteen-year-old.

"Of course, they all do. St. Thomas meant them to be in the context of righteous living and I see them in everyday life. Take prudence, for example, which is having the foresight to foresee the consequences of your actions. If I had prudence before going swimming, I wouldn't have broken my arm."

"I suppose that's one way of looking at it," said Denis. "What about justice?"

"Justice is easy. It is treating others the way you want to be treated. It's the Golden Rule."

"You have a good grasp of St. Thomas's message," said Denis. "He also asked that we be pure in our thoughts and deeds, for temperance."

Johanna interjected, "And he wanted us to have fortitude, meaning for us to be brave when there's a choice between good or evil." She was obviously happy with her recall and interpretation of her reading, and she asked, "Denis, are you proud of my schooling?"

"Indeed I am," said Denis. "What are we going to talk about next week?"

"I don't know, maybe I will read the New Testament," she said.

"Sounds fine, but remember to keep your arm still," cautioned Denis.

"I will," replied Johanna.

Denis said goodbye to Johanna and Judith and left to return home.

Thus Johanna spent the summer quietly and then eased back into doing her chores. At first she used only her left arm, but as the healing process continued she gradually regained strength in her right arm. By fall harvest, she had full use of her right arm, with little effect remaining from the injury.

* * *

Work at the blacksmith shop remained busy, as Denis spent most of the time preparing and trimming the horses' hooves for fitting the shoes. He was the farrier, whereas Andy was the toolmaker and worked the iron, pounding out the shoes. But for most of his time, Andy filled orders for tools, nails, chains and other iron farm items such as hinges and wagon parts.

In late August of 1835 a thunderstorm struck the area. Denis and Andy stopped working at the height of the storm to experience this light and sound event as it lit the streets of Peterborough with bolts of lightning and pelted the ground with raindrops as big as corn kernels. Out of the haze of rain approached a horse with a tall rider sitting high on his steed and headed towards the livery. Neither the horse nor its rider was affected by the intensity of the storm churning around them, and they sauntered at an even pace into the open door of the shop.

"Good afternoon, gentlemen," said the man, without regard for the soaking rain that now flowed off the brim of his hat down his full-length leather slicker onto the wooden floor.

"Hello," answered the two shopkeepers.

"Are you Dennehy?" he said to Denis in a direct and curt manner.

Andy spoke up, "I am." Like most blacksmiths, Andy was a burly fellow with great strength from lifting and pounding iron. He was not intimidated. "The name's Andy."

"I'm Bill Hogan from Lockport, New York."

"What can I do for you, Mr. Hogan?"

"I understand that you and Mr. McCarthy—I presume that's you?" he said as he motioned towards Denis.

"Yes, I am," answered Denis.

He continued, "I understand that you two fellows are very good blacksmiths and farriers."

"You came all the way to Peterborough for a blacksmith?" asked Denis.

"I came to Peterborough to hire a farrier or two."

"You heard about us in New York?" asked Denis.

"Actually, I'm travelling around the lake looking for labourers and tradesmen, and I heard about the two of you down the road in York. You have quite a reputation." He continued, "There's a canal through New York called the Erie Canal."

"Yes, we have heard of it."

"The canal traffic has reached its capacity and boom towns are springing up everywhere. Governor Marcy is planning to enlarge and expand the canal. I need people who are responsible and have strong backs."

"We are fine right here," both blacksmiths answered.

"I have a partner going to New York City to entice the Irish, Germans and Italians fresh off the boat to work as labourers. I'm looking for the experienced tradesmen. I will pay you a handsome sum to get you established."

"Our families are here and we have established a community. We do not need to move," replied Denis.

"Give it some thought. I'll be here for two days. Now, can I board my horse?" Mr. Hogan led his horse into the stall and dressed down the saddle. Shortly he left the livery for the hotel, walking through the rain.

Andy spoke as soon as Bill Hogan was out of hearing. "Denis, you should consider taking his offer. You haven't started a family yet, so the opportunity is right for you."

"Andy, I have my mother and brother here and I have a good job with you. Why would I want to leave?"

"Most people are settled here and soon the work will drop off. You may not have a job with me forever."

Denis rode home that night thinking about the offer from Mr. Hogan. He considered all he had invested in Peterborough with the job, family and friends. But he had suffered as well, losing his father, and he also knew he had to get over Máire, his lost love. He decided to talk to his mother about the proposal. That night Denis told her about the visitor to the livery. "I was thinking of asking for more details from Mr. Hogan regarding setting up a blacksmith shop."

"Denis, I would hate for you to leave Peterborough, but this may be good for you," his mother advised.

"I would come back and visit. And I have many friends here."

"Go," Johanna commanded.

"I will at least talk to Mr. Hogan tomorrow."

The next day, Denis talked to Andy again about leaving Peterborough, and Andy offered to hire him back if Denis decided to return. Denis left the shop and found Mr. Hogan at the market just up the square. The tall man with the long leather coat was easy to spot.

"Mr. Hogan, I was wondering if you could tell me more about the blacksmith shop."

"I come from a small city not far from Buffalo. The canal passes through this city, which rises sixty feet through a series of five locks, hence the name, Lockport. The locks are operated through gates that hold the water back—it's an astonishing mechanical phenomenon that water can be held at an upper level and controlled and released at will! Anyway, all this mechanical operation needs tools, hinges, gates and channels. Mule teams lead the barges and now the Governor wants to make it larger, which means more tools, more mules and more work. Denis, if you decide to come, I will pay you top wages for your experience. You are well respected throughout this region and I will be happy to have you on my team."

"I'll come for a year and see how I like it."

Mr. Hogan knew that Denis would like the people and the area around Lockport so he agreed to his terms.

"It's a deal."

* * *

In the ten years that Johanna Sullivan lived in Canada, she developed into a young woman approaching the age of adult maturity, and it was time to separate from the family. This girl of sixteen had combined the best qualities of her mother's quick intellect, her father's humour and both her parents' zest for life. Like most children, she watched and learned from older family members, trying to become the best she could and extract their finest characteristics. From her eldest sister Mary, she learned conviction and decisiveness; from Bess she learned compassion and child development as she watched her care for Martin; Ellen taught her patience, order and critical thinking; and with her younger brother she practised and honed these skills.

Neither could Denis's impact be ignored as an influence on Johanna's development, as children are the sum total of their experiences. The time he spent with Johanna made impressions beyond the imprint of family influences. He gave her a larger view of humankind through exposure to literature, religion, geography, nature and arithmetic.

Throughout this development phase, her mother was always in the foreground, as she was for each of the children, directing, correcting and ensuring each sibling had the proper coaching and schooling for their success. Judith saw the opportunities for her children that had never existed before, especially in Ireland, to escape from a pauper's existence into substantial lives. Johanna, the sum total of all her favourable and unfavourable influences, developed into a mature and well-adjusted young woman.

Most of all, she had a playful nature. Once, when Edmond was ploughing, he found an exposed rabbit's nest at the edge of the field. In the nest were two apparently abandoned baby bunnies, which he brought home rather than leave as easy prey for a hawk or effortless sport for a fox.

Johanna cared for the babies and Ed built a cage behind the house to raise them as pets. One night during dinner after everyone was seated, Johanna snuck one of the rabbits into the house under her sweater and placed it on the floor within easy view of the two young boys. Martin, who was four years old at the time, yelled with glee at the sight. John, at eight years of age, was out of his seat and started chasing the rabbit around the table. Rabbits have natural evasive instincts and John's swirling action in and out of the chair and table legs was not successful in capturing the confused rabbit. Johanna sat on the floor and watched John scramble around. Ellen, who wanted to restore order, assisted John in trying to apprehend the pet.

Edmond reached down in a suave, calculated move to entice the rabbit with a breadcrumb but the rabbit would not co-operate with the sophisticated manoeuvre. Judith sat quietly at the head of the table letting the antics go only so long, and then nodded to Johanna to put an end to the ruckus. Johanna, who had some clover in her pocket, pulled it out and waved it in view of the scampering hare. The rabbit recognized his friendly caretaker who offered food and tranquility.

"The rabbit stays outside," was Judith's command.

Johanna giggled as she returned the rabbit to his comfortable home in the back yard. Such was her nature—to play and have fun with the routine of farm life.

* * *

Denis's trip to the Sullivan house to bid them farewell was long and troublesome for the twenty-eight-year-old. He had developed a rapport with the children as a teacher but also a deeper friendship with the family that was exceptionally strong and hard to leave, as was his closeness with his mother and brother. By the time he arrived in Emily, his heart was heavy with the announcement of his move to New York State. He took Judith aside first and told her while most of the children remained outside either working or playing.

"I have a job with great pay and a promising future in Lockport on the canal."

"Well, I am happy for you, Denis. I guess I knew this day was coming."

"It was a difficult decision."

"I am sure it was. Do you want to tell the children or do you want me to tell them after you leave?"

"Oh, I will tell them. I couldn't leave without saying goodbye."

The two adults went outside to disclose the news. Denis took a deep breath. "I am leaving for New York."

Ellen immediately responded off-handedly, "Oh, all right, have a nice trip. See you when you get back."

"No, I'm moving to New York State."

This statement caught their attention. Denis explained, "I have a job there where I can run my own shop. It's in a small town on the canal where all the boats have to go through a series of locks and it's a natural place to have a blacksmith shop. The canal is the future of the western United States so there will always be work for me. But I'll come back and visit. I promise."

The children did not see the logic of moving to a new job when he already had one, so their reaction was emotional rather than understanding of the economically sound strategy. "You can stay here and work, can't you?" asked Johanna.

"Yes, but here I'll be working for someone else. Down there I'll be working for myself. And Mr. Dennehy may not always have work for me," explained Denis.

"We don't want you to go," said Ellen.

"Yeah, stay here," Johanna said firmly, almost as an order.

"I'll come back to visit," repeated Denis.

Once the impact of the announcement settled in, Judith, Ellen, Johanna, Denny and John started to stroll with Denis towards the top of the hill. "We had a lot of fun times since coming to Upper Canada," said Denis, looking towards the top and knowing the panoramic view of the lake was coming.

"Yes we have," said Judith, "and you've been an important part of this family, Denis. I appreciate all you've done for us."

"It was nothing, you are very close to being family," he replied. At the top Denis looked out over the landscape and saw the blue lake with the contrasting green hillside dotted with a few trees just starting their autumn hues of yellow and orange. "I'm going to miss it here," he said.

The hilltop was adjoining their property: Judith had traded it away for the mules to Mr. Seaver ten years earlier. Ellen frequently walked up here to enjoy the view of the lake. "Mother, you traded away the best ten acres for the mules."

Judith explained, "He got the view of the lake but you got a view of the world." She looked at Denis. The education for her three children far exceeded the limited view of Pigeon Lake; she knew they got the better part of the deal.

After returning to the house, Denis said goodbye to each of the children with handshakes and hugs. When Johanna, who was now sixteen years old and blossomed into a fine, intelligent and handsome young woman, came up to him, she threw her arms around him and said, "Thank you and I love you."

Denis was taken aback by the words from the ever-unpredictable Johanna, but he quickly returned the sentiment: "And I love you too, Johanna. Goodbye."

Denis and Willy left the Sullivan house in mid-afternoon for the twelve-mile ride back to the house on the 11th line in Smith Township. The memories of the past ten years with Judith and the Sullivan children passed through Denis's mind as Willy carried him over the watery terrain.

He thought how Judith had given him permission to discipline the children for bad behaviour. Only once did he use corporal punishment, and that was a spank on John's behind when he was six years old and sassy. Denis was so disappointed in himself that he never did it again. If he had continued to spank for each wrongdoing, the momentary pain would cause long-term damage to their relationship. After that incident, he vowed to find a better way to control the children.

He quickly learned that giving them respect and listening to their ideas created a deeper connection to their souls, and they, in return, respected and obeyed him. It was parental leadership he was learning. Slight transgressions only needed a small correction that sent the message, "I don't like this behaviour."

Denis learned that such methods of discipline needed to develop over time between child and adult, and he saw that Judith had used it with her children all along. Thinking through his own childhood, he realized his father and mother had espoused the same approach. Denis had observed many child beatings on the ship's voyage and while living in the tent city, and with each one he felt the child's spirit was being broken. The punishment was minor but the destruction of the spirit was major, and often the child was not given the time or attention to rebuild their spirit and belief in their own goodness and self-worth.

He thought about how Johanna was always the most attentive and responsive to his views and questions on the topic of the day. As she grew older, the thoughtfulness and respect she showed was constant and sincere. He had not realized the depth of the relationship between them until now.

These thoughts led to the words Johanna had said when he left, and they rang through his head during his trip home. He was riding up the 11th line and saw his house and then looked further down the road to where his land stood vacant, and all the old dreams he had for the land and raising a family came rushing back. He stopped for a moment.

Denis leaned down and stroked the mule. "Willy, we're going back."

He pulled the reins and Willy turned around. Denis rode back to the Sullivan house with confidence and clarity of purpose. His feelings for Johanna had coalesced into a solid convergence of affection. Now he became aware of all the pieces of their relationship: respect, compatibility, humour, integrity, personal history, and the maturity of the young woman he had come to not only admire but truly love.

He could feel his own excitement increase as he approached the house. At the same time, he felt his face become flushed and his breathing increase. Denis reached behind him and gently slapped Willie on the rump to encourage a faster trot; Willie quickened his pace as they travelled up the last hill to the Sullivan household.

Denis called for Johanna as soon as he arrived. She came running out the front door before he dismounted and he quickly flung his leg over the back of Willie and lowered himself to the ground.

Johanna met him as his feet hit the ground. His first words were "Johanna, I love you, too." This time he said it with more intensity and meaning and then added, "Please wait for me to return."

"I will," she promised. The two embraced, which might have been awkward at any other time, but today, the two former friends emerged as lovers with their sentiments in complete synchronization. "I will wait for you," she said again.

* * *

Within a week, Denis left Peterborough for his trip to Lockport. He had one bag containing a few tools and a change of clothes strapped to Willy. He threw his wool overcoat over the top of the bag and walked south towards Cobourg on the shores of Lake Ontario, where he caught a ferry to Niagara. The lake in early September was rough and the small ferryboat was tossed on the waves. These waves were different from the ones he had experienced on the ocean, which were wider spread; the lake waves were shorter, which made for greater heaves and more severe rocking. Denis managed, but he spent most of his time in the stall where Willy was unstable with the rocking.

Both of them were happy when the boat turned in to the protective mouth of the Niagara River and safely landed just up the river at Lewiston. As soon as he left the boat, government agents met him at the edge of the dock. He was led into a small building where he registered his entry into the United States. Denis could tell immediately that the agent was British.

"How come you live in the United Stated and not Canada?" Denis asked. He felt it was a logical question since Canada was a possession of the British Empire.

The agent detected the Irish brogue and he didn't have the same friendly response, nor did he take the question as friendly. "That's nothing you need to worry about." The agent continued in a condescending voice, "I'll fill in your entry."

"No need, I can write," Denis replied, and then added, "I can read, too, and you spelled my name wrong; it's Denis with one n." This conversation had taken an unpleasant and challenging turn.

"In English and in my register, it's Dennis with two n's."

"Clearly, you are marking down the wrong person entering today."

"As far as the United States government is concerned, you have two n's."

Denis shrugged his shoulders. "You can change the spelling but you can't change me."

The agent looked up and frowned. "It's the way I spell it that counts."

Some prejudices are not easily left behind, thought Dennis. However, all of Dennis's documents thereafter had the two n's. Dennis climbed up the hill to the town of Lewiston and found a hotel for the night.

The next day, the trip to Lockport was a short twenty miles, with even terrain: they proceeded along a ridge formed long ago by the receding waters of Lake Ontario. Willy liked the United States. He wanted to stop and graze on the fertile grasses along the road. Dennis prodded him along until the next stop for a snack. Soon they climbed a steep hill and entered the village of Lockport. In the centre of town, he found the office for the canal project and asked for Mr. Hogan, who greeted him warmly.

"Dennis, glad to see you. How was your trip?"

"It had some rocky spots."

"I have you set up in a temporary house with some other workers, up the Transit Road. Come, I'll show you to your room."

The house was one block north on Transit Road at the corner of Niagara Street, where Dennis was introduced to other men hired for canal work.

"You'll start tomorrow," Mr. Hogan informed Dennis. "I'll meet you in the lobby at seven a.m. and we'll go for breakfast."

"Fine. See you then."

* * *

The next morning Bill Hogan took Dennis around the corner to Main Street and treated him to breakfast at Bridget's Diner. The meal was a feast to the immigrant, who usually calculated and rationed every food serving. Today he delighted in eggs, toast, bacon, sausage and oatmeal served with a pot of hot tea.

"Do you always eat like this?" asked Dennis.

"No, usually just tea and oatmeal, but today is special because of your arrival. I am happy you agreed to come and work with our crew."

"I'm eager to meet your group."

After breakfast, Bill took Dennis down to the locks and explained the operation of raising and lowering the boats inside the chambers. He talked as a boat was going through, explaining how the water was fed into the lock or drained out, causing the boats to change height.

"That's an amazing feat." Dennis was astounded at the design and function of these mechanisms which could move such big and heavy boats through the locks.

"There are five locks the boats traverse before getting through," Bill explained. "That takes time and patience for the captains and their crews. We have placed a blacksmith shop just upstream to service the boats and their animals. Yours will be a second blacksmith's shop as we already have one."

"I can handle that," said confident Dennis.

The men headed up the edge of the canal through the village as the waterway flowed on towards Tonawanda. A freshly built blacksmith's shop sat on the edge of the towpath.

Bill pointed to the new building. "We just finished construction. All it needs is a furnace, and you should have that by the end of the week."

"Good," said Dennis. "I'll start setting up."

Dennis spent the week stacking firewood and hay, which was brought by boat down the canal. Masons were laying the brick for his forge and in a short time he was ready to fire up the furnace.

The work was hard. Dennis thought he already knew the strength and endurance required for this job, but this town was busy with activity and he was constantly behind in his orders. Mr. Hogan understood the workload but he also wanted to keep pace with the canal traffic. He did not want Lockport to be known to slow down the movement of cargo, and he encouraged Dennis to keep pace. In late summer and early fall many crops, grains and flour were being shipped and time was important, especially with winter approaching.

Dennis discovered that the canal shut down during the winter but the orders for the blacksmith continued and the shop serviced the village animals. Many people did not shoe their horses during the winter as the snow protects the hooves naturally, but work was plentiful. And Dennis appreciated the steady employment.

In late November, Dennis asked Mr. Hogan if he could have time off to go home for Christmas: "Mr. Hogan, I think I would like to head north to visit my family next month, if you don't mind."

"You mean for the holidays? I see that business is slow. Of course you can, but are you planning on coming back?"

"Yes, of course, I'll be back. I appreciate it. My mother will be glad to see me, I'm sure."

"I want to be sure that the best blacksmith on the western end of the canal will be returning."

"Yes, I'll be back. I just want to see my mother and brother in Peterborough."

Dennis left for home in mid-December. He took the land route around Lake Ontario. It was a long, cold and tiresome journey but he cherished the change from pounding iron all day. He stopped in York to purchase gifts for his mother and brother, and he bought a beaded coat woven by a native of the Mississauga tribe for Johanna. He continued on to Peterborough. But an early winter storm struck while he was on the road. He hunkered down in a grove of spruce trees that protected him and Willy from the sharp icy winds. It was bitter cold, and he took Johanna's coat from his pack to give him an extra layer of warmth. He was glad he had the coat.

The next day he started out in eight inches of new snow. Willy struggled in the deep snow, so Dennis walked beside him. For Dennis, too, each step was a struggle to raise his foot out of the wet packed snow and take another stride towards Peterborough. The trip went slowly.

When he arrived in the village of Peterborough, he thought of picking up a ham for their Christmas dinner, but the thought of the wolves on the road many years before made him reconsider the idea. A dressed and spiced ham might be trouble.

The trip continued to be a slow struggle as he headed north, but he made it home in time. The path north out of Peterborough towards Smith Township had all the familiar sights and feelings of past days. The turn at the lake to head up to the 11th line brought a smile to his face as he thought of his many trips on these roads.

As the house came into view, he could see the smoke rising from the chimney, and the comforting smell of the burning wood gave him a warm and happy welcome. When he reached the front door, he knocked twice and opened it. His mother was the first to see him.

"Dennis," she announced from the kitchen table where she was cutting carrots for the dinner pot, and she moved towards the door with arms extended to welcome her son. "So good to see you. I was hoping you were coming home for Christmas."

"Here I am," he said.

Dennis turned to his left and Jeremiah was suddenly standing next to him. "Jeremiah, I didn't see you there. How are you?" He patted his brother on the back, as a brotherly hug was not a typical McCarthy display of affection.

"Good, Dennis; you're just in time for my special rabbit stew."

"It smells good, and I could smell the fire coming up the road. Now I'm hungry," Dennis said.

Shortly they sat down as a family to celebrate the season and the homecoming of Dennis with Jeremiah's stew and bread fresh from the oven.

"How are things in Lockport?" asked Johanna.

"Work is steady and the canal is always busy. Even the people I work with are fun. There are a lot of Irish who live there and travel up and down the canal, but they're different from the Irish that moved here to Peterborough."

"How so?" asked Jeremiah.

"A lot more drinking—the whiskey flows night and day."

Johanna raised her eyebrows in relief. "I am glad neither of you drink in excess."

"By the way, how are Uncle Jerry and Aunt Liz?" asked Dennis, knowing that each of their five daughters had left the house to marry and have their own families.

"They're fine, but lonely without the girls around," said Johanna, "and the girls are doing well too."

After dinner Dennis announced, "I will be staying in Lockport because of the consistent money I am making."

"We understand," said Jeremiah, looking at his mother for confirmation. She made no acknowledgement.

"Why don't you move to New York and stay with me?" asked Dennis.

Jeremiah let the question go, knowing Johanna would answer that invitation. "No, I'm afraid we cannot move away from here. Have you forgotten that your father is buried behind the house?" Johanna had a sharpness in her voice, implying that she had no intention of leaving Thomas.

"No, of course not," answered Dennis.

"Well, I am going to stay here, and I want to be buried next to him." She looked at Jeremiah.

"You will be, Ma," he reassured her.

The moment froze in silence: there were no doubts about moving or where Johanna wanted her final resting place.

Dennis started again to announce his intentions. "Anyway, I am going over to the Sullivan house tomorrow to see the family."

"How nice," said his mother.

"I was thinking of asking Johanna to marry me."

"Oh, really?" said Jeremiah. "You've known her long enough. I saw her last month in town and she's as friendly and lively as she always was."

"I think the time is right," said his mother firmly, and then added her approval. "She's a fine woman."

"I have thought of Johanna constantly during my time in Lockport and I am anxious to see her again."

"Dennis . . ." Johanna started to make a reference to Máire and her refusal many years ago, but thought better of it. "Dennis, you deserve a fine girl like Johanna Sullivan."

Dennis didn't need any reminders of Máire. The memory of standing in her kitchen was as fresh as the day it happened. It was not missing Máire that bothered him; it was the rejection showing he had misread the depth of the relationship. In contrast, he had known Johanna Sullivan since she was six years old frolicking in the tent village. He knew her genuine love that had been expressed openly and passionately through the years.

The day after Christmas, Dennis set out to visit the Sullivan family in Emily Township. He left early in the morning to find Johanna's eldest brother, Edmond, to ask permission to marry his sister. Since Sully had passed away, Dennis thought Edmond was the proper person to ask even though Judith was clearly the head of the household. Dennis had decided to follow tradition and approach the elder male. Since Edmond lived close to Judith this first stop was not out of his way.

Willy knew the route by heart and walked along as Dennis became lost in his thoughts again, just as he had walked this path months ago. Even though he had rehearsed his words, he was afraid to propose marriage to Johanna. This deeply rooted fear was too familiar. The last time he proposed marriage, nearly eleven years earlier, he had been rejected and humiliated. He tried to reason that his relationship with Johanna was much different than his short association with Máire but fear gripped him nonetheless. He was not only distressed mentally but he also felt an ache deep within his stomach.

As he crossed the bridge over the Pigeon River which flows into Pigeon Lake, Dennis stopped to gather his thoughts and his courage. He was nervous, and began trembling at the thought of suggesting marriage to Johanna. Even though panic gripped him, in his heart he knew he had to ask. He had spent many lonely hours and days thinking of her in Lockport; now, he reasoned, was the time to make the commitment. He set out on the road again to Edmond Sullivan's farm.

He found Edmond going into the barn as he approached. "Good morning and Merry Christmas, Ed," said Dennis.

"Hey Dennis, Merry Christmas," he replied and stuck out his hand for a shake. Edmond led Dennis into the barn to feed the mules while they talked.

"What brings you this way?" Ed asked.

Dennis went right to the point. "I was heading over to your mother's house and while I am there, I wanted to ask Johanna to marry me."

"Oh," replied Edmond and then stopped working, giving the statement some thought.

"I wanted your blessing before I asked," Dennis added.

"I see," said Edmond. "She's a bit of a handful, you know."

"I do know, and that's one of the things I like about her," said Dennis.

"Does my mother know yet?" asked Ed.

"No, not yet. Should I talk to her first?"

"No, if she says anything, tell her you talked to me first."

"So you approve of me asking?" repeated Dennis.

"Oh of course; you two will be great together," said Edmond.

"Thanks, Ed. I'm going to head over there now," said Dennis, as he turned and left the barn. He added as he walked out the door, "Say hello to your family for me."

"I will, and we may see you later at Mother's house," answered Edmond.

"Good," said Dennis as he left the property and turned onto the lane where the remaining Sullivan family lived.

Little John, who was not so little any more, was the first to see him coming.

"Here comes Dennis," he yelled.

Within moments, Johanna was out the door and running towards Dennis. Her arms outstretched, she hit him in full stride and nearly knocked him over. He lifted her in a hug and swung her around. All fear left him. "I missed you," they both said to each other.

Finally, Dennis placed Johanna's feet back on the ground as Ellen and John came to greet him in the front yard. He said "Hello" to the other two Sullivans, but his attention came immediately back to Johanna.

"How have you been?" he asked.

"Lonely, waiting for you," she replied.

"Yeah, she has been talking about you all the time," John said.

"Look at all of you standing out here without coats," Dennis said. "You need to go inside before you catch a death of cold." Dennis grabbed a package for Johanna and they headed back inside, where Dennis met Judith standing at the doorway.

"Hello, Mrs. Sullivan," he said with a smile.

"Merry Christmas, Dennis. We are happy to see you," she replied. "Come in and sit by the fire for some tea."

"Ah yes, it was a cold ride up here. I shivered all the way."

John took Willy around to the barn and out of the exposed weather.

It was a gay celebration and reunion as the family sat to hear Dennis's stories of New York and life along the canal.

"I have met rich people travelling the canal in luxury and I have met people with nothing in their pocket, hoping to settle in western New York or Ohio and make a living. Every day packet boats go by with goods going back and forth from east to west and west to east. They grow apples and grapes. It's an exciting place." Dennis picked up the brightly decorated package he had brought with him and handed it to Johanna. "I thought you would like this."

"What is it?" she asked, ecstatic that Dennis thought of her when they were apart.

"Open it," said the equally excited Ellen, who knew the special relationship between her sister and Dennis.

Johanna slowly and carefully pulled the wrapping apart, savouring the moment of excitement and anticipation. Finally she peeked into an opening and saw the beaded cloth, and haste overcame her as she rapidly pulled the remaining wrapping off the coat.

"It's beautiful," she breathed, as she examined the fine, colourful needlework.

"It's very warm too," said Dennis. "I got caught in a snowstorm leaving York and I wrapped up in the coat to keep me warm through the night. I was glad to have it."

"I love it," she said.

"It is beautiful, Johanna," said Ellen. Johanna looked over at her older sister and smiled at her approval. Johanna thought how glad she was Ellen had decided not to enter the convent and continued living at home. The two sisters remained as close throughout their adolescent years as they had in their earlier youthful days.

After a while, Dennis asked Johanna to go for a walk. He had learned the last time that intimate questions deserve privacy.

Judith watched and smiled, for she knew, or at least hoped, what was coming as the two bundled up for a walk in the cold.

Johanna reached for her new coat, which she thought was both fashionable and practical for the frosty Canadian winter. "I feel proud and have a special joy that this coat kept you warm during your trip."

"It looks better on you," Dennis replied.

The crisp air lay still but chilled their noses and ears as they walked up the hill for a view of the lake. The conversation started casually.

"Your family seems good," he began.

"And how's your family?" Johanna said.

"All are well," Dennis said. "I want you to know how nice Lockport is, with great people living there, and the traffic makes each day exciting."

"Yes, it sounds exciting," Johanna said. "Maybe someday I can visit." There was coyness in her voice and a playful challenge for him to say more about living in New York.

Dennis felt the tempo building with an emerging discussion about future plans. "Johanna, there's something I want to ask you," he began hesitantly.

"Yes?" she replied with enthusiasm, trying to cover an immediate smile.

"I was wondering if . . . well . . . now that you are older . . . I was wondering if you might like living in New York State?" He thought an indirect reference might be a good way to start.

"I might, but I've never been there."

"I was really wondering if you would marry me and we could live there together." There, I said it, he thought. Whatever happens, happens.

"I think . . ." She hesitated. "I think . . ." she started again, toying with her reply. "I think we could live anywhere you want. Of course I'll marry you." She threw her arms around him again with all the passion and joy she had shown through the years.

He knew her well. "Were you making this hard for me?" he asked playfully.

She mischievously answered, "No, never—I was just thinking about my answer."

"Yeah, well good, that settles that," said Dennis. He was relieved the ordeal was over and he was overjoyed at the eagerness and clarity of Johanna's reaction. He realized his life's plan had worked out for the best. He was overjoyed.

Johanna initiated the intimacy that Dennis found difficult to verbalize. "I love you," she said and moved her lips in close to his. Dennis reacted and closed the gap as their lips met. His arms extended around her waist and drew her in, completing the embrace. Excitement and relief reverberated through the couple.

Even though their winter coats pressed between them, the magical energy of love flowed through their joined bodies. After several seconds, Dennis released and stepped back, grabbing hold of Johanna's hands. He smiled and pulled her back in for a second kiss. This time Johanna pulled back after a few seconds and dropped her head down. Dennis understood the message as a caution against public intimacy.

"And by the way, Edmond gave us his blessing for the marriage."

"He did, did he?" said Johanna. "He didn't ask me if he could get married."

"Wouldn't you've been surprised if he had?" asked Dennis.

"I suppose," replied Johanna. "Anyway, I'm happy you asked me," and she threw her arms around Dennis again for a hug.

"All right, all right," said Dennis, pulling back. "Let's go tell your family."

They returned to the house hand in hand, telegraphing the news before their arrival with their giddy behaviour and dance-like walk as they swung their arms and did an occasional jig, kicking their feet in the fast-tempo Irish dance. The release of internal energy and joy was driving their exuberance as they walked and hopped towards the house.

Once inside, Johanna couldn't hold the news. "Dennis has asked me to marry him."

Ellen jumped up. "Oh that's great news, I'm so happy for you."

"Yes, congratulations," said a happy Judith, indicating her approval with her smile and the tight embrace around Johanna.

The day continued with Christmas and pre-wedding celebrations.

Johanna McCarthy was happy when she learned that young Johanna had accepted her son's invitation to marry. She knew the relationship between Dennis and Johanna Sullivan had evolved from teacher and student through the years to a strong bond of friendship. The Sullivan family had deeply rooted ideals and values, which made Johanna and Dennis a perfect union of personality, humour and intelligence.

Even though Johanna was thirteen years his junior, their time spent together had united their thinking. In these days of the mid-nineteenth century, such an age difference was not uncommon, nor was Johanna's youth troublesome. Both mothers of the intended couple were not only satisfied with this marriage, they had expected it and they cherished its harmony.

Not surprisingly, these two families had connected in ordinary social bonding because both the McCarthy and the Sullivan families lived simple, humble lives with no extraordinary traits that made them stand out. They were law-abiding, industrious folks with high self-discipline, almost to a fault, who valued education and the ability to create their own opportunities. While other children ran off to devious mischief, the children of these families faithfully followed their indoctrinated values and upheld their family reputation. They did not feel they had missed something but took pride in being and doing good.

Of course everyone has their faults and shortcomings, including the McCarthy and Sullivan families, but their transgressions were relatively small in nature, and uncomfortable until made right. Once congruent again, the emotional stress was relieved and the equilibrium restored.

* * *

Dennis planned to return to Peterborough in the spring after the winter thaw and take Johanna to see Lockport. After that trip, they planned a summer wedding based on the farm schedule of the two families and availability at the blacksmith shop.

"I prefer the wedding to be in the United States," Johanna said, "our new home. After all, our current parish of St. Peter's in Chains in Peterborough is building a large new stone structure. Once the older church is moved our connection with the current church will be gone."

This statement caused an argument with her mother. "It's easier for Dennis to come here for the wedding than all of us to travel there," Judith insisted.

"But, Mother," Johanna insisted, "I will be living in New York and that is going to be my home. It would be like getting married in St. Martin's Church in Kilworth and then leaving."

Judith understood the analogy of St. Martin's Church, which she had left eleven years ago for the trip to Canada. She missed her home parish in Ireland and understood Johanna's concern about connectedness. But there were other issues to consider.

"But that is a big trip for all of us. We cannot afford the fare."

"Maybe we can just get married on our own," Johanna said softly.

The classic mother and daughter conflict was developing without hope of a resolution. Johanna insisted on being married in New York and Judith stuck with a marriage in Canada. Judith conceded to travelling as far as Cobourg on the shores of Lake Ontario, and then the two could sail off as newlyweds. "The notion," she said, "is romantic."

"I don't see the humour or the romance," countered Johanna.

The stalemate continued, as Johanna was still under Judith's influence and she did not have full independence yet. Dennis, who was in Lockport, was outside the conversation but shortly thereafter Johanna received a letter from him informing the family of trouble at the border.

"I am sure you have heard that some Canadians are trying to gain independence from Great Britain, and a number of skirmishes have occurred especially along the New York border. They are receiving support from some Americans, so people are having a difficult time at the Niagara border. It may be easier for you to travel here with your family than for me to leave. I believe if you cross on a ferry from Cobourg to Rochester, all will be safe. I will meet you at the Rochester dock on August 26 and we can wed in Rochester on August 27. Your family can return promptly to Canada. I travelled to Rochester on a packet boat and spoke to the priest and the date is set. Also, I am sending the same message to my mother. Looking forward to seeing you.

All my love,
Dennis"

Johanna read the letter to her mother and then added, "That's settled."

* * *

Just before summer, Dennis learned about a settlement of new homes—small shanties actually—that were being built on the west end of town for the Irish labourers. Dennis purchased a plot on Michigan Street and began construction of their new home. Construction would be finished in time for the wedding and Johanna's arrival, and the house would become the permanent McCarthy homestead.

By mid-August, Jeremiah realized he would be unable to travel with his mother to the wedding because it was necessary for him to harvest the cabbage before it rotted. He immediately sent a letter to his brother informing him of his inability to travel: "Dennis, I cannot be with you on your wedding day. May the Lord be with you. Jeremiah."

At the end of August, Johanna, Judith, Ellen and John Sullivan travelled to Peterborough and met Johanna and Jeremiah McCarthy for the trip down the Otonabee River to Rice Lake and on to Cobourg.

At the station their tickets were waiting for them. Dennis had purchased the tickets at the Charlotte station servicing the Rochester port and sent them to Cobourg. As planned, Dennis was waiting for the two families on the Rochester dock.

"Welcome," he said, and led Johanna and the others to a waiting carriage. "Did you have a good journey?"

"The lake was rough half-way across with waves that heaved the boat pretty bad, but eventually it calmed enough so nobody was sick," said Judith.

Dennis's mother asked, "Do you have a witness to replace Jeremiah?"

"Yes, a friend of mine from Lockport, John Trahy, will be the witness."

Once the carriage was under way the driver transported the travellers ten miles along the Genesee River to the centre of Rochester. They settled into a hotel not far from the canal and spent the evening discussing the news while having dinner.

"Who is the priest?" asked Judith.

"Father O'Reilly," said Johanna.

After dinner, the women retired to one room for the night with the two mothers sharing the bed, and the girls found room on the floor. The men stayed in another room down the hall.

St. Patrick's Church on the corner of North Plymouth Avenue and Platt Street was quiet on the cloudy, overcast day of the wedding. The large oak door creaked when Dennis pulled the oversized brass handle to enter the sacred House of the Lord. A blanket of darkness made them squint as they passed through the vestibule into the main section of the church. Now light filtered through the tall stained glass windows lining each side of the church, which gave this place of worship a majestic feel compared to the rustic rural chapel in Peterborough. The finely chiselled marble altar was representative of the sophistication Rochester had developed in the past thirty years since its founding. The Genesee River and the Erie Canal had accelerated the growth and development of the area, and St. Patrick's Church was an example of its rapid progress.

Dennis and Johanna walked up the aisle with their mothers behind them. The three siblings straggled behind, examining the ornate statues and carvings of the Stations of the Cross. Father Bernard O'Reilly, the parish priest, saw the group coming from a vantage point at the edge of the Sacristy and walked out to the Communion Rail. "Welcome," he whispered.

Dennis whispered back, "Good morning, Father."

"And you must be Johanna?" continued the priest, not only to meet the bride but also to verify her identity for the official recording of the marriage.

Other introductions were made but Father O'Reilly soon said, "Let's start," and switched to Latin: "In nomine Patris et Filii et Spiritus Sancti, Amen." All present made the Sign of the Cross.

Ellen stood beside her sister and John Trahy stood by Dennis as the Mass began. Following the Gospel and a short sermon, Father O'Reilly conducted the wedding ceremony. Dennis reached down and squeezed Johanna's hand as they became one in marriage. Both of them had such a long-standing devotion for each other that, when Father O'Reilly asked the crucial question, "Do you take this woman . . ." and "Do you take this man . . .?," their "Yes" was swift and natural.

Afterwards the entire family had dinner in the hotel restaurant to celebrate the occasion. Dennis and Johanna bid their families good-bye as the guests climbed into a carriage to return to the ferry for a late-night voyage back to Cobourg. Once the families left, Dennis and Johanna caught a westbound packet to Lockport. Luckily the packet had several musicians on board and when they realized a couple of newlyweds were travelling with them, the party started. The Captain broke out a couple of hidden bottles of poteen, Irish moonshine, and by the time Dennis and Johanna woke in the morning, they were in Lockport.

* * *

The newlyweds settled into their new home, town and life during the fall and winter of 1836. In the spring of the following year, after all the snow melted and the ice in the Niagara River broke up and flowed towards the St. Lawrence River and on to the ocean, they decided to go to Peterborough to visit their families.

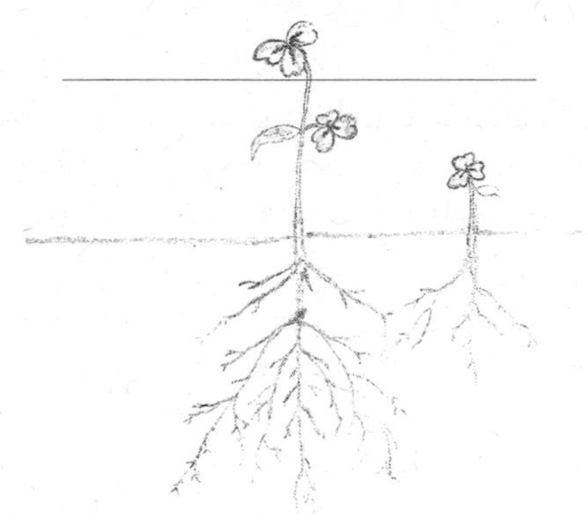

Epilogue

In late April 1837, Dennis and Johanna began their journey to their former home in Peterborough. The daily coach to Lewiston left Lockport early in the morning, which allowed them to board a boat by noon and sail across the lake to the newly named city of Toronto. Once in the Canadian city, they headed up to Claretown, an Irish neighbourhood along Queen Street West, to find a hotel for the night.

"We should be able to find a coach in the morning to take us to Peterborough," said Dennis.

"We came a good distance today. Hopefully tomorrow will be an easy ride home," said Johanna.

In the morning, the sun was still low in the eastern sky when Dennis and Johanna left the hotel to find the stage coach depot. Dennis was dressed in a simple travelling suit with a tie, indicating he had become a man of modest means. Johanna wore a long travelling dress with her hair tied up under a travel bonnet, which gave her the sophistication of a fine woman. As Dennis predicted, they found a stage leaving Toronto for Peterborough, and they were the only passengers on board. Their driver, an older man named Jake with long, thin, greying hair, had a quick wit about him, which Dennis discovered in a hurry.

"Where are you headed?" asked Dennis.

"Didn't you buy a ticket to Peterborough?" asked Jake.

"Yes," answered Dennis.

"Then I am going to Peterborough," replied Jake in a good-natured way.

Dennis decided to play the bantering game with his driver. "Are you sure you know the way?'

Jake laughed. "Do I know the way? I was travelling through the back hills of Upper Canada while you were still a baby in Ireland."

"Why do you think I was born in Ireland?" Dennis asked, half serious.

"Are you fooling with me? Between that accent and going to Peterborough where the Irish landed eleven years ago, that was an easy question. Give me something harder to figure out."

"What time are we going to arrive in Peterborough?" asked Dennis.

"Now that's a little harder. We should be there by nightfall, if all goes well."

"What do you mean, if all goes well?" asked Johanna, as she handed her bag to Jake for storage on top of the carriage.

"Good road and good weather," was Jake's explanation, followed by "Hop in, we're off."

The road to Peterborough started smooth and comfortable. After about two hours of riding, the passengers heard Jake call the horses to a stop: "Whoa." The carriage stopped. Dennis looked out the window and saw a young couple standing by the side of the road. Jake moved slowly to rise off the driver's bench and find his footing on the rungs of the steps to climb down. Before he reached the bottom, Dennis opened the door of the coach and stepped out. Johanna decided to take the opportunity to stretch her legs and followed Dennis out of the carriage. Dennis turned back and took Johanna's hand for stability as she brushed aside her travelling dress to find her footing.

"Hello," Dennis greeted the young man.

"Hello," they both answered back.

"Here Jake, let me help you," Dennis said to Jake as he grabbed the driver's arm to steady his step onto the ground.

"I'm fine," the driver replied with a tinge of grouchiness.

Dennis laughed. "Who's going to drive this coach if you fall and break your leg?"

"Whippersnapper," was the reply in a mellower tone with a half smile.

The driver turned to the young man. "Can you drive if I pass out, fall down, get kidnapped by Indians, jailed by the soldiers or trampled by runaway horses? This guy thinks it's my first trip down this road and some dreadful fate awaits me." The two were clearly having fun with each other.

Dennis struck back. "The next time you can fall off the coach and I'll be standing here saying, 'I told you so.'" They all laughed.

"So where you going?" the driver asked.

"Peterborough," replied the young man.

"Good, because that's where we're going."

Even though the tempo was light-hearted, they all realized the serious nature of wilderness travel. At any moment conditions could change, especially in early spring.

The driver loaded the bags in the back of the coach and turned to his passengers. "Let's go before the horses leave without us."

Dennis extended his hand again to Johanna. "Thank you," she said appreciatively.

However, Dennis did not follow her in but waited and offered his hand to the young woman. She took it as she climbed the step into carriage. The young man stepped forward and Dennis withdrew his hand, comically saying, "You are on your own." The young man grinned at Dennis's sense of humour.

Dennis turned his attention to the driver. "Jake, can you get up on your own or am I going to have to get a rope and pulley?"

"Young man, this old body can manage just fine. And get yourself inside or you'll be running behind for the next fifty miles."

Dennis stepped in and yelled out the door, "Jake, I'm in but we're still missing the comfortable chairs you promised."

"Hee yaw," Jake shouted, and with a snap of the reins, the horses pulled the coach into a jerking start.

The passengers settled in their seats. Dennis looked at the young man.

"You're going to Peterborough?"

"Yes," he said cautiously.

"Good town. We lived there for a while. Do you have family there?"

"No, not exactly. We are looking for someone there."

"Oh, who's that? Maybe I can help. I know just about everyone." There was a comfortable feeling among the four people and the new passengers seemed at ease.

"The daughter of a woman we were travelling with. The woman's name was Sarah Hurley. We don't know the name of the daughter."

"Well, there are some Hurleys in Peterborough," replied Dennis.

"I am afraid that she does not go by the name of Hurley any more because she is now married," explained the man.

"That could be tough. What do you know about her?"

The man seemed to know who he was looking for. "I know she moved to Peterborough about seven years ago and she grew up in Ireland in a small town called Crookhaven."

"Maherly O'Keefe is who you are looking for. Her husband is Michael O'Keefe. She lives in Peterborough, not one of the settlement towns adjacent to the village."

"How do you know this?"

"I lived in Peterborough for eleven years. I was a farrier with the town blacksmith. That's how I know the people." Dennis started to turn towards Johanna to continue the story but stopped and said, "I'm sorry, I've not introduced us. I'm Dennis McCarthy and this is my wife Johanna. We were married last year in Lockport in New York," he added proudly.

The young man replied, "This is Kathleen and I am Connor Meighan. We were married a month ago in the middle of the Atlantic Ocean."

"How romantic," said Johanna.

"Yes, it was romantic, but we have been on the move ever since. We can't wait to settle down," added Kathleen. "We stopped in Lockport while travelling the canal; it's a nice town."

Dennis explained, "Yes, we like it. We've decided to make it our home because of the work there. We're going back to Peterborough to visit our families. We haven't seen them since our wedding."

"You were born in Canada?"

"No, both of us were born in Ireland, County Cork, and brought to Canada by the English to start a new life," explained Dennis.

"The English? That's unusual."

"Yes, it was, and we appreciated the opportunity to start a new life. I'm afraid neither of our families would have survived the conditions in Ireland had we stayed," Johanna said. "My father died on the ship coming over and my mother had a difficult time starting a new life with seven children. My mother never recuperated from her grief. She always introduced herself as 'the widow Sullivan.' Dennis lost his father too but his mother's nature was stronger and her grief turned into determination."

Dennis broke in before Johanna's emotion overcame her. "The English helped many families go from starvation to self-sufficiency. The settlement program was a wonderful opportunity for many people. However, many lost mothers, fathers or children in the process of moving from Ireland, so upon arrival in Upper Canada there were no familiar family members to assist with clearing land, planting, harvesting and raising children."

"We miss our families, too," said Connor.

"They call this the New World, and we all have new lives here, whether we like it or not," added Kathleen.

"Sounds like you've had some trouble along the way," said Dennis.

"Yes, we have," said Connor.

The carriage moved along the lake on the main road with little difficulty. However, when they turned off the major east-west route and headed north in the less travelled direction towards Peterborough, the road was uneven, narrow and less well maintained.

The path leading to Peterborough was muddy from recent rains and the coach bounced in and out of water puddles. The conditions slowed the horses to a careful walk. The passengers felt the exaggerated bouncing, which at first was funny but rapidly became a nuisance. The terrain was rough in this remote area heading into the interior of the land away from the lake. Clouds rolled in and the sky darkened as the threat of more rain loomed. Jake pulled the team to a halt.

"Bad weather ahead," he announced. The passengers heard Jake climbing around on the top of the carriage.

"Anything I can do to help?" yelled Dennis out the window.

"No, I'm just getting my rain gear and securing the luggage from any dampness. Do you know how to close the flaps on the windows?" asked Jake.

"Yes. We'll take care of it," Dennis answered back.

The rumbling of thunder could be heard in the distance as the coach inched forward. The storm hit quickly. Lightning, thunder, heavy rain all appeared instantly. The horses kicked and reared under the tumultuous weather. Jake was working hard to control and calm the horses. At the peak of nature's tempest, Jake pulled the carriage to a stop and disembarked from his bench on the top of the coach. The passengers expected him to open the door and climb in. Even Johanna started to squeeze in closer to Dennis to make room but the door did not open. They could hear Jake's voice; he was calming the horses. The carriage would make slight jerks forward as the agitated horses reacted to the nearby flashes of light and the pounding thunder.

The passengers peeked out from the flaps to get a look at the intensity of the storm, only to quickly close the flaps when volumes of rain pierced the interior. The wheels had sunk into the waterlogged dirt roadway, and as the horses pulled the carriage began to rock. It released with a sucking sound from the muck and the carriage moved forward. Jake was in between the horses with his hand on their bridles to pull and coax them. He was soaked through his coat with a draining flow of dirt, mud and water down his pants and into and out of his boots. Between the resistance of the mud and the skittishness of the horses, the coach moved slowly.

The front of the storm passed by and the lightning and thunder drifted into the distance. The rain, however, continued. The horses settled down but Jake still had his hands full, making calming strokes on the horses' necks and keeping them on the move. A half-hour passed and the carriage had advanced only a short distance. Jake was afraid to stop for fear of the carriage sinking further into the mud while stationary. He knew of a small opening in the trail ahead and headed into a wider, grassy area to stop. The horses followed Jake's lead into the open part of the road that had firm ground among the thickly rooted, clumpy grass.

The rain remained steady through the day as Jake waited for clear weather. The passengers passed the time playing cards in the coach. The cards, dampened by the humidity, stuck together, but they made the best of their circumstances. By late afternoon the rain had stopped. Jake pulled out an extra set of dry clothes and changed. He had one pair of boots and his feet remained soaked.

He approached his passengers. "If we leave now, the road is wet and muddy and we will not likely go far. So we will wait until the road can dry up and drain. We will set up camp here for the night." The carriage had provisions for emergency stops such as this and Jake prepared a small dinner of bean soup. The rear of the carriage had a foldout bed with a canopy for two passengers and the interior of the carriage allowed one person on each of the cushioned bench seats. Jake slept on top with a tarp.

No additional rain occurred through the night and in the morning the road was passable enough to set out. The journey continued and the road dried as the sun became more intense. The McCarthys and the Meighans rekindled their conversation once the coach was under way and again the talk came easily between the two couples. Dennis spoke of his job in Lockport working on the canal.

"The work is hard but steady."

"Are there opportunities for people like myself?" Connor asked. "We met Bill Hogan, who said that he would hire me because of my strong back."

"Yes, I know Mr. Hogan; he is always looking for good, strong, honest workers. Especially those who don't let the drink get the better of them," Dennis said.

"You should consider coming to Lockport to work," said Johanna.

Connor looked at Johanna. "We will consider it. We talked about the possibility of heading back to Lockport."

* * *

Without their realizing they had stopped, the door suddenly flew open and Jake was standing there.

"Are you going to get out or am I taking you back with me?"

Dennis looked out the window and saw the familiar town where his family had settled. "Jake, you are a fine driver to get us here with hardly a bump in the road." Dennis remained playful after a difficult journey.

"Yeah, yeah, come on and get out so I can keep my schedule."

Dennis jumped out first so he could turn and assist the women from the coach to the street. Connor was the last to exit, as Dennis turned to the stationhouse. He was surprised to see Jeremiah standing there.

"Jeremiah, good to see you."

"Hi Jeremiah, how have you been?" Johanna asked.

"Dennis, I'm fine, and how are you two?" answered Jeremiah.

"Good. I would like to introduce you to Connor and Kathleen Meighan, who just arrived in America from Ireland."

"Nice to meet you." Jeremiah turned back to Dennis. "What took so long? I have been checking the station every day for a week. I have been waiting for you." Connor observed that Jeremiah looked up to his brother and most likely missed his presence in Peterborough.

"Late start. I had to get some work done before we left. How's Ma?"

"Very good. I have been checking on Mrs. Sullivan like you asked me to. They're all good too," replied Jeremiah.

"Thanks for doing that, Jeremiah." Dennis turned to Connor, "By the way, Maherly O'Keefe lives down Water Street in a yellow house. Is it still yellow, Jeremiah?"

"The O'Keefes' house, yes, but why would anyone want to go there?"

"It's their business, Jeremiah."

Dennis pointed towards the hotel. "You can find a room over there."

"Thanks," said Connor.

Dennis added, "I would like to introduce you to the rest of the McCarthy family. Would you have dinner with us tomorrow?"

"Sure, thanks for the invitation," replied Connor.

The two couples separated, Dennis extending his hand in farewell to Connor. "Welcome to the Americas. Good to meet a fellow Irishman."

"Indeed," replied Connor. "We are looking forward to meeting your family tomorrow."

"Good, tomorrow I will come by and pick you up," finished Dennis.

Dennis, Johanna and Jeremiah walked down the street in their fine clothes, carrying their luggage to head to their farm on foot. Connor noted there was no carriage; they were still a poor family struggling to fulfill a dream.

The air was clear as they headed north on the main roadway towards the McCarthy shanty on the 11th line in Smith Township. The often-travelled road with its muddy lanes seemed short, as Jeremiah talked of the farm and the concerns of his aging mother. She continuously missed her beloved Thomas as well as grieving Catherine's passing at the end of the voyage. Now that Dennis had moved to New York State, the loss of her family made her age faster than her biological years. Her heart was in constant ache even though Jerry and Lizzie lived close by on the next road and the five nieces still lived in the Peterborough area. Jeremiah, like his cousins, was establishing his home in Upper Canada.

Upon arriving at the farm, Dennis felt the warmth of home as Johanna came out to meet the young couple. "Hello, Ma," he said as usual.

"Dennis and Johanna, welcome home," Johanna McCarthy said warmly, with a hug for her son and daughter-in-law.

"Thank you, Mother," said her daughter-in-law.

They spent the evening talking and relaying news of their respective homes. "We have a small house on the edge of Lockport where many Irish families live," Dennis began.

"Sounds familiar," said Johanna.

Dennis continued, "The work is steady and there is an amazing amount of traffic on the canal; all day long boats are going back and forth with supplies, lumber, grains and people."

Jeremiah added his stories of the woods and working the land. "The moose are hunted heavily and are starting to shy away. It's not as easy to find the big game any more."

"Stick to raising corn, potatoes and the other crops and you won't have to chase them as far as a moose," advised Dennis.

"Yeah, I guess," said Jeremiah, who preferred the woods to the open fields.

Eventually they called it a night and Johanna laid out mats on the floor for her son and his wife. Just before lying down, Dennis informed his mother, "We met a couple on the stage coach coming from Toronto. By the looks of them, they are pretty weary of travelling, so I invited them to have a meal with us tomorrow night. I hope that's all right with you, Ma?"

"Where were they travelling from?" she asked.

"They came from the West of Ireland, just off the boat in New York, but they had business to tend to in Peterborough."

"Why didn't they come through Quebec and Upper Canada?" asked Johanna.

"I don't know, Ma," answered Dennis, "some things you don't ask."

"I will be pleased to meet them," she said. "What are their names?"

"Connor and Kathleen Meighan," answered Dennis.

"We are always willing to help," said Johanna. "Good night, and

I'm glad you're home."

* * *

The next day Dennis walked back into town to pick up Connor and Kathleen. He found them at the inn and asked if they minded a six-mile walk in the mud. Kathleen replied, "We have been riding in ships, boats and coaches for seemingly months. I am ready for a long walk."

They started their journey north to Smith Township.

"Did you meet Maherly O'Keefe?" asked Dennis.

"Yes, we found her. Thank you for your help."

"A pleasure. Did you get your business done?"

"We did. Again, thank you for your help," replied Connor.

"Sure," said Dennis, not pressing for the details of their visit with Maherly O'Keefe. He thought to himself that in due time the purpose of the visit would be known.

They continued up to the 11th line to the small McCarthy shanty situated twenty paces off the lane, which Johanna McCarthy still called home with Jeremiah.

The dinner and evening with the two Johannas, Jeremiah, Dennis, Connor and Kathleen were pleasant with talk of Ireland and the voyage over the ocean.

Kathleen explained how she and Connor met on the ship, "We met on ship and Connor took care of me during the voyage. We fell in love." She turned to Connor with a smile and he nodded back. "And the captain married us at sea."

"How romantic," said the younger Johanna.

Kathleen quickly added, "But we are going to get married again in a Catholic Church as soon as we can settle down."

"That's good," said the elder Johanna.

Connor indicated they had boarded a ship in unusual circumstances, but he was evasive about the details. "I was lucky to bargain my way onto the ship and work my passage over."

"Oh, they allowed that for passengers?" asked the elder Johanna.

"It wasn't a passenger ship, it was a merchant ship," said Connor, who stopped abruptly.

"The two of you were passengers on a merchant ship?" asked Dennis.

"Yes, but now we are here," said Connor, indicating a further explanation was not coming. "We are looking for a place to settle down and start our home."

Dennis turned to his mother. "They travelled through Lockport on the canal and thought about returning to Lockport to make their home."

The elder Johanna said, "How nice. It sounds like a good place to find work."

Connor and Kathleen said simultaneously, "Yes, we are looking forward to settling in Lockport." They laughed at their joint statement.

The next morning, Dennis and his wife Johanna walked part of the way back to Peterborough with Connor and Kathleen, until they reached the turnoff for Emily Township, where they planned to head up to see the Sullivan family. Before departing, they made arrangements to meet again in town for the return trip to Lockport.

"We are going to see Johanna's family for a day but we will meet tomorrow at the hotel," said Dennis. "And then we will head down to Cobourg for a ferry ride to Rochester in New York."

"Yes, we remember Rochester on the canal," said Kathleen.

"See you then," said Johanna.

The arrival of Dennis and Johanna at Judith's home lacked the excitement encountered in years past as the children were mostly grown, married and on their own. John still lived with Judith and the others were close, but the exuberance of the Sullivan household had subsided to the calm of mature serenity. Nevertheless, Judith's wide smile and outstretched arms at the arrival of her daughter and her husband had not changed and was reminiscent of the warmth and familiarity of childhood.

"You look so well," she greeted the two.

"Mother, you look good, too," Johanna said.

The three sat at the kitchen table with a pot of tea and traded family news as they had the day before at Dennis's home. Judith stared at Johanna and opened her mouth slightly, indicating she wanted to say something. They waited.

In her soft and tender voice, she said, "I wish Sully was here to see you two. He would be so proud of both of you and the happiness you share. I'm sure he's watching with great delight."

"He is with me always, as you are too, Mother. I often think of you both," said Johanna. The conversation was the vocal appreciation between parent and adult child so rarely spoken, but Johanna and Judith found the right moment to take the risk of an uncomfortable exchange of admiration.

John volunteered to ride over to the town of Lindsay and pick up Ellen. "I will bring her back for a night of celebration."

"You be careful on the road," warned Judith.

"I will," said the fifteen-year-old to his mother. Within a couple of hours, John returned with Ellen, who was now a teacher in Lindsay.

Dennis gave a big hug to his former student. "Good to see you again, Ellen."

"And you too, Dennis," she answered, and then she turned to her sister. "Johanna" was all she said before they wrapped their arms around each other. The two girls had been inseparable during their childhood in spite of their opposing personalities, but now they had a strong and mature admiration for each other.

"You're teaching?" asked Dennis.

"Yes, I am teaching young children and I hope to make enough money to attend a college."

"Have you given up on the idea of entering the convent?" asked Johanna.

"I think so," Ellen answered, "at least for now."

The evening was enjoyed with card games and talk before settling down for the night. Ellen left early, before sunrise, to travel back for her day's classes, but everyone was up to send her on her way.

"Goodbye, come and visit us in Lockport," Johanna said.

"I just may do that," said Ellen.

They hugged and she left for town about six miles to the west. Soon after, Dennis and Johanna left the house for Peterborough. Judith and John wished them well. "Have a safe trip back."

"We will," answered Johanna.

Once in Peterborough, Dennis and Johanna went to the hotel and met with Connor and Kathleen. They gathered their bags and boarded a coach to Cobourg.

"Did you have a good visit with your mother?" Kathleen asked Johanna.

"We did, and we saw my sister and younger brother, too," answered Johanna. "It is odd how we grow up and want to move out of our parents' home and as soon as we do, we can't wait to go back."

"Yes," said Kathleen. "I could go back now, but on different terms."

"I agree, we have experienced freedom," said Johanna. "And our parents realize we have separated and changed, too. There's more of a respect as equals, I mean."

"I hope so," said Kathleen. "I have not been back yet and quite frankly, probably I never will see my home in Ireland again."

"'Tis sad," said Johanna.

The two couples arrived at the dock at Cobourg and made their way to the ferryboat for the trip back to the United Sates. The official presence was light and they boarded the waiting steamboat without any hassle. Connor seemed nervous. He stated, "I don't like going through official inspections." Other than an agent asking for their destination and tickets, no other official inquiry occurred.

The steamboat pushed its way out of the harbour and headed southeast across Lake Ontario for the Charlotte harbour, some fifty miles distant. Johanna was looking back at the shoreline of British North America with Dennis standing next to her. He noticed a half-smile on her face as she stood poised against the cool westerly wind blowing into her face, and he could tell her mind was working with a thought that brought a degree of confidence. He waited.

"Blessed are the meek," she said with softness yet conviction.

"Blessed are the meek?"

Her eyes pierced the shoreline as she was leaving her home once again. "I am looking at all the families that came with us who held their quiet strength under the mighty thumb of the Crown. They persevered from the humblest beginnings, where they kept their faith in God and themselves. People doing hard work using quiet strength—the meek: they have inherited the earth."

Dennis put his arm around her shoulder and pulled her in to his chest but her eyes never left the shoreline. He was no longer the teacher; they were contemporaries, sharing life's struggles through their shared knowledge and experience. The boat moved forward.

Ag deireadh
(The End)

References

Bennett, Carol. (1987) *Peter Robinson's Settlers*. Juniper Books Limited. Canada.

Bennett, George. (1869) *The History of Bandon*. Munster Works. Cork, Ireland. Online at: http://www.paulturner.ca/Ireland/Cork/HOB/hob-main.htm

Byrne, Mary E. (800 AD) *Be Thou My Vision*. http://www.musicanet.org/robokopp/eire/bethoumy.htm

Clan MacCarthy Society, series of articles. (2000) http://mccarthy.montana.com/Articles.shtml

Courtmacsherry Hotel web site. (2008) http://www.courtmacsherryhotel.ie/index-8.html

Craig, Gerald M. (1968) *Upper Canada: The Formative Years, 1784-1841*. McClelland and Stewart. Toronto.

Cronin, Mike. (2001) *A History of Ireland*. Palgrave. New York.

Dickson, David. (2005) *Old World Colony, Cork and South Munster 1630-1830*. Cork University Press. Cork, Ireland.

Douay-Rheims Bible. (2004) http://www.drbo.org/

Eaton, Alex C. Personal Interview. October 2007.

Grimm Brothers. *The Wolf and the Seven Little Kids, Grimm's Fairy Tales* as reported http://www.literaturecollection.com/a/grimm-brothers/553/

Guillet, Edwin C. (1933) *Pioneer Travel in Upper Canada*. University of Toronto Press. Toronto.

Haurin, Don, Richens, Ann. (1998) Richens Academy of Irish Dance (Ohio) http://www.geocities.com/aer_mcr/irdance/irhist.html

Hopkins, Kerriann. (2008) *Margaret King, Lady Mount Cashell and Mrs. Mason: A Biography of One Woman*, University of Notre Dame, Open Course Work, http://ocw.nd.edu/political-science/mary-wollstonecraft-and-mary-shelley/lady-mount-cashell.

Kingston Chronicle, Friday June 24, 1825. Page 3. Column 1.

LaBranche, Bill. (1975) *The Peter Robinson Settlement of 1825*. Total Graphics Limited. Peterborough.

MacDonagh, Oliver, (1987) *The Hereditary Bondsman: Daniel O'Connell*, St. Martins Press. New York.

MacUistin, Liam. (2002) *Celtic Magic Tales*. The O'Brien Press. Dublin.

Newton, John. (1772). "Amazing Grace." http://www.constitution.org/col/amazing_grace.htm

Nisbet, I.C.T. (2002) "Common Tern (*Sterna hirundo*)." *In The Birds of North America*, No. 618 (A. Poole and F. Gill, eds.). The Birds of North America, Inc., Philadelphia, PA. http://www.birds.cornell.edu/AllAboutBirds/BirdGuide/Common_Tern_dtl.html

O'Murchadha, Diarmuid. (2001) *Crosshaven, a Literary Portrait*. Tower Books. Skibbereen.

Oracle ThinkQuest Education Foundation. (2006) http://library.thinkquest.org/05aug/00374/history.html

Rappoport, Angelo S. (2007) *Superstitions of Sailors*. Dover Publications. Mineola, New York.

Read, D.B. (1900) *The Lieutenant-Governors of Upper Canada*. Williams Briggs. Toronto.

Robinson, Peter. (1825-1827) Personal records and letters. Microfilm Archives of Ontario. Toronto.

Saint Mary's Catholic Church. (2009) Lindsay, Ontario http://www.stmaryslindsay.ca/history.htm

Sea Angling Ireland, http://www.sea-angling-ireland.org/

Spillane, Jerry. Personal Interview. February 28-29, 2008.

Stephen, L., Lee, S., and Smith, G. *Dictionary of National Biography*, Vol. XXII. (1890) MacMillan and Co. New York.

Swiggum, S., and Kohli, M. (2005) *Peter Robinson Settlers from Cork to Canada 1823 & 1825* http://www.theshipslist.com/ 1997-2008.

Traill, Parr Catharine. (2007) *The Backwoods of Canada*. IndyPublish. Boston.

Marquis Book Printing Inc.

Québec, Canada
2010